NORTHLAKE PUBLIC LIBRARY DISTRICT

3 1138 00154 9147

W9-BZO-570

DATE DUE

AG 10 '0?			
OC 26 '05			
MY 15 '06 SE 21 '07			

DEMCO 38-297

WAR AT HOME

ALSO BY KRIS NELSCOTT

A Dangerous Road
Smoke-Filled Rooms
Thin Walls
Stone Cribs

WAR AT HOME

Kris Nelscott

St. Martin's Minotaur ≋ New York

WAR AT HOME. Copyright © 2005 by White Mist Mountain, Inc. All rights reserved. Printed in the United States of America. No part of this book may be used or reproduced in any manner whatsoever without written permission except in the case of brief quotations embodied in critical articles or reviews. For information, address St. Martin's Press, 175 Fifth Avenue, New York, N.Y. 10010.

www.minotaurbooks.com

ISBN 0-312-32527-4
EAN 978-0312-32527-5

First Edition: March 2005

10 9 8 7 6 5 4 3 2 1

NORTHLAKE PUBLIC LIBRARY DIST.
231 NORTH WOLF ROAD
NORTHLAKE, ILLINOIS 60164

For Dean with love.

This book is as much yours
as mine.

ACKNOWLEDGMENTS

Once again, I could not have written this book alone. I owe a debt of gratitude to the staff at St. Martin's Press, Kelley Ragland, John Cunningham, and so many others, who have believed in these books. Also, I couldn't work on this without the support of Merrilee Heifetz. Thanks, too, to all the booksellers who championed this series from the beginning.

I also owe thanks to people who helped with various parts of the research, from the Malibu Brain Trust to Christine Valada and Carl Skalak. Thanks are due also to the staff at the various libraries, from Yale's Sterling Memorial Library, the New Haven Free Public Library, the Harold Washington Branch of the Chicago Public Library, and the New York Public Library. As always, any errors are strictly my own.

Once again, Paul Higginbotham and Steve Braunginn have taken time from their busy lives to review the manuscript. Thanks, guys.

Kelley Ragland's insight and understanding of Smokey have made this book much, much stronger. I'm so glad she's part of this project.

Finally, I have to thank my husband, Dean Wesley Smith, whose fertile mind always finds the best solution to the corners I box myself into.

We were bent on revolution right here
on earth, right here in America.

—**BILL AYERS**, *Fugitive Days*

WAR AT HOME

ONE

The blast shoved me backwards. I tumbled down the steps and hit the wall on the third floor with such force that my breath left my body. I slid down and landed, feet out.

Clouds of dust gathered around me. I was covered in dirt, bits of door, and blood.

I hadn't expected this. Anger, a gun, maybe, but not a bomb. The air was white with plaster dust. I was coughing, which hurt my ribs. I couldn't see anything ahead of me. My eyes were dry and chalky, and the inside of my mouth tasted like paint. I closed it, and my teeth ground against chunks of plaster.

The world was eerily quiet. I couldn't even hear myself breathe. Then I realized that the concussion had knocked out my hearing. If someone was crying, someone was calling for help, if someone was coming to the rescue, I couldn't tell. I hadn't realized how much I relied on my hearing until it was gone.

I moved slowly, feeling for problems. My back felt like someone had slammed it with a two-by-four. I guess a wall was infinitely more serious than a two-by-four. My left arm burned. My chest hurt, but I attributed that to the loss of air. I could now take shallow breaths, but they were filled with plaster dust.

The coughing continued. I could feel it digging into my throat and rib cage, but I couldn't hear it. I felt like I was alone in a blizzard, a soundless hot blizzard of white.

A jagged piece of wood stuck out of my thigh. A small piece. I wrapped my fingers around it and pulled. It came out easily, followed by only a little blood. The wood hadn't hit anything vital.

I touched my face, felt bits of stuff fall onto my lap, my fingers slick with blood. But I couldn't find too many wounds.

Maybe the blood wasn't mine.

I hadn't been the one closest to the explosion anyway. I'd just left the third floor. I was on the fifth or sixth stair, heading to the landing. The stairs then made a ninety-degree turn to the left, and continued upwards to the fourth floor.

I'd heard voices discussing unlocking the door, the click of a handle—or maybe the lock itself—and then the explosion.

It had to have been a powerful blast to hit me. The concussion had gone outward, and I had been protected by distance, and a plaster-and-lath wall.

God knows what would have happened if I had been on the landing.

I'd probably be dead now.

Shouldn't someone have come up the stairs? Out of the other apartments? Was the building more destroyed than I thought?

I couldn't tell.

I slowly got to my feet, bracing my hand against the wall. The wall seemed sturdy, but I couldn't see it clearly. The dust still swirled, giant clouds of it. Debris fell near my feet, some of it heavy enough to send vibrations through the floorboards. It felt strange not to be able to hear the thumps as the wood, the hardware, the whatever it was, landed.

I was in some kind of shock—not thinking as clearly as I could—but I wasn't sure what that meant. I wasn't sure what had happened to the others.

Wouldn't they have been blown backwards like me? Down the stairwell, landing in a pile?

I climbed up the stairs, keeping one hand on the wall as a brace, the other extended toward but not touching the railing. I wasn't sure what the explosion had blown loose. I reached the top step and swayed just a little; the wooziness hadn't disappeared. I made myself breathe, but the air tasted of smoke, and blood.

The landing had been ripped to pieces. The stairs going to the fourth floor disappeared into the clouds of white. I wheezed—at least, I think I did—and coughed some more, then I got on my hands and knees, distributing my weight as I crossed the ruined landing, heading for the ruined stairs.

Someone had to see if anyone survived.

It took me a long time—forever—to crawl up those stairs, using what was left of the wall to brace myself. My hands kept brushing nails and jagged bits of wood. I tried not to put too much weight on my knees—I didn't want to puncture any more skin.

The dust was as fine as baby powder. My eyes were finally starting to tear, to work the dirt out. I still couldn't breathe very well, and I had never been so dizzy in my life.

Then I reached the fourth floor.

Puffs of debris, like fog, floated in the hallway. The door itself was gone, blown open, leaving a gaping hole in the wall.

On the opposite side of the hall was an even larger hole. One that seemed to go on forever. Inside, a fire burned. No walls remained. That apartment was mostly gone.

The blast had gone outward, leaving wood and bits of shrapnel in the wall across the hall.

Wood, metal fragments, bone. My fingers shook as I reached toward the blood-covered whiteness sticking out of the plaster wall. My mouth was dry and I couldn't get the charred smell of the hall off my tongue.

I made myself look away from the bone fragment, down the dusty and ruined hall. No one. Maybe the others had gotten blown into the next apartment. Maybe they had already gone for help.

But even as I had those thoughts, I knew they were wrong. Beneath the piles of wood—the shattered plywood door, the bits of plaster from the walls, the ruined tables—were two people.

I crouched and started lifting the debris, one jagged piece at a time, hoping to find them.

Praying that they were alive.

TWO

One month earlier, I sat in the basement of a church. For the past half year, the church had donated this space to Grace Kirkland's after-school sessions. Grace taught the neighborhood children at the local parents' request. The after-school program was monitored by my good friend Franklin Grimshaw. He made certain that every parent paid Grace, either in cash or in kind. For her part, Grace made certain the children got the sort of education the Chicago public school system promised but didn't deliver.

The basement was long and narrow. It smelled faintly of chalk and damp, and had a chill despite the warmth of the June day. Sitting in one of the desks designed for children, I felt like a giant. I had to turn my legs sideways so that I would fit. Grace had already apologized for the lack of adult chairs.

She was a petite woman with ebony skin and a delicate manner that belied the steel inside her. Somehow she managed to keep a roomful of kids, ages six to sixteen, fascinated for three hours a day. As far as I was concerned, she had worked miracles since she had been running the program.

That afternoon, she had called me down to talk about Jimmy. Jimmy was, for all intents and purposes, my son. I hadn't formally adopted him because that would have meant we'd have had to go through legal channels, and we couldn't. We were living in Chicago under false names, trying to stay one step ahead of the Memphis police and the FBI.

Grace leaned against the desk the church provided for her, rested her hands on the surface, and crossed her legs at the ankles. She had fine legs, even though they were half covered by the conservative blue dress she wore.

Grace went to a great deal of trouble to hide her good looks. When asked, she identified herself as a mother of two boys, not as a teacher. And she never took credit for the fact that one boy was at Yale on a scholarship and the other was a straight-A high school student who was taking supplemental classes at the University of Chicago.

"I don't want to sugar-coat this, Bill," she said, using my alias. My real name is Smokey Dalton, but most folks around Chicago knew me as Bill Grimshaw, a relative of Franklin Grimshaw. Everyone thought Jimmy was my natural-born son, something I did not disabuse them of. I was as proud of him as if I'd raised him from the moment he was born.

Still, I had a feeling this conversation wasn't going to be easy. The public school term was over, and Grace was meeting with the parents, trying to see if there was enough support for a summer version of her after-school lessons. At the same time, she wanted to do a parent-teacher conference, so that we would know how our children were progressing.

So far, my meeting with her wasn't going as well as I had hoped.

"Jimmy is perhaps the brightest student I have ever come across." Her voice was soft, but there was a frown line between her eyes. "On a good day, I might even characterize him as brilliant."

"But?" I asked, trying not to shift in that too-small chair. I felt young and at the mercy of my teacher, instead of like the person who had hired her.

"But," she said, "he doesn't apply himself, and he drifts in class. I get the feeling that I'm not even reaching him. I try to catch his interest, but he does what he does to please me, not himself."

That sounded about right. With authority figures, Jimmy was eager to please—most of the time. That was how he got in trouble in the first place. He had been on Mulberry Street in Memphis on the day Martin Luther King, Jr., was shot. Jimmy had seen the shooter, and it hadn't been James Earl Ray.

So Jimmy, like a good citizen, reported what he saw to the nearby police. They tried to shove him into a cop car as if he were the criminal, and probably would have helped him disappear if I hadn't happened along at that moment.

Jimmy and I had been on the run ever since.

"He's had a rough year," I said.

Grace nodded. "Moving is always traumatic on children. But I have a sense that something else is going on. I know your job is dangerous, Mr. Grimshaw. Have you ever considered going back to the hotel work you were doing, for nothing more than Jimmy's peace of mind?"

I suppressed a sigh. Franklin Grimshaw had been after me to do the same thing ever since I had quit my job working security at the Conrad Hilton Hotel. But I wasn't set up to work for other people. I preferred being my own boss.

"I have some regular clients now," I said. "I've only had a few dangerous cases."

"A few might be too many." She touched her left cheek, obviously referring to the still-fresh scar on my face. I had gotten it during an attack in December. The scar was a visible reminder of my unconventional life, my unconventional work.

"My job is my job, Grace," I said quietly.

Something in my tone must have reached her, for she leaned her head to one side and sighed. Then she pushed away from the desk, walked across the dirty linoleum floor, and sat in the desk next to mine, turning it toward me the way she probably would with a student.

"I'm just at my wit's end with Jimmy," she said. "I don't know how to engage him, and he seems so sad. He has so much potential, Bill. I feel like I'm failing him."

I shook my head. "You're not failing him. We read together every night now instead of watching television. He devours the newspaper, and he helps me with the bills. His math skills have improved a lot, thanks to you. He's not the same boy he was in December."

She gave me a small smile, then twirled her finger on the kidney-shaped desktop. "It looks like we'll have a summer program. If you let Jimmy come, I'd like your help in developing a curriculum for him."

I didn't move. I wasn't ready to commit to summer school. I wasn't ready to commit to anything. I had been restless since Easter—the first anniversary of Martin's death—although the anniversary had less to do with my restlessness than Chicago itself.

The city had become a war zone. On the South Side, where I lived, 250 people had been shot and 28 had been killed since January in gang-related incidents. Some of the dead were police, and many of the dead were children.

I had made a devil's bargain with the gangs to help me avenge a friend and to keep them away from Jimmy. The Blackstone Rangers knew me, considered me one of their own, and were happy with me.

The minute that happiness ended, Jimmy or I could end up among the dead.

6

"Bill?" Grace asked, her head still tilted sideways. "Did Jimmy learn that habit from you?"

"What habit?" I asked.

"You faded out for a second. I asked you about the summer session."

I sighed. "My summer plans aren't finalized yet."

"It would do him good," she said. "The two of us together might be able to come up with something that would make Jimmy a participant in rather than a recipient of his own education."

"At this moment, I'm just happy he's getting an education." When I had met him, Jimmy lived on the street part-time. His mother had disappeared—which was not unusual for her—and his older brother would later abandon Jimmy in favor of drugs and a local gang.

"I think with Jim we should strive for more." She pushed herself out of the desk. "But it's not my call."

Her words sounded conciliatory, but her tone wasn't. I understood why the kids—even the big teenage boys—listened to her. She didn't brook disagreement.

But she didn't intimidate me. I was used to strong women and, although I knew her heart was in the right place, I was privy to information that she wasn't. Jimmy had been increasingly fragile all spring. My injury around Christmas time had shaken him up, and so had the anniversary of Martin's death. The world was still a difficult and frightening place for Jimmy, and all I could do was give him a little safety in the middle of the chaos.

I stood, too, struggling a little to get out of that tiny seat. Grace smiled just a bit as she watched me, then her smile faded.

"Can I ask you a personal question?" The toughness was gone from her voice now.

I had thought the discussion was already personal, but I didn't say that. Instead, I said, "Sure."

"I—ah—I'm having some more trouble with Daniel."

Daniel was her oldest son, the one who attended Yale. I had met him just before the Democratic National Convention last summer. He had come to Chicago with a group of protestors and hadn't told his mother. But his younger brother Elijah found out and ran away to be with him. Grace hired me to find Elijah, which I did. I brought both boys back to her, and she had never again hinted that there were any more problems.

"What kind of trouble?" I asked.

"It's not something I'm . . ." Her voice trailed off. "I'm sorry. Here I go chiding you about your work and then I ask you for help."

She noticed the irony; I appreciated that. "One conversation was about Jimmy. This one's about you. And I have an expertise that it seems you need."

She nodded, then looked down. She rubbed her hands together. They showed her age. The skin was tough, darker than the rest of her, and slightly wrinkled.

"Daniel's missing." Her voice was soft. Color rose in her cheeks and I understood that one, too. She'd been lecturing me on now to raise my child, then turned around and asked for help with hers.

"Another protest?" I asked.

"No." She kept her head bowed.

I waited. Sometimes silence worked better than twenty questions.

"I got a letter last week," she said. "They're withdrawing his scholarship." That startled me. "Why?"

"Seems he enrolled in the fall, but didn't finish his classes. Seems he didn't even bother to enroll in the spring term."

"What does the school say?"

She raised her head. Her eyes blazed, but her voice remained soft, almost emotionless. "They said such things aren't unusual. They said Yale is a cultural experience, and some boys—no matter how bright—don't adapt well to the culture."

Tears lined her eyes, but only for a moment. She blinked them away.

"They didn't even say they were sorry." Her voice was nearly a whisper now. "And when I asked them why they hadn't notified me when he had gone missing, they said that he was an adult and they weren't required to. I said that I bet they notified white parents, and they got all hissy on me, like I was the one at fault. 'We make accommodations for scholarship students, Mrs. Kirkland, but sometimes they just don't fit in.'"

I could almost hear the male voice with its upper East Coast WASP accent, calmly informing Grace Kirkland that her son was missing and it was her fault.

I walked over to her and put a hand on her shoulder, leading her to her desk. She leaned on me for just a moment, then smiled and moved away.

"Did you call his friends?" I asked.

"And his roommate, for what good that did. The boy was just about to leave for Greece and couldn't have cared less what happened to Daniel."

"Did the roommate know?"

"I don't think so. I got the sense they didn't get along." She sighed. "The thing is that they are right and he is an adult. But it's not like him to just disappear."

Actually, it was just like him. The boy I met, with his oversize Afro and antiwar rhetoric, hadn't even noticed the sacrifices his mother had made to keep him in such a prestigious school. He had taken a protest bus last summer without letting her know he would be in Chicago. The fact that he had dropped out during the school year and hadn't told her didn't surprise me at all.

But I didn't challenge her. I didn't see the point. "What did you want to ask me?"

She took a deep breath, then glanced at the row of desks as if they were full of students. "I called the New Haven police. They couldn't help me. They said the same thing the school did, that he was an adult and what he did was his business. So I called a private detective in New Haven. I got his name from the operator. He wanted to charge me half a year's salary, and he made no guarantees. When I told him I couldn't afford that, he suggested I look myself. Only I don't know how, Bill. I've done everything I can think of. I was wondering if you would mind—I mean, I'm taking advantage here, but I thought maybe you could tell me what to do next."

She surprised me. I had expected her to hire me like she had done before.

"Let me make a few calls," I said.

She put a hand on my arm as if she were going to physically hold me back. "No, really. I'll do this. He's probably on some bus going to some rally. I just need to know."

"When will they take away his scholarship?" I asked.

"September first if they don't hear from him," she said. "And he needs a good reason for not going to class last year."

She had less than three months to find him. America was a large country. People could easily disappear inside its borders. Jimmy and I had proven that.

"That's not a lot of time," I said.

"I'm sure it's just a misunderstanding. I keep thinking that maybe Elijah knows, but I worry about losing him, too. I don't want him to go searching for Daniel all on his own. Not again."

I nodded. I didn't want that either. If anything, the country had become more dangerous since last summer.

"Let me make some calls," I said again.

She licked her lower lip. "I'll pay you for your time."

She sounded relieved that I had made the offer. Relieved and a little embarrassed.

"Let's see what I come up with first," I said. "Then we'll decide if payment is even necessary."

"I believe in compensating people for their work," she said.

"You are." I smiled as warmly as I could, trying to reassure her. "You're worrying about my son. That's compensation enough."

THREE

By the time I got home, all of the Yale business offices were closed. New Haven was an hour ahead of us, and obviously, Yale had summer hours.

I didn't. I worked as much as I could. Our money situation had improved greatly this year, but not enough for me. I had two dreams, one I talked about all the time, and one I never spoke of.

I wanted Jimmy to go to college, and not just any college. A good school. That was the dream I spoke of. The one I kept to myself was the dream of owning a house again.

I still owned a home in Memphis, but I couldn't return to it. A friend of mine, Henry Davis, rented it out for me and put the money in a savings account that I secretly thought of as Jimmy's college fund.

At the moment, Jimmy and I lived in a three-bedroom apartment on Chicago's South Side. Since I started working as a sometime building investigator for Sturdy Investments, I had learned that our apartment was large and spacious by South Side standards.

The apartment didn't seem that way. The bedrooms were cramped, and the living room also served as the dining room. A half kitchen stood off to the side.

I had one of the bedrooms, and Jimmy the other. The third served as my office. I had furnished it with used pieces I bought at garage sales. I'd managed to find a large old-fashioned desk, a metal office chair on rollers, and some excellent filing cabinets. The office looked official, and I kept it neat, since I occasionally met clients there.

This last month, I had splurged and bought myself an electric typewriter, which sat on a credenza to my right. When I typed, I had a view out the window, not that I saw much more than the next building over.

I doodled on the blotter as I waded my way through a variety of Yale phone numbers. When that failed, I called the New Haven Police Department. I put on my best white man's voice, and claimed to be something I wasn't—a licensed private detective. I'd never been willing to go through the state bonding procedures in Tennessee, and I felt that I didn't dare jeopardize my position here in Chicago by bringing myself to the attention of the authorities.

The New Haven police didn't keep records of missing students. The police saw the college students as upper-class transients and didn't concern themselves with any missing persons cases, except those involving very rich families.

Grace had gotten the same information. But I took the call a step farther than Grace had. I asked if the police had a record of arrests involving a Daniel Kirkland.

"He your college kid?" the desk sergeant asked.

"Yes," I said.

"I told you. We don't keep records on these kids."

"Not even arrest records?" I asked.

"You know how it is," he said. "No sense pursuing something that ain't gonna stick."

I had a hunch Daniel Kirkland wasn't going to get mistaken for a rich college student, but I had already goofed in my conversation with the desk sergeant. I had mentioned Yale, and no amount of backtracking would get him to look up records for me.

So, on a whim, I called the jail and asked if they had records of holding a Daniel Kirkland. They did not—at least, none in the past few months.

Grace had already covered the hospitals. Aside from speaking to the registrar and other authorities at Yale, there was little more that I could do until the next day.

The following morning, I finally reached Edward St. James of the Yale Registrar's office. I used my white man's voice again, and introduced myself as Mr. William Grimshaw of the University of Chicago. I claimed to be reviewing a Daniel Kirkland's application for admission.

"He seems excellent on paper, but I have run into a few problems," I said, purposely rustling the files on my desk so that it sounded like I was working. "I understand that his national scholarship is in jeopardy, although the scholarship people tell me they're not at liberty to say why. So I assume something must have happened at Yale."

St. James made a noncommittal sound on the other end, showing attention and little more.

"And," I said, lowering my voice conspiratorially, "while I know that the University of Chicago is one of the best schools in the nation, I also know that Yale is even better. So I do find it curious that Mr. Kirkland would abandon your fine education for ours, even if it is in his hometown."

"I'll see what I can find." St. James sounded distracted "Would you like to hold while I look up the file or call back?"

As distracted as he sounded, I figured I'd better hold. He excused himself and the phone clunked as he stepped away from it.

I leaned back in the chair. I understood St. James's distracted tone. I had a hunch he got these calls a lot. Many students had given up on conventional schooling to protest. Harvard had shut down in April as students rioted, taking over the campus. So had San Diego State and Columbia. Student riots had become so common that most of them never reached the national news.

Even those that included burned and bombed buildings—and there were several—seemed to only merit a single paragraph mention on the national page of the *Chicago Tribune*.

"Mr. Grimshaw?" St. James had returned to the phone. "I have your file."

"Good," I said as I heard him turn pages.

"It seems . . ." His voice trailed off. He cleared his throat, obviously uncomfortable. "It seems that your Mr. Kirkland is no longer a student here."

"When did he leave? I don't have that in my files."

"You said you're considering his application?" St. James no longer sounded distracted.

"Yes," I said. "Normally, I wouldn't call, but I just have a sense—and it is only a sense—that things don't add up here."

"Indeed they don't," St. James said. "Give me a moment to examine these documents."

I heard more paper rustling on his side. I tapped my pen on the blotter, then hauled a legal pad out of my top drawer. Something in St. James's tone made me think I needed to take notes.

"It appears," St. James said, "that Mr. Kirkland had a less-than-exemplary record with us."

"I suspected as much. I figured there had to be some trouble for him to return home."

"Some is a bit of an understatement." St. James lowered his voice. "You realize he was a scholarship student?"

"Yes," I said. "I also understand his scholarship is in jeopardy."

"I should say." St. James sounded disapproving. "Most full scholarships, especially those like his—given to students based on merit and nothing else—require back-to-back enrollment with only the summer break, or barring that, some sort of explanation for time off."

"His application says that he didn't attend last semester, but doesn't give a reason," I said.

"Well," St. James sounded even more conspiratorial, "he was asked not to return."

"He was expelled?" That caught me by surprise.

"No," St. James said, "we don't expel, exactly. Usually we come to a mutual arrangement. You understand, either the school isn't right for the student or the student isn't right for the school."

I tensed. "Is that what happened with Mr. Kirkland?"

"Looking through the file, it seems that the admissions committee had concerns about him from the beginning. Apparently, he comes from quite a disadvantaged area and most of our colored students generally have a more middle-class background. His admission was part of our new outreach program. Until a few years ago, we hadn't been sending recruiters to public high schools."

"Previously, your—" I couldn't bring myself to say "colored," in this context, no matter how much I was pretending. "Your black students came from private schools?"

"Or schools that rated quite high academically," St. James said. "His school is in the middle of one of the more disadvantaged areas of Chicago, yet his SAT scores were quite high, and his essay was phenomenal."

"So," I said, trying to put all the doublespeak together in my mind. "You had hoped he would perform better academically? I have his SAT scores, his IQ test score, and his high school records in front of me, and I see nothing wrong with his mind."

"He has an excellent mind, Mr. Grimshaw," St James said, "and quite frankly, his academic performance, at least during his first year, was above expectations."

"So I don't understand," I said. "If he was getting good grades, why did you conclude that he wasn't right for the college."

14

"He's—how shall I put it?—an agitator. Trouble followed him, Mr. Grimshaw. He didn't participate in things. He started them."

"Riots?" I asked.

"We don't have riots at Yale." St. James all but sniffed that last. "But we have had difficult moments in the last few years, and Mr. Kirkland was always in the middle of them."

"But if he was making his grades, attending his classes, and not breaking any rules or laws, I don't understand the problem," I said.

St. James sighed. "Let me speak frankly, Mr. Grimshaw. Yale College was founded as a Christian school more than two hundred and fifty years ago. Even though we have become more secular, we keep many of the traditions of our founders. We don't merely teach young men letters. We teach them a way of life. We have found, as our admissions policy has become more open, that the young men who have the most difficulty with our system are the impoverished, the colored, and the Hebrew student. They do not participate in the social life, which is so much a part of Yale. Consequently, they aren't well known enough to join the various societies, and rarely participate in extracurricular activities. Young men learn how to be leaders here, Mr. Grimshaw. You can't lead with only one side of the equation. You must become a well-rounded human being."

I was clutching my pen tightly in my right hand, so tightly that my fingers hurt. "You expelled Daniel Kirkland because he wasn't popular?"

"On the contrary," St. James said, "he was quite popular. He simply didn't fit in. He kept trying to change things. We do accommodate the colored students, just like we accommodate the Hebrew students. The Hebrew students have their own rabbi now, and the colored students were allowed to form their own organization. But Mr. Kirkland wanted more. Black studies programs, more Negro professors, and an historical context that we don't believe will help our young men become the next leaders of this great country."

"I still don't understand—"

"Mr. Kirkland was not polite in his requests," St. James said. "He used language we do not find acceptable, and made demands of people whom he shouldn't have contacted at all. Presidents visit our university, Mr. Grimshaw, and we make them available to the students—"

"He insulted President Nixon?"

"One of the president's advisors visited Mr. Kirkland's college last fall. Mr. Kirkland was not a good representative of Yale."

"I can't imagine that a lot of the students were," I said.

"Those students didn't choose to attend the special luncheon," St. James said. "It's documented in the file. Frankly, I would have spoken to him sooner and not allowed him to come to the luncheon. But we attempt to be egalitarian here."

"I'm sure you do," I said, and then bit my lower lip. I hadn't meant to let the sarcasm out.

"While the University of Chicago is a different type of school," St. James said, oblivious to my comment, "you still have important visitors and well-known professors who have participated in things Mr. Kirkland does not believe in. He might do well academically, but at what cost to the university?"

"Things he does not believe in," I said. "The war?"

"The war, the current administration, the socioeconomic system." Paper rustled as St. James turned the page. "The white patriarchal society. I could go on, Mr. Grimshaw."

They had documented a lot, apparently expecting trouble from Daniel. I wished I could get my hands on that file. "So you asked him not to return for spring semester, but how did he do in the fall?"

"Our conversations began before midterms," St. James said. "Mr. Kirkland was skipping many of his classes and encouraging others to do so. He flunked two of his courses because he did not believe the 'garbage' the professors were teaching."

"And the other fall courses?"

"Much to the irritation of his professors, he succeeded in getting Bs without attending the last month of classes. He said it was proof that Yale's vaunted academic difficulty was a myth."

"Too bad a mind like that is being wasted," I said, more to myself than to St. James.

"My point exactly," St. James said. "If you believe the University of Chicago can get him off this path and make him a reliable citizen, more power to you."

"Thank you for your candor," I said.

"Believe me, I wouldn't have spoken up unless it were an extreme case."

I did believe him, and I knew he was dancing around the edges of something, something that he couldn't tell me from the file. Taken together, Daniel Kirkland's violations at Yale were a lot less than other students had done in the past few years at Columbia, Harvard, and other Ivy League schools. Many of the students who closed down buildings hadn't been expelled from their campuses. I couldn't believe that Daniel Kirkland would be tossed out for speaking plainly—if rudely—to the administration.

"May I ask one more question?" St. James's roundabout way of speaking was rubbing off on me.

"Certainly," he said.

"Did you inform Daniel's mother of your decision?"

"Our view is that our students are adults. We inform the parents if they foot the bill for the education, but for the most part we let the students themselves handle their own affairs."

At least the scholarship students, the "colored" students, and the "Hebrews." All of the undesirables to WASPy Yale.

"So no one outside of Yale and Mr. Kirkland know that he is persona non grata?"

"Unless they specifically ask, as you have, Mr. Grimshaw, we have no need to tell them."

"Not even his scholarship administrators?"

"They received a copy of the file," St. James said with a hint of satisfaction. No wonder Daniel's scholarship was being revoked.

"I don't suppose there's any way I can get a copy of the file," I said.

"I'm sorry." St. James sounded prim again. "Only the university and the financial aid providers are entitled to this information."

There was nothing left to ask him, so I thanked him for his time and hung up.

I had no idea how I would tell Grace all of this. She knew Daniel was involved in the antiwar movement, and she didn't appreciate it, but I doubted she had ever thought of him as a troublemaker.

I hadn't liked his attitude last summer, his unwillingness to let his family know he was home, his assumption of ignorance by all of us who weren't involved in his cause, but he didn't seem like a young man who would get thrown out of a prestigious college. If anything, I would have expected him to disappear, to fade away as if he hadn't been there at all.

Apparently, I had misjudged him as well.

FOUR

After I hung up the phone, I sat at my desk for a long moment, staring out the window at the building next door. Judging from St. James's comments, Daniel had had to deal with incredible bigotry at Yale, not just based on skin color, but also on the poverty in his background. Had Daniel been afraid to contact his mother? And if so, what had he done with his time since he left Yale?

This case couldn't be resolved with simple phone calls and, as Grace said, she couldn't afford an out-of-state investigator. Even if she could afford it, I doubted one would take the case when he found out that Daniel was black.

I leaned back in my chair and templed my fingers, a bit startled at my own reaction. I wanted to take the case, not so much for the work, but as an excuse to leave Chicago.

The thought of leaving Chicago had been floating around my mind since I became involved in a shooting in the worst part of the city, a section known as the Gaza Strip. Chicago hadn't been the haven I had hoped for. The schools were crumbling, riots had become common, and the violence in the south and west sides made this city one of the most dangerous places in the nation.

I had come here initially because I had nowhere else to go. Laura Hathaway lived here, and even though we had not been seeing each other at the time, I had subconsciously picked Chicago as my destination because of her.

But Chicago wasn't fulfilling my hopes for it. Jimmy still had nightmares. If anything, they had grown worse. I had developed community ties, but Grace was right: My cases often led me deeper into danger, something I couldn't afford with an eleven-year-old child as a dependent.

I had saved quite a bit of money from my work with Sturdy and the cases I had taken for various black insurance agencies. Part of me had been subconsciously planning to leave for a while now.

And Jimmy and I weren't in as much danger from the authorities as we had been. Even though the FBI had issued an APB describing us, that APB was over a year old. Other fugitives took priority. Jimmy and I had solidly established identities. I could portray Bill Grimshaw for the rest of my life, if need be.

We could see if other cities, other places, suited us better.

This case might provide an excuse to explore.

First, though, I had to talk to Grace. She might know more than she realized.

Grace Kirkland lived only a block away from me, and when she wasn't teaching, she was at home. I left the apartment and hurried down the stairs. Jimmy sat on the stoop outside, talking to some of his friends.

They moved furtively when they saw me. I wondered what they were up to.

"Jim," I said. "Everything okay?"

He glanced up at me. His face was lightly coated with sweat, and the back of his T-shirt was damp. He wore a pair of hand-me-down shorts from the Grimshaws.

"Yeah," he said.

His friends, two boys who lived across the street, watched me with big eyes.

I couldn't see anything out of place except their guilty attitude. I decided not to push my luck. "I'm heading to Grace's. Please be here when I come back."

Jimmy nodded. The other boys didn't move.

I stepped past them, and walked quickly down the block. Grace's apartment building, like mine, had been built before World War II. Unlike my building, however, hers hadn't been maintained. The white brick was a musty gray, the grass out front was overgrown with weeds, and the main door had nearly come off its hinges.

Grace's apartment was at the end of the hall. She had lived there for years, maintaining a garden in the back, surrounded by a fence that she had built herself. Even though the building was run-down, her apartment wasn't—showing a pride that I always associated with Grace, an ability to make the best out of anything that life had given her.

I knocked. After a moment, I heard rustling behind the door.

It opened, revealing not Grace, but her youngest son, Elijah.

He had grown since the previous summer, looking more like a teenager than a young boy. A wispy mustache graced his upper lip, and stubble covered his chin. However, his cheeks were still as smooth as Jimmy's.

"You come for Mom?" he asked, and his voice was deep and startling—a baritone in a tenor's body.

I nodded as he shouted for her.

Grace came into the narrow hallway. She was wearing an apron over a white sleeveless dress, and she was carrying a towel. When she saw me, she smiled.

"C'mon in," she said, gesturing with the hand holding the towel.

I stepped inside. The apartment was cooler than the hallway and smelled faintly of cinnamon.

"Don't tell me you're baking on a day like today," I said.

She shrugged. "I learned a secret from my momma. Bake before the sun comes up, and you'll have sweets for the heat of the day. Want a cookie?"

She had chocolate chip and snickerdoodles and good old-fashioned sugar cookies. I took one of each, and a cup of coffee, which sounded good despite the heat.

Elijah grabbed a chocolate chip, then disappeared down the hall, probably heading to his bedroom.

"He's become a teenager," I said.

"Overnight." She sighed, and untied her apron, hanging it on a peg in the half kitchen. Then she led me to the table, which she had placed in front of the glass patio doors, one of the few features of her apartment that I liked better than mine.

"I made those calls," I said as I sat down on the nearest wooden kitchen chair, "and I was wondering if I could see that letter about Daniel's scholarship."

A slight frown creased Grace's forehead, but to her credit, she didn't ask me any questions as she went to the small desk pushed up against the wall. She thumbed through a pile of open envelopes until she found the one she was looking for.

Then she handed it to me.

It was exactly as Grace had reported to me: Because Daniel hadn't completed his fall semester and hadn't enrolled for the spring semester, he would lose his scholarship if he didn't enroll in the upcoming semester, which was fall of 1969.

"That's odd," I said.

"What is?" Grace sat down across from me. She had poured herself some coffee, but now she pushed the cup away from her, as if she couldn't bear to drink it.

"I spoke to a man in the registrar's office who told me that Daniel had completed the fall semester. He even mentioned the grades."

I would have thought that St. James was looking at the wrong file if he hadn't mentioned where Daniel had grown up and the color of his skin.

"He did?" The news brightened Grace considerably. "That sounds more like Daniel. He always completes what he starts."

"But he still didn't register for the spring semester," I said. "He's not at Yale."

Her lips thinned, and that brightness faded just as quickly as it had come. "How come they never contacted me? Aren't they supposed to?"

"I don't know," I said. "Everyone I spoke to made a point of reminding me that Daniel is an adult. And he is, Grace. He has the right to make his own choices. Even the police had no record of him, at least in the last few months."

Grace sighed. "I can't imagine him dropping out without telling me."

I could. But I wasn't his parent. I wondered if I would become this blind about Jimmy—or if I already had.

She stood. "I can't believe he would give up all that we worked for. That scholarship was everything. He knew that."

She shoved her hands into the pockets of her dress, pulling it across her back.

"What kind of example is this for Elijah? How am I supposed to make something of other people's children when I can't even control my own?"

"You got him there," I said. "What he did after that is his business."

She shook her head. "College wasn't the end. He knew that. He had proven that a black boy from a bad high school could get into one of the best schools in the world with his smarts, his willingness to work outside of class, and his stick-to-itiveness. I used to tell him that if he could get into a college, he'd fought part of the battle. That would show the world that he was good enough for all the perks a college like that provided. He could be a lawyer or a doctor or anything white folks could be, only he could be better."

She spoke with so much force that her body shook with each word. Yet she still didn't face me as she talked.

I was glad that she didn't. Her words echoed St. James's. Daniel had taken the view she had expressed and twisted it, trying to mold the university into a place that would be his ideal school. He had been following Grace's plan, only in a more militant fashion.

She sighed, pulled her hands out of her pockets and threaded them together as she turned around.

"I guess I should thank you," she said. "I'll just wait until he calls me."

"There's one other choice." I heard the words come out of my mouth before I planned to say them. "I can go to New Haven and see if I can track him down."

Grace shook her head. "I can't afford to pay for that, Bill. I wish I could, but I'm barely making it as it is. All my extra money is going into Elijah's school fund now. I just hope he doesn't follow his brother's example—"

"We can trade, Grace," I said. "I know Franklin's talked to you about teaching next year. I'll keep a ledger, like I do for regular clients. I'll bill you for expenses and my time, and you do the same."

She teared up, then sank into her chair. "Would you do that?"

I nodded. I might never take advantage of the barter. If Jimmy and I decided the East Coast was better for us, I would lose money on this deal. But I was willing to take that risk. I had a son to protect, too, just like Grace did.

"That means all of this would come out of your pocket," she said. "You can't afford that."

"I've been working steadily for the past several months," I said. "I have some money saved up. I should be fine."

"You're being too kind." Her gaze met mine. It was steady, as if she could see through me.

"No, I'm not," I said. "I'm feeling restless. I figure some time away from the city might be good for me."

Her gaze didn't waver. "You don't like it here."

I shrugged. "This isn't my home."

"Neither is the East. I hear the South in your voice."

I gave her a small smile. "Just part of it. I grew up in Atlanta, but I went to school in Boston. I'm more familiar with the East than I am with the Midwest."

"And you like it better."

I took a bite from the snickerdoodle. It was fresh and soft and tasted like childhood. Then I chased it with some coffee, fighting the urge to tell her just how much I wanted to leave.

"I haven't given this place much of a chance. Jimmy and I were broke when we came here. We haven't had much, and our opportunities are limited. I don't like living like that."

I regretted that last sentence the moment I spoke it. Grace's opportunities had been limited, too.

"You told me once that Jimmy spent a lot of time with his mother," Grace said. "You're not used to having a child."

"No, I'm not," I said.

"It restricts you." Her voice was soft. "But it's worth it. Most of the time."

I knew she was thinking about Daniel when she said that last.

"I don't regret a thing I've done for Jimmy," I said, "and I love raising him. But—"

"What're you going to do with him while you're gone?" she asked. "Is he going to spend the summer with your family?"

She meant the Grimshaws.

I hadn't given it much thought. But I knew that I couldn't leave Jimmy in Chicago. "He'll come with me. See more of the world."

"And who'll take care of him while you're looking for Daniel?"

I hadn't even thought of that.

"I'd offer to come," she said, "but I can't. Elijah might need to see the world, just like Jimmy, but I need the work. If I left now—"

"I'm not asking you to, Grace."

"But see, you're not thinking of Jim. There'll be places an eleven-year-old shouldn't see. You know that." She sighed. "I could watch him, if you want him to stay here."

It was a generous offer. Grace would be a strict guardian, but a good one. Only I couldn't take her up on it. Last summer I had left Jimmy in Laura Hathaway's care and had put them both in danger.

I couldn't do that again. Not to Laura—who would always be my first choice to care for him, not to the Grimshaws, and certainly not to Grace and Elijah.

"Thank you," I said, "but I know a lot of people back east. We'll find a way to cope."

Grace gave me the same look she had given me in the basement of the church—as if I were an unrealistic, misguided man who didn't understand his child. At least this time, she was too polite to say anything, especially considering the offer I had just made her.

We talked a bit longer, and I asked for several things from her. I needed a photograph of Daniel. I also wanted a copy of Daniel's application for Yale, copies of his scholarship questionnaires, and any other material he had sent the college. Fortunately, Grace had those in a file in her desk; she had insisted that Daniel type his materials using carbon paper. The copies were difficult to read, but legible.

Then I asked her for any letters he had sent home, not just to her but to Elijah as well. She said it would take her a while to find those, and I knew she'd argue with me about taking them out of her apartment.

Finally, I asked her to sit down with Elijah and make notes about the conversations they'd had with Daniel since he left for school—any and all details, no matter how trite. I wanted hints of where he would be and what he might be doing, leads that I could follow with or without finding someone in New Haven to talk with me.

I didn't tell her that I still had the lists she'd made for me last summer when Elijah had gone to Lincoln Park looking for his brother. Then Grace had given me the names of their local friends with a D, an E, or a G beside the listings. I had noted at the time that there were very few E's, but there were a number of D's. Daniel had known a lot of people in Chicago, and I wasn't going to rule out that his local friends knew more about his life than his mother did.

Grace offered to let me talk to Elijah, but I wasn't ready to yet. I needed to put everything into a context. I also needed to get my own affairs in order. I had to either finish the cases I was working on for the various black insurance companies in town or give them back, and I had to talk to Laura, taking a leave from my work inspecting houses for Sturdy Investments.

All of that would take time.

As I walked back to my own apartment, I saw the kids sitting on the front lawn. They were playing cards, which surprised me. Jimmy was sitting sideways, concentrating as he set one card down and picked another up.

Gin rummy. That was why they looked guilty. A month ago, I had to stop Jimmy from taking Keith Grimshaw's lunch money in weekend poker games.

I sighed. Grace was right. I couldn't take Jimmy with me on each visit I made in New Haven. And missing persons cases, while difficult, often went in unexpected directions. I needed the opportunity to follow each and every lead.

I was also heading into a college. I would have to talk to young people. I learned last summer that when I walked into a room filled with college students and war protestors under the age of twenty-five, I was immediately suspect.

If I was serious about leaving Chicago and doing a good job for Grace, I would need someone young to come with me. Someone who could talk to college students and whom I could trust with Jimmy when I had to investigate. Someone who had enough freedom to leave Chicago for a week, a month or the entire summer if need be.

For that, I needed Malcolm Reyner.

FIVE

Malcolm Reyner was an eighteen-year-old orphan whom Franklin Grimshaw and his family had taken in last summer, initially at my request. They treated him well. In May, he had gotten his GED, and now he was working as a short-order cook at one of the local restaurants. Sometimes he worked for me, too, helping me with a few of my cases, doing jobs that I needed a younger, more active person for.

Jimmy was happy to leave his gin game to go to the Grimshaws' house. As I suspected, he had been playing for money, but he was losing for once. One of the older neighbor boys who usually didn't play was taking Jimmy for all he was worth.

It was easy to get Jimmy to talk about his conquests on the way to the Grimshaw house. He was proud of his card-playing ability. I wasn't sure how I felt about it. I did know, however, that by the end of summer I would have to find a way to convince him that preventing other kids from eating a healthy lunch by taking their funds was not a good thing.

That would take some diplomacy on my part. Jimmy felt like he wasn't good at most things. To take away one of the few things he did well would be a blow to his ego.

I pulled up in front of the house. It was large and well maintained, loved in that way that people who appreciated what they had gave their homes.

The Grimshaws didn't own the house—Sturdy Investments did—but the place was a great improvement over the three-bedroom apartment the family had been living in last summer.

The woman I was seeing, Laura Hathaway, ran Sturdy. It had been her father's company, and she had taken it over last December, trying to cure the mismanagement and corruption her father and his cronies had built into the company. One of her first acts had been to rent the Grimshaws this house at below-market rates.

Her investment was paying off. The Grimshaws were making improvements to the home as if it were their own.

A large front porch encircled the place. The lawn was mowed, and someone had trimmed the plants beside the sidewalk. Peonies budded near the front porch, and someone had planted bleeding hearts beside it. Pansies peeked out of pots that Althea had placed along the stairs.

As I got out of the car, I heard yells and screams and children's laughter. I couldn't see the kids, so I assumed they were in the backyard. So did Jimmy. He immediately ran around the house to see what games the kids were playing.

Franklin's wife, Althea, sat on the porch, shucking peas into a bowl. I hadn't seen anyone do that in years. She looked like the matriarchs of my youth, sitting in her rocking chair, surveying the neighborhood as she worked.

"You growing your own peas now?" I asked.

"Franklin got them in trade from a downstater," she said. "Apparently he's giving everyone advice these days."

Franklin consulted with various black businesses and politicians. He loved the work, and was quite successful at it, but he was also taking night classes for a law degree.

"Is Malcolm home?" I asked.

"Just got off shift," she said. "I'd say he'd be out of the shower by now."

She didn't ask me what I wanted Malcolm for, and I didn't tell her. Malcolm had assisted me in previous cases, and Althea had never approved. But unlike Grace Kirkland, Althea didn't repeatedly talk to me about her disapproval. Nor did she try to change me.

I appreciated that.

I went inside the house. It was warm, and smelled faintly of baking bread. Unlike most of the women I knew, Althea didn't work—not even when the Grimshaw family had been crammed in that tiny apartment.

She saw her job as raising children and saving the family money, from baking the bread to finding creative ways to use leftovers. Last summer, I learned a lot from Althea about bargain shopping and raising a child on a budget. I was good with money, but I couldn't make a dollar stretch in six different directions the way Althea could.

Malcolm was coming out of the bathroom. He wore only a pair of blue jeans. His feet were bare and he was toweling off his hair.

"Malcolm?" I said.

He jumped half a foot. "Jeez, Bill, I didn't see you. Don't sneak up on a guy like that."

He looked tired and he had burns along both forearms. I recognized those burns. They came from grease spatter. I'd had a few myself during my first years in Memphis when I had to have a second job to support myself while my own business took off.

"I didn't mean to surprise you," I said. "Can I talk to you?"

He kept toweling his hair, his gaze not meeting mine. "Is it important?"

Malcolm usually wasn't reluctant to talk to me.

"Yeah, actually," I said. "I have a job for you, but it's unusual and it might require some thought on your part."

"A job." He draped the towel around his neck. Some of the shower water beaded on his forehead. "I guess we can talk about that."

I wondered what he had thought I was going to discuss with him, and then decided not to ask. If he came with me to New Haven, we would have plenty of time to talk in the car.

He led me into the kitchen and slid a chair back with his bare foot. "Have some iced tea. I've gotta get a shirt. Althea's rules."

I knew about Althea's rules. They kept the household civilized, and you broke them on pain of death.

I poured myself a glass, while Malcolm pulled open the door that led upstairs. The house was old enough to have existed before central heating. Doors blocked all sections of the house so that heat could remain in each area. The Grimshaws didn't use most of those doors, but they did keep the one leading upstairs closed, probably to keep the downstairs noise from bothering those children who had to go to bed early.

As I waited, I peered out the window into the backyard. In the middle of the yard, an old coffee can sat on top of a mound of dirt. The children were playing kick-the-can. Jimmy was the only kid I could see, which meant he was it.

When Noreen, at six the youngest and most pampered Grimshaw, appeared at the edge of the garage, Jimmy ignored her. I knew that he had seen her, because his head moved ever so slightly. But he kept his back to the can and continued his search of the trees at the back of the property.

Noreen ran across the yard at top speed, her pigtails flying, her sneakers kicking up dust. When she was only a foot or two from the can, Jimmy pretended he had just noticed her and started toward her.

She squealed in terror and kicked the can so hard that it flew onto the back patio, landing with a thunk. Then she grinned and waved her arms at Jimmy.

"I beated you, Jim!" she shouted.

He frowned, but the frown was as fake as his attempt to stop her had been. "Guess you did."

Malcolm thumped down the stairs. I turned, still smiling from my brief view of the game. Malcolm hurried into the kitchen, his mood visibly improved.

"I wouldn't mind a job," he said, buttoning the short-sleeved white shirt he had put on. "Be nice if it paid enough so that I could quit the restaurant."

He'd been talking like that more and more. Malcolm didn't like the cook's job. After he got his GED a month ago, he had thought he would get better work. Even though he applied for other jobs, no one wanted to hire a young black man for anything other than menial labor.

"Pay is an issue," I said.

He sighed.

"Listen to me first before you make up your mind." I handed him a glass from the cupboard, and he poured himself the last of Althea's iced tea. Then he grabbed some tea bags, filled the pitcher, and set it on the back patio in the sun.

When he finished, he came back in, picked up his glass, and sat down like a man who had worked a full and tiring day.

"So I'm listening," he said.

"Daniel Kirkland has disappeared."

"I know."

Malcolm's response surprised me. "You know?"

He nodded. "I heard Mrs. Kirkland talking about it. I figure he's probably off fighting some other white man's cause."

Malcolm had no respect for the antiwar movement. He felt that it was run by wealthy white kids who had nothing else to do with their time.

"But I did look for him a little," Malcolm said.

That caught my attention. "You did?"

He shrugged. "Mrs. Kirkland's really helping everyone out here, and I had the time. I figured if I found him, I'd be doing her a favor."

He constantly surprised me. He was a good kid, who liked helping people. "That was kind of you. Did she know about it?"

He shook his head.

"I take it you looked for him here," I said. "Does that mean you think he's in Chicago?"

"Most of his friends are. Haven't you heard?"

I shook my head. I wasn't sure what he was referring to.

"The SDS is holding their national meeting at the Chicago Coliseum."

I frowned. I had heard that, but I hadn't paid much attention to it. The Students for a Democratic Society had been influential in organizing the protests at the Democratic National Convention the previous August. Daniel had come to that convention early. I never determined if he had been an SDS member; in fact, I had never thought to ask.

"You think Daniel's there?" I asked.

"I did, but he's not."

"How do you know?"

Malcolm smiled at me. "I went there. The whole thing is nasty and pointless and stupid, but to my surprise, Daniel isn't part of it."

"Did you spend a lot of time there?" The Chicago Coliseum was a large place.

"Enough," he said.

"Enough to be sure Daniel's not in Chicago."

"Yeah." Malcolm grinned at me. "That's one palefaced group of radicals, Bill. There are blacks, sure, but they stick out like raisins in a bowl of sugar. I talked to everyone who could've been Daniel or could've known him. He isn't there."

I sipped my tea. Althea had sweetened it like the southerner she used to be. "Did you talk to anyone who was here from Yale?"

Malcolm nodded. "They don't like him."

Somehow that didn't surprise me. "Why's that?"

"I guess he told them they were a bunch of idiots who wouldn't know revolution if it bit them in the ass."

I let out an involuntary laugh. "That's one way to make friends."

"That's our Daniel," Malcolm said. Malcolm and Daniel had gone to high school together. Malcolm had had to drop out to take care of his dying mother; Daniel went on to Yale. Malcolm never quite forgave him for that.

"Did you get any idea where he might be?"

Malcolm shook his head. "I talked to his friends here, too. They haven't heard from him."

Then he set his iced tea down and grinned at me.

"So I've already done the job, right? You don't need me after all."

"Actually, I do," I said. "I'm thinking of going to New Haven personally to see what I can find."

"Out east?" Malcolm frowned. "That's pretty far. Can Mrs. Kirkland afford that?"

"No," I said. "That's why money's an issue."

"You got her the teaching job, Bill. You don't owe her anything."

"I owe her a lot," I said. "But I have other reasons for wanting to head east."

Malcolm studied me for a minute. Then he nodded. "The Blackstone Rangers."

He was the only one among my friends who knew the depths of my involvement with the gang. He knew that I had made not one but several bargains with them, and he'd been around gangs long enough to know that the bargains would come back to haunt me.

"Yes," I said.

"You leaving for good?"

I shrugged. "If I can find some place better. But don't tell anyone please. That's up to me."

He rolled the iced-tea glass between his hands. "So why're you talking to me?"

"I'm taking Jimmy," I said. "I'll need help caring for him when I'm working and I'll need help finding Daniel Kirkland."

"You're serious about this?" Malcolm asked.

I nodded. "If I can provide Grace with a few answers, I'll be able to pay her back for the kindnesses she's shown Jimmy over the past few months."

"I don't think she's done for him more than she's done for anyone else," Malcolm said.

"That's my point," I said. "She's been amazing."

He sighed. I could almost hear his thought. She'd been amazing with her own children as well. Only it hadn't stuck with Daniel.

"Money's an issue because she's not going to pay you," he said after a moment.

"That's right," I said.

"So you can't pay me."

"That's right, too," I said. "But I'll pay all the expenses. You won't have a dime out of pocket."

"How're you gonna afford that, me and Jimmy and all that traveling? Your rich girlfriend?"

I'd never heard Malcolm refer to Laura that way before. It startled me. "I have some of my own money put away. The last few months have been lucrative."

He took in that information. He seemed to understand that I was serious. "What if you stayed east and I didn't want to?"

"We'd get you a bus ticket home," I said.

He continued spinning his glass between his large hands. "How long would I be gone?"

"I don't know that. Maybe a week. Maybe a month. Maybe all summer. Finding someone who doesn't want to be found is nearly impossible, particularly if they're smart."

My breath caught as I said that last. It almost felt like a confession.

Malcolm didn't notice. "Daniel's smart." He drummed his fingers on the table. "What if you don't find him by the end of summer and you want to come back?"

"Then I'll tell Grace I did all I could."

"You taking Elijah, too?"

"No," I said. "Grace needs her other son to stay home."

"He's not going to like it that I'm going and he's staying."

"He's too young."

"Jimmy's too young," Malcolm said.

"Jimmy stays with me."

Malcolm tilted his head slightly as he looked at me. "Someday you gonna tell me where all this comes from?"

"What?"

"Your—I don't know—protectiveness, I guess. Most folks would just go on doing what they're doing, you know? You don't. You're always surprising me."

I smiled. "Sometimes I surprise me, too."

Malcolm picked up his tea glass and drained it. Then he wiped his mouth with the back of his hand. "The Grimshaws aren't going to like it either."

"That you come with me?"

"That you're even going. They worry about you. And Jimmy. Jimmy a lot. They say he needs stability."

"What do you say?"

Malcolm got out of his chair and took the glass to the sink. He stood with his back to me. "I'd trade stability for another summer with my mom any day."

His voice was quiet as he said that. But I knew what he meant. I spent the last half of my childhood thinking the same thing. My parents were lynched when I was ten, and I grew up with wonderful adoptive parents who never quite felt like my own. I would have traded anything to get my own parents back, even for an afternoon.

"You want to come?" I asked.

"Hell, yeah," he said as he turned around. His eyes sparkled for the first time that day. "When do we leave?"

NORTHLAKE PUBLIC LIBRARY DIST.
231 NORTH WOLF ROAD
NORTHLAKE ILLINOIS 60164

SIX

Given the chance, I would have left the next morning. But I had a few loose ends to tie up first.

And I hadn't even told Jimmy my plans. I did so at dinner that night. I didn't mention that I was thinking of leaving Chicago permanently. I figured I could tell him that when—if—we found some place we liked better.

"I dunno," he said without meeting my gaze. "Me and Keith was planning on swimming this summer."

Keith was the Grimshaw boy closest to Jimmy's age. They were best friends.

"Swimming?" I asked.

Jimmy nodded. "They got Jackson Park open. We thought maybe you or Franklin or Malcolm could take us there. Keith's never been swimming in the lake."

"Never?" I asked.

"His mom says it's too cold."

Lake Michigan was cold, but that was precisely why most Chicagoans loved to swim in it during the city's sweltering summers. If Althea didn't want the children to swim in the lake, she probably had other reasons—pollution or dangers near the swimming area.

"You're going to swim all summer?" I asked.

Jimmy nodded, his mouth full of macaroni and cheese. When it got hot, I didn't like to cook. When we'd gotten home, I'd boiled the noodles, fried some sausage, and had a meal on the table within fifteen minutes.

"You can probably swim in the lake before we leave," I said.

He swallowed, chased the food with some milk, and started to wipe his milk mustache off with the back of his hand. Then he noticed how closely I was watching him. He picked up his napkin and dabbed at his lips, missing the mustache altogether.

"Can't Mrs. Kirkland find somebody else?" he asked.

"She can't afford anybody else," I said.

"If she can't afford anybody else, how can she pay you?"

Out of the mouths of babes. I sighed. "We'd probably trade services. My work for hers."

"More school," he said, and slumped in his chair.

I nodded. "If we stayed, you'd be going this summer anyway. Franklin and Mrs. Kirkland came to terms this afternoon."

"Nobody goes to school in the summer," Jimmy said.

"Lots of people do," I said. "That's why it's called summer school."

He wrinkled his nose, slid back up in his chair, and dug into the meal, holding his fork in his fist. He had been hungry after the long game, and he was dirty. I made him wash his hands and face before we ate, but he would still have to take a shower before bed.

"What'll I do when you're working?" he asked.

"That's something I'd have to figure out. For the most part, you'd come with me."

He wrinkled his nose again. "I'd rather swim."

I understood. I would rather give him the carefree childhood he'd never had, the kind he played at this afternoon. But Jackson Park wasn't far from gang territory, and the Blackstone Rangers had a reputation for getting in deeper trouble in the summer. They'd started mugging people on the El last month, apparently to fill the Stones' coffers with extra money.

"What about Laura?" Jimmy was asking about Laura Hathaway. He had become quite attached to her in this past year. They were friends, independent of my relationship with her.

"What about her?" I asked.

"Would she come?"

"Probably not," I said. "She has her own work to do."

"You work for her. Don't you got to stay?"

"I contract with her," I said. "I work for myself."

He probably didn't understand the distinction, but he nodded anyway.

"Won't she miss us?" he asked.

"I suspect she might."

"Then maybe we should stay."

"It's not final yet, Jim," I said. "I just wanted you to know what I was thinking."

He sopped up the last of the bright orange sauce on his plate with a piece of sausage. "Could Keith come?"

"I don't think the Grimshaws would approve."

He sighed. "What about Mrs. Kirkland? If she's teaching, maybe I should stay."

"I'm not talking about moving," I said. At least, not yet.

"Yes, you are," he said. "You don't like it here anymore. You got scared in April, and you haven't liked it ever since."

I set my fork down. I hadn't realized Jimmy had been watching me so closely. I shouldn't have underestimated him.

"I am worried," I said. "And, to be honest with you, I'm not sure this is the best place for us."

"But we gots friends!" He usually lapsed into bad grammar to provoke me, but I had a sense that this time, the lapse was caused by his distress.

"Yes, we do. We don't lose friends because we move."

"You did."

I looked at him.

"That nice minister guy in Memphis, we never saw him again. You don't even call him."

Jimmy was referring to Henry Davis, who had helped us leave town. I'd contacted him a few times, most recently from a pay phone when a case had taken me to Indiana, but Jimmy didn't know that.

"Maybe that's our biggest problem," I said.

Jimmy frowned at me. "What?"

"That we've begun to feel safe enough to forget why we're here in the first place."

Jimmy looked down. He pushed the last piece of meat around on his plate.

"I'm sorry, Jim," I said. "I have to do what's best for us, and sometimes it's not pleasant."

"I know," he said, his voice nearly a whisper.

"There's no guarantee that we're moving," I said. "I'm not even sure we're going on a trip, but it's a possibility. I promised you I wouldn't lie to you, and I've kept that promise."

"I know." His voice was even softer.

"If we do go, we'll keep the apartment here and tell everybody we'll be back."

"But what if we don't come back?" Jimmy asked, raising his head.

"Then we'll call and explain why," I said. "It won't be like Memphis. We can stay in touch with everyone here."

"I don't want to move, Smoke."

"Noted," I said. "But what would looking at a few other towns hurt?"

He shrugged, not meeting my gaze. "Can I be excused?"

"Yes," I said.

He picked up his plate and his glass, carried them to the sink, and then walked, head down, to his bedroom. It was my turn to do the dishes, but I let them sit for a few minutes.

I sighed. Sometimes this parenting thing seemed like the most complex job I had. I had no idea if I should have told him my plans or not. But I had promised not to lie—and sometimes I even doubted the wisdom of that.

After a moment, I got up and went into the living room. I called Laura, and asked her to come over the following night, for one more difficult dinner.

SEVEN

I spent the next day tying up loose ends. I organized my finances, paying as many of July's bills in advance as I could. I got traveler's checks. I had traveled with a lot of cash before, and it made me nervous. I didn't really want to do it again, even though I worried about cashing the traveler's checks. I figured I'd be able to find a sympathetic bank somewhere.

I also traded in my rusted Impala for a panel van. I cleaned out the back, bought three sleeping bags and a cooler, along with a tent. If we couldn't afford a motel room, I figured we could sleep in the van or, if we found a place to camp, we would pitch a tent.

I wrote reports, closing a few cases for the various insurance companies I worked for. I told the companies I would be available again toward the end of summer.

Jimmy spent the time packing and repacking his clothes. The thing that surprised me and pleased me as well was that he wanted to take an armload of books "to read for Mrs. Kirkland."

Apparently Grace had given him a summer reading list. Jimmy viewed it as his work for the trip, and I didn't try to talk him out of it. I made room in the back of the van for a box of books and reminded Jimmy that if we carried the weight, he would have to do the work.

All too quickly, it was time for dinner.

Jimmy and I planned the meal together and, considering it was so hot, finally decided to barbecue. We had custody of the Grimshaws' old grill—they hadn't wanted to move it—and we used it on nights like this. Althea had taught me to marinate the hamburger patties in beer and melted butter before I cooked them, and that gave them an extra flavor that made them seem irresistible. I added Kaiser rolls, potato chips, and a tossed salad. Jimmy declared it a perfect meal.

Laura arrived around seven. The heat had wilted her blond hair, and she had washed off her makeup. She had also changed into a pair of shorts and a cotton shirt that accented her figure.

I kissed her lightly, gave her a Coke, and offered to sit outside at the communal picnic table in the back if the apartment was too hot for her. She seemed tempted. Then she noticed that Jimmy had set the table, placing a bouquet of wildflowers in the middle.

"I think here is just fine," she said.

Jimmy grinned. She had pleased him. I went down to cook the hamburgers while the two of them sat inside, conversing about whatever it was that they felt they had in common.

When I got back, they were laughing. Jimmy glanced at me sideways, as if he were trying to give me a message. I got it. But I had other considerations besides our friends in Chicago. And as I had told him before, Laura could travel. We would see her again.

I set the plate of steaming hamburgers on the table between the pickle relish and the sliced onions. Jimmy got the ketchup and mustard out of the refrigerator, setting them beside the plate of Kaiser rolls. I tossed the salad and placed it in the very center of the table.

"Fancy," Laura said.

"Like a five-star restaurant," I said, and we both smiled.

"It's the best," Jimmy said. "Smokey makes the best burgers in the whole world."

"That's a tall order," Laura said as she grabbed one of the rolls, split it open, and applied ketchup to the bottom. She added lettuce, onions, and a slice of cheese but no mustard. I served salad to myself and Jimmy, knowing if I didn't he wouldn't eat any of the green stuff.

Jimmy waited, fidgeting until Laura was done, then assembled his own burger, using everything on the table. I went last, my stomach rumbling.

"You sounded serious on the phone," Laura said to me.

"Eat first." Jimmy spoke with his mouth full of hamburger and bun, barely understandable. He swallowed, and added, "Then Smoke gets to talk to you."

"Coward," I said.

Jimmy shrugged. "It's your idea."

"What is?" Laura asked.

So I told her about Daniel Kirkland and Grace's concern for him. I told her that missing persons cases were tough, and I told her that the case might take the summer to solve.

She listened closely, then looked at Jimmy, who throughout my monologue had concentrated on inhaling his burger. "And you want me to take care of Jimmy?"

"He's coming with me," I said.

"On a case?"

"I can't ask you or anyone else to watch him for the entire summer."

"I don't mind," she said, "and he might like it. I'm not far from the lake, and my place is air-conditioned. I still have his room—"

"No," I said before Jimmy could chime in. "He's coming with me."

"This doesn't sound like a good idea, Smokey," she said. "Your cases aren't always safe."

"The case is an excuse." Jimmy reached for another bun. He hadn't touched his salad. I shoved the bowl toward him, and he wrinkled his nose. But he took a bite, just to show me he understood.

"An excuse?" Laura set her hamburger down. She frowned, then her shoulders sagged. "You're leaving Chicago."

"I don't know for sure," I said.

"I wondered if that was going to happen. You've been so restless since April."

Everyone seemed to have noticed my discontent.

"Chicago's getting worse," I said. "Twenty-eight murders in the last six months, most of them only a mile or so from here. Kids, adults, cops, it doesn't matter."

She glanced at me on that last. She knew about my role in one of the deaths last spring. She also knew that it haunted me.

"You can both move in with me," she said. "It's safer at my place, you know that. The neighborhood's better."

"Not for us," I said. Laura lived in Chicago's Gold Coast. Most of the inhabitants of that section of Chicago were wealthy and white. They'd always reacted with suspicion when they saw me going into the front door of Laura's Lake Shore Drive condominium complex. I couldn't imagine the reaction if we lived there.

"Smokey," she said. "If you're willing to leave Chicago, why don't you consider this first?"

"You know why," I said. "Even if we decided to live up there, I'd still have to come down here to work."

"You would only have to work for Sturdy," she said. "You wouldn't have to take all the other jobs—"

"The other jobs are the ones I enjoy." I spoke softly.

"But if you're thinking of Jimmy, a new place can't be good for him. He'd have a new community to learn, new friends, new relationships."

"Maybe a better school and a nicer house, a safer community—for blacks as well as whites. Chicago is the murder capital of America, Laura. I'm sure we can do better than that."

Jimmy was watching us as if we were participating in a tennis match, and it was clear from his expression that he wanted Laura to win. "Maybe Laura could hire a detective for Mrs. Kirkland. I mean, in trade for me going to school with her and all."

"In the same neighborhood we're trying to leave," I said. "You'd come back for school?"

"I couldn't leave my friends or Mrs. Kirkland." Jimmy spoke simply. I looked at Laura as he said the words, and for the first time, it was clear she understood.

No matter what part of the city we lived in, we were tied to the South Side of Chicago. I couldn't forbid Jimmy to come here; he wouldn't listen to me even if I felt I had grounds to stand on. We would be better off remaining in our apartment, in our little neighborhood, then going to Laura's fancy uptown location and having Jimmy sneak El rides south to visit his friends.

Jimmy set aside half of his second hamburger. To my surprise, however, he reached out and put his hand on Laura's.

"Smoke says you can come see us no matter where we are. He says you gots enough money that it doesn't matter where we live, you can find us. So it won't be like leaving Memphis and never seeing nobody again."

She put her hand over his, then smiled. He didn't seem to notice that the smile didn't reach her eyes. "Smokey's right about that. I can come see you no matter where you are. I'd just miss seeing you every day."

"You don't see us every day now," Jimmy said. "It'll be okay, Laura, really. If Smoke says we gots to, then we gots to."

He was defending me. I hadn't expected it. I knew how much he wanted to stay.

She squared her shoulders. "I take it Mrs. Kirkland is paying you?"

"No," I said. "I have enough saved."

"Then let me pay your fees," Laura said. "Or at least your expenses. You can fly out east, rent a car, stay in nice hotels—"

"Laura," I said.

"You have to be comfortable, Smokey," she said.

"We will be. But we're driving. I don't want to rent a car, and Grace and I have already handled the fees. I'm not taking charity."

She rolled her eyes. "I hate it when you use that word. Technically, the charity wouldn't be for you, it would be for Grace Kirkland."

"It would be for me. You wouldn't offer if I weren't involved."

Laura sighed. "You're not going to let me help in this at all, are you?"

"No," I said.

"So if you do decide to move out of Chicago, do you have enough for the trip and for a security deposit?"

"You're getting way ahead of the program, Laura."

"No, I'm not," she said. "You have to be ready for all contingencies. You have—"

"As it stands right now," I said, "we're going to be gone until we find Daniel Kirkland. Then we're coming home. If we decide to stay in Connecticut or Indiana or Pennsylvania, then we'll worry about the other details. We certainly didn't have any money when we came here, and it worked out."

Her eyes filled with tears and she turned away. Jimmy tightened his grip on her hand. His knuckles were turning white.

"Don't cry," he whispered. "We won't like no place better. You'll see."

She slipped her hand from his, grabbed his face, and kissed him on the top of the head. Then she stood and looked at me.

"I don't make these offers to patronize you, Smokey. I make them because I love you and I worry about you and I want you to be okay. But you don't seem to understand that."

"I understand it," I said. "I just don't like the inequality in this relationship."

"Which inequality?" she asked. "The financial one? You don't like me to have more money than you? Or the racial one?"

"They're both factors, Laura."

"Because you make them factors," she said.

"I'm not the only one," I said.

"I *don't*," she said. "I never have. I've stood beside you. I don't care what color you are or whether you have money. I'm in love with you. I have been since Memphis and you don't understand that."

"I do understand that," I said. "And I'm not saying you're the one who makes them factors. Society makes them factors. Other people—"

"Other people have no place in our business," she said.

"No, they don't," I said. "But that doesn't stop them from looking or commenting or getting in the way. I'm in more danger when I walk the streets of Chicago holding your hand than when I'm chasing down some criminal on the South Side. And you've never really understood that."

She was shaking. One tear fell down her cheek, leaving a light mascara trail on her skin. "I understood it. I always thought you had the courage to face anything. Guess I was wrong."

She chucked Jimmy under the chin, gave him a watery smile, and then let herself out the front door.

I wasn't breathing, and my hands were clenched together.

"You go apologize," Jimmy said.

"For what?" I asked. "For telling her the truth?"

His mouth got small and his eyes narrowed. For a minute, I thought he was going to cry, too.

Instead, he stood up.

"You're really stupid sometimes," he said, as he let himself out of the apartment. I could hear him run down the stairs, calling Laura's name.

But I didn't go after them. I ate the last bite of my cold hamburger, washed it down with my warm Coke, and then stood, putting the dishes beside the small sink.

Sometimes being courageous wasn't about walking into the middle of a fight. Sometimes it took courage to retreat, to look for safe ground.

Sometimes being courageous meant turning your back on everything you knew, and starting over.

Jimmy and I had done it once before.

We could do it again.

EIGHT

We left on Saturday afternoon, June twenty-first.

I had chosen my route carefully. I used Franklin's *Chicago Negro Almanac* to look for the largest black communities on the way east. That way, I could eyeball them as a prospective new home.

On that first afternoon, we drove from Chicago to Cleveland, taking our time along the way. I had been to a number of the places in Indiana, and knew that I had no interest in that state. I also didn't want to go to Detroit which, news reports told me, had as many problems as Chicago did.

Before we left, I had set my sights on Cleveland. I hadn't heard anything bad about the city. I knew it was the first major American city to elect a black mayor, having done so two years before. And Cleveland had the largest black population in Ohio. Those three facts made it my first stop.

I had also decided, before we left, that we'd stay in a hotel the first few nights. I wanted Malcolm and Jimmy to be comfortable and to enjoy the trip. The ride in the van was more difficult than I expected. The back got hot in the middle of the day, and we'd overpacked it. I had thought Jimmy could ride back there, but as it turned out, he was more comfortable up front.

It took us a while to find a place to stay. I wasn't familiar with Cleveland,

and I had to drive a bit before I saw a neighborhood with some black faces. I had to drive even more before I found a hotel that looked like a place we could afford and be safe staying in it.

The hotel was on the corner of Central and Fifty-fifth. It was a five-story monstrosity that anchored the entire block. The neighborhood was run-down, but not alarmingly so.

Our room was on the third floor. The elevator was cranky, and once we got off, we had to carry our bags the length of the floor. The room itself was square with one window overlooking the street. The two double beds sagged in identical places, and the room smelled strongly of cigar.

The beds were covered in thin chenille, and separated by a small end table with a bubble lamp. A table and two chairs stood beside the door, and across from that was a low-riding dresser with a television on top of it.

Jimmy had the television on before I could set my suitcase on the metal luggage rack.

"Not yet," I said. "We need dinner first."

I set the suitcase down and turned around. Malcolm was still standing by the door, staring at the room. He looked like he had never seen anything like it before. It wasn't that remarkable, except that it was cleaner than most and had a little more space.

"Everything okay?" I asked.

"Yeah." He gave me a small grin. "Just didn't expect it to be so . . . normal. You know?"

I blinked, thought, then realized that Malcolm had never been outside of Chicago. He hadn't acted like someone seeing the flat Indiana and Ohio countryside for the first time. When we'd hit the Ohio turnpike, he hadn't seemed too surprised by the tolls, even though the tolls were cheaper and the toll booths less intrusive than the ones around Chicago.

I smiled at him. "Well, these rooms are designed to make you comfortable."

"I guess," he said, and set his suitcase down. He pushed on one of the beds, as if testing it to see if it was real. Then he sat down, bounced, and his grin widened.

"You're right, Bill," he said after a minute. "This is going to be an adventure."

I wouldn't have used that word, but it seemed oddly appropriate. Adventure.

I only hoped it would turn out well.

We were up early the next morning. We found a pancake house nearby, and I treated us to a large breakfast, along with the morning paper. I read it back to front, trying to get a sense of this city from a short night's sleep and a few hours' drive.

The paper made me wonder why I hadn't heard much about Cleveland in Chicago. Mayor Carl Stokes, up for reelection, was having trouble in his own community for something called the Glenville shootout, a three-day riot that began when the police tried to bring down a black militant group the previous summer.

And Stokes wasn't as effective with the white political establishment as people wanted. Apparently, the black community had expected miracles from him, and was disappointed when he managed only to do a good job.

Or so it seemed. I was making a lot of judgments from a few column inches and some editorials. Other articles caught my attention: A group of blacks were calling for a boycott of McDonald's because a black man had applied for the franchise store in the Hough District and had been turned down. And in nearby Akron, a minister who let the SDS meet in his church had been fired. Local ministers and lay people weighed in on whether something like that could happen in Cleveland.

Midway through breakfast, Malcolm slid a section of the paper toward me, folded to show a picture and an article. The picture was of a white man, standing on top of a stone structure. He was young and thin, wearing glasses, his head turned down. In his right hand, he held a gun, pointed away from his body.

I grabbed the section and read the article. In Pittsburgh, this twenty-two-year-old man, who had just come out of the Air Force, climbed a bridge and shot at people below. The paper listed the shooter's service record and time in Vietnam.

Malcolm had his hand wrapped around the diner's white coffee cup. "We going to Pittsburgh?"

I had thought of it. I had toyed with taking the long way through Pennsylvania, getting a meal in Pittsburgh and spending the night in Philadelphia before heading north to Connecticut.

"Why?" I asked.

"Just doesn't look like the kinda place we want to stop," he said.

I shoved the paper back at him. Jimmy reached away from his pancakes and grabbed the section before I could stop him.

"Don't worry," I said. "We're going through Pennsylvania today, but I promise we won't stop in Pittsburgh."

Malcolm gave me a relieved smile and went back to his paper. Jimmy looked at me from the other section, nodded toward the article, and frowned. He didn't get Malcolm's objection. But Jimmy had seen a lot more than Malcolm. Jimmy'd faced white men with guns, and survived. He'd also traveled a lot more, moved to a new community, and started a new life.

He knew how to deal with differences.

Malcolm didn't.

I found that troublesome. I had brought Malcolm along so that he could help me. I didn't want to take care of him.

Despite Malcolm's worry, the drive across Pennsylvania was relatively uneventful. True to my promise, I didn't go south to Pittsburgh. Instead, we drove on Interstate 80 across the middle of Pennsylvania. I got a bit turned around after we left the Ohio Turnpike. The interstate wasn't finished through Youngstown, and the maze of roads and the lack of signs were very confusing.

But once we hit Pennsylvania, I was all right, taking the driving one hour at a time. There was a lot of traffic, most of it elderly people on Sunday drives or families enjoying a day off. There were also a lot of small towns just off the interstate, which made me leery.

Up north, the small towns were generally white, generally suspicious of anyone who didn't belong—and it was pretty obvious, right from the first glance that I didn't belong—and unwilling to accommodate newcomers, particularly black newcomers.

I had known from the start that this part of my trip would be difficult. I made sure our gas tank was full before we started into Pennsylvania, and as I drove, I kept an eye not just on the landscape, but also on the other drivers around me.

In some ways, the panel van gave us protection. We rode higher than most cars, and because of that, our skin color wasn't immediately obvious. Judging by the reactions I got at gas stations and at one of the restaurants in Cleveland, no one expected three black males to get out of a van. I guess the stereotype had us in finned Cadillacs or the kind of dilapidated car my Impala had been.

We stopped twice at waysides. On both occasions, I picked stops that had few cars, instead of the ones that were packed. Jimmy, who had a small bladder, complained once when I passed a stop, but when I mentioned that there were three trucks in the parking area, he said he could hold it.

Malcolm looked at both of us as if we were speaking a strange language, and maybe we were. But Jimmy and I had had a couple of bad experiences with truck drivers after we had fled Memphis, and neither of us wanted to repeat that.

We had dinner in Scranton at a roadside diner that I saw a black couple enter just as we were driving past. The meal was adequate, and the prices reasonable.

The last part of the trip, from Scranton into New York and then on to Connecticut, proved more difficult than I expected. My Sinclair map, which I had gotten because Jimmy loved the dinosaur on the cover, showed Interstate 84 as completed. But my map was optimistic. The road was supposed to be completed by 1969, and in the way of all good road construction, it was behind schedule.

We sat through single lanes and long traffic lines, driving past construction workers who looked uncomfortable in their work uniforms, sweat pouring down their faces.

I felt at a distinct disadvantage not knowing the area. When Jimmy and I had driven north from Memphis, I had deliberately followed the Old Gospel Trail, knowing I would find friendly motels and a lot of black faces. It had been the black migration route when the jobs left the south and moved north.

But I knew so little about Indiana, Ohio, and Pennsylvania that I had mostly guessed. The back section of *Chicago Negro Almanac* listed black population centers in the country by state. There seemed to be a pattern: Cleveland to Pittsburgh to Philadelphia, which had been my original route.

But when I changed my mind, and decided to push directly to New Haven, I forced us into uncharted territory. And my little Sinclair map, which was about as trustworthy as a page of imaginary lines, said the largest town between Scranton and New Haven was either Middletown, Newburgh, or Danbury, which were nothing but names to me.

The road construction continued most of the way through New York. The workers had left by the time we reached Maybrook. The new interstate, with its half-opened lanes, became a ghost road a few miles later—dug into the earth, but not yet paved, and we found ourselves detoured to 17K leading into Newburgh. I nearly stopped for the night then, but I didn't see an obviously friendly neighborhood.

It was growing dark as we crossed the Hudson River into Beacon.

I wished we hadn't taken this route after all. The interstate had been planned to bypass the main highways, so we found ourselves on back roads that led to places I'd never been with names like Fishkill and Poughquag.

The back roads weren't direct, either, like the interstate was supposed to be, so we went at least fifty miles out of our way north to catch Highway 22, which took us south to US 6 which finally took us into Connecticut.

I'd never been a fan of Connecticut. The state was too white and too rural for me. I'd been in and out of it a few times as I'd traveled to New York from Boston. But I was relieved to see the white and black Connecticut road signs appear in my headlights. Danbury wasn't far, and if New Haven hadn't been less than an hour from there, I probably would have stayed in Danbury despite my misgivings.

I was getting tired, my eyes hurt, and I had been on the road too long. As it was, we had to stop just outside of Danbury to let Jimmy pee on the side of the road. He got a little thrill from doing something forbidden in the dark because I wasn't going to let any cop catch a glimpse of our skin color from our headlights.

We took US 6 to Connecticut 34, going through sleepy small town after sleepy small town, filled with expensive homes and barns and silent streets. Malcolm kept looking at me nervously, and I kept ignoring him. I didn't want him to see how uncomfortable I was.

Route 34 was supposed to dump us in New Haven, and I wouldn't have realized that we had gotten there if it hadn't been for Jimmy, yelling and pointing at the tiny NEW HAVEN, POPULATION 136,000 sign that was pushed up near a tree on the side of the road.

Like the rest of Connecticut, the buildings were dark here. But the area was dilapidated. Warehouses and storefronts, many made of brick, had boarded windows and barred doors. Streetlights were either burned out or knocked out.

Ours was the only car on the road.

"You know where we're staying?" Malcolm asked.

I shook my head. I felt at a loss. I hadn't called ahead, because I hadn't known New Haven and wasn't sure what part of town we would stay in. But I had expected to arrive in daylight.

Another sign told us we were headed toward the Yale Bowl, and I continued on the same route. I figured if we got close to the university, we had a chance of finding a motel that might take us.

Since the university was integrated, black parents had to stay somewhere.

So I doubted any of the nearby motels would throw us out, especially if I assured them we'd only stay one night. My bigger concern was prices. Yale was an expensive and prestigious university, so I expected the hotel prices in New Haven to reflect that.

"Hey, Smoke!" Jimmy scooted forward in his seat. "There's a place."

He was pointing at the right side of the road. There, not a block ahead of us, was a motel, built into the shape of a U. The center had trees and a carport. Someone had placed lights at decent intervals, revealing a small group of cars parked at one end.

I turned into the parking lot. The place didn't look full. A neon VACANCY sign had a burned-out V, and no one had turned on the YES or NO below it.

It was nearly midnight, but I decided to take my chances.

I parked beneath the carport. A wrought-iron fence framed the north and south sides of the carport, and the front door of the office had the same wrought-iron design.

That door was closed and obviously locked. But someone had taped a handwritten sign to one side of the door.

I got out and walked to the door. The sign, above the doorbell, read:

FOR AFTER-HOURS SERVICE, PLEASE RING BELL. AND BE PREPARED TO WAIT!!!!!

I pushed the button. A paint chip fell off into my hand. From inside, I heard a loud buzzer, obviously designed to wake someone from a sound sleep.

Then I took a step back from the door, just in case I startled the hotel manager. I had no idea what the ethnic makeup of New Haven was, nor did I know what this neighborhood was like, even though it looked transitional at best.

I turned slightly, so that my right profile faced the door. No sense in letting the manager find a large black man with a scarred face at his door. Better to let him assemble the parts of me slowly.

Across the street, there were several long buildings and even more parking lots. Behind them, a football stadium rose against the night sky, dark and forbidding.

That had to be the Yale Bowl, and the buildings around it all those support facilities that big sports arenas usually had.

Down the road directly in front of me seemed to be some kind of dead end. Or maybe it was just darkness, no streetlights at all.

A lock turned. The wooden door swung open, and it was my turn to be surprised. A black face peered out at me.

The man was as tall as I was, but older, with red pockmarks from a skin condition. His hair was silver and straight, which was a surprise given how dark his skin was.

"Yeah?" he asked.

"Do you have a vacancy?" I kept my voice soft. "I'm looking for a double for me and my sons."

I had decided along this trip that most people would think of Malcolm as my child. It would be easier to explain than the real rationale behind what we were doing.

The man pushed open the screen door. He wasn't wearing a robe, like I expected. He wore dark blue pants and a short-sleeved shirt. The only thing that gave away the late night was the tan slippers on his feet.

He padded across a vinyl runner that led to the front desk. The interior smelled like cigarettes, ammonia, and pine deodorizer. The desk was long and blond, one end covered with brochures.

"How long you staying?" he asked as he went around the desk.

"That depends." I glanced over his shoulder, saw the door to the back was closed. "I plan to be here for several days, but level with me. Should we stay in this neighborhood or is there someplace a little friendlier?"

He opened a register. Several spidery signatures already filled the page.

"Checking out Yale?" he asked.

"How'd you guess?" I said.

He shrugged. Obviously that's what most people did with their kids when they came to New Haven.

"A room here's nineteen dollars a night for a double. That's the cheapest you'll find within fifteen minutes of downtown. You might be a bit cheaper heading out Whalley, but honestly, depending on the place, you might run into some trouble there."

I nodded, not knowing where Whalley was, but figuring I could find it on a map.

"Otherwise, you're gonna want to be either in the Hill or along Dixwell. I don't think there's much on the Hill any more, but I know of a few places on Dixwell. You can give 'em a look if you want."

"But?"

This time it was his turn to glance over his shoulder. And he looked behind me, as if he were checking for other paying customers.

"Ain't none of those places black-owned, even if they're in our neighborhood. So you got smaller rooms, no real upkeep, and higher prices for less. At least here, you got nice rooms because we do good business."

"And we're not going to have a problem if we stay here a week with, say, the day manager?" I asked.

The man smiled. His teeth gleamed in the fluorescent light. "That day manager got canned. You'll be okay."

It was my turn to smile. "You said nineteen dollars for a double?"

Nineteen was expensive. I had hoped for less.

"If you stay the week, I can bring it down to fifteen a night."

He was doing me a favor, and I knew it. Still, I wasn't sure where my investigation would take me.

"I'd like to say I'm going to, but it depends on whether we can get all the meetings we've been planning, since the Fourth is coming up." I let my smile ease into a grin. "I promised the boys camping if we got done early."

The manager nodded. "That last summer before college's an important one. I'll make a note on your file. We'll charge fifteen if you're here for six nights."

He slid the register toward me, then grabbed an index card.

"Pay tonight's up front, and you won't owe nothing till you check out. We'll settle then."

"All right." I took out a twenty and handed it to him as I pulled the register closer. I picked up the pen and then paused. I was tired. I had nearly signed my real name.

I signed, put down my address and phone number, as well as Malcolm and Jimmy's first names, and then slid the register back toward the manager. Out of force of habit, I skimmed the other names before releasing the thick book. I didn't see any I recognized.

He had me sign the index card, too, after I saw him make the note about the possible lower rate. Then he recorded that I paid $19 for the first night, and reached into a drawer to get me my dollar change.

"You'll be in 1171," he said. "It's in the back, away from the street and the noise. There's a good walking trail to the park, and in the summer, the park's pretty nice. If one of your kids is young, he might like it. It's got swings and a merry-go-round, some picnic tables."

"Thanks," I said. "And thanks for letting us in so late."

He nodded. "You're lucky I was on tonight. Not many places in town open their doors after ten."

"I'll remember that."

"Best you do," he said. "This ain't Chicago."

So he'd already looked at where I was from. He was more watchful than I had expected.

"I'll remember that, too," I said.

NINE

Room 1171 was part of another building, tucked into the back. This building was older than the one up front, and had been built to look like row houses, attached on each side. The building was made of red brick and the doors had been painted a crisp white. Each door had a light above the entrance, a nice touch that made the place feel secure.

The room itself was the same size as the one in Cleveland, but cleaner and with newer furnishings. It also lacked the musty odor that underlay the cigarettes. This room had a faint smell of fresh paint, and didn't smell institutional at all.

"Cripes," Malcolm said from the bathroom. "They even put a paper banner around the toilet."

"Sanitized for your protection," Jimmy said from his spot on the bed.

"How'd you know?"

"Seen it before."

And had been as astonished by it the first time as Malcolm now was. I unpacked us, turned the window air-conditioner on low, and told the boys to prepare for bed.

They argued, but not strenuously. The drive had tired them out as well. It had exhausted me. After I closed my eyes, I still saw headlights coming toward me. We had been lucky; we hadn't run into any small-town traffic cops or anyone trolling for unfamiliar faces.

I didn't expect our luck to hold for the entire trip.

The next morning, after breakfast, I called Grace. I told her where we were staying and asked her for permission to pose as her ex-husband. His name had been all over the application and other documents that Daniel had filed with the university, mostly as a person who wouldn't contribute to Daniel's education.

"Why would you want to do that?" Grace asked.

"I figure the authorities here will accept me better as a member of Daniel's family than as an investigator."

"Darrel would never check up on Daniel," Grace said. "I'm not even sure Darrel remembers he has children."

"That might work for me then," I said. "If anyone calls you and asks if you sent your ex-husband here, tell them you did."

She agreed. After we exchanged a few pleasantries, I hung up and called some of the names on the list she had given me before I left. I never reached the people I wanted. Instead I was informed that they were out of town, or in one case, decided "at the last minute" to spend his summer in Venice.

On my last call, I managed to reach Daniel's college master. I felt odd talking to someone called a "master," even though I knew that the name came from the English university tradition and had nothing to do with slavery.

The master—or special master, as he called himself—would be in his office, and we set up a time to meet. When I hung up, I told Jimmy and Malcolm that we were leaving.

Jimmy and I would go to the meeting. Malcolm would explore, talk to anyone he met, and hook up with us at a designated spot.

The special master had given me instructions on how to get to his building. He told me to find the New Haven Green, and his directions proceeded from there.

The Green wasn't hard to find. It was the exact center of New Haven, a large square park filled with trees and sidewalks. Three churches dominated the east side of the square, their spires rising into the clear blue June sky. On the west side, Yale University began, hidden behind an ivy-covered stone wall that looked as intimidating as it was supposed to.

I found a five-story block-long concrete parking structure on nearby

Temple street, and left the van inside it. Malcolm went off on an investigation of his own, promising to meet us on the Green in two hours.

Jimmy and I went in the other direction, through the big Tudor arch that led us onto Yale's campus. The great stone buildings behind us blocked the traffic noise from College Street, and it felt like we had entered a whole new world.

Ahead of us lay well-mowed grass and lovely pathways. To our left, a long Colonial building was dwarfed by the mock-Tudor buildings behind it. A statue of Nathan Hale stood outside the Colonial, and it turned out that Mr. Give-Me-Liberty-or-Give-Me-Death had lived in that Colonial building when he was a student.

I wondered how Daniel had felt when he first came here. Like Malcolm, he had never lived anywhere except Chicago's South Side. Knowing Daniel, he had probably researched Yale, but research wasn't like reality.

This place had been designed to intimidate those who didn't belong.

There weren't a lot of students on the grounds. The handful that we saw weren't going from class to class but instead were lounging against the large trees that gave the area its character. Obviously, there was summer school, but equally as obvious, not that many students attended.

It didn't take us long to reach Daniel's college. Yale followed the Oxford and Cambridge model, dividing the students into twelve residential colleges. The master lived on site, as did, apparently, the dean of that college and a handful of professors.

We had to ring a doorbell and get buzzed through yet another archway to enter the college. The Gothic architecture and all the stone spoke of wealth to me. It seemed exotic to Jimmy, who couldn't stop touching the curved walls.

The archway opened into a wide quad. There were more students on this patch of green grass, many of them sunbathing as they read thick tomes. A game of touch football went on along the far end, the boys laughing and jumping with ease. Someone had hooked a bicycle rack to the stone courtyard in front of one of the doorways, ruining the medieval look. Above us, a stereo blared the rhythms of the Beatles' "Sergeant Pepper."

Jimmy didn't seem to notice that so far all of the students we had seen were white. Usually this many white people made him nervous, but he was too intent on the university itself to pay much attention.

The masters' quarters were in one of the Gothic towers. We went to the thick wooden door as instructed, and I pounded the brass door knocker. Jimmy had never seen one, and wanted to give it a try. I let him do it once, and then we waited.

I slipped on my suitcoat, trying to ignore the weight of the wool.

After a moment, a student opened the door. He was short, white, and clean-cut, with dark greased-back hair, and an acne-scarred face. He wore a long-sleeved white shirt that didn't have a spot of sweat on it and black pants with shiny black shoes.

"I take it you're the Kirklands," he said.

I nodded, and the student led us inside.

The interior was startlingly monastical. The floor was marble, the walls the same stone as the exterior. The student led us up a flight of stairs that eventually opened onto a carpeted hallway.

The walls were paneled. Shelves stuck out at odd angles, and photographs, many of them black-and-whites of professional quality, rested on each. I noted a lot of familiar faces as I went past those pictures: President Dwight D. Eisenhower, Senator Prescott Bush, and President Richard Nixon mingled with George Balanchine, Margaret Mead, and David Frost. After a moment, I realized that many of the photographs had been taken at Yale.

The student pointed toward a set of double doors at the end of the hall. "That's Master Robinson's office. He's expecting you."

"Thank you." I put my hand behind Jimmy's back and led him forward.

I pushed the doors opened, half expecting the student to announce us as if he were an English butler. But the student disappeared into one of the other doors along the hallway.

Jimmy and I stepped into a two-story library that smelled of leather. A large oak desk sat toward the back, an area rug and two chairs before it. Books rose around us on all sides, and Jimmy gaped, just like I wanted to do.

It took me a moment to notice the man behind the desk. He was small, white-haired, and balding, with that translucent skin some older white people get. He stood when he saw us, and came around the desk.

He wasn't dressed for the weather either, although his suit coat was lighter than mine. That's when I noticed how cool the room was. I couldn't see an air conditioner, and wondered if the coolness came from the stone and the room's lack of windows.

"Darrel Kirkland, I assume?" the man said.

I stuck out my hand, sliding into my role as the nervous friendly father of a missing boy with more ease than I expected. "You must be Ludlow Robinson."

He bowed slightly, but didn't take my hand. "At your service."

Although as he said the words, they didn't sound subservient at all. More the condescending politeness of a great man to a supplicant.

"This is my youngest son, James," I said, pushing Jimmy forward. To my surprise, Jimmy bowed, too.

Robinson laughed. "It's nice to see a young man with manners," he said, and swept his hand toward the heavy leather chairs in front of the desk.

We took our seats as he took his behind the desk. His graceful movements made me realize I had seen him before. Not in person, but on television. I hadn't recognized his name, but he was one of those experts who was constantly interviewed by the nightly news programs.

"I understand you've come about Daniel." He elongated the name, gave it some class.

I nodded. "My ex-wife, Grace, called me when she found out he was missing. She asked me if I could check things out."

Robinson took a pipe from the ashtray that sat on a small table beside the desk. He tapped some tobacco into the bowl. "I do hope you didn't come far."

Meaning he didn't have a lot of news for me. But I pretended I didn't speak the same subtle language that he did.

"I took some vacation time I had coming," I said, not answering him directly, but sounding as eager as I could. "Grace is pretty worried about him."

"You're not?" Robinson moved the pipe away from his face.

I put my hand on Jim's shoulder. "May I be honest with you, sir?"

"Certainly," he said, and it seemed that for the first time, I held his interest.

"Grace and I divorced over a decade ago, and she raised my older boys. I don't know them as well as she does. When she says that it's not like Daniel to disappear, I have to take her at her word."

"Yet you came here."

I shrugged. "She couldn't afford it. And I do owe him. Both my older boys, if you know what I mean."

Jimmy glanced at me. Someone watching him would think that he was surprised by my words, but he was playacting as much as I was.

Robinson used a small silver tool to push the tobacco down. "I do understand. In life, we all make difficult choices."

And he clearly didn't approve of the one he thought I had made. I didn't approve of it either. No one should abandon a child. But that was the role I had taken on, and I would use it as best I could.

"Grace says he never showed up last semester, but he didn't tell her. She hasn't heard from him in a long time, and she's worried."

Robinson pulled a file out of a lower desk drawer. The illusion was supposed to be that all student files were at his fingertips, but he had probably had that student assistant look up Daniel's case when I called.

"I can't tell you where your son is right now, Mr. Kirkland. If that's what you're here for—"

"I need to start somewhere," I said, adding a touch of desperation to my voice. "All we know is that he was here, and then he left. So I'm starting here."

Robinson sighed. "I do remember Daniel, of course. We get to know all of our students in the college. Unfortunately, my first interactions with him were . . . difficult, to say the least. You do understand our system here?"

"Four-year school, one of the best in the country, lots of prestige. I know the kid was damn lucky to get a scholarship that covered it."

Robinson picked up his pipe again, running his fingers along the stem. "I'm sure you know we've been in a state of flux. Universities all over the country are reevaluating their policies and curriculums, and we're no different."

Jimmy squirmed beside me. The initial ruse had been fun for him, but now the discussion was serious and he wasn't interested. I squeezed his shoulder, then let go.

"The reason I'm here this year, and not up on the Vineyard—"

Was the Martha's Vineyard reference a put-down to me or an unconscious reference? I honestly couldn't tell.

"—is because of one of our president's concessions to the students. Yale has come under fire for being one of the few all-male colleges left. We were going to have a co-educational program with Vassar, but the school refused to move to New Haven from Poughkeepsie."

He made it sound like Vassar's administration wanted to remain in hell.

"Then we—"

"What does this have to do with Daniel?" I had expected to hear about the black studies program, not about coeducation.

"Well." He set the pipe down. "President Brewster decided that the school would become coeducational in 1972, and the administration went along with it. That would give us time to build facilities, give the women their own college, perhaps, and allow—"

"I'm sorry," I said. "I still don't understand."

"Perhaps if you let me finish." He pulled the file closer to him and opened it. "The students protested last fall, and as a result, we will have women attend this fall, as members of the class of 1973. Because of the student protests, these women will be scattered all over the colleges. I'm here to facilitate the changes in this college, so that the women are safe from predatory males and—"

"You think Daniel was one of the predatory males?"

"No," Robinson said. "He was one of the protestors. The first time I met him was at a college luncheon that we held to discuss the women issue, shortly before Coeducation Week, which was in November. Daniel was convinced that Yale would block the admission of black women. He claimed they were the most discriminated class of people in the United States, and unless there was some guarantee that our admissions policy would bring in a specific number of black women, he would make sure that Coeducation Week went badly."

"Coeducation Week?"

Robinson's lips thinned even more, which was his way of letting me know that if I allowed him his lecture, I might learn what Coeducation Week was.

"We did an experiment last fall. For one week in November, we had girls on campus. If that experiment failed, then we might not have opened the admission."

Which probably would've gotten his vote.

"Or we might have followed the original plan and brought in the first female class in 1972."

"What's wrong with girls?" Jimmy asked, startling me. I had asked him not to speak unless spoken to.

"Jim," I said warningly.

"It's all right," Robinson said. "There is much to be said for an all-male institution, young man. You're old enough to know what a distraction the female can be."

Jimmy frowned. He wasn't quite that old.

"Add to that their undisciplined minds, and the fact, in truth, we'll only be producing overeducated housewives, and you will see why this entire idea is so ludicrous."

"The girls I know are really smart," Jimmy said. "And Laura, she runs a business all on her own. So does—"

"Jim," I said, and he stopped. I knew where he had been going. He almost mentioned Grace. Only he would have called her Mrs. Kirkland.

His cheeks flushed. "Sorry," he said, and bowed his head.

"Not all women become housewives, that is true," Robinson said, "and studies have shown that educated women produce intelligent children. But there are other institutions for those women. Yale breeds leaders. We have produced many of the nation's presidents, senators, and congressmen. Yale Law has been well represented on the Supreme Court, and if you look at the captains of industry, you will see a Yale domination. We don't need to deny this sort of education to future leaders just to accommodate a few women."

I clasped my hands tightly on my knees, concentrating on the pressure in my fingers instead of my building temper. "So let me get this straight. Daniel approved of admitting women, but he was going to disrupt Coeducation Week."

"If we didn't insert some guarantees that black women would be admitted as well."

"I'm sorry, sir," I said. "But it seems reasonable to me."

His lower jaw tightened. "It was his tone. That became the problem with Daniel. His tone. He made pronouncements. He didn't listen."

"So he yelled at you," I said. "I've been reading about schools where students close down buildings. Yelling seems kinda minor in today's world."

Robinson stood, grabbed his pipe and paced toward the books. "This is Yale, Mr. Kirkland. Those things do not happen here. As I said, we're training future leaders."

"And Daniel didn't fit in," I said. "He was black, he was poor, and he was opinionated, so you guys tossed him out."

Robinson gave me an alarmed glance. My voice had more edge in it than I expected.

"Not exactly," he said, returning to his chair. "I was merely telling you about my encounters with him. I should perhaps explain my job here. As special master, my main function at the college is to serve in a cultural capacity."

"Huh?" Jimmy said, and I almost applauded him. I hated the vague language of power.

"It means, young man, that I arrange for guest lecturers and special seminars, host luncheons with important guests—I'm sure you saw some of their pictures in the entry—and I throw parties for the more successful students."

The richer ones, at least.

"Even though I do act as the college's link to the administration, my interactions with the students should be primarily social. Your son, Mr. Kirkland, saw me as someone who made policy, as someone to push against, not someone to work with. And that is what I meant by his tone."

"Daniel was thrown out because he was rude to you?"

"I never said that young Mr. Kirkland was thrown out of Yale. I'm not sure why he's no longer with us, only that he did leave." He thumbed through the file. "There are many reprimands here, a few disciplinary actions, and one somewhat egregious incident last fall. According to the file, the university and your son mutually decided that they were not suited for each other."

"You make it sound like you weren't involved."

"I wasn't," Robinson said. "The dean handles the administrative tasks. You should really be talking to him."

"He was on my list," I said. "I haven't been able to reach him."

"Because he's been in meetings on this coeducation matter," Robinson said. "But let me set up an appointment with him. He'll be better able to answer your questions."

"Maybe I could just take a look at the file—"

"It's for Yale only," Robinson said. "Besides, I read you the pertinent language. I'm sure Dean Sidbury will know the exact incidents and probably some of the other precipitating events. I do know that young Daniel wasn't happy here. That became painfully obvious. We assumed he went home after he left. It was Christmastime, after all. There's nothing in the file after that."

I swallowed. A bead of sweat ran down one side of my face. The room wasn't as cool as I had thought.

"Daniel couldn't afford to go home for Christmas," I said softly. "Surely your file would tell you that."

"My file tells me he had a full scholarship, he was a straight-A student his first semester, his grades went down slightly in the second, and that he participated in some of the more radical societies on campus. He stopped attending all but a few classes in his third semester, became quite active in Bee-Say—"

"What's Bee-Say?" I asked.

"B-S-A-Y," he said, enunciating each letter. "It is the Black Student Alliance at Yale. BSAY is an informal group that the students originally put together. Over the years it has become militant, making demands and protesting the smallest slight. This afternoon, a handful of the BSAY students still on campus are at the courthouse, protesting the arrest of some Black Panthers who murdered one of their own this spring."

He shook his head.

"If Daniel were still in New Haven, I would expect him to be there, not here."

I nodded, suddenly wanting to get out of this oppressively opulent room.

"Where's the courthouse?" I asked.

"On the corner of Church and Elm," he said, obviously glad he had diverted me. "Across from the Green. Not far from here at all."

I stood. "Come on, Jim," I said. "We'll see if we find him there."

Jimmy stood, looking a bit confused. I hadn't gotten my questions answered, but I wasn't sure if I could talk to this man much longer and remain polite.

"I'd still like that appointment with your dean," I said, putting my hand on Jimmy's shoulder to lead him out of the room.

"I'll get in touch with you," Robinson said.

"Is it possible to set it up now?" I asked. "I'm hard to reach. We're in a motel."

I stressed the word "motel." Robinson had probably never stayed in one in his life.

"Let me call his secretary." Robinson picked up the phone. Jimmy and I walked toward the books on the far wall.

"He didn't say nothing," Jimmy whispered. "Just a bunch of junk about girls."

I smiled at him. Jimmy had never really helped me on a case before, and he was putting his entire self into this.

"Sometimes it's what people don't say," I whispered. "I'll tell you when we leave."

Jimmy grunted. He hated nuance more than I did.

"Mr. Kirkland?"

I turned. Robinson still had his hand on the top of the phone. "He'll see you tomorrow at eight A.M. sharp."

I nodded to Robinson. "I appreciate your help. If you find out anything else, we're at the Motor Court near the Yale Bowl. Or you can call Daniel's mother. She'll be able to get in touch with us."

Robinson closed the file. "I'm sure Dean Sidbury will be of more help. Good luck finding the young man."

Neither Robinson nor I tried for other amenities. This time, I didn't even offer him my hand. I opened one of the double doors and let us out.

"Jeez—," Jimmy started as the door closed, but I put a finger over his mouth.

"Outside," I said.

"Okay," he whispered and ran ahead of me down the hall. Jeez was right. If these were the attitudes "young Daniel" faced, I was amazed he had survived even a year at Yale.

Jimmy and I headed down the stairs and out of the building. When we reached the quad, I pulled off my suit coat, wishing I could remove my sweat-stained shirt as well.

"Jeez," Jimmy said again, louder than he should have, probably because I had stifled him before. "That guy was a jerk."

I grinned. "Better brace yourself, Jim. I have a hunch he's not the only one we're going to encounter on this trip."

"How come you didn't ask him more questions?"

"Because he was making me mad, and I can't do a good job when I'm angry. If I need to, I'll talk to him again."

"I'm glad I know Laura," Jimmy said. "So that I know all rich people aren't like that."

"Here's a tip, Jim. That man isn't rich."

Jimmy looked up at me. "But he lives in a mansion."

"Paid for by the school. Owned by the school. For his name, which is a famous one, and the work he does for the school."

"Wow," Jimmy said. "Wish I could get a job like that."

"You can," I said. "It takes a lot of education and a specialty in an important field. Anyone can do it, if they want to."

Jimmy's eyes lit up. "And they pay you to live here?"

I nodded.

"That's just cool," he said and ran ahead of me down the path, through the students.

Of course, it wasn't as easy as it sounded, but that was the first time I'd seen Jimmy interested in anything that had to do with school.

I followed him across the quad, happy to be leaving Yale, and hoping we'd be lucky enough to find Daniel at the courthouse.

TEN

The courthouse was hard to miss. It was a massive stone building that wasn't Colonial or Federal, but appeared to have been built at the turn of the century.

Initially, the courthouse had been white, but time, dirt, and pollution had turned it a dusky gray. Still, it had a grandeur that a lot of other old buildings lacked. Big stone columns, marble steps, and two statues bridging those steps like guardians. I didn't recognize the men who formed the statues, but I didn't look that hard.

The sidewalk was relatively empty. No one protested on the steps, and no large group of black students stood near the entry.

Jimmy and I entered, and stopped in surprise.

The interior was stunning. The ceiling was vaulted, with amazing amounts of light. Bridges and mezzanines floated above us, like some kind of Escher drawing.

"Wow," Jimmy said, his voice echoing in all that stone. "How come they don't have stuff like this in Chicago?"

I didn't know the answer to that, so I didn't even try to guess. Instead, I walked to the information board, which listed the day's uses for each courtroom.

The grand jury room was on the second floor. I took Jimmy's hand, pulling him forward, and we walked up one of the staircases.

I couldn't hear the sounds of protest coming from any level. And if someone spoke too loudly in these hallways, the sound would carry. It probably wouldn't be understandable, but it would be audible.

We reached the top, and I turned right. Jimmy ran to the railing so that he could look down at the main floor, then up at the vaulted ceiling.

"C'mon, Jim," I said, still heading forward.

No group of black students stood in the corridors. In fact, no one was in the corridors at all, except a few lawyers scurrying to their next court date and a couple of bailiffs guarding the doors.

I figured that behind one of those doors would be the Black Panthers. Jimmy hurried after me, catching up as I reached the grand jury room.

One of the bailiffs stood in front of it. He wore a gray uniform, a black belt with a truncheon and handcuffs, and a walkie-talkie. His skin was darker than mine, and as I approached, he watched me out of the corner of his eye.

"Can I ask you a couple of questions?" I asked as I approached.

"Information's downstairs."

"I know," I said, "but this'll only take a minute."

"Downstairs," he repeated. I knew what he was thinking; he worried that I would distract him so that I—or a cohort of mine—could cause a disruption in the grand jury room.

"I was told by one of the professors at Yale that the Black Students Alliance had planned a protest here today."

The bailiff snorted.

"I'm looking for a missing student, and I thought he might be with them."

"He's my brother," Jimmy piped up.

I hadn't planned to use the Kirkland identity here, but Jimmy's comment caught the bailiff's attention.

"Where's he missing from?" The bailiff spoke to Jimmy, not me.

"Yale," I said. "He didn't report for the last semester, and we only just found out about it."

"So they sent you here?"

"One of the so-called special masters."

The bailiff's gaze caught mine. He clearly disapproved of the title these men held as much as I did.

"We didn't have no protest today," the bailiff said, moving his gaze to the far wall. He hadn't moved from his position near the door. "Those students haven't come near here all summer. Last seen students in May."

"Black students?" I asked.

He nodded. "When those Panthers got arrested, the students came as a 'show of support.' "

Again, he didn't seem to approve.

"You think the Panthers are guilty," I said.

He shrugged. "That's what this's for. To see if there's enough to indict 'em. There'll be another grand jury tomorrow, but it'll be in Middletown. Looks like they get the murder charges, not us."

I frowned. "What's the case?"

"One of their own got found, murdered, in a marsh. Looks now like the killing might've happened in Middlesex County, not here. So we're getting kidnapping, at least that's what the DA said."

"How many Panthers are being indicted?" I asked.

"That's for the grand jury," he repeated.

I hadn't asked my question correctly. "How many were arrested?"

"Eleven." He shrugged one shoulder. "Them kids—"

Meaning the students.

"—they see it as a cause."

"What do you see it as?"

"Trouble," he said. "Most the time, folks around here just don't notice us. Then the militant kids come along, and suddenly, it's a black-white thing."

"You don't have racial problems in New Haven?"

He looked at me like I'd grown a third head. "Where're you from?"

"Chicago," I said.

"You live rich, there, right, you and your kid? Buying Yale and all, trying to be white?"

I tried to think of a way to answer without letting him know that I bristled at his tone.

"We ain't rich," Jimmy said. "He got here on—whatsit?—school money."

"Scholarship." The bailiff gave him a tolerant look. "We been seeing all kinds of stuff. They say New Haven's protected from the—y'know—violence and stuff because the kids here are rich and from good families. Me, I think it's that university president, Brewster, you know? He stops stuff just as it starts. And there's still trouble. But you don't hear about it none."

"How could I find out?"

"Your kid in trouble?" he asked.

"I didn't think so at first, but I'm not so sure now," I said. "He's been involved in the antiwar movement, and his 'special master' said he was also in the Black Students Alliance."

"Them BSAY kids." The bailiff shook his head.

"They've come through the courthouse?"

"Not except to put up bail money for protestors. And mostly, they been outside, talking about how unfair the system is. Like they know."

I let that pass. Just because a black student got a privileged education didn't mean he was privileged.

"You said I wouldn't hear about the problems," I said.

"Town's buttoned up. You noticed that, right? Read the *Crow*?"

"The *Crow*?"

He nodded. He was looking at both of us now, not paying attention to his job.

"I've only been in town since last night," I said.

"It's supposed to be our paper," he said, meaning the black paper. "But you read it and you won't understand it. It's all black businesses and how good stuff is. That's New Haven. Don't say bad stuff about nothing."

"Even if it is bad," I said.

"Especially if it's bad." His voice was close to a whisper.

"So how do I find out what's going on?"

"You got to know folks, and you don't."

I sighed. "All I want to do is find Daniel."

"Best thing, you go through the reports, ask some questions. The paper'll help you so long as they ain't on record. Nobody'll go on record."

"Not even you," I said.

"A job is a job." He seemed to remember his. He resumed his military posture in front of the door. "But use your eyes. Look who's got what jobs around here. And how come no one says nothing to them masters of yours."

I shuddered at the phrase. They weren't my masters.

"They have the paper at the library?" I asked.

"Just go down to the offices. They're on Goffe, the hundred block," he said. "And there's one other place you might want to check out. There's a place on Washington where kids live, mostly townies, but I heard stuff. You can't miss it when you work here, you know."

"Do you know exactly where?"

"No," he said. "Just ask, though. They been calling it a 'Teen-Inn' locally. Won't be in the papers, but the neighbors'll know."

"And they'll talk to me?"

His gaze met mine. "It's not so much how you look. It's that you don't live here. You gotta tell them this kid is missing, maybe in trouble. They're not gonna feel no compassion, but the fewer troublemakers we got in this town, the better."

His tone had shifted. There was an underlying tone of anger, and it felt like he directed it at me, as if I were in the wrong for even talking to him.

"Thank you for your help," I said.

"Give me his name," he said, "and I'll keep an eye out. You can check back if you don't find him."

"Daniel Kirkland." Jimmy spoke up. He, apparently, hadn't heard the undertone. Or maybe he was ignoring it.

"Don't sound familiar," the bailiff said, "but I'll keep my ears open."

"Thank you," I said.

"You checked the Panther roster, right? He ain't with them."

I hadn't checked it, but I couldn't imagine it. Of course, I couldn't imagine jeopardizing a full scholarship anywhere either. "No, I haven't."

"He ain't one of these guys, but that don't mean he don't know them. These kids're playing at stuff they don't understand."

I thought of the Panthers I'd seen in Chicago. I never had the sense they were playing at anything.

"Thanks again," I said, and put my hand on Jimmy's shoulder, to lead him out of the corridor.

"You be careful," the bailiff said. "Just because stuff don't get talked about here, don't mean it don't happen."

I appreciated the warning anyway. Just because the town was smaller than I was used to didn't make it any safer.

I was glad Jimmy heard the warning as well.

He needed to remember to keep his eyes open, just like the rest of us.

ELEVEN

Jimmy and I waited for Malcolm on a bench across from Yale. After twenty minutes, I sent Jimmy off to get us ice cream cones, since I was sweltering in the June heat. My wool suit itched, and even though I wasn't wearing the jacket, I was extremely uncomfortable. I couldn't wait for Malcolm's return so that I could go back to the motel and change clothes.

Malcolm arrived from the Elm Street side, walking toward us from our right. He was upwind from us, and as he got close, I caught the sickly sweet odor of marijuana. Apparently Jimmy did too, because he slid sideways, away from me, obviously anticipating my reaction.

"Sorry I'm late," Malcolm said as he reached us.

"Smells like you found something," I said, taking the last bite of my cone, balling up the napkin and holding it in my right fist.

Malcolm sighed. "It's not like it seems."

"Oh, really?" I asked. "How is it?"

"I didn't smoke anything."

I raised my eyebrows and looked at him. Even though the smell was strong, his eyes were clear—not unfocused or bloodshot.

"What happened then?"

Jimmy leaned forward, elbows on his knees, watching both of us as he nurtured his cone. White ice cream dripped down the sides, onto his fingers and pants. Eventually, I would have to find a Laundromat.

Malcolm looked all around us. Then he crouched, getting as close to us as he could so that he wouldn't have to speak too loudly.

"Hooked up with some students in there." Malcolm pointed toward the arch that we had gone through. "Let them think I was dealing, you know?"

My fingers tightened on that napkin. That certainly wouldn't have been my approach.

"Told them I was establishing my turf, and I was wondering who would need my services." He grinned. He seemed very pleased with himself. "I figured if Daniel was into bad stuff, these guys would know about it."

Logical. Jimmy bit his lower lip and looked at me. He remembered my reaction from over a year ago when I found him running drugs for his brother. Jimmy was probably expecting me to yell at Malcolm.

"And did they?"

Malcolm shook his head. "These white boys are really laid back, you know? They don't care who knows their business. I got five names and ten different places to go. I went to a couple, found out some of those guys were gone for the summer, but a few were hanging around. They were in Silliman College, which took me a while to find. No one wanted to tell me where the college was. They told me the names of the guys, but when they found out that I wanted to go to the college and I wasn't a Yalie, they got really worried."

"Yeah," I said softly. "So did you find the place?"

"It's that way." He nodded toward Elm, the direction we had come from. "A few blocks down, but it's hard to tell because everything's fenced off. Like they don't want anyone to see in their precious little houses or buildings or whatever."

"They don't," I said.

He sat down cross-legged, apparently tired of crouching. "Once I got in the college, I found six guys smoking weed under one of the trees. Like no one cared if anyone saw them. I was freaked."

His language was looser than usual, so he probably inhaled some of that weed. I didn't say anything, though. Jimmy munched on his ice cream cone, his gaze going back and forth from me to Malcolm.

"I made like I was interested in buying, but I didn't have any cash on me. I strung them on for a while, but these guys were so focused on money. They almost didn't talk to me when I told them I'd have to come back to my apartment to get some."

"But they did talk to you," I said.

"A little." He ran a hand through his hair. "They knew Daniel."

That caught my attention. "They did? Did they know where he is?"

"They haven't seen him since winter break, whenever the hell that is."

"Christmas," I said. "Sometime in there."

"They didn't like him. He liked weed now and then, but he didn't buy, and he wasn't into the other junk."

"What other junk?" I asked.

"These guys sold some acid, too, and some ludes. The stuff looked better than the stuff I've seen in Chicago."

I decided to let that pass.

Jimmy crunched the last of his cone, then licked off his fingers. He wiped them dry on his pants. He kept his gaze on us, looking worried.

"Daniel was pretty straight. Most of the guys hadn't even seen him drunk, which I guess is unusual here. And he's righteous—their word, and they didn't mean it nice. They meant it like he was holier-than-thou. They thought he was a real jerk."

We agreed on that, then, but probably not for the same reasons. "What did they tell you?"

"That there was some trouble with a girl. Rhonda or Rhondi or something like that. Back in the fall."

"What kind of trouble?" I asked.

Malcolm shrugged. "They wouldn't say. Something about Coeducation Week."

"That master guy talked about that," Jimmy said.

I nodded. "I heard about the week, just not Daniel's involvement in it."

"Sounded pretty heavy, but no one knew exactly what he was doing. Said he flirted with the SDS but left it for some other organization. Said he got real militant, too, by the end, screaming about rights and privileges and the way that the system had to change before anybody got the rights they deserved, which didn't play well with these guys."

"You'd think it would," I said, "given what they were doing."

Malcolm shook his head. "I got the sense that they weren't into any kind of revolution except the one going on in their own heads. They were doing more than weed because they forgot about me after a while. Except one guy, who really wanted his money. He started screaming at me, and I got out of there."

"So we can't talk to them again."

"*I* can't talk to them again," Malcolm said, "and I doubt they'd let you get near them. But I think I got most of what I needed from them. They haven't seen Daniel since he left campus. But they gave me a few partial names. The girl's and a couple of other people's. They think some of the guys are still around, so I'm going to see if I can find them."

"Smoke don't like drugs," Jimmy said softly, as if he couldn't keep silent any longer.

"I'm not real fond of them either," Malcolm said, "but they have their uses. Those guys are pretty plugged in because they have to be. But I didn't expect to find these guys so easily. I thought it would take a couple of days. It sure would've at home."

The differences between our lives and that of the privileged class. "Let's get back to the van," I said. "I'll explain what happened to us along the way."

We rode back with the windows open. I took one of our duffels inside the motel room to use as a laundry bag. Malcolm wasn't wearing those clothes again until we had a chance to wash them.

I showered first, though, and changed into something cooler. I was going to head to the *Crow* on my own. I wanted Jimmy and Malcolm to rest. Besides, I wanted the freedom to go to a few places I didn't feel comfortable bringing an eleven-year-old.

Jimmy complained, but I promised I'd be back for dinner. I told Malcolm to use the phone book, see if he could track down any of the names that the Yale students had given him.

He was in the shower when I left, and Jimmy was watching an old movie that seemed to feature women in scanty costumes and men dressed up as giant bugs.

I got into the van and headed toward Goffe. It didn't take me long to find the *Crow*'s offices. They were in an old building that looked like it was about to fall down. The rents here were obviously cheap, and judging from a sign on a nearby corner, the buildings would eventually vanish.

The sign promised a firehouse here, along with some more housing and some town houses. A design map of the plan was enlarged, along with the slogan "New Haven Working for You," which I highly doubted.

I parked near a building that announced itself as the Goffe Special School—whatever that was—and walked the half block toward the *Crow*'s building. The *Crow* shared the building with other businesses. I would have driven right by if it weren't for the address painted in black letters above the door and a small crow sign in one of the windows.

As I got close, I realized that the crow sign was actually a hand-painted reproduction of the newspaper's logo. Beneath the name and the crow drawing were these words: *The Crow Will Speak the Truth and the Truth Will Make Us Free.*

I certainly hoped so.

The door stood open, letting in the warmth of the day. A large desk sat right near the entrance, and in back were smaller desks, two of them with manual typewriters, one of the desks with just a phone. In the very back, were drafting tables, probably for layout. The place had the sharp smell of printer's ink.

"Help you?" The woman at the desk was about my age, with a pair of cat's-eye glasses around her neck instead of a necklace, and her dark hair in a modified beehive. Her lipstick was an incongruous orange, and she wore false eyelashes.

"I'm not sure," I said. "I'm trying to find out some information."

"About the paper?"

"No." I glanced around. A man in the back was studying me. "I'm new to town, looking for someone, and a man suggested that I talk to you."

"Is this about a news story?"

"Maybe," I said. "I'm just trying to get—"

"Can I help you?" The man had come up from the back. He was slender, his hair short and natural, his face covered with a neatly trimmed beard.

"I hope so," I said. "I'm kind of at a loss. My name is Bill Grimshaw. I'm from Chicago."

I extended my hand. The man took it.

"Reuben Freeman." He shook my hand once, then let go.

"Pleasure," I said. "Is this your paper?"

He shook his head. "Mostly I just report. What can we do for you, Mr. Grimshaw?"

"I'm looking for someone. He's been missing since last fall, and his mom hired me—"

"You're a private detective?"

"More or less," I said.

"The mother hired you, so I assume you're looking for a college student?"

I nodded.

"South Central, Southern Connecticut State, University of New Haven, or Yale?" he asked, listing three schools I hadn't heard of.

"Yale," I said.

"Black, I assume," he said. "Else she would have hired someone local."

Meaning most of the private detectives here, if not all, were white.

"Yes," I said.

"Missing since last fall." He led me through the desks to the one he was using in the back. It also had a phone, but that phone had been hidden by stacks of paper, another manual typewriter, and three legal pads. "That's a long time."

"I don't know exactly when he went missing. I'm trying to figure that out."

"Kids nowadays, they don't take things as seriously as we did." He shoved some of the papers aside.

"I've met this boy. Seems he took things too seriously."

"But she only sent you now," he said again.

"Yes," I said. "She didn't find out he was missing until she got notification that his scholarship was going to be revoked if he didn't sign up for this fall's term."

Freeman frowned. He sat in the metal chair behind his desk. "Pull over a chair."

I grabbed the nearest one, a heavy wooden chair that was probably as old as I was.

"What's his name?"

"Daniel Kirkland," I said.

"It's not ringing any bells. So he wasn't in the news much."

"You can check for me, though, right?"

"Do we look like we have a standard morgue? You're better off going to the *Register* or the *Journal-Courier* for that."

I sighed. "All right."

Freeman rubbed that beard of his, a slight frown marring his forehead. "Mom and kid weren't in close contact? I mean, how can she not know he was gone for half a year?"

"Long distance is expensive."

"But he sent her letters?"

"Not after his first semester," I said.

"He's what? Junior?"

"Sophomore," I said. "If he'd taken his spring semester, he'd be a junior."

Freeman sighed. "You don't know how many parents we get here, looking for their kids. The cops won't help. They're not even helping the white folks anymore. Unless, of course, the folks are from money."

"I hadn't heard that."

"You live here with a bunch of colleges in town, and even more in the neighboring cities, and you learn real fast what the kids are doing. Right now, they're dropping out and living their own way, not communicating with their parents, and throwing away their lives. You sure this kid wants to be found?"

"I'm not sure of anything," I said. "I talked to some folks from Yale before I came out here, which made me nervous enough to make the trip. Now that I am here, I'm finding that New Haven isn't as peaceful as it seems."

Freeman grinned. "Don't say that too loudly, especially in this building."

"What does that mean?"

"Meaning that we believe in bootstraps and entrepreneurial equality and working for the betterment of the community from within the community."

"In other words, don't stir things up."

He smiled. "You said it. I didn't."

The phone rang. The woman at the reception desk answered it, then put her hand over the mouthpiece. "Moxie Baker wants an ad for this week."

"Okay," Freeman said. "I have to take this. Why don't you look at a few back issues."

He waved his hand toward a stack of papers leaning against the wall. I had no idea how a newspaper could survive with that many copies still inside the building. Nonetheless, I picked up the top issue, with Saturday's date.

The paper was thin and had too much empty space, suggesting that the person who did the layout wasn't a professional. Most of the articles seemed to lack depth, and referred to people without describing who they were, apparently assuming the reader knew.

I scanned the editorials, which referred to more things I didn't understand, and nearly set the paper aside before an article caught my eye.

AIM Announces Drive to Explain Panthers

The American Independent Movement has announced an education program on the Black Panther Party to explain the purpose of the BPP. AIM believes that the BPP is an important and positive force in the efforts of working Americans to control their country and their lives. The Panthers' work is not racist but racism has been used as a powerful weapon against them, especially in the rumor-filled unproven press coverage of the recent arrests, AIM says. It is—

"Sorry about that," Freeman said. "It's mostly a one-person show around here. You just happened to catch me running it."

"It's all right." I folded the paper, but kept hold of the article about the Panthers.

"I'm not sure how I can help you on this," he said. "I'll do what I usually do. I'll give you the names of some contacts locally, let you know where the kids hang out, but that's about all I know."

I nodded. "You don't get police blotters or anything like that?"

His smile faded. "We're not doing that kind of news. You think he might be in legal trouble?"

"I don't know," I said. "I'm hearing rumors about Coeducation Week, and something that happened there. Yale says they mutually parted company with him, which seems odd to me."

"Yale mutually parts company with students who don't fit the mold." Freeman sounded bitter.

"But there are enough black students for them to form an organization," I said.

"BSAY?" Freeman sighed. "BSAY used to be the right kind of organization, but it's going the wrong way, too."

"Right kind?" I asked.

"Put together to help black students help each other. In the last year, it's gotten pretty militant, which I think is a risk. There're only about 250, maybe 300, black students—graduate and undergraduate—at the school. That's not even one percent of the total enrollment. It's supposed to get bigger next year—applications from blacks tripled when the university announced it was going coed, but tripled means they got 525 applicants."

"Interesting statistics to have at your fingertips," I said. "For someone who doesn't rock the boat."

He grinned at me. "Didn't say *I* didn't rock the boat. Said that the paper doesn't. Yale enrollment is a hot topic right now, with the women coming in. I'm doing articles for a variety of places all over the country. Most of my income is freelance. You just caught me on my volunteer day here."

"Volunteer?"

He shrugged. "We're trying to get this thing off the ground. What little money that comes in goes right back out to pay for typesetting and printing. Only a few people get paid, and that would make a pittance seem like a fortune."

I shifted the paper in my hand, keeping my finger on the Black Panther article. "Seems to me that New Haven is more than one percent black."

"Yep, and the other colleges around here reflect that. But Yale is not a local school. New Haven's a lot more diverse than our greatest industry would let on."

"Are there black professors?"

"A few," he said. "Haven't paid attention to the statistics on them. Not relevant in this year of the women. But no need to go to the professors. They won't tell you much about the black students. The key to survival at Yale is pretense—and getting involved with a militant black group won't help."

"You think BSAY is militant."

"By Yale standards, yes," he said.

I opened the paper to the Black Panther article. "You know what's amazing about this article? It's the stuff it doesn't say. It doesn't say that New Haven has a Black Panther office, just that some Panthers were arrested here. It doesn't say whether any locals were involved in that arrest, or even what the arrests were about."

He templed his fingers. "Your point?"

"The Panthers *are* militant. Are they associated with BSAY?"

"God, no," he said. "BSAY wouldn't get its Ivy League fingers dirty with the Panthers."

"But BSAY protested the arrests."

"No, they didn't. Where'd you hear that?"

"From Ludlow Robinson."

Freeman let out a small breath. "And that got you out of his office, didn't it?"

I nodded. "It also got me here. I talked to a bailiff at the courthouse. He told me about you, and he said that BSAY did picket when the Panthers were arrested."

Freeman looked down. "I told you, we don't handle the cop beat. So there's probably a lot I don't know."

"So why's this article here?"

"Talk," he said. "There's been lots of fear talk about the Panthers, afraid they're going to bring the wrong element to town. Then with the murder—"

"Tell me about it."

"We don't know a lot. Just that a young man was found murdered in a swamp near Middlefield. He'd been tortured, and soon we find out he was a member of the New York City Black Panthers. Rumor has it that he was going to inform on someone—I've never quite figured out who—and these eleven Panthers murdered him for it."

"So the Black Panther Party is active here," I said.

He shook his head. "Never really was. Just some misguided kids, you know."

"I've met some Panthers," I said. "I don't know if I'd use the word 'misguided.'"

"Here? In New Haven?"

"Chicago. They have a different perspective on the world. Not one I believe in, but they seem convinced."

"You sound like you respect them."

"You sound like you don't."

He shrugged, clearly unwilling to answer.

"Where's their offices?" I asked.

"Shut down," he said. "With the arrests. I have no idea where they are located now. You think this boy you're looking for is with them?"

"I'd heard that he got militant in the last few weeks of his stay at Yale, but I don't know what that means. You tell me BSAY is militant, so maybe that's all it was."

He sighed again. "You survive in this town by rumor. And even though I heard that BSAY has been talking about getting some black studies courses at Yale, that's about as militant as they've been getting."

"Which is too militant for you."

"They're rocking a pretty big boat. They're representing us in there—the more folks who get into these power networks, the better for all of us."

I leaned back. I'd heard that argument before, but I knew it had several sides. "You're saying they should turn their backs on who they are so that they get into the power networks?"

"Not at all," he said. "But change comes from above. You got to get above before you can make the changes. Only Yale alumni are on the admissions teams sent out to pick the new students. And mostly it's Yale grads who form the various committees at the university. You're never really inside here unless you came from here. So it's important that they don't rock the boat."

I studied him for a moment. "You believe that."

He nodded.

I stood. "Militants frighten you, don't they? They make the rest of us visible. Any kind of protest, it makes you nervous."

"I didn't say that." The good humor had left his face.

"Yes, you did. You a Yale grad?"

"You think I'd be sitting here if I was?"

I gave him a half smile. I wondered if he knew how bitter that sounded. "No, I don't suppose you would be."

"Look," he said, "if I find out anything, I'll let you know. Leave me your number."

He was doing me a favor, as best he could. I had to remember that. Even if we didn't have the same approach to the world.

"I'll contact you in a day or so," I said. "One more question. The bailiff at the courthouse, he mentioned a Teen-Inn on Washington. Do you know about this place?"

"I doubt your boy would be there," Freeman said. "It's for hippie kids, you know, the dopers and the ones who think they know everything about the war."

"Do you have an address for this place?" I asked.

"It's in a bad part of town."

I gave him a sideways look. "That doesn't bother me."

He shook his head slightly, but wrote the address on a piece of paper. As he handed it to me, he stood. "You realize this kid is probably just pushing his mom's buttons."

"I thought so at first," I said. "But I'm beginning to wonder if I might be wrong."

TWELVE

The address Freeman had given me was in the four hundred block of Washington, in a neighborhood that the receptionist at the *Crow* called the Hill.

As I drove into the Hill, I noticed that several buildings had condemned signs on them, and even more appeared abandoned. Near the empty buildings were development signs, explaining how wonderful the area would be when construction was finished.

The house wasn't too hard to find. It was a two-story frame house in the middle of a group of intact buildings. No signs here; it almost looked like this part of the neighborhood had been forgotten by the redevelopment committee.

Two yellow VW microbuses were parked on the street, along with an old Ford truck that someone had painted neon green. The back of the truck was painted with red flowers, and in the truck's bed were open boxes filled with tie-dye shirts.

A bunch of white kids sat on the lawn. Most of them had stringy long hair that fell to the middle of their backs. If it weren't for the clothing, I wouldn't have been able to tell the sexes apart.

The girls wore skimpy T-shirts over long skirts, and the boys wore the same shirts with blue jeans. The group was passing a pipe around, and I knew before I smelled it that they were smoking marijuana.

As I got out of my van, one of the kids looked up at me. "You here about the sink, man?"

I felt color flush my cheeks. He thought I was a plumber. I couldn't tell if the assumption came from my skin color, the panel van, or both.

"No, actually," I said. "I'm looking for someone."

"Second floor, back bedroom," he said. "Don't be surprised, though, if you catch him having a hairburger."

I almost asked what he meant, and then my brain caught up with the slang. "Thanks," I said, and went into the house.

The smell of pot clung to the walls. It was mixed with patchouli oil and incense. Candles burned despite the heat of the day. Kids were scattered everywhere, in various states of undress. I couldn't determine ages, partly because all I saw were white limbs tangled together.

The kids weren't moving. Most of them were in some sort of drugged state. A hi-fi played Country Joe and the Fish, a group I'd become familiar with thanks to Malcolm on the drive over. I still didn't know the name of the song, but I recognized it.

The stairs looked treacherous. They were made of wood and hadn't been shored up in a long time. The wood was thin in some places, scarred in others, and looked like it might collapse under my weight.

I debated whether I should talk to some of the kids on the ground floor, but they didn't look all that rational. The kid outside had sent me upstairs for a reason. He had no idea who I was looking for, but he made an assumption—and I had a good guess why.

I made it to the landing, which was remarkably people-free, but did have a table in the middle with more candles, burning next to an open window. Curtains blew inward from a breeze I hadn't even noticed. My innate caution made me pinch the candles out.

More music came from up here, a variety of types, all clashing so badly that I couldn't recognize anything. All the doors on the second floor were shut.

I knocked on the first door, didn't get an answer, and pushed it open. No one was inside. Just more candles, some incense burning beneath a picture of an Indian god, and a blackout curtain on the window.

I pulled the door closed and went to the next room, finding no one, and then the next.

Finally, I reached the last room. Remembering the kid downstairs's comment, I knocked first.

"Fuck off, man," came a male voice from inside.

I knocked again.

"Shit-fuck, man. We're busy."

I knocked a third time.

More swearing, but it was mostly inaudible. Then the door pulled open and I found myself facing a young man, naked and in full arousal. A naked girl lay on the bed, her body open to me. She was white. He was as dark as I was.

The room smelled of sex.

"Yeah?" he said, not seeming to care that he didn't know me.

"The guys downstairs directed me up here," I said. "I was looking for Daniel Kirkland."

"That pussy? Fuck." He shook his head. "He hasn't been here in a hundred years, man."

My heart rose. This was the first real lead I had.

"How long has it been really?" I asked.

The kid extended his hand toward the makeshift bed. It appeared to be several mattresses on the floor, covered with batik sheets. The girl sat up, keeping her legs spread.

"Like I care," he said. "I'm busy, man."

"I already interrupted you," I said. "You may as well take a minute and answer my question."

"You can come in if you want," the girl said. "But you gotta get naked."

I hadn't really been embarrassed until then. "Thanks," I said. "But I'm just here to find Daniel."

"I don't know where he is," the boy said.

"I didn't ask where he was," I said, although I really wanted to know. "I asked when he was last here."

"Fuck me, man, I don't keep him."

"Christmas," the girl said. "Him and Rhondelle. They got the tree."

I looked at her. Her eyes were wide and blue and bloodshot. Her black hair was tangled over her face.

"You're sure?" I asked, mostly because I couldn't believe someone in her state would know what they were talking about.

"Oh, yeah. They were gonna make it a special Christmas no matter what, but then Jax brought some smack and they got all pissed. Said they were going to find a place where people used their brains instead of fucking them up. Fucking losers." She flopped back down.

"You sure you haven't seen them since Christmas?" I asked.

The kid sighed. He didn't look as out of it as his girlfriend. "They got their own place near here for a while. Shared it with some other heavy types, you know?"

"No, actually."

"Activists, you know. They didn't belong here. We're more into the make-love side of things, you know." He looked over his shoulder at the girl.

"That seems obvious, although if he was with a girl—"

"Fuck me, man, you're even straighter than he is. He was getting that warrior vibe, you know?"

"What do you mean?"

"Bringing the war home, baby," he said. "Stupidest thing I ever heard. We don't need any stinking war. If everybody just loved each other, we wouldn't be so fucking fucked up, you know?"

I wished Malcolm was here to interpret for me.

"You're not coming in, right? I mean you can get your own downstairs, if you want it. We're kinda into our own thing." He was still talking to me.

The girl smiled at me. "I don't mind a three-way. Never done it with two black guys."

"Um, no, thanks," I said. "I'm just—"

"Looking for Daniel, I know." The kid shook his head. "Too bad, man. Wouldn't surprise me if he was dead by now, you know?"

Then he slammed the door in my face. I thought about knocking again, but wasn't sure what it would accomplish.

The girl laughed from inside the room, and then squealed. I turned around and headed back down the stairs.

I tried to ask a few other people questions, but no one seemed sober enough to speak to me. I felt a little off myself, and wondered if it was from the pot smoke in the air or from my rather surreal encounter with the couple upstairs.

I had a hunch it was from both.

THIRTEEN

The next morning had a damp chill in the air. The weather forecast said we'd get up to eighty degrees, just like the day before, but for now, the temperature hovered in the low sixties, making my wool suit bearable.

The night before, Malcolm had teased me about coming back to the motel smelling like pot, which I deserved. I told him and Jimmy about my afternoon—leaving out the racier parts—and Malcolm grew serious.

"Sounds like Daniel might be in trouble," he said.

I agreed. I felt a growing sense of urgency to find Daniel and, at the same time, concern that I might be too late.

When we finished breakfast, I took Jimmy with me to Yale for my meeting with Dean Sidbury. We dropped Malcolm at a Laundromat along the way.

Yale's campus was lively at seven-forty-five on a summer morning. I hadn't expected it. A number of students carried books against their hips, heading to class. All of them looked clean-cut, especially compared with the young people I had seen the day before. All those white shirts, black trousers, and short hair made me realize that the group I had seen the day before wasn't the norm. Kids still tried to get ahead. Only a handful of them rebelled in one way or another.

Dean Sidbury's office was in the main part of Daniel's college. Instead of going in a side door and up a tower, Jimmy and I went into the main double doors that led into a stone hallway. To our right was a door marked PRIVATE and straight ahead was a typical office setup, with a secretary in a reception area, lots of brown leather chairs, newspapers for those who waited, and a door with the words JONATHON LYON SIDBURY, DEAN across the center in hand-carved wooden letters.

The secretary looked up as we walked in. She had the same look as the secretary at the *Crow,* right down to the beehive hairdo, only this woman was white and much older.

Jimmy stayed behind with the secretary because she insisted that the dean would want to see me alone. Apparently she felt that the dean wouldn't want to discuss confidential matters in front of a child.

As I pushed the door open, I heard her ask Jim, "Do you color?" and I was glad I wasn't there for his response.

Dean Sidbury's office was as different from Robinson's as could be. A wall of windows had a view of the quad, and plants the size of trees stood in front of them on the inside. More plants hung off his desk, their leaves trailing to the blue shag carpet.

Sidbury was a slender man with a bony aesthetic face. Black hair covered the tips of his ears and touched the back of his collar. He stood when he saw me, and offered me his hand.

I took it, sensing no hesitation in him. "Darrel Kirkland."

"Jonathon Sidbury." He shook my hand once, then let go, indicating the chair beside his desk.

"Sorry I don't have more time," he said. "We're having all sorts of difficulties with the accelerated schedule for making Yale coeducational. Finding homes for the young women—safe homes—while still giving them the Yale experience is proving quite the challenge."

I nodded politely, not really caring. "I was told you could help me find Daniel."

"Yes, well." Sidbury cleared his throat. "Find him, no. Tell you his history, yes. I can't let you see the files, but I can tell you what's in them and what happened last fall."

"All right." I folded my hands in my lap and waited.

"I had high hopes for Daniel," Sidbury said. "He came in here like a ball of fire, ready to work, ready to conquer the world."

I could see that. That fit with the young man I had met last summer.

"He got straight A's in some of our more difficult freshman courses, although he struggled toward the end of the year. Skipping classes, that sort of thing. He blamed it on the political climate, and frankly, I could understand that. Dr. King's death shook up many of our students."

I nodded.

"Your son believed that Yale needed to be changed," Sidbury said. "We had many discussions. I agreed with him, in part at least. Our academics are geared toward a certain kind of student. Daniel believed that black history, black literature, and black achievements should be taught in all of the schools. He showed me black studies curriculum from various colleges, most of them out west, and insisted that Yale start training black leaders."

"It doesn't sound unreasonable," I said. "Especially since this school supposedly creates the future leaders of America."

Sidbury sighed. "That was Daniel's argument."

"And you kicked him out because he wanted you to examine your own cultural elitism."

"Um, no." And this time, Sidbury let his tone rise to that patrician level which I loathed. "First, let me tell you that we kick no one out. Yale does not expel students. And secondly, Daniel did not leave because of his academic complaints."

"So why did he leave?" I asked. "No one will tell me."

"It's not a pleasant story, Mr. Kirkland."

"How can I find the boy if I don't know what happened to him? We lost him after Yale. He's vanished."

"He is an adult—"

"I am quite aware of that," I snapped.

"Your son was asked to leave because he nearly beat a boy to death."

I froze. Daniel Kirkland struck me as misguided, but not violent. "Are you certain?"

"Quite." Sidbury clutched the file tightly, as if he were afraid I was going to grab it and read it. "I'll be as clear as I can. Daniel came to me at the beginning of the fall semester, representing some splinter group in BSAY— the black students' organization at Yale. They were angry about the war, claiming that it was people like us, people trained in the Ivy League, who were behind it, and that our 'cultural imperatives' led us to repress minorities worldwide. The war was just one manifestation of this repression."

Sidbury couldn't keep the sarcasm from his voice. I could almost hear Daniel making this argument, his fist shaking in defiance.

"Daniel said he believed in changing the system, but he preferred to do so from within. The first step would be to teach black studies at Yale as well as courses in communism and third world history. He had an entire list, from the history of Vietnam—with reminders that Ho Chi Minh had been our ally for nearly twenty years—to a list of black writers whom he felt we should study."

Sidbury shoved the file aside. He was clearly telling me his own opinions now, his own memories.

"I told him that his arguments had merit, but I was not the person to implement them. He wanted advice on who to speak to, and I told him that I would handle things with the curriculum committee. He didn't like that, but agreed to let me try."

"Did you?" I asked.

"I was consulting with others when Daniel came back, accused me of doing nothing, and decided to take matters into his own hands. He led campus-wide protests, talked to the curriculum committee himself, enlisted some of our more liberal professors in this quest, and seemed to be gaining a bit of ground."

"This sounds like leadership behavior to me," I said.

"It was disruptive, and your son was not polite about the way he handled things," Sidbury said. "Diplomacy requires politeness and patience. Daniel became well known on campus for being a troublemaker. By the time the incident occurred, he had few friends in the administration. That, more than anything, was his problem."

Sidbury seemed like he was on a roll. I didn't interrupt.

"Coeducation Week," Sidbury said. "November fourth to the eleventh. Seven hundred girls from twenty-two Northeast schools came to Yale for one week to see if our four thousand boys could deal with them. You have to understand, Mr. Kirkland, one mistake, one problem, and Yale would have been all over the national press. Coeducation wouldn't have happened here, and we would have been the laughingstock of the entire country."

As if that were the most important thing that happened in November of 1968. It seemed to me a lot of other things happened that month that the nation had focused on, not the least of which was the election of Richard Nixon and some failed Vietnam peace conferences.

"We were on eggshells here, and the boys knew it. Many of them gave up their rooms so that these girls could be scattered throughout the colleges. The security was intense. We did our very best, and so did the girls, going to classes, staying in the dorms, handling these young men who were used to being kings of their own hills, as it were."

Sidbury glanced at me nervously. His fingers toyed with the closed file.

"As you know," he said, "the experiment worked. Things did go smoothly, although there was an undercurrent of anger from many of the alumni and some of the boys. Students presented a petition for coeducation with more than seventeen hundred signatures on it, the national press corps seized on this, and that, along with the success of the week, made President Brewster decide to accelerate the coeducation of the college."

"What provoked Daniel?" I asked. "What caused this so-called incident?"

Sidbury cleared his throat, clearly a stalling tactic as he figured out what to say next. "There were no incidents, so far as I knew, in Coeducation Week itself. But there were a few afterward, mostly with local girls. We did our best to keep them quiet."

"I'm sure you did."

"Not for the sake of our reputation," he added quickly. "But because the decision had been made. We didn't want to scare the young ladies away."

"Are you saying that Daniel was involved in one of these incidents with the women?"

"Yes," Sidbury said. "Yes, he was. But not in the way you'd expect."

I had no idea what Sidbury thought I would expect. I knew what he expected. He would have thought that Daniel—angry, black, impolite Daniel—would have hurt one of the women, or done something worse.

"What did he do?" I asked.

Sidbury stood. He paced toward the window, then paused, and looked out. Finally, he said, "It seems that Daniel was dating one of the girls who came here from Vassar. She came from a good family in New Haven, and had decided to stay here through Thanksgiving."

"The girl's name?" I asked.

"Rhondelle," Sidbury said. "Rhondelle Whickam. Bright young woman. Black, of course."

"Of course," I said.

He gave me a nervous smile. "She came to visit Daniel after the announcement was made. That weekend, as a matter of fact. Emotions were running high. It was probably the wrong weekend to visit."

"Because?"

"There was some concern, particularly among the legacies, that young women would take away slots that should go to them. You have to understand, the number of legacy admissions had dropped from more than a fourth of the class to less than a fifth. The girls would simply bring that down farther, and Yale would not be the school it was."

I wasn't sure what he meant by legacies. It was a term I hadn't heard, although I could guess. I assumed it meant students who, because of family history or wealth, didn't have to meet the same stringent entry requirements as other students.

"What happened is this: Four young men learned that Rhondelle was here and decided to make coming to Yale an unpleasant experience for her, hoping she would let other girls know that Yale could be an uncomfortable place."

I didn't move. I had a hunch I knew where this was going.

"They didn't plan their attack well. Daniel walked in on them. He managed to get them away from her before too much damage had been done."

"And he nearly beat one of the legacies to death," I said, finally understanding.

"It was justified," Sidbury said, "but when added to his discontent, we simply felt that he didn't belong here."

"Even though he had stopped a rape."

"I wouldn't use such a harsh term," Sidbury said. "They were merely trying to scare the girl."

"Did they succeed?"

"I don't know." He sighed. "You'd have to talk to her father."

I hadn't expected that response. "Her father?"

"Professor Whickam. He teaches French."

"Her father teaches here?" I was stunned.

"You can see our dilemma. If this had gotten out, so close to Coeducation Week, then all the work we had done to bring young women here would be for nothing. The charges against the university would have been horrifying—with legacies involved, one of our minority professors, a young woman, and a discontented young man."

"No," I said. "I don't see your dilemma. You had four boys gang up on a young woman, threaten her at the least, and assault her at the worst, and you covered it up?"

"I wouldn't use that phrase," he said.

"You threw Daniel out of school," I said.

"We did not. We mutually agreed that he shouldn't return."

"Did you mutually agree that the other four boys shouldn't return?" I asked.

"Two of them." Sidbury's face had grown red. "We dealt with the other two in a different manner."

Suddenly I knew exactly what legacy meant. "The other two. They were the legacies, weren't they? You can kick out the scholarship students and the students without powerful parents, but you can't kick out the children of alumni."

"It wasn't my decision."

"But you approve of it." I lowered my voice, trying to take some of the threat out of it.

He closed his eyes, and shook his head. "There are ways things get done here. One of the boys was beaten badly, as I said. He was one of the legacies. We explained to the parents what happened, and they assured us it wouldn't happen again. He did not return for the spring semester—ostensibly recuperating—and I haven't received notification that he will return in the fall."

"And the other legacy?"

"His father is quite well known, and a major supporter of the university. He assured us that nothing like this would ever happen again."

"You believed him?"

"What I believe doesn't matter." Sidbury gave me a meaningful look. Someone else, someone higher up, with more authority, believed the father. "His son returned for spring and didn't get into any trouble. I'll have my eye on him this fall. He's being housed as far from the girls in this college as possible."

I shook my head and turned away, disgusted.

"Daniel was as upset by this turn of events as you were, even though we talked the other young man's father out of pressing charges. Believe me, when a man like that wants the law to go after someone, it happens. We managed to avoid that."

"At the cost of Daniel's scholarship and education."

Sidbury didn't answer me directly. He swallowed, then bent his head forward.

"When I saw Daniel after all of this, told him that no charges would be pressed against him, he asked about charges against the others. I told him that it looked like three wouldn't return, but when it was clear we could do nothing about the fourth, he had some choice and colorful things to say about the way things worked here at Yale and within the establishment. He accused us of discrimination, threatened to go public with this, and I told him, as I had been instructed, that if he did, then the legacy's father would pursue him with the full force of the law. Daniel understood that he couldn't survive this man's wrath, no matter who was in the right."

The poor kid. I had been unfair to him. He hadn't abandoned his education for his so-called political stances. He had been forced to leave by a combination of activism and injustice.

"Daniel said he wanted nothing to do with an institution that supported such people, that this was exactly what he was talking about, this kind of elitism and privilege, and if we had listened to him in the first place, taught black studies and the other things he had mentioned, showing the result of these attitudes on real people—his words, 'real people'—then things like this wouldn't happen."

Sidbury was talking too fast.

"But, he said, he could see now that he had been naïve. He used that word, not me. And he said that he felt the only way to turn this country around was to start from scratch. The entire system had to be torn down before there'd be any justice, real justice in the world. His last words to me were that he had been stupid for being a believer. The dream, he said, was really just that. A dream."

"Martin's dream," I said, more to myself than to Sidbury.

"Yes. Doctor King's dream. I think Daniel saw himself as a martyr."

I couldn't keep silent any longer. "Daniel didn't see himself as a martyr. He finally understood that for all your talk of equality and open admissions and everyone having a chance at leadership, it's still all about the color of your skin, how much money you have, and who your parents are. Obviously, in the eyes of Yale, his parents don't measure up."

Sidbury's face was bright red and covered with sweat. "I can't tell you how sorry I am for all of this, Mr. Kirkland."

"Save your apologies," I said as I stood and headed for the door, "for someone who believes that you actually mean them."

FOURTEEN

I don't remember leaving Sidbury's office. I barely remember collecting Jimmy and heading out of the building. I do remember that by the time we reached the oldest part of campus, Jimmy was running to keep up with me.

"Smoke, wait," he said, sounding breathless. "Please, wait up."

I slowed, finding myself on a path near that statue of the pompous white guy surveying his world. I wanted out of there. I wanted out of there now.

Jimmy was breathing hard. I hadn't realized just how fast I was walking. "What happened?"

I shook my head, still too angry to speak. Besides, I wasn't sure what to tell Jimmy. There was still a part of me—the martyr part, I guess Sidbury would call it—that wanted to believe in Martin's dream, a part that wanted to protect kids like Jimmy from the worst of the racism in the hopes that some day it would just vanish.

"I heard you yelling," Jimmy said. "Was this guy a jerk, too?"

I smiled, despite my anger. And then I laughed. "Yeah," I said. "He was a jerk."

"I knew it!" Jim punched one fist into the palm of his other hand. "That lady kept looking at me like I smelled bad. I figured if he let her work for him, he had to be a jerk."

The anger was still there, but Jimmy had succeeded in taking the edge off of it. "Let's get out of here."

Malcolm was waiting for us outside the Laundromat, a neatly folded stack of clothes on top of the inside-out duffel bag. It looked like he had washed it too.

He was reading the morning paper, and leaning against the building, the only person on that side of the street. When we pulled up, he folded the paper, tucked it under his arm, and grabbed the clothes. Jimmy got out to help him.

As they climbed into the van, Malcolm said, "You read this morning's paper? They're rioting in Pennsylvania."

Pennsylvania was apparently becoming the symbol of his discomfort with traveling.

"Who's rioting?" I asked.

"We are," he said. "The cops hurt ten people and arrested even more just because some lady was protesting that she got picked up for something no white woman would get charged with."

I sighed. "Where's this?"

He thumbed through the paper. "Philadelphia."

I shook my head slightly, the lightness that Jimmy had helped me achieve gone. Philadelphia had been on my list of places to stop on the way home. I probably would have to look up the articles myself. One isolated event shouldn't be enough to stop my search for a new place to live.

"Smoke's mad," Jimmy said.

Malcolm leaned toward me. "What happened?"

I told him as succinctly as I could, trying to keep the anger out of my voice. Neither boy said anything, and neither asked any questions as we drove across New Haven. Instead, they just listened.

When I finished, Malcolm said, "I thought any school could kick you out for any reason."

"I suppose legally they can," I said as I turned the van into the motel parking lot. During the day, there were very few cars. At night, the place seemed to fill up. "But places like Yale like to pretend that everyone who comes here is perfect, and they make no mistakes. After all, how can you expel a student who qualifies for a place like this? That implies that someone got out of control, and an Ivy Leaguer wouldn't get out of control."

"You think Daniel could've gotten in trouble from this legacy guy?" Malcolm asked as he opened the van door.

I got out, and Jimmy slid after me. It seemed even warmer here, but that

94

was probably the effect of the sun off the pavement and the brick of the building. I pulled my suit coat off.

"What do you mean trouble?" I asked as I came around the side of the van to get the laundry.

"Dunno exactly," Malcolm said, "but my experience with gangs of guys is that if they get caught for something, they tend to blame somebody, and it's usually not one of their friends."

"I seen that too," Jimmy added. He had a room key, and unlocked the door for me and Malcolm.

I let out a sigh. I hadn't even thought of the repercussions of Daniel's actions among his peers. And I should have.

"It's possible," I said. "It's one more thing to investigate."

Malcolm slung the duffel over one arm and then lifted part of the clothing stack. I took the rest. We set them on the bed nearest to the window.

The maid had already been inside the room. The beds were made and the place smelled clean. I liked this feature of motel living. I often wished my apartment could get magically cleaned up while I was away.

"Nobody's gonna tell you what happened, Bill," Malcolm said.

"I'm not sure they'll tell you, either," I said.

"I meant the kids," he said, sorting the clothes by owner.

"I did, too," I said. "These are rich white kids, and if the controversy turned racial, they're not going to tell a black kid."

Malcolm looked at me sideways. "But if it's about a girl, they might."

He obviously had an idea on how to handle this. I'd let him.

"If I can have the van this afternoon," he said, "I can check out both that place on Washington and some of the kids at Yale."

"That's fine." I wanted to track down Professor Whickam, but I could do the preliminaries from the room. "Let me pick up some lunch for me and Jimmy, and then you can have the van until supper. If you get delayed, call here. The desk clerk should take a message if we're out."

"There's not a lot of places to go around here," Malcolm said.

"There's enough," I said, remembering the park. I could use some time in a peaceful setting. Sidbury, Yale, and Robinson had shaken me up more than I wanted to admit.

The afternoon brought only frustration for me. As the day progressed, I hoped Malcolm fared better.

Before Jimmy and I left for the park, I scanned the phone book. Only one

Whickam was listed, a René Whickam. I thought René was a woman until I got ahold of the Yale switchboard and asked for the first name of the Professor Whickam in the French department.

"*Wren*-ay," the operator said, as if she had been instructed on the proper pronunciation. Then she put me through to the department.

Professor Whickam wasn't due in his office until the following week, which I thought odd, since the following week was the week of the Fourth of July. No one answered at his home, either, and I got a bit worried. I wanted to wrap this case up as quickly as possible, and I had a hunch I needed Whickam to do that.

After I tried Whickam, I tried all the phone numbers that Grace had given me again, and got no answers. I would try again at odd hours, hoping to reach someone.

Then Jimmy and I went to the park, ate a bag lunch, and pretended to be indolent. I had bought a cheap softball at an all-purpose drugstore next to the grocery store, and we played a game of catch until I tired of it.

When we got back to the room, we read until Malcolm returned—Jimmy starting one of the books Grace had sent with him, and me reading the morning paper. The riot in Philadelphia sounded nasty. Things in Vietnam were not going well either, but the paper felt the biggest news was actress Judy Garland's death from a drug overdose.

I had finished the paper and was about to start another round of phone calls when Malcolm pulled up. He came into the room, looking tired and discouraged.

Aside from a few details, he had learned nothing new. He couldn't even find out the names of the boys who had been involved in the fight over Rhondelle Whickam. It seemed, as I predicted, that no one wanted to talk. But Malcolm had found a couple of crumpled antiwar leaflets with some local addresses.

That would be tomorrow's start.

FIFTEEN

Morning arrived in an unexpected torrent of rain. The weather was cool, and I found myself wishing that the rain had come the day before, when I had been trapped in my suit. That morning, I wore a short-sleeved shirt and thin tan slacks more appropriate for summer.

The three of us spent the morning together, going to the various addresses on the flyers Malcolm had found. Depending on how the buildings looked when we arrived, either Malcolm or I would go in.

I got the reputable and clean buildings; Malcolm got the seedy, run-down ones. The theory was simple: A long-standing peace organization wouldn't mind seeing a forty-year-old coming through the door. A student-run organization wouldn't talk to me and would be happier with Malcolm.

The flyers announced a vigil that had been held the day before to support a University of Connecticut student who had refused to be inducted into the armed services. The vigil had been organized by a couple of groups who worked in tandem—a peace organization that had existed since World War II and catered to housewives—and a local branch of the Students for a Democratic Society.

The housewives were as alarmed by me as the SDS would have been, only the housewives were polite. They gave me flyers for upcoming rallies and reminded me that there had been protests on the Green every weekend since the Vietnam War began. Obviously, not a lot of people paid attention, and as one of the women told me, they didn't even get press coverage anymore.

They had only been involved in the vigil the day before because it was nonviolent. The UConn student had wanted conscientious objector status, and the draft board had refused to grant it to him. The women felt justified standing up for him. They had planned the vigil, they said; the SDS had simply been along for the ride.

Of course, Malcolm had gotten another story from the SDS. They claimed they had contacted the women's group to get extra bodies at the induction center because there weren't a lot of students on campus in the summer. The vigil had gone off "without a hitch," they said, even though it seemed to me that they had accomplished nothing.

Neither group had seen Daniel at the vigil. The housewives hadn't met him, and Malcolm got no direct information about Daniel from the SDS. A few knew him, and didn't much like him. Apparently his fascination with the organization waned after the Democratic National Convention. The SDS, Malcolm told me when he came back to the van, didn't seem as interested in civil rights issues as Daniel was.

Malcolm did get some information: a couple of addresses where students could stay for a week or so if they needed to get back on their feet. Apparently, this happened from time to time, not because Yale expelled them, but because Mommy and Daddy cut them off. A few of the scholarship students ran out of funds between terms and used these places as well if they couldn't stay in their college rooms.

The first safe house was in the Hill area, not too far from the Teen-Inn that I had discovered on Monday. Malcolm went there, knocking on the door and asking for Daniel.

He was told that Daniel had never stayed there; Daniel had rented his own apartment on Dixwell. No one had an address to give Malcolm, although a few people thought it had been near the Winchester rifle company.

The next few steps would require the kind of legwork I often did in Chicago—checking records, talking to landlords, knocking on doors. I saw no reason to bring the boys with me on this part of the trip, so we went back to the motel to drop them off.

When we arrived, the door to our room was open. A squad car was parked outside. Jimmy clutched my arm, his fingers digging into my skin. My own heart was pounding hard.

"What the hell?" Malcolm asked, opening his door before I even stopped the van.

"Let me handle this," I said, blocking him with my arm. "You've never dealt with the police in a strange town before."

I got out of the van and walked to the room, breathing steadily to keep myself calm. I didn't want to seem too calm—I was supposed to be a middle-class father of two boys, presumably the kind of guy who didn't have a lot of contact with the police. But I also didn't want to let the police run over me. I had Jimmy to protect.

I got to the motel room door and leaned in. Two policemen—both white—were in the middle of the room. They had scattered our clothes all over the floor, upended the suitcases, and pulled open the bureau drawers. One of the policemen had just shoved a mattress off the box spring, and was looking underneath.

"Excuse me," I said, letting a bit of tremble into my voice. "You mind telling me what's going on?"

Both policemen looked up as if I had caught them doing something wrong.

"You Bill Grimshaw?" the one closest to the door asked. He was red headed, balding, and as tall as I was. The nameplate above his right breast pocket identified him as Officer Sanford.

"Yes," I said deliberately staying near the door. I wanted to be able to escape quickly if I had to.

"You're here on—?"

"My eldest son wanted to see Yale. He's thinking of coming next year. The only time I could get off was the two weeks around the Fourth. Why?" I was using my white-guy phone voice. I needed to sound middle-class and educated, without any trace of the South in my tones.

"Where were you today?" The other officer came forward. He was holding a battered white envelope and slapping it against one of his palms.

"We were driving around the city," I said, "trying to get a sense of the place."

"Driving around?" Officer Sanford made that sound like a crime.

I took a deep breath, as if I were trying to quell nervousness. Instead, I was trying to push down anger.

"I'll be honest," I said. "We're from Chicago, and I've learned that there are some places that just aren't amenable to blacks, no matter what the people who live there say. So I was being careful. I was making sure my son would have a community if he came here."

Officer Sanford blinked at me as if I had spoken a foreign language. The other officer came close enough that I could see his nameplate. Prauss. He was older, heavier, and obviously the one in charge. His pale blue eyes were small and bloodshot.

"You in Wallingford today?"

"Is that one of the neighborhoods?" I asked. I honestly didn't know.

"It's a town a little bit north of here," Sanford said.

"Then no," I said. "We didn't leave New Haven."

"Anyone verify that?" Prauss asked.

"Why would anyone have to verify that?" I let some of that anger into my voice.

The cops were crowding me, but I continued to hold my position just outside the door.

"How'd you get that scar?" Prauss asked, touching his left cheek.

"I got mugged," I said, telling something close to the truth.

"Where are your sons?" Sanford asked.

"In the van. You want to tell me what this is about?"

Sanford peered past me, looked at the van. If these cops headed toward the van, I'd do everything I could to stop them.

"You take them everywhere?" Sanford asked.

"No," I said. "Yesterday I went to a nearby grocery store without them. Why?"

"Mind if we take a look in the van?" Prauss asked.

"Yes," I snapped. "I do. I have no idea what this is about and I'm beginning to think I have to call my attorney."

"You have an attorney?" Sanford asked, as if I had told him I had been to the moon.

"His name is Andrew McMillan." Drew's firm had offices all over the country, and it was particularly well known on the East Coast.

"You're not rich enough to have a lawyer," said Sanford.

"What are you basing this opinion on?" I asked.

"The fact you're staying here, and driving that crummy van."

I glanced over my shoulder at the van. Malcolm was leaning forward, looking alarmed. He had his arm around Jimmy, who was so frightened that I could see him shaking from here.

"The van has camping gear in it. I promised them that we'd stay somewhere fun over the Fourth. And as for staying here, I've learned that ritzy hotels don't really like my skin color, so I don't push it much."

The cops were staring at me as if I were a new breed of black. Maybe I was to them. From the standards I'd seen so far in New Haven, I was being pushy and outspoken.

"Are you going to tell me why you're here?" I asked. "Or do I call Drew?"

"There was a bank robbery in Wallingford this morning," Prauss said. "Crooks got away with twenty-seven grand that don't belong to them."

"And the guys who robbed the place were black?"

"Probably," Sanford said.

"Probably." I had to struggle to keep my voice even.

"They were wearing ski masks."

I made myself breathe evenly. "And you're what—canvassing every motel room, seeing who has ski masks and a lot of cash?"

Prauss just stared at me. I felt a flush rise in my cheeks. It wasn't embarrassment that made the color rise. It was fury.

"Oh," I said after a moment. "You made a few calls, didn't you? Asked about suspicious characters, strangers who didn't seem to belong? Asked about skin color?"

"It's well known that Negroes are responsible for ninety percent of the crime in this country," Sanford said.

"Well known," I said. "Among law enforcement?"

"We're checking all our leads," Prauss said.

"Find anything here?" I asked.

"As a matter of fact." Prauss moved even closer. I could feel his breath on my skin. He started slapping that envelope again. "Who's Malcolm Reyner?"

"My son," I said.

"But his last name is Reyner and yours is Grimshaw."

"He's my stepson," I said. "My wife's from her first marriage. I raised him from a baby."

I hoped I wouldn't have to keep these lies straight for too long. I also hoped that Malcolm had kept the windows down in the van so that he could overhear what I was saying.

"How come you let him leave Chicago at a time like this?" Prauss asked.

"A time like what?" I was confused about this. Had something happened in Chicago that I didn't know about?

He handed me the envelope. It was addressed to Malcolm in care of the Grimshaws. The return address belonged to the Cook County draft board.

My hands shook as I pulled out the letter. I scanned it. It was dated last week, and it told Malcolm that he was to report for service as soon as he received the letter.

"I've never seen this before," I said truthfully.

"You ain't helping your kid run?" Prauss said.

"If I was, I wouldn't have brought him to Yale," I snapped. "Canada's a lot closer if you drive straight north from Chicago than if you go all the way to the Atlantic seaboard first and then go north."

"Your attitude isn't helping, Mr. Grimshaw," Prauss said. "Seems to me that it would be a good idea to get some funds to help your kid along if he was going to spend some time out of the country. Maybe rob a bank."

"And if we did that," I said, "what did we do with my other son? Put a ski mask on him, too, and give him a loaded water pistol?"

This was ridiculous. We hadn't done anything, not that that mattered. The cops would believe what they wanted to.

"He could've waited in the car," Sanford said.

"Car?" I asked. "We only have the van. You can call the Illinois DMV. That's the only vehicle I own."

They both peered at the van again, then looked at its Illinois plates.

"Mind if we inspect the vehicle?" Sanford asked.

I did, but I figured it might be the only way to get them out of here.

"And I'd like to look at your wallet as well," Prauss said.

"You think I have twenty thousand dollars in my wallet?" I asked.

"Twenty-seven," Sanford said.

Because the request was so outrageous, I handed him the wallet, mentally thankful that I had the traveler's checks and only a little cash. The rest of the cash was spread out between the two boys.

Sanford thumbed through the wallet, frowned, and handed it to Prauss. He looked through it, too, pulled out one of the checks, and studied it.

Then he slipped it back inside. "The van," he said again.

"Fine," I said. "Do what you need to."

They went to the van. Jimmy cringed against Malcolm.

I opened the driver's door. "Come out this way, boys."

Jimmy slid toward me, then slammed against me, clinging to me. He was covered with sweat and shaking. I held him close. Malcolm stood next to me, his gaze fixed on the envelope still in my hand.

The cops examined the entire van. They found no ski masks or sacks of money, but they did manage to trash our camping equipment and supplies as thoroughly as they trashed the motel room.

After a while, Prauss came over to me. "You're clean so far."

"I'm clean period," I said.

He shrugged. "Hope so."

Then he nodded toward Malcolm. "You're the one going to Yale?"

"Just checking it out." Malcolm kept his voice calm.

"Like it?" Prauss asked.

"I met a few people I like," Malcolm said. "Dean Sidbury's been really nice."

Great touch. I wouldn't have thought of that. I only hoped that the cops didn't check with Sidbury to see if he'd met Malcolm.

"Next week," Malcolm was saying, "I have an appointment to talk to Professor Whickam."

Prauss's tough-guy grimace faded. He obviously recognized at least one of those names and was beginning to realize he had made a big mistake.

Then he looked at me. "You see anything suspicious, you let me know."

I almost retorted, *What's suspicious? More black people in motel rooms?* but I bit back the response. Jimmy's tight grip on me reminded me exactly what was at stake.

Then the two men got into their squad car, and without an apology, drove away.

SIXTEEN

shoved Malcolm's letter into my back pocket, determined to discuss the contents with him after this current crisis passed. First, I had to deal with Jimmy.

He was so terrified he didn't want to move. He clung to me like a young child, his face buried in my waist. Malcolm was staring at him as if he'd never seen Jimmy before.

I kept a hand on Jimmy's back, rubbing it, trying to soothe him. He had dealt with police all right in Chicago—even challenging a white detective, Sinkovich, who had stayed with us a few nights. But that apparently wasn't the same as coming in on two officers searching our hotel room—our private place.

"It's all right," I whispered.

He shook his head.

"They're gone," Malcolm said.

Jim just held on tighter. I pulled him close, let him take his own time to disengage. I didn't dare hurry him.

"He gonna be okay?" Malcolm asked quietly.

I don't know, I mouthed, not wanting Jimmy to hear my pessimism. I hadn't anticipated this at all. Usually I prepared him for the things that could go wrong, but this hadn't even occurred to me.

I thought we had stayed under the radar. I thought we hadn't done anything to be noticed.

Then I wondered if someone from Yale had sicced the cops on us, and immediately dismissed the thought. There I was known as Darrel Kirkland, not Bill Grimshaw.

There were only two ways the cops could have known we were here. They could have followed our van, which didn't seem likely, since it looked like they'd been tearing up the room for some time, or someone in the motel told them.

"I guess I should start cleaning this up, huh?" Malcolm said.

"Leave it for a minute. We have a few things to take care of first."

Jimmy leaned back, wiped his eyes with a fist, and looked up at me. His face was blotchy, his eyelashes stuck together by tears that my shirt had probably absorbed.

"Let's just go." His voice was hoarse, as if he'd been shouting.

"Go where?" I asked.

"Home," he said.

Leaving sounded like a good idea, but I wasn't completely ready to head back to Chicago. "What about Daniel? We promised Grace we'd try to find him."

Jimmy shrugged. "We gots to be careful ourselves, Smoke."

He was talking about the reason we had left Memphis in the first place, the reason we had changed our names. He was referring to the fact that we were both still wanted by the FBI for "questioning" in connection with Martin Luther King's death.

"Yes, we do," I said, "and I'm not sure running is the right thing right now."

"I sure as hell don't want to stay here," Malcolm said.

"If we run, we look guilty," I said.

"Even though they didn't find any money or ski masks?" Malcolm asked.

I gave him a sideways look. "You know how fair white cops can be."

He sighed. "What do you want to do?"

"Get a few answers," I said.

"To what?"

"How they found us," I said.

"What if they come back?" Jimmy asked, his voice trembling. "What if they arrest us? What if they put us in jail?"

"We'll be fine," I said. "We have the resources to protect ourselves. It won't come to that."

"I don't know how you can be so sure." For all Malcolm's posturing, he was scared, too, just not as deep-down terrified as Jimmy. Malcolm had no reason for that kind of fear.

"If they were going to arrest us, they would have done so tonight," I said. "This was just a normal shakedown."

"Shakedown?" Malcolm asked.

"Normal?" Jimmy asked at the same time.

"Get my wallet, Jim," I said, nodding toward the dresser where Prauss had thrown it. "I'll show you what I mean."

Jim wiped at his face, and walked into the motel room, his back straight, his entire body on alert, as if he expected more cops to jump out of the shadows at him.

He climbed over a pile of clothes, grabbed the wallet, and ran back outside, tossing it to me as if it burned his hands.

I caught it with my right hand. The fake leather was slippery. Prauss's skin had been sweaty, and had left a film on my wallet. The thought disgusted me.

I opened the wallet, pulled out the traveler's checks, and then pulled the wallet wider. I bent slightly, holding the wallet open so that Jimmy could see inside the long flap.

"What do you see?" I asked.

"Nothing," he said.

"Exactly," I said. "I had fifty dollars in cash in this wallet when we drove up. Where'd the money go?"

"They stole it?" Malcolm breathed.

"What are we going to do after that little encounter? Run to the police station and accuse two of their officers of theft?"

Jimmy took the wallet from me and felt inside of it. Then he held his hand out for the traveler's checks. I handed them to him, and let him look through them as well.

"I have a hunch they were disappointed that we didn't have more cash," I said.

"How would they know you had any money at all?" Malcolm asked.

I sighed. "How many black people go to hotels expecting to write an out-of-town check?"

"You think the cops do this a lot?" Malcolm asked.

"I think these two do it every opportunity they get. If there's a robbery nearby, they 'investigate.' A murder, a kidnapping—any excuse they have to tear up a black motel room and find whatever cash is lying around."

"But they found us," Jimmy said.

"Yeah," I said, "and I think I know how. But I want a chance to confirm it."

Jimmy glanced at the room. "I don't know if I can sleep here."

"Other hotels aren't going to be any better," I said. "In fact, they might be worse. We don't know if Officers Sanford and Prauss have hit those motels. We know about this one."

Jimmy's lips thinned.

"Let me see if my hunch about them is right," I said. "If it is, we don't have much to fear from them."

"How can you prove it, Bill?" Malcolm asked.

"By having a little talk with the manager." I patted Jimmy on the back one more time, then nodded at the van. "Why don't you two straighten out the back of the van first? That way if we have to pack, we have room."

"We could always camp," Jimmy said.

"If we have to, we will," I said, and headed across the parking lot to the motel manager's part of the building.

The manager's apartment jutted out into the center of the parking lot. The overhang almost looked like a separate part of the building, the plants growing on the iron scrollwork looking perky after the morning's rain.

Puddles had formed across much of the lot, and I walked around them as I headed toward the main door.

The screen was open. Cool air from a wall-unit air conditioner blew outside. A radio played loudly in the back, blaring Nancy Sinatra, singing that her boots were made for walking.

Lucky I wasn't wearing my boots. The mood I was in they'd be made for kicking.

I pushed the screen door open, and shouted, "Hello!"

A skinny white man I hadn't seen before peeked out of the back room. He had a blond crew cut, and a birthmark on his right cheek. He was my age, with a face flushed either from too much sun or too much drink.

"Yeah?" he asked.

I turned around and gently closed the main door.

"Hey!" he said, and I could hear the fear in his voice. "Hey, what're you doing?"

"Trying to find out what your take is," I said, keeping my voice low.

"Take of what?" His gaze flicked toward the door, then back to me.

"When your little transistor radio told you about the robbery in Wallingford today, you called your two favorite cops and told them that you had some blacks staying the motel."

"Why would I do that?"

"So that they would trash our room, take what cash we had, and give you some of it."

He took a step toward the front desk. "Get out of here."

"You know," I said, "if I had a private detective friend of mine do some checking through the guest register, I bet we'd find some other black guests who've had the same problem here that I did today. I'd bet we'd find a series of black guests with that problem, and strong memories of Officers Sanford and Prauss."

The manager took another step toward the desk.

"If you have a gun in there, you might want to think twice about grabbing it," I said. "Shoot me, and my sons will report this incident, not just to the New Haven police, but to the press as well."

He stopped moving.

"There are several ways we can settle this," I said. "I know you don't own this motel, and I'm sure your boss would love to hear what you've been doing on the side."

I didn't know for certain that the man in front of me was only the manager, but it stood to reason. This behavior was too risky for the owner, especially near a big alumni and tourist attraction like the Yale Bowl.

The manager raised his head, and didn't deny my statement.

"Or you can get my money back for me," I said. "Or better yet, you can promise that this will never happen again and give us a break on the room price."

"What kind of break?" he asked, and I knew I had him.

When I left the manager's office, I had a receipt that showed that I had paid in full for the last four nights and paid in advance for the next two. I knew it was a risk to stay any longer, but I also knew the risks of moving to another motel.

Malcolm and I would take turns guarding the room at night, and from that moment on, we would keep most of our valuables hidden in the car.

And I had a measure of revenge planned as well. I wasn't going to let the motel's manager get away with this scam of his for very long. In the morning, I would go to the *Crow*'s office and see if Reuben Freeman wanted to pursue this story, not for the local market, but for the national. If he was too afraid to cover it (and that wouldn't surprise me if he was), then I would call Saul Epstein, a Chicago reporter and photographer who helped me with a case last December.

No matter what, I was going to make sure the manager and those two New Haven cops felt a little heat from all of this.

When I got back to the room, Jimmy and Malcolm had it mostly straightened up.

"Hey, guys," I said, "is the van locked?"

"You better believe it," Malcolm growled. I couldn't remember ever seeing him so angry. "You get the information you wanted?"

I closed the door, picked up one of the shirts that still remained on the floor, and then grabbed Jimmy in a bear hug. He resisted for a moment, then fell against me, his body still tense as a wire.

"Come on," I said, leading him to one of the chairs. "Let's just sit for a minute."

He took the bed instead, fluffing back the pillows. He looked like the picture of comfort until I realized that from that particular vantage, he could see out the window.

"Can we leave?" he asked.

I shook my head. "It's better to stay. This is a scam, like I thought, and I let the manager know that we wouldn't stand for it. In the morning, I'll do a few extra things, making sure we're covered in case something else happens. But I think from now on, none of us remain here alone, and we don't use this as a refuge."

"I still think another hotel would work," Malcolm said.

"We're getting this one for free this week," I said. "With luck, we'll have found Daniel, and then we'll be gone by Sunday at the latest."

"All right," Malcolm said, but he didn't sound convinced.

Jimmy just looked out the window, his face impassive. That was the expression he had had when we were driving away from Memphis. The loss had been so deep for him that he retreated somewhere inside himself to deal with it.

"Did you threaten the manager guy?" Malcolm asked.

"We came to an understanding," I said.

"He's not going to revisit that understanding in the middle of the night, is he?" Malcolm asked.

I shook my head. "It's in both of our best interest to forget this ever happened."

"I hate that," Jimmy mumbled.

"What would you like to do to handle it?" I asked. "Besides run?"

"You said running's okay sometimes," Jimmy said, finally looking at me. I saw anger in his eyes, directed at me.

"Yes," I said. "It is. Just not this time."

"They know where we are now," he said.

I nodded. "They know where Jimmy and Bill Grimshaw are, along with Malcolm Reyner."

I didn't look at Malcolm as I said that. We would deal with his letter after Jimmy fell asleep.

"If we left, they wouldn't know where any of us are."

"But they'd let other cops know, and maybe the state police," I said. "They've seen the van. They'd keep a lookout for us and probably harass us about that robbery or worse. It's better to stay here for now."

Jimmy sighed. "How come we gots this problem? How come it don't happen to other people?"

"It does," Malcolm said. "Just not white people."

"We should live with Laura," Jimmy said to me. "Then we'd be okay."

"I wish it were that easy," I said.

He grimaced, pulled his legs up, and wrapped his arms around them. Then he began to rock.

Malcolm looked at him, then looked at me, his eyebrows raised. "You want to tell me what's going on?" he asked softly.

"We left Memphis because he had a very bad run-in with the police." I spoke quietly, too.

"Can you tell me about it?" Malcolm asked.

I shook my head. "It's not something we discuss."

Malcolm gave Jimmy a long, sympathetic look. Then he said, "I'm sorry, Jim."

Jimmy didn't seem to hear him. He continued rocking. Malcolm glanced at him, then at me, and finally stood.

"You know," he said, "maybe we should get some dinner."

I couldn't think of anything better. "Yeah," I said. "Let's get out of here for a while."

Dinner seemed to break the cycle. Dinner, dessert, and an episode of *The Outsider,* which at first seemed to me like a bad choice. Darrin McGavin's David Ross was an unconvincing private eye to me—the kind of guy who had too much luck and jumped to the wrong conclusions too quickly.

But Jimmy seemed to like the quick solutions, and he found some comfort in the TV justice. Malcolm obviously enjoyed the distraction.

I took point in the chair by the window, keeping an eye on the parking lot while watching the inane plot unfold. I was the one who wasn't calm; I was annoyed. I wanted to be able to relax, even in this tiny room, and that wasn't possible.

Jimmy fell asleep during the news, curled up on the bed farthest from the window, his back to the wall. Malcolm got up and turned down the set, but left the picture running. It sent a flickering gray light throughout the room.

"So, you going to say anything to me or what?"

I pulled the letter out of my back pocket. "You mean about this?"

He nodded.

"What's to say?" I asked. "You're going home in a week or so and report, right?"

"I thought this trip might take all summer."

"It's a crime to skip out on the draft, Malcolm," I said softly, looking at Jimmy. His breathing was even, and his body still. He was asleep and not faking it. Still, I would have rather had this conversation out of his earshot. "A federal crime."

"I know." Malcolm took the letter, folded it, and slipped it into his wallet. "If they'd bombed us like Pearl Harbor or something, I wouldn't complain, but they're not. They're just some ignorant peasants, and we're supposed to murder them."

I moved my hand slightly, indicating that he should keep his voice down. "I didn't fight in World War II, Malcolm. I fought in Korea. And it was pretty similar to this war in a lot of ways."

"Then you should understand why I don't want to go."

"I don't think anyone wants to go," I said, wondering if that was true, barely remembering the man I had been before I left for Korea. I had been a dreamer, too—the kind of idealist that Daniel had denounced in his last speech to Sidbury. I had thought, since the army had integrated, that my life in it would be so much better than my life outside it.

I had been wrong.

I leaned the chair back on two legs. "Why didn't you tell me you'd gotten this before we left?"

"You wouldn't've brought me along," he said. "You need me this trip, now more than ever."

I glanced at Jimmy. I did need Malcolm. Unfortunately, that wasn't enough of an excuse to help him out of the draft.

"I'm not going back," Malcolm said. "Not till we find Daniel."

"And if we don't find him before it's time for you to leave?"

Malcolm was silent for a long moment. Then he said again, "You need me."

The choice, then, fell to me. I could take Malcolm home and abandon the search for Daniel Kirkland, which might be prudent given today's incident. But I felt like I would betray Grace if I did that, as if I hadn't really given this investigation a chance.

My other choice was to send Malcolm home alone and try to slog along without him, although I didn't know what I'd do if the search for Daniel became in any way dangerous.

"How did the draft board find you?" I asked.

"GED." Malcolm sounded bitter. He had wanted his high school diploma. He'd been proud to get it, afraid that he never would finish his education. And then, after the GED had been logged with the Board of Education, this letter came.

No wonder he felt betrayed.

He had no family to speak of, so he couldn't get a hardship deferral. He had no health problems and no history of mental illness. He had no money for college, so he couldn't get another student deferral. He couldn't even object on religious grounds. Even if he had an argument, which I didn't think he did, the government had made getting conscientious objector status nearly impossible.

"Let's say we get you back to Chicago on time," I said, "what would you do then?"

"I don't know." Malcolm was looking out the window now, and it was clear he wasn't seeing anything. "I really don't. I don't want to go to prison, I don't want to go to Canada, and I don't want to go to Vietnam."

"You can't just do nothing," I said. "Eventually, you will have to make a decision, or the government will make it for you."

"I know that, too," Malcolm said. "I just didn't expect this, Bill. I thought they'd never find me, not after Mom died. I figured I'd be okay."

"Well," I said after a moment, "you've got about a month before they start looking for you."

"I know," he said.

"You've used a week of it."

He nodded.

"We're going to have more than one discussion about this," I said.

"Yeah," he said. "Maybe by then, I'll have made up my mind."

SEVENTEEN

In the middle of the night, I left the motel room and walked to the office again. There I found the friendly night manager who had checked us in. I told him about our afternoon, watched his face go gray with anger, and then showed him the receipt the afternoon manager had given me.

The night manager confirmed that the receipt was good, and he assured me that he would personally vouch for our safety. I wasn't sure how he'd do that, but I thanked him anyway.

Malcolm had been awake when I left, and he was awake when I returned. He had guard duty for the first half of the night. I would take over near dawn.

Jimmy hadn't moved except to roll over once, about midnight. The day had caught up with me, and I surprised myself by falling into a sound sleep.

My dreams, however, were of cold and ice, and of carrying a dead man from a trench we had dug together back to the base, his blood hot against my freezing hands.

I woke shaking. I'd had that nightmare off and on since I'd come home from Korea, and I had always awakened disgruntled. In the past, it had been worse, and sometimes it acted as a warning. In this case, I hoped it was only a response to stress.

The morning paper didn't help my mood. The two cops had known that the bank robbers wouldn't be at a motel. Those robbers had arrived at the Wallingford Colonial Bank and Trust at eleven A.M., exactly the time when an armored car arrived at the bank to deliver twenty-seven thousand dollars.

Only someone who had spent weeks casing the bank would know when the armored car delivered, which varied from day to day, but did follow a pattern if observed over time.

I didn't show Malcolm the paper. He was upset enough.

We had a quick breakfast and headed downtown. I dropped Malcolm and Jimmy at the Green, letting them choose whether they wanted to ask more questions at Yale, go to the library and while away the day, or sightsee around downtown New Haven.

Me, I had a lot of legwork, none of which I was looking forward to.

I started at the *Crow*. Reuben Freeman wasn't there, but the receptionist remembered me and gave me his home phone number. Reuben was at home, working on an article for some education journal, but he wasn't sure that he wanted to expose the officers' motel scam, not even for a national byline.

The call wasn't entirely wasted: He gave me a list of buildings that catered to students and landlords who might be amenable to a visit from me. I used the *Crow*'s phone book and found a list of rental agencies that would also give me a place to start.

It soon became clear that I couldn't hog one of the *Crow*'s phones. I went to a nearby drugstore and bought a roll of dimes. Not far from the *Crow*, I found a phone booth with an intact glass door. When I pulled it closed, it locked out most of the street noise. Then I took over the phone booth as if it were my office.

My ploy was simple. I introduced myself with a fictitious name, claiming to be a landlord from nearby Branford. I told the people I talked with that I had had a tenant named Daniel Kirkland and that he had skipped out on three months' rent, trashed the place, and cost me enough in damages to make it worth my while to take him to court.

All I needed, I said, was an address so that my process server could find him.

My story was horrible enough that other landlords would check their records just to see if this Kirkland deadbeat was on their rolls. It didn't hurt to tell me as well.

That afternoon I went through half of my roll of dimes, and ended up with nothing. After my third call, I got smart enough to have them check for Rhondelle's name, and still I came up with zero.

I was beginning to get discouraged. I took five more dimes and called the numbers Grace had given me, getting no answer. And no answer either from Whickam's number at home or at his office.

Finally, I decided to call it a day. Deep down, I was very concerned for Daniel Kirkland and, oddly, the more roadblocks I ran into, the more concerned I became.

Jimmy showed up shortly after I arrived at the Green. He was out of breath and sweat-covered. I hadn't even seen him come toward me. Malcolm took his time reaching us, looking from side to side as if he were searching for someone.

"Didn't think you'd be here yet," Jimmy said.

"I needed a break," I said.

"Me, too. Malcolm promised ice cream. Want some?"

"I'd rather have dinner," I said.

"He deserves ice cream." Malcolm reached us, overhearing the last interchange. "He worked all afternoon."

"Doing what?"

"Skimming." Jimmy held up his hands. His thumbs and forefingers were black.

"He got the bright idea to go through the New Haven papers for the past year, searching for Daniel's name." Malcolm leaned on the bench's arm. "He said he didn't believe all those people who told you Daniel wasn't in trouble."

I looked at Jimmy. He shrugged. "Folks lie, Smoke."

"Did you find anything?" I asked.

"Not Daniel," Malcolm said. "But we found a couple of articles about Rhondelle Whickam."

"Really?" Now I was interested. "What were they?"

"The librarian gave me paper." Jimmy shoved his hand in his pocket. "I wrote it all down."

He handed me some crumpled sheets of scrap paper.

"Tell me anyway," I said.

"Her daddy said she's missing," Jimmy said. "They're searching for her."

Sidbury hadn't told me that.

"It was a short news article," Malcolm said. " 'National Merit Scholar Disappears.' I think the only reason they ran it was her dad's connection to Yale."

That made sense. "Anything in there?"

"It was really short," Jimmy said. "Just her name and that everybody was worried about her. It was in May."

"Near the Panther murder?" I asked.

"Before," Malcolm said.

I would have liked to see that article. "You said you found more than one article. Did they find her?"

"Nope," Jimmy said. "That was the newest one. But we found an old one, too. Malcolm did."

"I saw that she'd won a National Merit scholarship. I remember when Daniel got his national scholarship, it even hit the *Chicago Tribune*. So I figured the New Haven papers would cover hers. And they did. There wasn't a lot in that article either, just her address and her parents saying they're proud and all that and a picture."

Something in the way that Malcolm said "picture" caught my attention. "What about the picture?"

Jimmy giggled. "Malcolm says she's a fox."

"Did not," Malcolm said, his cheeks growing red.

"Said Daniel didn't deserve her."

"I did say that." Malcolm grinned at Jimmy.

"You were amazing," I said to Jimmy. "What made you look that up?"

"The sooner you find Daniel," Jimmy said, "the sooner we can leave."

I ruffled his hair. "Let's get you some ice cream. Then let me see those articles, see if I can find anything in them."

Jimmy grinned. Malcolm smiled, too. "We'll get the ice cream and meet you at the library."

"Deal," I said, and headed across the Green.

EIGHTEEN

The article about Rhondelle Whickam was only five paragraphs long, but it told me a few things I hadn't known. I learned that she hadn't returned to Vassar for the spring semester, although she had told her parents that she had. And they didn't find out until the school sent a letter inquiring whether she'd return in the fall.

The last time her parents had seen her had been the day she left for Vassar. She had called them once or twice since, but their letters had gone unanswered (and unreturned). Her parents had simply assumed she had become too busy to write.

When they found out, in May, that she was gone, they searched everywhere, but hadn't found her. The police had no leads, so they were turning to the community for help.

I couldn't find a follow-up story, which led me to believe there was none. I used Jimmy's scrawled notes to find the original news story about the scholarship. There wasn't really a news story per se, just a photograph of the National Merit Scholars from Connecticut. Only a handful of students were in the picture, along with the governor.

Rhondelle Whickam was the only black, and the photographer had her stand to the side, behind two boys who were taller than she was. The other girl stood up front, but she probably looked like Connecticut's idea of a

National Merit Scholar, with her pale skin and smooth blond hair.

Rhondelle's hair was smooth, too, but it had clearly been straightened or ironed. Her eyebrows had been plucked into an arch, accenting her delicate nose and the European look to her face. If it weren't for her hair and her lips, her skin color wouldn't be readily apparent.

I stared at the photograph for some time, committing it to memory. I wasn't the kind of person who would rip a photograph out of a library newspaper, although in this case I wished I was.

I finished with the papers quicker than I expected, feeling no need to double-check Jimmy's efforts. It pleased me that he had taken initiative. Part of his willingness to do this, obviously, had been his desire to leave New Haven. But a year ago he wouldn't have known how to help.

The work he had done with Grace Kirkland—reading, studying the daily papers, learning how to use a library—was really paying off. I felt like I owed her even more.

The next morning dawned sunny and warm. I had guard duty from three A.M. on, so I had plenty of time to plan my day. I used the motel phone to see if the Whickams had returned. They hadn't.

Malcolm offered to help me with my search, but I had little for him to do. This day would be a duplication of the day before—more phone calls and a lot more searching for information.

I wasn't going to leave the boys at the motel, either, although I might return to make some calls. We needed something for them to do on what was obviously going to be a hot day. I couldn't find evidence of a public pool (not that I looked terribly hard; what I was afraid of finding was a pool that "frowned on" the presence of blacks), and there didn't seem to be much else that New Haven offered for idle children.

Essentially, I had no choice but to drop them at the Green again. This time, I suggested that they visit some of the Yale museums and libraries, hoping they might find something to interest them. If nothing else, I said to Malcolm, they could explore the campus.

We set up a meeting time for early evening, and then I drove to Reuben Freeman's home.

He had given me his address the day before. He lived in an old house on Bristol. The street had an air of age and decay. Most of the houses were about a hundred years old, and they had clearly been broken up into apartments.

Freeman's was on the third floor of a narrow, faded building that showed its Civil War roots. The main door was propped open with a wooden box lying on its side. To the right, there was a narrow flight of stairs, obviously original. They weren't carpeted, and the wood was scuffed so badly that it shone white.

I hurried up the stairs. This building clearly didn't have air-conditioning. The second floor smelled faintly of garlic and roses, an interesting combination. Four doors opened onto the landing there.

A fifth opening revealed another flight of stairs. Only this one was even more narrow than the original, and I had to crouch as I climbed to avoid hitting the ceiling.

Freeman clearly lived in what had been the attic of this old house. There was only one door, and it was at the very top of the stairs. No landing, nothing to brace yourself on. The last stair touched the door's jamb.

I knocked, hoping I was early enough to find Freeman in.

"Yeah?" he shouted from somewhere toward the back.

"It's Bill Grimshaw," I said.

"Lordy, you don't let up."

I could hear his footsteps as he walked toward the door. Then I heard a deadbolt turn, and a chain lock slid back before the door opened outward. I had to step down to avoid being hit.

Freeman grinned. Obviously a lot of his visitors had that problem. "Welcome to my humble abode."

"Thanks," I said. "Sorry to drop in. I had a few questions."

"That you didn't want to discuss on the phone," he said as I walked past him.

I shrugged, letting him believe that.

The apartment was immaculate. The ceiling slanted, confirming my impression that this had once been the attic, but someone had put in extra windows and dormers, giving the room a sense of light and air. Freeman had plants hanging in front of each window and near two skylights that added even more light.

A fake Persian rug covered the hardwood floor, and a dark blue sofa that picked up the rug's main colors dominated the front room. A matching easy chair stood to one side.

A narrow hallway disappeared down the back, probably leading to the kitchen, bath, and bedrooms. The entire place smelled faintly of incense, surprising me.

"Have a seat," Freeman said. "I was just getting to work."

There was no resentment in his voice, no concern that he had been interrupted. He nodded toward a table pushed up against one of the windows.

A manual typewriter sat on top of the table and, next to it, a stack of papers and a pile of books. A folding chair, with a dented pillow acting as a cushion, was set at an angle, as if the user had just stood up.

He pushed the door closed. "I did some calling around. I guess what happened to you is pretty common, and pretty shocking, considering Yale's new 'open' admission policy. It doesn't happen at the more expensive hotels, though."

"That's not a surprise."

"Yeah." He shook his head. "Want some coffee?"

"Sure," I said, and followed him through that dark hall. The kitchen was a galley carved into the wall, across from a dining area with no window, only an overhead light.

He poured me a cup from the pot on top of the stove. "Cream? Sugar?"

I shook my head, and took the cup from him. There was no evidence of a woman in this apartment or a roommate, or anyone else.

"You checked," I said, "but are you going to cover the story?"

"Why's this so all-fired important to you?" he asked.

"Besides the theft and violation? And the fact that I can't go to the police?"

He raised his eyebrows.

"I can't let them get away with it," I said, "and I have to work on the Kirkland case. I don't have the time to go after two corrupt cops."

He poured himself a cup of coffee. "So you figure I'll do it. You think I have a death wish? I've got to live in this town."

"So publish the article in the national press."

"New Haven hates national publicity."

"Use a pen name," I said.

He bit his lower lip. The skin looked raw there, as if he had been doing it a lot.

"You can't be a crusading reporter if you shy away from the tough stuff."

"Never said I was a crusader." He took a sip, and closed his eyes for a moment, as if he had been waiting all morning for that coffee.

"You weren't happy with the way the *Crow* covers stories."

"There's a large distance between the *Crow*'s happy business tone and taking on New Haven's finest."

"I think that's New Haven's worst. But if you don't want to do it, I'll call a friend of mine. He's done some gutsy national stories. He'll love this one."

I hoped. If Saul had the time and energy to leave the Midwest and come east. He'd been badly injured in December, and although he was much better, he still had to rest a lot.

Freeman held up his hand. "The pen name is an idea. If I can get the interviews without blowing my cover, it might work."

"The victims would be a good place to start."

"I was thinking of the police," Freeman said. "They're not going to be happy."

"Sanford and Prauss won't admit anything. Don't go in person. Use the phone and your pen name, and talk to the department representative. Every police station has a press contact. They'll deny it, which is all you need. Then when the story breaks, they'll do more denying and, with luck, some investigation into their ranks. And then you can cover the story under your own byline for the *Crow* because that rumor you started would affect business."

"Man, you're one sneaky son of a bitch." There was admiration in his tone. He grinned. "Remind me not to get on your bad side."

"Done." My turn to sip the coffee. It was bitter and had been sitting too long, but I didn't mind. I figured I'd need a lot of caffeine for my day. "You ever hear of Rhondelle Whickam?"

"Professor Whickam's daughter? Sure." His smile faded. "Poor thing."

"Poor thing?"

"She's missing," he said. "No one can find her. It can't be good."

"Maybe," I said. "But she was involved with Daniel Kirkland, so maybe she's with him."

Freeman whistled. "That's interesting. You think the Pride of New Haven's black community voluntarily went AWOL?"

"It's a possibility. I've been trying to reach the professor, but he's out of town."

"He goes as often as possible, searching for his daughter. He's crazy over this. I heard talk that it's affecting his work."

"But you never investigated."

"We ran the missing-person story," he said. "There never were any calls or any follow-up. I just don't think folks care about a missing black girl."

"Not even the black community?" I asked.

He shrugged, and then changed the subject. "Those names I gave you yesterday pan out?"

"The ones I've contacted," I said. "I still have a heck of a list to go through, and for fairly obvious reasons, I don't want to call out of the motel."

"Afraid the cops'll come back, huh?"

"I doubt they're that dumb. But I'm not going to sit there alone waiting for them."

"I'd've left the minute they messed with me," he said.

"Most people would." I set the cup down beside the sink. "Thanks for the coffee and the conversation."

"If you're not calling from the motel, where're you calling from?" he asked.

"I found a pay phone not too far from the *Crow*."

"You probably pissed off half the neighborhood if you were hogging the booth," he said. "Lots of folks in that part of town don't have phones."

I hadn't even thought of that, and I should have. The phenomenon was the same in the poor areas of Memphis and in Chicago's South Side. The pay phone was most people's link to the outside world.

"I don't have a lot of choice," I said.

"I do. I have a deadline for a fluff piece I'm doing for the *Ledger*. You can use my phone. I won't be needing it."

I had hoped he would make an offer like that. I thanked him, and got down to work.

NINETEEN

I used Freeman's phone for nearly three hours. He had moved his typewriter to the kitchen table. About ninety minutes in, he came into the living room and listened to me work. When I hung up from yet another failed call, he said, "Man, you sure like fake names. You sure you're really Bill Grimshaw?"

My heart hit two extra beats, but I managed a grin as I stood. I reached into my back pocket, pulled out my battered wallet, and tossed it at him.

"Sometimes you gotta know how a door will open," I said.

He thumbed the wallet open and actually looked at my ID. It was legitimate. The birth certificate I had used to get the driver's license hadn't been. But people didn't routinely look at other people's birth certificates.

"I don't think I've ever met anyone like you before," he said, handing me back the wallet. "You're willing to take all kinds of risks to make sure a couple of corrupt cops won't get away, and you're striving pretty hard to find this kid, but you're willing to cut some interesting corners along the way."

"Yep," I said, replacing the wallet and sitting back down. "The line I walk is mighty fine."

In Chicago these last few months, the line had been nearly nonexistent. The agreements I'd made with the gangs made me feel like I had not only crossed that line, but that I was going to take up residence on the wrong side.

Freeman shook his head and disappeared back into his kitchen. After a few moments, I heard the rat-a-tat of the manual typewriter and went back to my calls.

I had only a few names left when I finally scored a hit. A rental agent with one of the firms that catered to students sounded appalled when she heard my lies about Daniel. She offered to check her records and get back to me.

I offered to hold on the line while she looked.

She was gone nearly fifteen minutes, and when she returned, her voice was shaking. "I rented him the apartment," she whispered, as if she didn't want anyone else to know. "I remember him. Usually we require extra identification and references from coloreds, but he had a Yale ID. He even showed me his transcripts from last spring, proving he'd been there. He said he didn't like the atmosphere in the colleges, and who could blame him with all those snotty rich kids?"

"Do you usually talk to your renters this much?" I asked.

"Well, he was unusual. I remember that much. And he was charming. So educated and funny. I figured my boss wouldn't ever see him, and wouldn't know that I hadn't gone the extra mile. What could it hurt?"

"Has he been paying you?" I asked.

"On time, every month on the twenty-fifth—so he was actually early. It's usually cash, because he doesn't have a New Haven checking account and we don't accept out-of-state checks. We have a cash arrangement with a number of our students."

"Aren't they worried that the cash might not get credited to their account?"

She didn't seem to take offense at the question. "One of his friends drops it off and gets a receipt. That was my idea, actually. I figured if my boss didn't see him, there wouldn't be the wrong kinds of questions, you know?"

"I know," I said, and hoped I didn't sound too sarcastic. "Is the friend a girl?"

"No," she said. Then she gasped. "He's not shacking up, is he? That's all we need. I'd be fired for sure."

Her voice remained low throughout all of that, but I could hear the panic in it.

"I know he has a girlfriend," I said. "I just don't know who his male friends are."

"His friend seems like a nice young man," she said. "He's here, like I said, at the end of every month."

"But you don't have a name," I said.

"I didn't think it was important."

I made some kind of noncommittal noise because I didn't know what else to say, then I asked her for the address. She gave it to me, if I promised to call her back, let her know the condition of the apartment, and if there seemed to be evidence of a girl living with him "without benefit of marriage."

I agreed, although I didn't plan to fulfill that promise, and hung up. Then I gathered Freeman for lunch. After we ate, I planned to go to Daniel Kirkland's apartment and see why he hadn't called home.

TWENTY

The address the agent gave me was in a neighborhood that she called the West Village. At lunch, Freeman recommended that I park and walk, and when I arrived in the West Village, I was glad he had. The Village wasn't too far from his apartment, but it felt like a whole other world.

I walked by several students, and an old man sleeping on the sidewalk. Another elderly man was leaning against a doorway, smoking, watching me as I passed. His clothing suggested that he had once had wealthier days, now lost to time and his old age.

The apartment was in a block of row houses on the right side of the street that had seen better days. The houses had wooden stairs and few of the original doorways. Most had replaced the windows. Only the top floors seemed to retain the intricate cornices and loopy designs that marked these row houses as a onetime upscale neighborhood.

The address was in the middle of the row, the building indistinguishable from its neighbors except for the wrought-iron railing and the brightly painted yellow door. I walked up the steps, redone recently in concrete, and stared at the mailbox. It listed two apartments inside, indicating that the narrow three-story house had been split in two.

I pushed on the main door, surprised to find it open, and stepped inside. Stairs ran along the right-hand wall, just like they did in Freeman's building, only these looked even more rickety. Mud-covered shoes sat on a rug at the foot of the stairs, and even more shoes rested haphazardly in front of a door at the end of the hall.

I glanced at that door first. It had a metal number one on the door. I wanted apartment two. Up the stairs I went.

These stairs also ended in a door, with the number two painted on it in white. I stood on the nearest step, knocked, then stepped back down, not wanting to get hit by the door as it opened outward. I also didn't want Daniel to see me and bolt through the back window, disappearing down a fire escape.

After a long minute, the door opened. A young man stood there. He was about twenty, with long blond hair and a wispy beard. A petite, brown-haired white girl stood behind him, peering over his shoulder.

"I'm looking for Daniel Kirkland," I said. "I understand he lives here."

"Not any more," the boy said, and started to close the door.

I caught it, glad that it did open out. "His family's worried about him. They haven't heard from him in more than six months, and they just found out he hasn't been in school. I've been hired to find him."

"Good luck," the kid said. "I haven't seen him since February."

February was a lot more recent than anyone else had seen him.

"Look," I said, "you're the first lead I've had in nearly a week. I'd like to talk for just a minute, find out what he did between December and January, and see if this case is worth pursuing."

"It isn't," the kid said, but he stepped away from the door as he did so. The girl scurried backwards as well, looking at me as if I were the most dangerous thing she'd ever seen.

I climbed the remaining few steps and walked into the apartment. It smelled of vinegar and spoiled milk. Clothes were draped all over a dumpy couch, and two wicker chairs with sagging seats were the focus of the room. The room was big and square and seemed to go on forever, except for the stairs, going up the right side, just like they had below.

More clothes hung off the wooden balcony. Black-light posters covered the walls, and lava lamps sat on two tables fashioned out of boxes.

The young man took some of the clothes off the couch, tossing them onto another chair in the corner. "We weren't expecting company."

"I wasn't planning to stay long," I said, not sure I wanted to sit on that couch. It seemed to be the source of the sour milk smell.

"Who told you Daniel lived here?" The girl's voice was quiet, but strong. I might have frightened her, but her fear hadn't lasted long.

"A woman at your rental agency," I said. "She seems to believe Daniel still lives here."

"Crap," the boy said. "I forgot he signed the lease."

"We can't change it now," the girl said.

The boy waved his hand at her, shushing her. And I knew, just from that interchange, that I wouldn't get their names without a struggle.

"You work for the agency?" the girl asked me.

I shook my head. "I work for Daniel's mother. I'm from Chicago."

"I thought his family was broke," the boy said.

"It is," I said. "I owe his mother a favor."

The boy whistled. "Some favor. But I guess you can go home now. I'd tell Moms that Daniel isn't worth her time."

He was serious, which surprised me. I had initially thought the deprecating language was just the way he viewed the world.

"I take it you and Daniel weren't friends," I said.

"Shit, man, we were tight once," he said. "But he's not the same guy I met last year."

"You met him at Yale?" I asked.

"We were roomies freshman year. He was one serious guy, always studying, trying to be the best at everything he did. Then he started to realize that being the best student didn't mean as much here as it did at home, that he had to play all these games, and Danny wasn't good at games."

"Yes, he was," the girl said with a touch of bitterness.

"Claire," the boy said, warning her.

The girl made a face at the boy. "Danny swallowed the revolutionary pill, you know?" she said to me. "He is one wacko guy. We couldn't keep him here, not with his stuff."

"Claire," the boy said. "We don't know who this guy is."

"Like I care," she snapped.

"I don't want us getting in trouble," he said.

"You won't. I promise," I said. "I am from Chicago. I have ID if you'd like to see it."

The boy started to ask for it, but Claire waved it away. I was beginning to get a sense of who was in charge in this relationship.

"If we get in trouble, Barry can say I told you so all he wants." The girl crossed her thin arms. "But I believe you. I think you just want to find Danny, although I'd be careful if I were you."

"Careful? Why?" I asked.

"Because we kicked him and his weapons out of here. The guns were creeping me out, but that stuff he had in his room— Barry said that you could make bombs from it. And I don't want a part of that. None of us did. So we threw him out."

I frowned. That was the second time I'd heard of Daniel's violence. Perhaps Rhondelle's beating had frightened him. "Bombs?"

The boy—Barry, apparently—shrugged. "I might've been wrong. I thought I saw some stuff that looked like C-4 and he had a lot of nails and stuff. But I didn't see a blaster or anything else you needed to make the things go off. It was the rhetoric more than anything else. I mean, you can only listen to so much about the honky-controlled system and how nobody gets a fair shake except the rich, and how the world has to explode to bring about a whole new reality. After time, it all sounds crazy, man."

It sounded crazy to me. "I met Daniel last summer. He didn't say anything like that."

"The convention was like the last straw for him," Claire said. "All those kids getting beat up and nobody apologizing, then Nixon getting elected. It was like Daniel saw on the national scale what he thought was going on here at Yale. You know, the underclass getting trashed, and the administration not giving a shit. Then there's the whole war, man, and that's just the same-old same-old. A white colonizing nation destroying the homes and livelihoods of people of color."

I shook my head a little, not certain if that was her rhetoric or his. "Did you agree with him?"

"About what part?" she asked. "That there's discrimination? Yeah. That it's bad? Yeah. That you need to destroy the system before you can rebuild it? Hell, I don't know. I just know I can't kill anything."

My frown grew. When she referred to killing, did she mean the war or something Daniel proposed?

"I don't think anybody in the house agreed with him except Rhondelle," Barry said.

"Rhondelle was here, too?" I asked. "I thought she was missing. There was an article in the *New Haven Register* about it last May."

Claire snorted. "Like Rhondelle would tell her daddy what she was up to. He wanted that girl to be whiter than all the debutantes on the social register. Vassar education, marry someone rich, speak with that Katharine Hepburn accent that showed *Kult-chur*. Rhondelle wasn't having none of it. She always thought her dad was jealous because she could pass and he couldn't."

I sighed. Skin color was important even among my people. The paler the skin, the higher the social status. It simply showed how infected we all were with the same disease.

"How many people lived in this apartment when Daniel and Rhondelle were here?" I asked.

"There're three bedrooms upstairs," Barry said. "All with couples, all Yale refugees."

"Except the girls," Claire said. "We're from everywhere. Mount Holyoke, Vassar, Radcliffe."

Yeah, everywhere, I thought, but didn't say anything. "And you all dropped out?"

"Some of us not voluntarily," Barry said. "My dad switched jobs and my folks couldn't afford Yale anymore. So they asked me to take a semester or two off while they looked for funding. But if I live on my own for a few years, without their help, I qualify for aid on my own income, which is for shit, if you know what I mean."

I nodded.

"So I wasn't going back because of money. Ira, he was having some of the same problems Daniel was, only they were over his religion. And the girls, all three of them were planning to transfer to Yale in the fall, even Rhondelle."

"She was the first admitted," Claire said. "By then, she didn't give a damn."

"When was that?" I asked.

"April?" Claire asked Barry. "Right?"

"But I thought you hadn't seen Daniel since February," I said.

"He moved out in February." Barry sounded annoyed. "He was back a few times."

"Then why'd you say that you hadn't seen him since February?" I asked, pressing the point.

"I don't know," Barry said. "I hate thinking about him, man."

"What happened that angered you so much?" I asked.

"Besides the rhetoric? Besides the guns and the bomb stuff and the way he screamed at me when I confronted him?"

"I guess," I said.

Barry walked away from me. He flopped on the couch, put his feet up and closed his eyes, as if willing me away.

"Danny told Barry he would never get it," Claire said softly. "That last day, they had this hideous fight, you know? And Danny said that Barry was just as much a pawn in the game as everybody else. He'd rebel for a while, then he'd realize that the system benefited him—you know, tall, handsome white kid—and Barry said it wasn't like that, he wouldn't sell out, and Danny said that Barry didn't have to. That he was already part of the system, being a rich Yale baby and all that."

I glanced at Barry. His face was flushed, and it wasn't from the heat. In fact, I noticed for the first time that the apartment was cool. This place had an air conditioner, which surprised me. It had to be in one of the back rooms because I couldn't see it or hear it.

"Barry," Claire said, her voice rising—obviously this discussion had made her indignant, too—"didn't qualify for some special scholarship. His parents aren't rich, either, and they're really sacrificing to send him to school. He didn't have a lot of breaks. Danny's throwing his away, but Barry, he's just struggling to hang on, you know—"

"Claire," Barry said wearily. "Shut up."

"—and they really got into it. Danny screaming at Barry that he didn't know what real poverty was, and Barry screaming at Danny that he didn't know what real opportunity was, and then I had to get between them because I thought they were going to kill each other, you know?"

I did know. Those two boys had cared about each other, but their differences had gotten too much for them. And it sounded like neither one of them knew how to resolve those differences and maintain their friendship.

"Anyway, we all voted, and the decision was that Danny had to leave. Rhondelle went with him, even though she didn't have to. I think for Ira and Louise it was the bomb and gun stuff that made them think Danny shouldn't stay, but for Barry and me, it was the attitude. We just couldn't play the enemy any more."

"Any idea where he and Rhondelle went?"

"No, thank God," Barry said from the couch. "And I don't want to know. It's better if you don't find them either. Tell Danny's mom to let him go. He's nuts."

Barry said all of that with his eyes closed. Somehow, his relaxed posture and his immobile face added power to his words.

"I'm this far," I said. "I'll see if I can find him. And then I'll tell her what I think she needs to know."

This time, Barry did look at me. "What the hell does that mean?"

"His mother is a good woman," I said, "and if you're right, I don't want her coming out east to find him surrounded by weapons and talking about revolution. But I've known a lot of guys who've gotten in deeper than they expected and sometimes they just need help getting out. If that's the case, then I'll see what I can do."

That was what had happened with Malcolm. Franklin and I had gotten him out of the gangs in time. Of course, Jimmy's brother Joe had been in a similar situation, and he refused to leave.

Barry snorted. "Danny never gets in too deep. He's the one digging the goddamn hole, man."

Claire had gone to a nearby table and was looking through stacks of paper. "I've got an address around here somewhere. I've been forwarding mail."

Finally, I was getting somewhere.

"Did Daniel ever talk to you about the incident with Rhondelle after Coeducation Week?" I asked Barry.

Barry took his feet off the coffee table and hunched forward, losing any illusion of being relaxed. "No, but Rhondelle did. She wasn't sure she was going to apply to Yale after that. She did eventually, I think because her dad forced her."

"Did you know who the boys were who threatened her?" I asked.

"Threatened?" Claire asked. *"Threatened?"*

"That's what Dean Sidbury said. He said that Daniel stopped things before they became too serious."

"Prick," Claire muttered.

"I wasn't there, but I heard it was pretty ugly," Barry said. "Those guys, they trapped Rhondelle in the room, said some nasty things, forced her into a corner, and started going for her clothes. She was kicking and screaming and fighting back when Danny came into the college. I guess he heard her, ran upstairs, and got in the middle of it."

"Do you think Daniel's obsession with weaponry could have been caused by that?" I asked.

"It would seem logical, wouldn't it," Barry said, "if it'd started there. But it started earlier. He'd come back from Chicago with some kind of handgun. I didn't know what it was. Then I found some books on explosives in his room. He said it was for a class, but he didn't have any real science classes that semester. I think the Rhondelle thing was an excuse for him to leave school."

"It bothered her, though," Claire said. "She would never say why."

"I was wondering if Daniel and Rhondelle still felt threatened by those four boys," I said.

Barry shook his head. "One's still in and out of hospitals, the other two are out of Yale, and the last guy, he's the kind who's not going to bother you if you're not in his face. Unless Danny goes to Yale, he's not in any trouble from them."

"But would he believe that he was?"

"Who knows?" Barry slipped down on the couch again. "Like I said, Danny's crazy."

Claire had gone back to digging through the papers. She finally pulled out a slip with Magic Marker writing on it. "Got it. Let me write it down for you."

She bent over the desk, grabbed more paper, and wrote the address for me. Then she handed the paper to me. Her handwriting was neat and well formed, not at all like the Magic Marker writing she still had clutched in her hand.

"Don't tell Danny that we told you where he was," she said. "I don't want him or his new friends to know that we ratted on them."

"New friends?" I asked.

"You don't need to be a weatherman to know which way the wind blows," Barry said.

At the time, I had no idea what he meant.

TWENTY-ONE

was late meeting Jimmy and Malcolm. I had warned them that I might be, that our early evening meeting time was a bit flexible, but still I worried as I drove to the Green. Jimmy panicked when I was late picking him up from the Grimshaws'. I had no idea how he would react in a strange town with no friends at all.

I needn't have worried. Jimmy and Malcolm were sprawled on the grass, leaning against one of the big trees. A group of folding chairs had been set up in the middle, and a college student was walking among them, setting out music stands.

Jimmy and Malcolm were watching as if they had never seen anything so fascinating.

"You guys ready for dinner?" I asked as I crouched beside him.

"Not really," Jimmy said. "We don't want to lose our spot."

"Your spot?" I asked.

"Free concert," Malcolm said. "We thought maybe we'd stay for it, if you don't mind."

"What kind of concert?" I asked.

"I dunno," Malcolm said. "The kind my mom would've liked, I guess."

I studied him for a moment. He rarely mentioned his mother. He was still devastated by her death.

134

"What kind of music would that be?" I asked. "Jazz?"

"Classic," Jimmy said.

"Classical music," Malcolm said softly, as if he were embarrassed by it. "My mom made me listen. I kinda . . . It's snotty, but cool . . . Mom always wanted me to . . ."

His voice trailed off. I wasn't going to push him to continue. I remember what it was like mourning parents; sometimes the memories became too much to deal with, and so you just had to stop.

But Jimmy didn't have that compunction. "Your mom wanted you to what?"

Malcolm looked up at Jimmy as if he had forgotten that Jimmy was there. "She, uh, loved music, and wanted me to be as musical as she was."

"Were you?" Jimmy was interested. So was I. I suddenly realized how little Malcolm talked about himself.

"I liked church choir." Malcolm shrugged. "I taught myself a little piano. I'd heard that college . . ."

His voice trailed off again. I was going to put my hand on Jimmy's shoulder, to silence him, but didn't reach him in time.

"You heard that college what?" Jimmy asked.

This time Malcolm didn't look at him. This time, he was staring at the makeshift stage. "College sometimes loaned you instruments, so that you could learn. At least for piano. Drums, too."

There was so much longing in his voice that even Jimmy heard it. Jimmy looked at the chairs, lined up on the Green, then back at Malcolm.

"How come you never told Althea? She'd get you into choir."

A little boy's solution, with a little boy's simplicity. Malcolm gave Jimmy a fond look, and that seemed to break the spell.

"Could you imagine me practicing vocal scales in that house?" he asked. Then he sang one, revealing a voice that had incredible purity. "You guys would've laughed me out of there."

"I wouldn't have." Jimmy was looking at Malcolm with as much awe as I felt.

I'd had musical talent as a child, enough to sing a solo at the very last concert I'd performed in, the weekend my parents died, but I'd never had the dream that Malcolm seemed to. Malcolm seemed to have set aside that dream and accepted that he would never achieve it.

Yet here, sitting on this long lawn, with trees three times older than all of us combined, and churches hundreds of years old along the edge of the common, Malcolm's dream resurfaced. I couldn't deny him an evening of music.

"I'll get some takeout," I said. "You guys stay here."

They did. I left, and stood in a long line at a nearby diner that offered a Concert on the Green picnic special. I brought it back, and we spent the warm summer evening listening to the New Haven Symphony Orchestra playing mixing crowd-pleasers like Anderson's "Bugler's Holiday" and less common pieces like Gottschalk's "Night in the Tropics."

For the first time, it seemed like a vacation, even though I knew the feeling wouldn't last.

On the drive back, I asked Malcolm if he thought Daniel was violent. Malcolm leaned his head against the back of the seat, as if he was thinking hard.

Then he shrugged. "I've never seen him do anything violent. But then, the thing about Daniel is that he'll do what it takes."

"What it takes to do what?"

"Whatever he wants. If he wants a scholarship, he'll study his ass off. If he wants some girl, he'll charm her until he gets her."

"What would he gain from violence?" I asked.

Malcolm sat up, looking at the road ahead of us. "I don't know," he said softly. "Daniel usually works with his brains. I can't imagine him walking around beating people up."

But guns and bombs weren't about beating people up. They were distance weapons, and someone with a brain could make a plan involving them.

I felt very unsettled as I drove. Until this afternoon, I had felt like I was gaining an understanding of Daniel Kirkland. Now I wasn't sure I knew who he was at all.

TWENTY-TWO

That night was filled with sirens. They seemed to go on forever. Every time one ended, another began.

Sirens—fire, police, ambulance—were a way of life in Chicago, and I hadn't noticed they were missing here until they ran from about eleven P.M. until about two A.M.

I had late-night guard duty, and I was especially watchful. If another major crime had gone down, I would be prepared this time for Sanford and Prauss. And this time, they wouldn't get into the hotel room. In fact, this time, they'd get more than they bargained for.

But no cops showed up, despite my vigilance. We spent a goodly part of Saturday morning in the hotel room while I made my phone calls to Grace's list—which I was beginning to think was worthless—and to the Whickam house and office.

No answers, of course. I tried to reach Grace, too, but no one answered at her place either.

We headed out, making sure we left nothing in the hotel room, and after some luscious pastries at a local bakery we went back down to the Green.

I dropped the boys at the library, and then I went out to see if I could find the address Claire had given me. The address was on the corner of DeWitt and Putnam, in an area of houses that had been condemned.

The building I was looking for was an old sprawling Victorian. Outside, the building looked like one good wind would knock it over, but someone had fixed up the interior. The stairs had been repaired with new boards supporting the old. Holes in the wall had been patched but not painted, and a number of the apartment doors had shiny new deadbolt locks on them.

The door to the third-floor apartment was open. Someone had placed an old table fan on the floor, blowing air into the hallway. The heat up here was intense.

A slight clanking made me understand why: The radiators still worked, and they were on. No one had shut them off for the summer. Maybe no one knew how.

The entire place smelled of dirty clothes and human sweat. I was getting tired of those odors. At least the scent of marijuana didn't overlay them.

I knocked on the door, leaned in, and called, "Hello!"

No one answered, and my voice echoed enough to make me worry that the apartment was empty. I shoved the door open the rest of the way, and stepped past the fan into a messy kitchen. Dirty dishes sat on the counter, and had been there so long that they no longer had an odor. Water dripped into the sink, leaving a rust stain.

A table with a broken leg was propped against the only wall without cupboards. Sunlight poured into the hallway from the rooms beyond. I shouted hello again and still got no answer.

The apartment got hotter the farther in I went. A window was open in a bedroom off the kitchen. Dust bunnies covered the hardwood floor, and a shirt lay crumpled in the corner. To my right was a bathroom. Another door opened into it, probably from the next bedroom.

I opened the door to that second bedroom. This room looked lived in. Clothes strewn everywhere, an unmade bed, and papers on every surface. I was about to step inside when I heard the floor creak behind me.

I turned. A white woman was standing at the very end of the hall, her arms crossed. She was young, maybe twenty, her long hair going all the way past her hips.

"Who the hell are you?" she asked.

"My name is Bill," I said. "I'm looking for Daniel Kirkland."

"Danny's not here," she said.

"When will he be back?" I asked.

"Not ever," she said, then raised her eyebrows for emphasis. "And I'm moving out, too. This building's been condemned."

"I know," I said. "Look, I'm here from Chicago. I'm searching for Daniel for his mother. There's a family emergency, and she can't seem to find him."

"Should've called the police," the girl said, obviously not buying my story.

"She did. Then she called me. I specialize in finding things."

"Danny's not a thing," she said.

"He's not easy to find either," I said. "If he doesn't live here anymore, where is he staying?"

"Why should I tell you? I don't know you. You make claims, but I have no clue if they're correct." She hadn't moved from her position at the end of the hall.

"I have identification, if that helps." I reached into my back pocket.

"A license?"

"Not a detective's license. Grace didn't want anything that formal or that expensive. She doesn't have a lot of money."

The woman's eyes narrowed. I pulled out my wallet, removed my driver's license, and held it between two fingers so that she could look at it.

"You can at least see that I'm being truthful about my name and my address," I said.

She didn't leave her position at the end of the hall. I suddenly realized that she was afraid of me. Her position gave her courage: It covered her back and gave her two doorways to escape through, should she need them.

We were alone in this apartment; her behavior told me that.

I took two cautious steps toward her, then leaned forward so that she could take the license from me. She did, looked at it, then handed it back.

I slipped it inside my wallet and replaced it in my pocket.

"I don't deal with narcs," she said.

"I'm not a narc. If you can get him a message, that would be fine."

She didn't make any promises. Instead, she raised those eyebrows again, as if she were encouraging me to continue.

"Tell him that Bill Grimshaw's looking for him. I'm at the Motor Court across from the Yale Bowl, and I'll be there at least through Monday. I need to talk to him about his family."

"If there's a family emergency, then shouldn't he just phone home?"

"That'll do, too," I said, although it wouldn't resolve my work in the case. A phone call from Daniel might put Grace's mind at ease, but I wasn't happy with all of this talk of bombs and guns. I wanted to find Daniel myself if I could.

She shook her head, then held up her hands. "I'm not involved in his stuff any more, to be honest. You'd be better off talking to someone else."

"Is there someone else to talk to?" I asked.

"I'd head to the Barn, if I were you," she said.

"The Barn?"

"Out by Branford. That's all I know. That's all I want to know."

Something in her tone alerted me. "What's the Barn?"

"Don't be a square, man," she said. "Just head out there, take care of your business and leave. And I'd bring some backup with you. They might take you for a cop."

"What kind of place is this Barn?" I asked.

"Frickin' dangerous, man," she said. "I wouldn't get near it. I don't even know exactly where it is, only that most of the group moved there in May. Maybe BSAY knows or the SDS down on campus. But I'm not telling you anything else."

"Is Daniel in some kind of trouble?"

She laughed, but the sound had no amusement in it. "When isn't Danny in trouble?"

"What does that mean?" I asked.

"You know he nearly killed a guy last fall, right?"

"Yes," I said, and she started with surprise.

"Then you probably know that he's only gotten worse," she said. "I was glad when he left, him and his friends. I was glad to have this place to myself."

She flushed, then bit her lower lip. She didn't want me to know she was alone. Maybe she wasn't planning to move out after all. Maybe she was squatting here.

"Why?" I asked. "Was it the guns that bothered you?"

"You know about the guns?" she asked, sounding surprised.

I nodded.

"That isn't good." Her voice was soft, and I doubted the comment was meant for me. She grabbed her long hair, gathered it into a ponytail, then let it fall down her back.

I waited. The warmth and the quiet of the building made us seem like the only two people in the world.

"It wasn't the guns or the . . ." She paused, as if she caught herself. "Or the rhetoric. It was . . . it was me. I couldn't take it any more. I got clean, and once you're clean, if you want to stay that way, you have to change some habits, get rid of the people around you who use."

"I heard that Daniel didn't use."

Her smile was bitter. "Maybe not drugs, at least he didn't take them. But he used them with other people. He bought, then doled them out, so that other people would do what he wanted. And when you used, man, that seemed like the best thing. Free cake, free ice cream, no real cost. Until you find yourself doing things you don't want to do."

"Like what?" I asked the question softly so that I didn't startle her and stop the confession.

"Getting stuff. Components . . . doing stuff you wouldn't normally do just for favors. Things I don't want to remember."

I shivered. I didn't like what I was hearing. "Why did he leave?"

"Two reasons," she said. "He thought the cops were on to us, which wasn't the main thing. The main thing was that I'd come back from the drug clinic, and there's Danny, offering me junk again. And I lost it. I mean, lost it. I grabbed one of his guns and threatened him with it. Chased him out of here so damn fast, he didn't know what hit him. When he tried to come back for his stuff, I wouldn't let him in."

"What about his friends?"

She shook her head, as if the memory bothered her. "They didn't want to live with a crazy woman. And some of them didn't want to be junk-free. So some of them went with Danny. A few came with me to the clinic. We've been pulling it together. I've got a job now, and enough saved so that I can get a real apartment come fall. Maybe I'll even be able to go back to school next year, if I can stay off the stuff. The pressure gets to me, you know?"

I nodded, mostly to encourage her to continue.

"So there you have it," she said. "That's why I don't want to give Danny your message, why I don't know exactly where the Barn is, and why I don't ever want to see him again."

Without waiting for my response, the girl disappeared into one of the side rooms.

I stood there for a moment, looking at the dust floating in the sunlight-filled hallway. Her shadow crossed the floor, growing large, then small again as she checked to see if I was still there.

I was, but only because my stomach was churning. Guns and bombs and using people. If all that I'd been hearing was true, Daniel was planning something.

But what?

TWENTY-THREE

When we got back to the hotel, I called Grace. This time, she was home.
"Did you find him?" she asked.

"I have some leads." I wasn't sure how to broach the topic of Daniel's violence. I didn't want Grace to get angry at me, but I needed some questions answered.

"Good ones?"

"Ones I'm not sure I believe," I said.

Malcolm and Jimmy, who were sitting on the edge of one of the beds, looked at me questioningly. I hadn't yet told them about my day.

"What did you hear?" Grace asked.

"I've heard twice now that Daniel's violent. Has he ever hit something when he lost his temper or gotten into fights?"

"Daniel?" Grace laughed. "He's always said that anyone who can't talk his way out of a fight is stupider than he looks."

That was my sense of Daniel as well.

"Has he ever condoned violence?"

She didn't answer me. I wished I could see her. I didn't know if she was thinking or if the question had disturbed her.

"After the convention," she said slowly, "he said something about how this country only understands violence. But it didn't sound like he was condoning it."

"Did he buy a gun then?"

"Daniel?" She sounded shocked. "No, of course not."

I sighed, but not loudly. I didn't want her to hear me. "If you remember anything, would you let me know?"

"What's he done?" she asked.

I had no answer for her. So I told her the truth. "I don't know yet, but I'm doing my best to find out."

When I hung up, Malcolm wanted to know what I had learned.

"Let's get some dinner," I said, "and I'll tell you."

We ended up having pizza in the park, sitting outside because I didn't want to talk about Daniel anyplace we could be overheard. I had to relay part of what happened the day before, because I hadn't had a chance after the concert. As I told them about the first apartment, I mentioned the reference to weather.

"Oh, man," Malcolm said, "we're getting in way over our heads."

I looked at him. The sun was going down, casting shadows through the trees that surrounded us. The three of us were sitting on the merry-go-round. Jimmy was the farthest back, leaning on the very center. Malcolm and I sat in opposite slices of the metal pie, cross-legged and facing each other. The pizza—or what remained of it—was on Jimmy's section, sitting uneasily on the bumpy metal top.

"This weather reference means something to you?" I asked.

"Oh, yeah," Malcolm said. "I saw the damn document."

"What document?"

" 'You Don't Have to Be a Weatherman to Know Which Way the Wind Is Blowing.' " He said that with great contempt.

Those were the words Barry had used the day before.

"Should this mean something to me?" I asked.

"Probably not. I didn't tell you about it because I didn't think it was important." Malcolm rested his slice of pizza on his right leg, and reached for his can of root beer. "Remember that stupid SDS convention?"

"Yeah," I said.

"That's where the document was. I told you everybody at the convention was fighting? They'd split into factions. One was the National Organizers, the other was the Progressive Labor people. They fought, then it looked like the Progressive Labor people were going to win, and they didn't want a lot of black involvement, which they called militant, which might not have been wrong, since I seemed to be the only person of color there who wasn't a Panther."

I froze. "You didn't tell me that the Panthers were there."

"Because it wasn't really important. It was just a lot of stupid speeches, and then these National Organizers wrote this paper about how important it was to be militant, and how they wanted to bring down the government, and how they wanted to revolutionize the United States, and how the only way to take on the Establishment was through violence, and all that crap. I thought it was really stupid, especially when a bunch of them stayed up all night and wrote their thoughts down in this mimeographed document they expected everybody to read."

"How did that reach New Haven so quickly?" I asked.

"The split was already here. That's the point. This was just the first time the splits were visible nationally, at least so far as I can tell." He set his root beer down.

Jimmy leaned forward, grabbed it, and took a sip.

"Hey!" Malcolm said.

"I'm out," Jimmy said.

"Next time, ask first, Jim. Don't presume," I said absently.

"Sorry," he mumbled.

"Anyway," Malcolm said, "at the convention, everyone started calling the militants the Weathermen and the Progressive Labor people and everyone else who didn't like want to bomb the entire planet the Running Dogs. And the names kinda stuck."

A chill ran down my back. "Do you actually think Daniel's joined the militants?"

"That's what it sounds like, right? And they might not have called themselves Weathermen until this last week. Maybe they don't even call themselves that. Maybe everyone else does. I mean, that's all anyone talked about on campus this week, right, Jim? The bust-up of the SDS."

"I thought it was some rock group." Jimmy picked the anchovies off his pizza and tossed them onto the concrete playground.

Malcolm watched him for a moment, then sighed. "All I'm saying is that if Daniel's actually using guns and buying drugs and making bombs, why're we looking for him?"

"What if he's not?" I asked quietly. "If I talked to anyone about you last summer, they would have told me you had been in a gang all fall, that you were a lost cause, and that I should give up."

Malcolm flushed. "This is different."

"Is it?" I asked. "You were with that gang because they gave you a place to sleep. You hadn't gotten completely co-opted. You were too smart for that."

"But Daniel's always been political," Malcolm said. "Even you said you could hardly talk to him last summer. He was clearly SDS then. He's involved now."

Malcolm was probably right. I knew that. I also knew that I wanted to believe, for Grace, that Daniel had flirted with the violent faction of the SDS and moved on.

If he hadn't, I wasn't sure what I would do.

"What if he is a Weatherman?" Malcolm obviously wasn't willing to let this go. "What'll you tell Grace then?"

"He'll say there's nothing you can do and that sometimes you have to take care of yourself and hope he'll grow out of it, right, Smoke?" Jimmy had plucked an entire lump of cheese off his pizza. The cheese dripped tomato sauce onto the merry-go-round.

Malcolm stared at Jim as if he'd never seen him before, but I recognized those words. I didn't know how many times I'd said them to him about his brother, Joe. Joe had been dealing drugs, lost in a gang, and willing to let his little brother go instead of cleaning up his own act.

"Yeah," I said. "That's probably what I'll tell her."

But that wasn't all I would do. If Daniel was involved in something illegal, something that could hurt innocent people, I would have go after him—or make sure someone else did.

"We got to be real careful here, Bill," Malcolm said. "These guys, they're on some whacked-out mission to save the world, and they don't care who they hurt. This isn't the place for Jimmy."

"It doesn't sound like the place for any of us," I said. "But if my information is right, all we have to do is find that barn. Daniel will probably be there, I can check him out for myself, and then we can leave. Will that work for you?"

Malcolm unfolded himself and pushed off the merry-go-round, sending it on a slow spin. He walked to the edge of the concrete. As the merry-go-round came back toward him, his gaze caught mine.

"You know," he said, "sometimes it just gets me. Daniel gets the scholarship, Daniel gets the good family, Daniel gets all the opportunities, and what does he do? He tries to blow up the fucking world. Me, I got to fight for every goddamn crumb. I finally get a break and what do I get? Drafted. It's not fucking fair."

He walked off into the park. Jimmy stuck out a foot and stopped the merry-go-round from spinning. "We got to go after him, Smoke."

I shook my head. "What do we say? He's right. He would have taken everything Daniel got, used it, and made even more of himself. It's not fair, and lying to him and telling him it'll be all better isn't going to comfort him."

Jimmy glared at me, then jumped off the merry-go-round. He ran after Malcolm, catching up to him near the swings. Malcolm kept walking, and Jimmy remained at his side, like a determined little brother.

I dug my feet into the concrete holding the merry-go-round in place. Was that what I had set up? Another brother for Jimmy to look up to and then be abandoned by him? I hadn't meant it. All I'd meant to do was bring Malcolm along so that we could find a better place to live.

New Haven certainly wasn't it. And, as Malcolm pointed out to me, neither was Philadelphia or Cleveland. Nor, I noticed from yesterday's paper, was Kokomo, Indiana, where another riot had broken out in the black community, or Omaha, or Cairo, Illinois. All filled with violence, and rioting, and the deaths of countless innocent people.

The entire summer seemed like it was going to rage forward. And there was little I could do to stop it.

TWENTY-FOUR

We decided that I would care for Jimmy the next morning, while Malcolm went back to Yale to see if he could find the local SDS chapter. He figured he might be able to sweet-talk them into telling him where the Barn was.

Jimmy seemed excited by the prospect of having me around all day. Since it was Sunday, he asked if we could go to church. Apparently he had promised Althea he'd keep up with his religious work.

I didn't want to sit in some stuffy New England church, rising and singing with inhibited white people who had no idea how to properly conduct a church service. But Jimmy pressured me and, after we had dropped Malcolm at the gates of Yale, we ended up on Dixwell, in the United Church of Christ, whose bulletin said that this church was the descendant of the first black church in New Haven.

After church, Jimmy and I returned to the motel to change out of our Sunday best. I took a minute to use the phone, trying the phone numbers that Grace gave me one more time. Still no answer at any of those, but when I called René Whickam, I was startled to hear someone pick up the phone.

I asked for Professor Whickam.

"This is he," a deep, slightly accented male voice said.

"Professor Whickam," I said, "my name is Bill Grimshaw and I'm an investigator from Chicago. I'm working for Grace Kirkland, Daniel Kirkland's mother. She hasn't heard from him in more than six months, and she's worried. I've been asking around, and I understand he spent some time with your daughter, and that there was an incident. I was wondering if I could speak to you about it."

Whickam was silent for so long after I spoke that I began to wonder if he had hung up. Then he said, "Where are you?"

"I'm in New Haven," I said. "I'm staying near the Yale Bowl."

"Let me come to you," he said, and no amount of argument would change his mind.

Jimmy wasn't happy with me. He had planned an entire day of sightseeing New Haven places that could only be reached by car and spending time doing "things" that he wouldn't describe.

I told him that we'd be able to start as soon as the professor left. Even if the professor gave us tips as to where Daniel might be, I wasn't about to follow up on them with Jimmy at my side.

Professor Whickam arrived about a half hour after we spoke on the phone. He drove a brand-new Ford station wagon that he kept so clean it looked like it was never used. I watched him get out of the car. He was a bald, lanky man who wore loose-fitting white cotton clothes that made him seem vaguely counterculture.

As he scanned the rooms looking for mine, I opened the door. "Professor Whickam?"

He seemed surprised at my appearance. His gaze ran up and down my khakis and short-sleeved shirt. Jimmy peered out next to me, startling Whickam further.

"I'm Bill Grimshaw," I said. "This is my son, Jim."

Whickam came closer, extended his hand, and introduced himself, although it wasn't necessary. His accent was very faint but noticeable. I couldn't quite tell its origin, but the softened consonants led me to believe he was either from Europe or from one of the Caribbean islands.

"Forgive me," he said. "I thought you were some kind of professional investigator. I did not realize that you were a family man."

"Professional investigators can be family men," I said with a smile. "Until I got here, I actually thought this would be an easy search. I had hoped to have a bit of a vacation with Jim after we found Daniel, but it's not proving that easy."

"I do understand." Whickam stood awkwardly in the doorway. The warmth of the early afternoon floated in on the breeze.

148

"Come on in," I said, indicating the chair beside the table.

Whickam sat. Jimmy crawled onto his bed and leaned back, closing his eyes like we had discussed. I figured it might be easier for Whickam to talk if he thought Jimmy was dozing.

I took the chair across from Whickam. I told him a modified version of my search for Daniel, leaving out some of the more graphic details, but not sparing the Yale administrators in any way. Then I told him that I had tracked Daniel through a series of apartments, with one left to check.

"Where is it?" Whickam asked. "I'll go with you."

"I wish I knew," I said. "It's a place called the Barn."

He blinked. "I have never heard of this place."

"Neither have most people. I'm tracking it down now." I leaned back, I hadn't told him that I knew Rhondelle was missing. "A number of people told me that Daniel and Rhondelle were an item. I was wondering if you knew where she was. I figure if I can find her, she might lead me to Daniel."

Whickam ran a hand across his mouth. For a moment, I thought he wasn't going to tell me about his missing daughter.

"I have not seen Rhondelle since Christmas," he said. "She left just after the break, telling me she was headed back to Vassar, but she never arrived. In fact, she hadn't even registered for the semester. I didn't discover this for weeks, and by then I had no way to find her. I have been looking. I have hired a private detective in Poughkeepsie who charges a small fortune and tells me nothing. My wife has gone to every fair and festival within a two-day radius. She looks through the crowds of young people, hoping to see Rhondelle. I spend my own vacation time searching. But I cannot find her."

"I'm sorry," I said quietly.

He raised his chin. "She is our only child, and we are frightened for her. She has not been the same since that incident this fall."

"I had heard that it was nothing more than threats."

"Perhaps to people who were not there." Whickam glanced at Jimmy, then back at me, apparently satisfied that Jim wasn't paying attention. Still, Whickam lowered his voice. "Rhondelle would not talk to me about it. The one time we did speak of it, she demanded that I quit my job at the fascist university. That is what she called it. Just last summer, she hoped to be transferred here. Those boys damaged her somehow, but no one will tell me exactly how. Even Danny, he says to me, 'Professor, I took care of it, you need not worry.' As if a father cannot help but worry."

He twisted his hands together. I tried not to look at them, long and thin and manicured.

"How well did you know Daniel?" I asked.

"How well does any father know his daughter's boyfriend? I had seen him at school. He was in my first-year French seminars, very driven, quite focused. He learned quickly and never seemed out of line—at least, not until his second year. There is such anger in him, Mr. Grimshaw. I fear for my daughter if she is with him."

"Do you think he'd harm her?"

Whickam folded his hands together, almost as if he were offering up a prayer. "The police, they say he nearly ripped that boy apart."

"That boy hurt your daughter," I said.

"Yes, I probably would have attacked him as well. But it takes a particular kind of man to so damage another, does it not?"

It did. A man who felt a very deep rage and had finally found an outlet for it. But I saw that rage differently than Whickam did. From what I had heard, Daniel had suffered humiliations at Yale he had never faced before. I suspected the attack on Rhondelle—particularly by legacy students and rich kids—had finally broken Daniel.

"I am concerned," Whickam was saying. "No one has told me the entire story, so I do not know if that young man's injuries are justified or if they are some kind of overreaction on Daniel's part."

"How did Rhondelle act around Daniel afterwards?"

Whickam waved a hand, then shook his head. "My daughter, she is in love with him. To her, he can do no wrong."

"Did you search for her here in New Haven?"

"She went to Vassar," he said.

"So that's a no?" I asked. "You haven't looked here in New Haven."

"If she were in New Haven, why wouldn't she come home? We made flyers. We even put an announcement in the paper. Why wouldn't she come forward?"

I didn't know how to answer that. Rhondelle had never been my focus. But I had some difficult things to say to her father now.

"In the last few days, I've encountered a number of people who said that Rhondelle and Daniel were together and living in various apartments in New Haven."

"I would have seen her."

"She probably knew how to avoid you," I said.

"Why do you insist on telling me that my daughter would not come home?" he asked.

"I'm wondering if there was another incident over Christmas, perhaps a break within the family, maybe even a fight over Daniel."

Whickam shook his head. "Daniel was always well behaved in our home, although my wife asked him not to discuss politics. His attitudes offended her."

"But not you?"

Whickam gave me a small smile. "I grew up in Paris. People there, they argue about all things. It is a form of entertainment."

"You're French, then?" I asked.

"I am American, born to American parents, raised in France because my parents believed in equality. They could not receive it here, so they joined the expatriate community. They will never come back."

"But you're here."

He nodded, extended his arms, and looked around. "I am here, a college professor at an Ivy League school. Well respected, well treated, things my parents did not have and could not have."

"I've run into discrimination in New Haven," I said.

"I am not saying it does not exist," Whickam said. "But here it is more of a class issue than a race issue."

"That's not what the black students say. I understand they formed their own group to protect their rights."

"To expand their rights," Whickam said. "They do not realize they are a part of the international community, that they must learn about all culture, white and black and any other color you might designate."

That sounded like a canned speech. I wondered if he had given it to Daniel. "Has Rhondelle lived here her whole life?"

"She has spent most summers with her grandparents in Paris," he said. "But she was born at Yale-New Haven Hospital. She is truly a local girl. That is why I have trouble believing that no one would come to me if they had seen her in town."

"Let me give you the addresses," I said. "The second is in the Hill. You probably don't want to go to either alone. But the first is in a neighborhood not far from Yale. Check it out. Then we can talk."

I wrote down the addresses and the few names I had learned. I slid the slip of paper toward him. He studied it for a moment, then folded it and put it in his pocket.

"Did your private detective look for her here?" I asked.

"He did work by phone," Whickam said. "He wanted to come, but I assured him she couldn't be here. I would have seen her."

He put extra emphasis on those last five words. He was wedded to his denial.

"Would you mind bringing me a picture of Rhondelle?" I asked. "Maybe I was mistaking her for someone else."

He smiled, then nodded once, a courtly gesture. "I shall bring several. I have one of her with Daniel from the holidays that I might part with. Perhaps that will help as well."

Whickam touched the folded slip of paper in his pocket. "Do you believe that my daughter is here with Daniel?"

"I believe they were together as recently as April," I said.

"What could they be doing that would cause her to give up her life, her future?"

"I don't know," I said quietly. "When I called you, I had hoped you could tell me."

TWENTY-FIVE

A fter Whickam left, I woke Jimmy and we drove to the Green to meet Malcolm. He had had a more successful day than I had. When we met him on the Green, he came with three separate addresses for the Barn, all of them vague and none of them in Branford. He also discovered other rumors, the most common being that Daniel and his group had left New Haven in May, after the Black Panthers had been arrested for murder.

The conflicting rumors on Daniel's departure all agreed on one other thing: that he had taken the group to the center of "imperialistic capitalism" in the United States. I certainly hoped that wasn't true, because tracking Daniel in New Haven was difficult, but tracking him in New York would be almost impossible.

We decided that Malcolm would have the van the next day. He would drive past all three addresses, see which if any of them looked like the Barn, and let me know. He would also see if he could track down the New York rumor, and maybe get some kind of address.

An early morning phone call changed my plans. After he had left me, Professor Whickam had gone to the row house and learned that his daughter had indeed been in New Haven. Then he had gone to his office at Yale, looked up Daniel's file, and gotten Grace's phone number. Whickam called Grace, and she had spoken highly of me.

Whickam wanted to meet me at the motel. I told him I would be downtown, and he offered to meet me in front of the Beinecke Library. When I suggested his office instead, he said no. He would rather talk with me away from the prying ears of his secretary.

The Beinecke Library was somewhere between York and Grove Streets. Jimmy and I wandered until we found it—an astonishingly ugly building that looked like it had been made of papier-mâché and glue. It had no exterior windows and seemed like some architecture student's semester project.

Whickam was already there, sitting on one of the concrete benches outside the Memorial Hall. I didn't approach him immediately. Instead, I stood and stared at the names carved in the granite, names of Yale men who had died in the various wars. Of course, Vietnam wasn't up there yet, but I was certain I'd find Korea if I looked.

Usually, I tried to honor the other veterans, the ones who had made the greatest sacrifice, by reading their names on the memorials, but that morning, I didn't have time. I did notice, with great disgust, that someone had spray-painted the word "Murderers" across one of the columns, and someone else had spray-painted the word "Killers" along another.

The implied violence against men who had only done what their country had asked of them made me turn away.

Jimmy glanced up at me, frowning. "You okay?"

"Yeah," I said, a bit more curtly than I meant to. We walked over to Whickam, who had been watching us from a distance.

"I had thought perhaps you were not going to speak with me," he said.

"The memorial caught me." I sat down beside him. "You surprised me when you called this morning."

"You surprised me yesterday," he said. "I had not thought Rhondelle could be so cruel, and yet you were right. She had remained here."

I didn't have any words to comfort him for her betrayal.

"You have done more in a few days than the detective I hired in Poughkeepsie," he said. "I would like to talk with you about hiring you to look for Rhondelle."

"I'm already working on a case," I said, not wanting the conflict. If she had gone one way and Daniel another, I didn't want to feel torn between my loyalty to Grace, and my need for an income.

"Daniel and Rhondelle seem to be together. I understand your need to put Daniel first. I respect that. But I do not want to lose your leads. I would like notice of them, so that when you are finished with Daniel's case, you may look into Rhondelle's as well."

Apparently Whickam had already thought of the potential conflict.

"I would have to charge more than my usual rate," I said. "Expenses alone will be quite high on this trip, and I'll have to go slow, since Jim is with me."

I nodded toward Jimmy who was standing in front of the ugly library reading one of the signs.

"I understand," Whickam said.

"If I don't find her by the beginning of the fall school year, I will have to resign from the case." I made that stipulation because no matter where I ended up, Jimmy had to be in school. And I didn't want him starting late. He was at enough of a disadvantage as it was.

"I understand that, too," Whickam said. "We will agree that I will hire you, and pay the expenses pertaining to Rhondelle, for the next few months only. At that point, you will turn over to me what you have found so that, if I need to, I will be able to hire someone else."

"All right," I said. "I'm going to need a lot of information from you. I'll need Rhondelle's history, that photograph I requested, any letters you might have or other writings that might pertain to this case, and I'd like to be able to talk to her friends and her mother."

"It is already done." He took a stiff manila envelope off the bench beside him. "I anticipated some of your needs and brought them. The rest I shall deliver to you by the evening."

"I'll also need a retainer," I said, "and I'm afraid, since I'm so far from home, it'll have to be in cash."

"I shall bring that also." He opened the envelope and pulled out a glossy eight-by-ten black-and-white photograph. Rhondelle, looking young and beautiful, was posed with her head tilted to one side, her hair flipped outward like Laura's had been the first time I met her. "I believe you might need this. The photograph of Rhondelle and Daniel is inside also."

I took the envelope, holding the photo up as if I could see through it to the place Rhondelle had run off to.

"High school graduation?" I asked.

"Yes," he said. "We spared no expense with her. Perhaps that was our mistake."

Who knew anymore? I certainly didn't. I took the envelope, feeling like a double agent in a James Bond movie, then got up to collect Jimmy. We spent the rest of the afternoon exploring Yale, a place Jimmy was falling in love with—all the hidden nooks and crannies, the way the buildings turned inward and were invisible from the streets, even the ivy growing on the walls.

I let him show me his favorite parts of campus and didn't try to dampen his enthusiasm. Nor did I encourage it. The way he was going right now, he would never have the grades to get into a place like this, nor would I have the income.

But I said none of those things. Instead, I listened to him chatter as I clutched the manila envelope holding another father's hopes, another father's dreams.

TWENTY-SIX

When Malcolm picked us up, he reported that all of the buildings that could have been the Barn were abandoned. Malcolm stopped at each one and found nothing—no sign of recent habitation, no sign of illegal activity—until he reached a derelict building not far from the scrap metal yard.

There he found some things that made him nervous, things he was afraid he was misinterpreting. He wanted to take me there immediately, but I couldn't go. We had to wait for Whickam to arrive at the motel. If he came early enough, we'd go out to the Barn. If he didn't, we'd have to wait until the next day.

Whickam came about seven, and brought his wife. She was as pretty as her daughter, only with darker skin and prominent lips. Her hair was professionally straightened, and her sundress crisp despite the day's heat. Her name was also Rhondelle, only her husband called her Rhondi.

They crammed into the small motel room. I gave the Whickams the chairs, and I sat on the edge of the bed. Malcolm and Jimmy had gone to the park to give us a little privacy.

The additional photographs, paperwork, and lists they brought me seemed superficial, even though I would look the items over carefully. As the interview wore on, I heard parents who saw the daughter they wanted to see and ignored anything else that she might have done wrong.

Finally, I asked the Whickams if they had any ties to New York City. Whickam frowned as he looked at me. "I have gone there in the past for business. A professor at Columbia and I collaborated on a series of French-language textbooks. The books were completed years ago, but we occasionally have to revise and update them."

"Have you done so recently?" I asked.

Whickam shook his head. "I have not been to the city in nearly a year, and I probably will not return for another year or more."

"What about you, ma'am?" I asked. "Do you go to New York?"

"No," she said softly. "I am not fond of the city."

"Did Rhondelle ever go?" I asked.

Mrs. Whickam folded her hands. "We did not believe in subjecting her to that place."

"She has never been there?"

"As a young teen, she went a few times," Mrs. Whickam said. "On school field trips to the Museum of Natural History, places like that."

"But that's it?" I asked. "She's never gone with you?"

Mrs. Whickam shook her head. "We even protested the school trips. New York is not a place for an impressionable child."

"But Paris is?" I asked.

"Yes." She straightened in the hard-backed chair. "Especially for a child of color."

"Where do you stay when you go to Columbia?" I asked Professor Whickam, figuring that I might need some place to start if and when I went to New York.

"My parents own an apartment on Sugar Hill," he said. "They bought it in the twenties and have kept it all this time, only allowing friends and family to use it."

"Your daughter would know about it, then," I said.

"She knows about it," Mrs. Whickam said, "but she would have no idea where it is. She's never been there."

"Would she know the address?" I asked.

"I doubt it," Professor Whickam said. "If she knew anything, she knew it was in Harlem, but that's it."

"Do you have a key?" I asked.

"Of course," Whickam said.

"Where do you keep it?"

He fished his key ring out of his pocket. The ring had half a dozen keys on it. He thumbed through them until he found one old brass key. He held it up to me.

"Is that the only key?" I asked.

"My parents have theirs," he said. "A neighbor has another."

"Would the neighbor give the key to your daughter?"

"Of course not," Professor Whickam said, "I am not even sure that he knows Rhondelle. He is under strict instructions not to give the key to anyone or open the apartment to anyone without contacting us first."

"You've been gone," I said. "Could he have tried to contact you?"

"He would have left a message with my secretary," Whickam said. "Or he would have contacted my parents."

"And he's done neither," I said.

"That's right," Whickam said.

I sighed. "I would like the name of the neighbor and the address of the apartment, just in case."

"You think Rhondelle is there?" Mrs. Whickam sounded confused. "Why would she go there?"

"We've been hearing rumors that Daniel is in New York," I said. "Maybe she went with him."

"Oh, dear," Mrs. Whickam said. "Harlem is such a horrible place these days."

Whickam took his wife's hand and held it in his own. "Rhondelle knows we do not want her in the city."

"She also knows you want her to attend college," I said as pointedly as I could.

He shook his head, eyes downcast. Mrs. Whickam sighed.

"Why don't you call the apartment?" I said. "Use the phone over there. Maybe we'll get lucky."

"My parents never had a phone installed," Whickam said. "I never saw the need. When I was working there, I used the phones at Columbia or the pay phone outside."

What a great way to escape the family, I thought. Both for him and for his daughter.

"Do you really think she's there, Mr. Grimshaw?" Mrs. Whickam asked.

"I don't know what to think, ma'am," I said. "But it's a possibility. We have to investigate all possibilities."

"This is why I hired him, Rhondi," Whickam said. "He is much more thorough than that man in Poughkeepsie."

Mrs. Whickam blinked back tears. "I never would have thought Rhondelle lied to us. I was always afraid that something happened to her on the way to school. I would have thought that news of her would make me feel better, but somehow this makes me feel worse."

I said nothing. Perhaps if they had seen their daughter clearly in the first place, none of this would have happened.

"If you go to the city, you will report back to us?" Whickam asked.

"I'll send you an expenses sheet along with a cursory report each week," I said. "Or, if things are too hectic for that, I'll call."

Whickam grabbed one of the pieces of paper, and wrote down his various phone numbers. He also wrote the address of the apartment in Harlem, and the name of the neighbor.

"I don't have his phone number," Whickam said. "But if you're going to the city anyway—"

"I don't know if I'm going yet," I said, "but with his name, I can get the number."

"I never thought Daniel would be the boy to lead her astray," Mrs. Whickam said, not so much to me, but to her husband.

"I'm not sure he did," I said. "It sounds like a bunch of factors came together to change both of their lives."

"The incident," Mrs. Whickam said.

"If I had to guess," I said. But I wondered if it was as simple as that. I wondered what else I might find, the more I looked.

TWENTY-SEVEN

Tuesday morning, I called Whickam's neighbor in Harlem. The neighbor, an elderly man, said that he hadn't seen anything suspicious, but he lived half a block away. He would check the apartment for us, and I would call him the following morning.

After I hung up, Malcolm, Jimmy and I got into the van. Malcolm took us to the only promising place he had found. The address was in Fair Haven, on the Quinnipiac River. From a distance, Fair Haven seemed pretty. Lovely old buildings nestled against a hillside, with just a few smokestacks rising above the trees.

But once we got into Fair Haven proper, the illusion of beauty vanished. Most of the buildings on the wide street were boarded up and covered with graffiti. Many of them had broken windows or empty storefronts.

People loitered outside, watching the cars go by and catcalling. A number of the loiterers turned away from the cars, hiding their faces. If I'd wanted to buy drugs, I had a hunch I could have had an easy time of it here.

We headed toward the smokestacks. The closer we got, the hazier the sky grew. White smoke drifted out of the stacks, almost like trapped clouds escaping darkness. The effect would have been pretty if it weren't for the acrid odor that seemed to permeate everything.

Rusted scrap metal and junk lined the river's edge, obscuring the view of the picturesque harbor. Children played in the dirt beside the scrap heap, and I shivered at such a careless disregard for their safety.

Malcolm had me turn down a street that followed the river. The street was old and narrow, with broken pavement that denoted a road of long use. Beside it, broken-down buildings, most of them empty warehouses, lined the harbor.

But a few were unusual: they were raised up on narrow cellars that appeared to be dug into the nearby banks. The shore was right beside them, and, in a few cases, water lapped against the lower stone wall. These buildings were old—centuries old—and had probably been the cornerstone of the area.

Malcolm had me slow down. We rounded a sharp corner, and found ourselves in a varied neighborhood. A once-fancy Victorian tilted sideways, its windows covered with thick plywood, its door barricaded by long wooden slats. Next to it sat one of the old raised-up houses, and beside it, a ranch house that had clearly been moved from some other location and was now falling apart.

No cars lined the street, and all of the houses seemed empty. Malcolm had me park the van at the base of a small rise.

"The place is up there," he said, pointing at yet another of the raised houses. Only its arched roof and its faded red paint did make it look like a midwestern barn. "I think Jim and I should wait here."

"No way!" Jimmy said. "You guys get to do all the stuff. I get to wait and read and sit and watch and it's just dumb."

"That's right," I said. "Someone could be in that place, and then what would you do?"

"Run," he said.

I grinned, and slipped out of the van. Jimmy made no move to follow me. Malcolm was leaning forward, gesturing, obviously still making my point.

I walked toward the house. The day was already turning hot, and this area carried not only the stench of the factories, but the stink of dead fish and a slow-moving river. I rubbed my nose with my fingers, wishing the smell would go away.

Then I stopped in front of the building.

A long staircase led to the front door. I looked from that to the harbor. This reminded me of some old dwellings I'd seen in Boston, based on the English model. Boats were usually docked next to these old buildings, just as cars would be parked outside houses today. When the tide was high, the boats would go out, and fish or net lobster or do whatever it took to make a living here.

These steps were chipped, broken, and worn down by water. The door wasn't barricaded, but the upper-story windows had been boarded up. The lower windows were closed and covered with newspaper.

As I climbed the steps, I peered at the newspaper. It had yellowed, but the date on one of the sheets was from April. Someone had lived inside recently.

The door was a sturdy wood that time and weather had splintered near the knob. I knocked, waiting for an answer, then knocked again. The knock had a hollow ring, the kind usually heard in an empty building.

I glanced down the steps at the van. The sun shone off the windshield, hiding Malcolm and Jimmy from me. But Jimmy wasn't striding up the street defiantly, so I figured they were waiting below.

I knocked one final time, listening to the hollow sound echo through the house's lower floor. Then I grabbed the knob and pushed the door open.

Dust motes floated toward me, along with the faint smell of old cigarettes and a fresh scent of mold. As I put my foot down inside, the floor creaked, and I wondered if it would hold my weight. The top of my skull brushed against the ceiling, and I bent at the waist so that I wouldn't hit my head again.

The low ceiling and narrow room gave me a hint at the building's age. It probably had been built in the eighteenth century. I'd been in many eighteenth-century buildings in Massachusetts, and all of them had had impossibly low ceilings.

It took a moment for my eyes to adjust to the darkness. I left the door open for what little light it could give me. The main room had no furniture except a broken chair that looked as old as the house.

A central, freestanding fireplace made of brick dominated the room. Thick wood beams supported the low ceiling. The walls were made of long boards that had cloth stuck in between the slats for insulation.

I walked around the fireplace into the next room. A large metal table was pushed against the wall. Beside it, empty boxes were turned on their sides. The boxes extended almost to the center, like discarded garbage.

I used my foot to move a box toward the light. On one side, someone had stenciled: *Danger, Explosives*. On another, someone had written: *Dynamite: Handle with Care.*

My heart started beating hard. I examined the others, moving as slowly as I could so that I wouldn't accidentally hit something I shouldn't have. The boxes were stenciled with names: Douglass and Sons, Bower Builders, and Tucker Construction were the first ones that I saw.

Beneath the empty boxes were a few full ones. I stuck my fingers in the hem of my shirt to keep my fingerprints off the cardboard, and then pulled a box open. I saw books piled on top of each other haphazardly. I slid the box toward the door, so that I could see what was inside, then inspected the other full boxes.

One was filled with cotton batting and chicken wire. Another was filled to the brim with nails. And a fourth had briefcases with *U.S. Army* stenciled across the top.

Among the boxes I also found electrician's wire, duct tape, and a partially disassembled alarm clock.

I peered into the remaining room. It had once been the kitchen. Beer bottles lined the countertop, their labels missing. An empty box of detergent stood beside them, along with some ripped cloth for cleaning.

I went deeper into the room, smelling something faint and pungent that was almost familiar. Then I found the source of the smell. An empty gasoline can and, beside it, an empty can of motor oil.

My instincts told me to leave. The last thing I wanted was to get caught by the police in this building. The police would arrest me first and ask questions later—if they asked questions at all.

But I hadn't seen everything. I had to see if I could find anything that tied Daniel to this place.

I felt slightly dizzy, but I kept going, finding the stairs leading to the second floor. Up there I found some discarded clothing and crumpled sheets of paper. I picked one up, unfolded it, and saw that it contained writing. I put it in my pocket. Then I grabbed the rest, holding them as if I had found a bootleg version of the Gettysburg Address.

On one wall, someone had scrawled *Bring the War Home!* Beneath it, I saw some fresh footprints in the dust. So this was probably what had convinced Malcolm he had the right house.

I hated the thought of Malcolm in here. He had been lucky that the building was empty. Who knew what would have happened to him had he caught the people who collected this much bomb-making material at home.

I went through the entire second story, finding a ripped blanket, some filthy socks, and little else. Then I went back downstairs and examined the kitchen and the back room again.

My foot brushed against something near one of the counters, making the scratching sound of metal against wood.

I crouched, used my shirt as a glove, and picked up the item with my left hand. A blasting cap. I hadn't seen one in years. Gingerly, I set the cap on one of the empty countertops, and eased out of the room, wiping my prints off the doorknobs as I went.

Thank heavens Malcolm had enough sense to stay behind with Jimmy. Thank heavens I hadn't allowed Jimmy along. With all the combustibles in that building, one wrong move could have set it alight.

I hoped that my information was wrong, that there was nothing to tie Daniel Kirkland to that building. I clutched the wadded-up sheets of paper in my right hand.

They could be nothing.

They could be everything.

It took all of my willpower to hang onto them, because I wasn't sure I wanted to see what kind of information they held.

TWENTY-EIGHT

I left the house in a hurry, my back aching from the unusual posture I'd had to maintain while inside. The sunlight blinded me, and the heat seemed even more oppressive than it had before.

But I couldn't smell the stench of the nearby harbor or the acrid scent of smoke. My nostrils were filled with the odor of gasoline, and it was making me light-headed.

I ran down the steps, a headache building across my eyes. It took me a moment to see the van. Jimmy and Malcolm stood outside of it, their hands shaded over their eyes as they stared up at me.

They had heard me banging out of the house. I made a terrible racket in my effort to leave quickly. I slowed down, took deep breaths, and tried to calm myself. I didn't want to panic Jimmy.

But the paraphernalia in the house had only one use.

Bomb making.

When I reached them, Jimmy stared up at me, his expression neutral, as if he were the adult and I was the upset child.

"What is it?" he asked.

We were all in trouble, three black males standing outside a panel van on a mostly deserted street. I had just come from a house filled with bomb-making equipment.

I had papers clutched in my hand.

"We have to leave," I said. "Now."

"Smoke—" Jimmy started.

"In the van. *Now.*"

I didn't raise my voice, but the boys seemed to catch my panic. They got inside and slammed the doors. I climbed into the driver's seat, handed the papers to Malcolm, and started the van.

Then I checked the mirrors to see if anyone had been watching the house.

There were no obvious observers. But I couldn't tell if the nearby buildings were occupied or not.

I pulled into the street, but made sure I didn't speed away. I wanted to draw as little attention to us as possible.

"What's going on, Smoke?" Jimmy asked.

"You didn't tell me the place was filled with bomb-making equipment," I said to Malcolm.

"I said it had weird stuff," he said.

"In every room. On every floor." I glanced in the mirrors again. Still nothing. We weren't being followed.

"I didn't know what most of that stuff was," Malcolm said.

"It's all for making bombs," I said.

"So you think what everybody's been saying about Daniel is right?" Malcolm asked.

"I don't know," I said. "I don't know if he lived there or not."

"Oh, he did," Malcolm said. "Believe me. I know he'd been there."

My breath caught. I didn't want to know this. "What makes you so sure?"

"The T-shirt," Malcolm said.

Jimmy was watching the mirrors too. He had caught my fear, and knew how to respond.

"What T-shirt?" I turned onto Fair Haven's main street.

"The one bundled up against the wall?"

I had seen the discarded clothes, but I hadn't looked through them.

"What about it?" I asked.

"It's a Museum of Science and Industry T-shirt. Daniel got it for being in the all-city high school science fair the museum sponsored four years ago."

"Was he that good at science?" I drove the car toward the bridge. I wanted out of Fair Haven as quickly as possible.

"Yeah," Malcolm said. "He placed that year. Everyone wanted him to join the next year but he wouldn't because the company that sponsored the competition was one he didn't approve of."

My mouth was dry. The van's wheels sang along the metal bridge. I glanced at the mirrors again. We were alone on the road.

Sweat ran down my back.

I had underestimated Daniel. I had ignored the evidence around me. I had believed Grace, who was as deluded about her son as the Whickams were about their daughter.

And I had deluded myself.

I had thought that someone as competent as Grace couldn't raise a boy like Daniel, a boy dedicated to overthrowing the government, a boy who left Yale to start a real war at home, a war he would start with bombs and guns and the death of innocents.

"Now what, Smoke?" Jimmy asked.

"We have to find him," I said. "Before someone gets killed."

TWENTY-NINE

I drove to one of New Haven's newly built parking garages, figuring if we were followed, the tail would have to come inside. I stopped the van on the third level and rolled down the windows.

I waited a few minutes, but no other car showed up. We were alone on this level. Once I was convinced no one had followed us, I examined the papers I had found inside the Barn.

Most were just doodles. Bridges, buildings, a few with jaunty stick figures walking past. One was a page ripped out of a book. Another was a political cartoon from an old newspaper. It showed anarchists blowing up a building.

The sweat turned to ice against my skin.

Malcolm was uncrinkling some of the pages as well. Jimmy had taken one and was studying it.

" 'Of all of the good stuff, this is the stuff,' " he read. " 'Just stuff the stuff into an inch pipe, plug up the ends, and—' "

I snatched the paper away from him. This, too, had come from an old book. It was a recipe for a pipe bomb—an old-fashioned pipe bomb, one that didn't take wire and blasting caps, but one that used dynamite and gunpowder.

My hands were shaking.

"This is just sick." Malcolm set more sheets of paper on the seat. One sheet had a crudely drawn bottle, with the ingredients of a Molotov cocktail written along the side in a back-slanting hand. Another hand wrote, in blue pen: *If we add detergent into the mix, make it sticky, it becomes a flammable paste.* And someone else wrote beneath that: *Napalm!!!!!!!*

But the sheet in my pocket was the one that made me the most nervous. Torn from a street map of Manhattan, several places were circled in red. One had an exclamation point through it, and a 74 beside it.

I didn't let Malcolm or Jimmy see that. I simply looked at it, then shoved it back into my pocket.

My headache had grown worse. I couldn't, in good conscience, call the police, not while I was still in New Haven. I was afraid they would come after me, particularly if someone saw the panel van with its Illinois plates on the nearby street.

But someone had to know about this building. Someone had to know how dangerous it was.

"Now what?" Malcolm asked.

"Now I guess we head to New York," I said.

THIRTY

I wanted to leave New Haven quickly, but I knew better than to check out of the motel so late in the day. Someone would notice. Someone would think we had left in a panic.

When we got back to the motel, I took a shower in an attempt to get the dust off me and the stench of gasoline out of my nose. I wasn't sure how much of that smell came from my own dislike of explosives or from an actual gasoline odor in the house.

Once I had cleaned off, I tore up the papers and flushed them down the toilet. The last thing I wanted was to have another visit from the New Haven police, and have them find pages describing bomb-making.

I sent Malcolm out to get us some pizza. Then I called Professor Whickam. I told him we'd confirmed the lead in New York.

After we finished eating, I took the van out for a drive. I stopped at my old phone booth on Dixwell Avenue, and took out the rest of my dimes. I had several long-distance calls to make.

The first was to Whickam's neighbor.

"Haven't seen any activity," he said. "But folks say there's a light on in the apartment at night. They just figure Whickam left the light on the last time he was here."

"When was that?" I asked, trying to gauge how truthful Whickam had been with me.

"Beats me," the elderly gentleman said. "He doesn't report his comings and goings to me. He only calls when he needs something."

I thanked him. A light was better than nothing. It was a lead.

Then I called a number I hadn't dialed in more than a decade. I was amazed I remembered it. The phone rang, and I was beginning to think I'd been wrong, when someone answered.

The voice was a man's, deep and throaty, but with an edge that marked it as young.

"Is Gwendolyn Cole there?" I asked.

"Yeah," he said. "Just a minute."

The phone line crackled and thumped as he set the receiver down. I clung to my own phone, watching the cars go by on Dixwell. The phone booth was stiflingly hot, but I wasn't willing to open the door. I didn't want anyone to overhear the conversation.

Then the phone crackled some more, and a woman's voice said, "Yes?"

The voice should have sounded familiar, and it did, in a half-forgotten way. I would have said that her voice was higher pitched, that her New York accent was less pronounced.

"Gwen?" I said. "It's Smokey."

"Smokey *Dalton?*" she said. "Good Lord, Smoke. You fell off the face of the earth. Never thought I'd hear from you again."

"Things have changed," I said, not knowing what to say. My relationship with Gwen had gone from intimate to a few letters to nothing in the space of fifteen years.

"I *guess,*" she said. "Where've you been? What're you doing? It's been so long."

"I'm on a pay phone, Gwen," I said. "But I'm planning to come to the city in a few days, and we can catch up. I was wondering though if you knew who I could call to get a short-term apartment. I can't remember the name of the agent I used to use."

"You can stay right here," she said.

Sweat trickled down the side of my face. I leaned against the glass wall of the booth, hoping to feel something cooler, but the glass was as hot as I was.

"Much as I appreciate the offer, Gwen, there's three of us. I can't put you out like that."

"You're not putting me out," she said. "Normally I've got room for four, but Alex is here on leave, so the three of you would have to share."

I blinked, trying to concentrate. The gasoline headache never entirely left, and now the heat was making it worse. "What would Lionel say if I stayed there?"

"Lionel don't say nothing." She sounded offended. "I haven't seen the son of a bitch in five years, and I hope I don't see him ever again."

"I'm sorry, Gwen. I had no idea."

"What'm I supposed to do? Write you a Christmas card saying the guy I dumped you for wasn't Prince Charming after all?"

I had forgotten her edge. It was one of the many things I liked about her.

"Didn't mean to be so sharp," she said without pausing for breath. "I'd love to see you and your friends."

"I think it'd be more comfortable for both of us, Gwen, if I found less personal lodgings." The words sounded stiffly formal, but I meant them. I didn't know how to explain my circumstances to Gwen without talking about the past year, and I didn't know how to explain Gwen to Malcolm or Jimmy.

"Afraid of your past, Smoke?" she asked.

"We didn't part on the best of terms, Gwen. I wasn't exactly the sanest in those years, and I certainly don't want to bring up bad memories for Alex."

"He was *six*, Smokey. He's twenty now. And in the army, for God's sake. He can handle anything."

"That was Alex who answered the phone?"

"Yep. He's back for two weeks. The idiot signed up for a second tour just before Nixon announced he was bringing back the troops."

"A second tour?" I said, trying to imagine the little boy I'd last seen as a grown man who'd already served in the military. "He's in Vietnam?"

"Not at the moment." For the first time, her voice wobbled. "I wouldn't mind seeing you. And if you're worried about your wife meeting me, I'll be the soul of discretion."

"Wife?" I said, then understood how she'd interpreted my mentioning three people. "I'm not married, Gwen. I'm traveling with my son and a friend."

"She's got nothing to worry about from me, that's all I'm saying." Her voice had recovered its strength.

"It's a male friend. He's helping me take care of Jim while I work on this trip."

The operator interrupted, demanding more money. I plugged in dimes, listening to them clink-clink. Then I said, "Gwen, I don't have enough for a longer call. Can you give me the name of an agent?"

"Yeah," she said. "Hang on."

She set the phone down. I counted my dimes, hoping she'd return before I had to plug the phone again.

She did. She gave me a name and number, which I dutifully wrote down. "If he doesn't have anything, you come here, Smokey," she said, and gave me her address.

I promised I would.

"Don't be a stranger," she said. "If you're in the city, I want to see you."

Oddly enough, I wanted to see her, too.

After we hung up, I kept my hand on the receiver. The phone spit back some coins, but I didn't dig them out of the coin return.

I was shaking. That had gone better and worse than I had expected. Gwen was the first person from my past I'd spoken to in a long time. But I knew she was safe. We hadn't been in contact for several years, since I'd called her in 1960 on a trip to New York, just after I'd inherited some money.

Gwen had still been married then, and she had whispered into the phone that seeing me wouldn't be a good idea, that Lionel was jealous even of the mention of my name. He tore up my letters to her—not that they'd been very personal or informative—and he didn't want her to have contact with me, not then, not ever.

So I'd honored that request until now, knowing that of all the people I had known, Gwen Cole was one who wouldn't have shown up on the FBI's list. If old friends or my family had even mentioned her, they would have called her by her maiden name, Gwen Daines. But I didn't recall ever telling anyone much about her. When I'd known Gwen, I hadn't been talking to people at all.

I stayed awake for hours that night. I took first guard duty, figuring if anything was going to happen, it would happen around midnight.

I sat in darkness, watching the parking lot. I would be happy to leave New Haven. I hated this place. Both Memphis and Chicago had had communities that would have adopted me, Malcolm, and Jimmy in a moment.

From what little I'd seen of New Haven's, it was repressed and frightened, and only peripherally aware of how to fight back. Those that had the power to fight, like Whickam, had convinced themselves that racial problems happened elsewhere, not in his comfortable little corner of the world. I wondered how Freeman was doing on his story about the police and hoped I hadn't gotten him in too far over his head.

About twelve-thirty, a bevy of sirens rushed by, their sounds magnified by the silence around me. I stiffened, watched the parking lot for multicolored lights, and, as the sirens faded, relaxed only slightly.

From that point on, the silence grew. I finally woke Malcolm around three for his turn at watch, then fell asleep myself.

The nightmare brought its usual chill, only the dream ran backwards. Instead of carrying my friend out of the trench, his hot blood dripping all over my hands, I carried him into it. I was still covered with blood, which steamed in the cold Korean night.

We stood in the trench and watched as a sergeant showed us how to use grenades. Only he wasn't using grenades—not real ones. He was making Molotov cocktails. He was going to have me stuff cloth into the liquid-filled bottles, until he saw that my hands were covered with blood. So he gave me the matches instead.

I couldn't light them, but somehow the cloth caught fire anyway. The bottles blew, and I woke up, a scream caught in my throat.

Malcolm was watching me as if he had never seen me before. "You okay?" he asked.

I nodded, got up shakily, and went into the small bathroom. I grabbed the only clean terry washcloth, flowed cold water over it, and slowly bathed my face, trying to slow my heart.

These days, Jimmy usually had the nightmares. Now I was the one whose dreams revived the horrors of my past, and I wasn't sure exactly how to stop it.

THIRTY-ONE

We checked out of the hotel just after dawn and drove out of New Haven. Just outside of town, I stopped at a space-age Mobil gas station. It had a round umbrella-like roof over the conical gas pumps, and the square concrete building had a red Pegasus painted on the sign.

The boys waited while I used the pay phone to call the New Haven police. I gave them the address of the Barn, said I'd been inside, and that I had found components for making bombs.

Then I hung up and headed out as quickly as I could, disappearing down the road toward New York City.

The day promised to be muggy. Even though the sun was out, a haze hung over everything. I had to squint as I drove. The diffuse light was brighter than it seemed.

Jimmy bounced on the seat across from me, happy to be leaving New Haven. Malcolm hugged the window, his knees pressed against the dash. He looked nervous and uncomfortable. I remembered how frightened he had been to drive through Pennsylvania, and I wondered how frightened he was now.

"I think it's good that we're leaving New Haven," I said to him.

"I was getting tired of that room," Jimmy said. "Kinda felt like my mom's place, that last one, you know."

The one that she had abandoned him in. The one his brother had left him in as well. The one that had locked him out when the rent money hadn't been paid, the one that nearly made him live on the street.

I hadn't wanted him to remember that. But his past was as vivid for him as mine was for me.

I wondered how Daniel felt about his past. Disconnected from it? Empowered by it? I couldn't tell from the few clues I'd found. He had become more of an enigma to me in these last few days.

I hadn't called Grace to tell her we were leaving New Haven. I wasn't sure how to talk to her. The evidence in the Barn put me at odds with my initial mission.

Finding Daniel was no longer enough. I had to stop him. I had to do everything I could to keep one of those bombs from going off.

The road twisted past a junkheap of discarded train parts. Old cars with holes through their sides, torn-up track, and warning lights were mixed in with old tires and piles of organic garbage. Gulls picked through the wreckage. Beyond it, one of the rivers glistened.

"Chicago's not this ugly," Jimmy said.

"Chicago's bigger," I said. "You haven't been to all parts of the city."

He frowned at me, as if he didn't want me to contradict him, and then rested his arms on the dash, peering out the windshield.

Malcolm said, "I heard New York is the worst."

"The worst for what?" I asked.

"Dirt," he said. "Garbage. Crime."

"I've always liked New York," I said, and that was the truth. I always felt hopeful in Harlem. The first time I'd climbed out of a subway platform onto 125th Street, I stopped and stared in awe, knowing that this was the place where Langston Hughes had lived, the place where Duke Ellington had gotten his start, the place where W. E. B. DuBois published the *Crisis*. W. C. Handy, father of the blues, left Memphis to come to Harlem, where he made his name, and played with Eubie Blake, among others. Once upon a time in Harlem, on any given afternoon, you could see Zora Neale Hurston or Madame C. J. Walker or A. Philip Randolph. And then there were the nightclubs—Small's Paradise, the Rhythm Club, and Connie's Inn.

Harlem was also a place of scandal—a place where blacks performed for slumming whites at the Savoy Ballroom and the Cotton Club (which didn't integrate until long after its heyday). Riots happened here, and assassinations—Malcolm X got shot at the Audubon Ballroom only four short years ago, even though it felt like a lifetime had passed.

Like most people who'd spent time in Harlem, I loved it and I hated it, and still it called to me. I had nearly settled here once. Only that horrible breakup with Gwen, which left me adrift and wandering, led me to Memphis, my odd jobs, and the first real home I had ever had.

When I'd been at Boston University, I'd come down to New York almost every weekend—at first to get away from Boston, and later to see Gwen. We had been intense for nearly two years. Then I'd moved to Harlem for one brief summer, and everything changed.

Malcolm was looking at me. I felt my cheeks heat, as if he had seen each memory, each thought pass across my face.

"Give New York a try," I said. "And don't believe everything you hear."

He grunted, and I left him to his silence. He would have to make up his own mind about the city.

I certainly had.

I parked the van in one of the lots at the Newark Airport. We took our small bags, hid everything else under a blanket, and locked the van up tight. Then we headed into the terminal as if we were going to fly somewhere.

Malcolm had never been in an airport terminal. He looked at the milling people, the ticket counters, and all the luggage as if it were a miracle. Jimmy kept close to me. He hated official buildings and the crowds inside them. So far, we hadn't seen any security guards, but there had to be some, and we knew, by virtue of our color, that we'd be instantly suspect.

We took the stairs down to baggage claim and followed the brown signs that led us to public transportation. A number of cabs were parked along the curb, but I wasn't even going to try to take one. When I had lived in New York in the 1950s, cab drivers refused to pick up blacks. If you were somehow lucky enough to get a ride, the driver would deposit you at 110th Street rather than enter Harlem.

Instead, we took a bus. I paid the fare for all three of us, and we sat in the back, mostly to avoid trouble. We kept our suitcases on our laps like shields. Jimmy peered out the window, but Malcolm stared straight ahead, ignoring everything around him.

He looked intimidating, but I knew, just from the set of his body, how terrified he was.

The Port Authority Bus Terminal in midtown didn't help matters much. We got out on a lower level filled with garbage and smelling of diesel exhaust. I led us along a vaguely remembered route, trying to find the subway trains that would take us to Harlem.

The walls were filthy and covered with graffiti. Junkies shivered near garbage cans, and more than a few had their hands out for money. A busker played his guitar a few yards from a newspaper kiosk. His guitar case was open and dotted with scattered coins, probably his own, to encourage other people to add some. He was playing some rock tune so badly that I couldn't figure out what it was, and I hoped he wouldn't start singing until we were past him.

The train ride to Harlem was uneventful. The farther north we went, the darker the faces became in the car. That helped Malcolm relax just a little, but he still clutched his suitcase as if it were the only weapon he had.

When we got off, we climbed up to the street level. The city's noise hit me first, then the smell of diesel and exhaust, and finally the sidewalk, surrounded by buildings.

We stepped away from the subway entrance. Malcolm stood beside me, biting his lower lip. He wasn't looking at the skyline in the distance, but at the graffiti-covered buildings beside us. He looked like he had never seen poverty before in his life.

"Think Daniel's here?" he asked quietly.

"I do," I said.

Jimmy stood on his toes beside us, turning slowly, taking it all in. "Looks like Chicago."

I didn't think it did. The cities had different energy, different looks, different layouts. But the red brick and graffiti were the same, at least in certain sections of both cities, and so were the tall buildings off in the distance.

Only here, a wide body of water didn't dominate like Lake Michigan did in Chicago. The rivers and the bridges were a presence, but they were overwhelmed by the city itself.

"It's nothing like Chicago," Malcolm said. "Nothing at all."

Jimmy looked at him, surprised. Apparently Jimmy hadn't noticed how much trouble Malcolm had had on the trip to New Haven. But Jimmy was noticing now.

I picked up my suitcase and Jimmy's and headed down the sidewalk.

"Do you know where we're going?" Malcolm asked.

I nodded. "I lived in Harlem for a while. It's a pretty easy place to get around in."

He didn't answer me, but he had stopped biting his lip. He followed, as if he were covering our backs.

The stench of urine was strong, and someone had strewn garbage all over the sidewalk. This was not at all like Chicago, and I waited for Malcolm to say so. Instead, he wrinkled his nose and kept walking, following me to the cross street.

Harlem did look different. It was dingier than I remembered. A number of the nearby buildings had broken or boarded windows, but still showed signs of habitation.

Jimmy moved up beside me, pretending to want his suitcase, when I actually believed he wanted my protection.

"This a bad part of town, Smoke?" he asked quietly.

"It depends," I said. "Harlem has neighborhoods just like the South Side. I haven't been here in nine years, so I'm not sure which neighborhood is good or not anymore. I'm sure we'll be able to figure it out, though."

Malcolm didn't say anything. He frowned and kept walking, his head up, his eyes scanning for any sign of trouble. I did the same, seeing loiterers and people going about their business.

Our suitcases branded us as outsiders, and the quicker we got rid of them, the happier I'd be. At least here, however, we blended in, and that made us less likely targets for anyone who was thinking of mugging us.

I softly explained to both boys how to get around in the city, the way that natives spoke of cross streets and main streets, and how New York, outside of certain areas, was pretty logical—the numbered streets running east-west and the avenues, also numbered, going north-south.

We were going to Lenox Avenue, between West 120th and 121st Streets. Lenox was the name Sixth Avenue got north of Central Park. Jimmy thought the information fascinating, especially after having learned Chicago's convoluted streets. Malcolm didn't venture an opinion at all.

The rental agent operated out of his own home, half a block from Mount Morris Park. The agent's apartment was in the center of a group of brownstone row houses that had distinctive mansard roofs. I'd loved those buildings when I'd first seen them years ago, and I loved them still, despite the grime that time and the city had deposited on them.

Still, no graffiti decorated the building's sides, and no garbage cluttered its walks. Someone spent time keeping this place cleaner than the other blocks we'd walked down.

I took the steps to the main door two at a time. Malcolm and Jimmy waited on the sidewalk while I pushed the bell. When I identified myself through the intercom, the door buzzed open. I held the door as Jimmy and Malcolm hurried into it.

The air was cool inside, and the hallway was narrow. A secretary sat in a small room to the side. She smiled at me, had me leave my "companions" and our suitcases in her room while I met with the agent.

He was a small man with tight curls and a fake smile. His suit cost more than I'd earned all spring. He shook my hand like we were old friends and told me that Gwen had contacted him, begging him for a good location, not some place filled with hookers and junkies.

"The problem is," he said to me, "my weekly apartments aren't in the best neighborhoods. To do a favor for my friend Gwen, I need to put you in a boardinghouse or set you up as lodgers. Maybe even get you a suite at the Olga Hotel. What do you say?"

Boardinghouses wouldn't work for us. We'd have to stay in separate rooms and eat at a set time with the other boarders. Lodgers were in even tighter quarters. While we were in the city, I didn't want that kind of scrutiny.

"I'll take the hotel if that's all you've got," I said. "But I'd prefer an apartment. We may be here all summer, maybe even into the fall, but I won't know that for a few weeks."

His eyes twinkled for the first time. I knew I had caught him exactly where he could be caught—in his pocketbook.

"Tell you what," he said. "I have one apartment on West 114th, between Seventh and Eighth, not far from the Twenty-eight Precinct. I won't lie to you. The neighborhood is in transition. But it's transitioning upward. It got model cities money five years ago, and six million dollars later, respectable families are taking the place back over. All the apartments on that block have been fixed up at government expense. It even has air-conditioning. And the cops patrol regularly. It couldn't be safer."

The muscles in my back tensed, but I didn't move. I didn't like the idea of cops patrolling, but I also knew that a lack of police protection in this part of the city was just as bad. Besides, the New York police had no idea that Jimmy and I were on the run. The APB went out over a year ago, and I was certain that if anyone had looked at it, they had round-filed it long ago.

My silence must have seemed like rejection to him. He said, "Tell you what. You stay there a couple of weeks and find out you'll be staying longer and need a real place, you call me and I'll give you a great apartment in a better section of Harlem for a rent-controlled price. I'm not supposed to do that—when an old-timer moves out, we're supposed to let the apartment go to standing rates—but we have ways, you know. And my good customers, they benefit from it. I'm one of the few black landlords in this part of the city, and I help our people."

I wished I could believe him. He probably did better than the anonymous white landlords who owned so much of Harlem, but that wasn't saying much.

"I'll tell you what," I said, mimicking his tone. "We'll take the apartment on 114th sight unseen, and if we don't like it, I'll come back here for something better without any penalty. We can talk about the future later. What do you say?"

The twinkle left his eye, but his smile remained. "If that'll make you happy. I have an agreement right here."

He walked back to his desk and slipped a paper forward. On it, he wrote the address at 114th Street. "Name?" he asked.

I felt relieved that Gwen hadn't told him everything, just that a friend of hers was coming. "Bill Grimshaw."

"Permanent address?"

"Here," I said. "Let's make this easy."

I took out the driver's license that I'd bought in the name Bill Grimshaw.

When he'd finished filling out the form, he slid it toward me along with a pen. I read it, saw that the rent could go up each week if he so chose, that we could be evicted without notice, and decided to sign it anyway.

I paid him twenty-five dollars for the week in cash, along with a twenty-dollar security deposit that was supposed to be refundable. I got my receipt and carefully put it in my wallet.

The agent went to a full board in the back room, and returned with two keys to the 114th Street apartment.

"We're here until five," he said, "should you have any problems."

I had problems, but none of them were with the apartment. I didn't want to walk the path I'd set for myself, but I would. And I didn't want to hurt Grace, but I had a hunch I would do that, too.

I clutched the keys and got the boys, taking the first step toward finding Daniel, and his bombs.

THIRTY-TWO

he apartment was a third-floor walk-up in an old brick building that had been recently renovated. Inside the main door was a small entry with a locked door, security buzzers alongside apartment numbers, and a working intercom. A young man, his clothes so filthy that they looked like they'd been crusted to him, slept against the wall.

The building manager had been told to expect us. I pushed the bell to his apartment, and the door buzzed without him even checking to see who was standing outside. For all he knew, the smelly young man could have been trying to get in.

The hallway was wide and well lit. The paint on the wall had a few handprints, and moving scrapes from furniture being carried past, but no graffiti. The stairs were new and didn't creak as we went up. The railing was made of a sturdy metal that wouldn't buckle under repeated use.

Despite the stink in the entry, the hallway smelled of dryer lint and laundry soap. A sign pointed down a flight of steps, indicating that the building provided its own laundry facility.

Malcolm glanced over his shoulder, as if he had expected someone to follow us inside. No one had. We went up the steps, Jimmy taking them two at a time. He held one key in his right hand, reciting the apartment number under his breath as he hurried.

"Wait for us," I called at the main landing.

Jimmy didn't wait, though. He skipped ahead, and I heard him as he reached the third floor.

"We're right near the stairs."

He made that sound like a good thing. I supposed it was in case of fire, but for day-to-day living, it would be annoying. Malcolm and I had reached the landing between the second and third floors when I heard the apartment door open.

"Cool, man," Jimmy said, his voice fading. "This is cool."

Malcolm followed him. I rested a moment, wiped the sweat off my face, and hoped that the promised air-conditioning was working. Then I carried my suitcase up the remaining steps.

The hallway was dark. The light was either burned out or turned off. At the far end, a window opened onto a fire escape. The other apartment doors were closed, but the one nearest the steps was open.

Jimmy stood in the living room of our apartment, his suitcase on the floor beside him. The room was long and rectangular with double windows at one end. The windows had a window seat built below them, and beneath the seat someone had installed cabinets.

The furniture was cheap and threadbare, but adequate. The couch was pushed against one wall. Two easy chairs faced the window. End tables with old lamps stood on either end of the couch.

"I don't see no TV," Jimmy said.

"There isn't one," I said. "This isn't a hotel room. If we want TV, we have to buy one."

"People rip them off." Malcolm had set his suitcase down as well. He walked through the living room to the small kitchen beyond. The kitchen had a butler's window that opened into the living room. To one side, a tiled area marked a square dining room. The table was silver Formica, with arching metal legs, and four matching chairs.

I followed him into the kitchen. At the far end, near the stove, another door opened, leading to the bathroom. It was small and mean, without enough room for a bathtub, only a built-in shower. The toilet itself had no seat. Apparently, the money that had been used to fix this place up hadn't been spent here.

"I hope there's bedrooms," Malcolm said from behind me.

"He said there were two." I turned around, and looked, hoping to see the door. It was in the kitchen, painted white to match the walls. I had initially thought it was a broom closet.

Instead the door opened onto a short hallway. Two doors stood across from each other. Once this had been a separate apartment, or maybe two separate apartments, all sharing the bath with the apartment we were standing in.

Malcolm flicked on the hall light, then peered into one of the rooms. "Fancy," he said, and his tone was mocking.

I looked in, too. There was the promised air conditioner, as far from the living room as it could possibly be. Only the bedrooms could be cool, and only if we kept our doors open all night long.

The bed in the room with the air conditioner was a double, with two end tables on either side. The other room, smaller and with no window at all, had room only for a bunk bed.

"I get the top," Jimmy said as he came up beside us.

"I get the top," Malcolm said. "I'll hit my head underneath."

"It can't hold your weight," Jimmy said. "I don't want to die when you come crashing down on me."

"It'll hold him," I said, "And if you guys don't like sharing, one of you can take the couch."

"No thanks." Malcolm went around me and disappeared into the kitchen.

"He doesn't like any of this," Jimmy said.

"I know," I said.

"Maybe he should go home. I'll be okay by myself. You told me how to get around."

This was absolutely the worst place for Jimmy to be alone. He probably hadn't noticed the teenagers loitering in doorways, or the men leaning against walls, their eyes half closed in some drugged-out ecstasy. I knew he had seen the guy in the entry because we'd all had to step over him.

But Jimmy could have selective vision sometimes. He had seen a group of children his own age playing stickball up the block. He had also seen another group on the basketball court at the nearby school, playing as if their lives depended on it.

"Sorry, Jim," I said. "You're going to need to be with one of us at all times around here. This isn't a good neighborhood."

"I thought you said we'd stay some place safe."

"It's safe enough," I said, "but it's not somewhere I'd choose to put down roots."

"Didn't say I wanted to move here," Jimmy said sullenly. "We're not moving here, right?"

"Not permanently," I said. "Not this apartment"

"Yeah," Malcolm said, coming up behind us. "This is a cruddy place. There isn't even a phone."

"That's something else we'd have to pay for if we were staying," I said, remembering all the things the lease enumerated as our responsibility. "There's a pay phone across the street. We can use that if we need to make calls."

Malcolm took his suitcase into the room. He tossed the case on the top bunk as if to claim it as his own.

"It's safer for me to be up there, Smoke," Jimmy said.

"Let him," I said quietly.

"Jeez," Jimmy said. "No TV, and a stupid bottom bunk, and you guys gotta babysit me all the time. This is just dumb."

"Where are the books Grace had you bring?" I asked. "In the van?"

"Some," he said. That surprised me. I had expected a yes. "I brought three."

No wonder he had struggled with his suitcase.

"Three's a good start," I said. "Looks like between the books and the newspapers you're supposed to read every day, you'll have plenty to do."

"Can we at least get a radio?" Malcolm asked.

"That's probably wise," I said. "We'll pick up a transistor this afternoon."

For the moment, though, I wanted to get the air conditioner working. I wanted to sit down and rest for a few minutes, then figure out my plan.

I wanted, with an intensity that surprised me, to be somewhere else.

THIRTY-THREE

W e spent the rest of the day settling in and exploring the neighborhood. It wasn't as bad as it had initially seemed. Even though there were junkies in doorways, there was also a newly formed neighborhood watch.

The building's manager, a strongly built man in his midthirties, found me as I was coming down the stairs. He made a point, he said, of meeting all the short-timers, especially since the neighborhood watch had gotten so diligent.

I quizzed him about the area. Turned out that the rental agent had been right—the neighborhood was cleaning itself up. Even though half the residents were on welfare, they were mostly elderly people who had lived in the area since the 1920s. Many had been in the same apartment for more than forty years.

The rest worked. Most of the drug addicts had been routed from the apartments as part of the government's condition for cleaning up the place.

The manager had most of these figures courtesy of the government. This had been one of the first model cities projects in 1964. It had been designed as a working experiment in not just cleaning up the buildings, but improving the lives of the residents as well.

The apartments had been improved. The rats were mostly gone, at least inside, and so were the cockroaches, thanks to diligent spraying efforts. The locks worked, there were no exposed electric wires, and the buildings them-selves were as secure as the residents desired. Apartments had more than one room now, functioning bathrooms, and actual closets.

But the government's work had stopped there. The neighborhood watch had come out of a committee the residents had put together to force the government to fulfill its promises, promises to provide the drug center, the jobs, and adult education—the very things that would keep the neighbor-hood improving.

At least I didn't feel any despair here. Maybe the watch worked.

That night before it got dark, I showed Malcolm and Jimmy the way to the nearest subway station. I showed them how to read the map, and then I took them up to 135th and Lenox, where the public library was located. The neighborhood wasn't as good as I remembered, but it was all right for them to be here during the day, while I was working.

I checked the library hours for the Fourth of July, and noted that the building was closed. On that day we might have to make special plans.

The next day, I left Malcolm with Jimmy. I had Malcolm give me his esti-mated itinerary, so that I could find them if I had to, then I headed for Sugar Hill to see if I could find Daniel Kirkland and Rhondelle Whickam.

The address that Whickam had given me was in one of the older neigh-borhoods closest to the park. All of Edgecomb Avenue had a great view of the Harlem Plain, but this area had a quiet air of comfort.

Even though it was about nine A.M., the day was already getting warm. Traffic moved by quickly, as if the cars knew that they could overheat if they stopped for too long. Headlines on a discarded newspaper caught my eye: Hanoi was releasing three U.S. prisoners; four Arab jets had been shot down over the Suez Canal.

The entire world continued to burn, and here, in Sugar Hill, the radiant heat seemed to envelope everything.

I walked up the nearly empty sidewalks, stepping over broken bottles and piles of garbage in bags that sat out for collection. The stench was amazing—rotted food, spoiled milk, and other odors I couldn't identify mingled with the heaviness of the air.

Rows of wrought-iron banisters rose toward the row houses, looking identical despite the bicycles chained to some and the clothes hanging on others. From my sideways angle, the door arches looked like sculptures. If I squinted, I could almost see the past, when this neighborhood was in its prime, the red brick was clean, and people walked with pride.

I finally found the address I was looking for. I walked up the concrete steps to the small stoop and stopped. The door was made of fine wood, which had once been polished, but lost its luster to time and the elements. The door knocker had survived, though, and a wonderfully detailed lion's head with a ring in its mouth suggested the elegance that this place had once had.

I grabbed the ring and pounded it against the brass with force. For a moment, I didn't think anyone heard me. Then the door opened a slight crack.

"What?" a female voice asked.

"I'm looking for Danny," I said.

"He's not here," the woman said.

"How about Rhondelle?"

"What do you want her for?"

Finding them had been easier than I expected. I tried not to let my surprise show.

"I got some business to finish up," I said.

The door opened all the way. A young white woman, in shorts and a cropped T-shirt, held it open for me. Her dark hair was gathered at the back of her neck, and her eyes were red with exhaustion and maybe something else.

"C'mon in," she said, and moved away.

She didn't ask who I was or what I wanted. She didn't seem to care.

I stepped inside. The entry was ornate. A chandelier hung from the ceiling, the chain trimmed in gold. To my right, a floor-length mirror as big as a door was framed in mahogany, and brass clothes hangers hung in a square pattern on each side, waiting for coats. Just beyond that, stairs rose to the house's upper floors.

"She's having breakfast," the young woman said, motioning toward a hallway that disappeared toward the back.

Then she climbed the stairs like an elderly person. She didn't even look back to see if I had taken her direction. Her manner was odd and unnerving, and even though this place didn't smell of pot like some of the places I'd found in New Haven, I wondered if her lack of response was due to drugs rather than a natural lack of interest.

I felt uneasy. I had thought I would find no one here. I had planned to spend the day talking to the neighbor, searching for Daniel and Rhondelle, going through the same sort of wild goose chase that I had pursued in New Haven.

Now that I had found them, I would have to find out what was going on without alienating them.

I walked down the hall, the wooden floor squeaking beneath my shoes. Another door opened to my left, leading into a back parlor. I peered inside. Clothing was strewn all over the heavy Victorian furniture. The fireplace screen was being used as a drying rack for underwear. Dirty dishes sat on an expensive wood table. Above it all, someone had left yet another chandelier burning, its dusty globe sending a dim light through the room.

I continued forward. Ahead of me, an unprepossessing door remained closed. I pushed it open, and found myself in a long narrow kitchen. A utility sink with an orange base leaned against the wall, the top covered with copper dishes that had once been used as decoration.

The room smelled faintly of peanut butter and toast. A young woman sat at a small table toward the back, barely visible beyond the huge turn-of-the-century cast iron stove. She was hunched over the table, reading as she drank from a steaming mug. Her hair was frizzed into an oversized Afro that looked teased instead of natural.

"Rhondelle?" I said.

She jumped and faced me all in one movement. A bruise ran from her left cheek to her jaw, distorting her face. Her left eye was blackened. But she was still recognizable from that scholarship picture.

I hadn't expected the bruise. I tried not to stare.

She clutched her toast as if it were a shield. "Who are you?"

"My name's Bill Grimshaw. Your father hired me to find you." I kept my voice low so that I wouldn't scare her further.

"Who let you in here?" She was still pressed against the wall.

"A girl," I said. "She told me you were here, and then she went upstairs."

"She just let you walk in?"

"It's not her fault," I said. "I told her I had some business with you and Daniel."

"Daniel," she said as if the name were unfamiliar.

"Is he here?" Now that I'd found Rhondelle, I wanted to talk to him. I had a hunch she knew very little about his activities.

"Not at the moment." She bit her lower lip and glanced over my shoulder, then back at me.

I resisted the urge to follow her gaze. I hadn't heard anyone come up behind me. "When do you expect him back?"

"Why?"

"Because I'm working for his mother, too. Grace is really worried about him. She—"

"That's bullshit." The harshness of Rhondelle's words startled me. They seemed at odds with the fear she had shown a moment before. "Danny's mother doesn't care about him."

She seemed to believe that, and it seemed to matter to her. It would do me no good to argue Daniel's family dynamics with this girl. I decided to focus instead on the one thing that concerned only Rhondelle.

"Your dad thinks that something's happened to you," I said quietly. "He hired a detective in Poughkeepsie. He thought you were kidnapped on the way to Vassar in January—"

"Yeah, my dad would think that." She set the toast down. The fear had disappeared. Instead, her expression hardened. "So you're from Poughkeepsie?"

It wasn't a polite question.

"No," I said. "I'm from Chicago. I was initially looking for Daniel, and I had gotten a lot of information about you in the process."

"Really?" She looked away from me, picked up her coffee mug, and sipped from it. Her hands trembled ever so slightly. "What kind of information?"

"About the incident at Yale last fall," I said, "and all the trouble it caused."

Her shoulders relaxed. I wondered if she had expected me to say something else.

"Trouble." She scooted her chair so that she faced me. "Is that what my fascist father calls it?"

Her father didn't strike me as a fascist. I made myself take a deep breath before I spoke. "He was never sure what happened. No one told him."

She raised her eyebrows. They weren't plucked like they had been in that photograph. "*I* told him. I asked him how he could work there with all those bigots and fucking conforming Negroes, and he said that I didn't understand."

Her language didn't sound Ivy League to me. I was amazed that her father was as sympathetic to her as he had been.

"I'm not sure I understand either." I swept a hand to indicate my surroundings, which must have been quite expensive and modern in their day. "But it seems that your father came from a different tradition than I do."

She let out a contemptuous noise. "He thinks because he grew up in France, he's special. He never saw how the French treat us, like some kind of exotic animal. Whenever I went to see Grand-mère and Grand-père in Paris, I was treated like a piece of art or a sculpture, not a person. Something other, not human. I hated it."

"More than you hate it here?" I asked.

Her eyes narrowed. "I'm an American, just like everybody else. We shouldn't have to put up with the second-class citizen crap. It was a great ideal, this country, but it's fucked, you know?"

Of course I knew. I knew better than she did, with her privileged background and her protected upbringing. But I said nothing.

Instead, I took one step toward her.

She kept her back to the wall, watching me warily.

I touched my cheek. "What happened?"

"Nothing." But a look crossed her face, a slight frown, a memory. Something that showed she wasn't as tough as she pretended to be.

"You know," I said, "I met Daniel for the first time last summer. And while I thought he was pretty committed politically, I never knew he was violent."

She shrugged one shoulder and looked down. Then she wiped toast crumbs off her lap, as if I weren't even in the room.

"You can talk to me," I said.

"Oh, yeah?" I didn't expect the force of her anger or the fierce expression on her face as she raised her head. "Why can I talk to you? Because you know my father? Or because you say so? Because I can see you're a pretty crappy detective. I thought you knew about the incident last fall, and then you come in here and say, 'I never thought he was violent.' "

She did a fair mocking imitation of my voice.

"I know that he beat up that boy," I said, "but if someone was attacking my girlfriend, I might get violent, too."

"Danny nearly beat him to death," she said.

I nodded. "They were hurting you."

She rolled her eyes. "They were just trying to scare me. They did it to a bunch of the girls, trapped them in a room and told them all kinds of crazy stuff, most of which I knew wasn't true because I'd been around Yale my whole life. They weren't even scaring me, and they never touched me."

That was so different from the reports I'd heard that it took a moment for her words to register. Yale wouldn't have told me the story that she'd been attacked unless they believed it. I had certainly believed it.

Why would she lie to me now?

"So what really did happen?" I asked.

"I just told you." She glared at me defiantly.

"That boy did get hurt, right?"

"There you go," she said. "Expecting me to trust you."

"What do you have to lose?" I asked.

She didn't move for the longest time. Then she turned toward me, as if she were actually thinking about what I had to say. "Danny thought maybe the fight would start investigations into the way regular people were treated at Yale. He thought it would be the beginning of the end. It was just the beginning of *his* end."

Such contempt in her voice. She was still shaking, her hands clasped in her lap. I felt slightly off balance, uncertain of what I had walked into.

"So," I said, "Daniel came in the room while these guys were crowded around you, right?"

"Him and a bunch of lower classmen." Her eyes lit up when she noted my surprise. "Danny said that these guys had tried to rape me, and it became a huge fight. He didn't take on four guys like everybody made it sound. Just one, and he nearly kicked him to death."

Then she looked at me. Her lips were upturned ever so slightly. She was enjoying this conversation.

I felt a chill run down my back. "The others involved in the fight, they never spoke up."

"They had a lot to lose," she said.

"So did Daniel."

"Daniel hates Yale. He hates the Establishment. He hates what the world has done to us, all of us. He thinks everything has to change from the top down."

"What do you think?" I asked.

"I think things are pretty fucked," she said.

"And everything has to change?" I asked.

"It would be nice," she said, which wasn't exactly a ringing endorsement of Daniel's position.

"But you don't believe change will happen," I said.

"It's like Yale," she said. "Daniel went head-to-head with it, brought a scandal, hoped to get public attention, and instead, he got tossed out on his ass, and no one would listen to him."

"It sounds like the dean of his college listened to him."

"I mean the press, the government, the important people. No one listened."

"Maybe because he nearly kicked someone to death?" I asked.

Her lips thinned.

"Violence doesn't solve everything," I said.

This time, she touched her cheek, and she wasn't referring to her bruise. She was referring to my scar. "I suppose you got that in a nonviolent confrontation."

"I didn't duck fast enough when a white guy came after me with a knife."

"And I suppose you diplomatically talked him down."

It was my turn to smile, ever so slightly. "No. I defended myself. Sometimes you have to."

"Well," she said, "if you look at the world as one big confrontation between the haves and the have-nots, then you'll see that what we're doing is really a matter of defending ourselves."

With bombs? How involved was Rhondelle? "What are you doing?"

She blinked, as if she hadn't realized what she had said. She looked away, moved her plate, then leaned back in her chair. "I guess you could say we're trying to figure out the best course."

"The best course for what?"

Her eyes met mine again. Her eyes weren't really brown. They were more of a light brownish-green.

"What happened to the white guy who knifed you?" she asked, not answering my question.

"He's in prison," I said.

"What'd he do? Knife somebody else?"

She hit close to the truth, but I wasn't going to let her know that. "Sometimes the system works."

"That's the problem with you Establishment Negroes," she said, putting an ironic emphasis on the last two words. "You get one victory in the middle of a thousand defeats and think you won the war."

"We didn't used to get any victories at all," I said. "Change takes time."

"Time's what we don't have." She was spouting the party line as if she believed it, which meant that she probably believed as deeply as Daniel did.

She stood, picked up her plate, and carried it to the sink. As she brushed past me, I caught a faint scent of floral perfume. The scent surprised me. Unlike so many people I'd met in the past week, she still cared about herself and her appearance.

Which made that bruise seem all the more unusual. Maybe she had been posturing a moment ago. Testing me. Maybe she was afraid not to contradict Daniel.

"You can come with me," I said to her back.

She turned back toward me slowly. For a moment, I thought I had her. Then she laughed. "Oh, and go home? I could go back to my little girl's school and learn how to be somebody's really smart wife, and go to cocktail parties and smile nice and nod a lot, and raise two-point-five children—"

"Or you could go home, put your life back together, and figure out what you want to do," I said. "You're what? Eighteen? Nineteen? You can do whatever you want."

"I know," she said, "I want to stay here."

"I'll have to tell your dad I found you," I said.

"Fine," she snapped.

"He said you didn't have a key to this place."

"He's more stupid than he looks." She braced both hands on the countertop and leaned against it. "You know how easy it is to get keys made, especially when he leaves his key ring on the entry table every night when he gets home?"

I had suspected as much. But Whickam would probably be shocked at the daughter who was speaking to me now.

"He's not going to like the fact that you and your friends are here without his permission," I said. "It doesn't look like they're taking good care of the place."

"No one else was using it," she said.

"Even if you don't go home, your father might ask you to leave this building."

"Fine," she snapped again. "It's probably time for us to move on anyway."

I studied her. She seemed very young. But I had learned in Chicago that youth wasn't any guarantee of innocence. I wondered if I should ask her about the explosives I found in the Barn or if I should wait until I saw Daniel. I didn't want to scare the group away from here too quickly, but I also didn't want them to do anything stupid. First, I needed to figure out how to stop them.

"When's Daniel due back?" I asked.

"What's it to you?"

"I want to talk to him," I said.

"I'll tell him you were here." Rhondelle crossed her arms.

"I need to talk to him, for his mother's sake. Even if he chooses not to go home, I need to tell her I saw him."

Something passed across Rhondelle's face, something sad and lonely and filled with regret. Then she blinked up at me, the expression gone.

"Let me take you home," I said so softly that for a moment, I wondered if she heard me.

"Why?" she asked, and this time, she didn't laugh at me.

"Because," I said, "you don't deserve to be treated like this."

She shook her head slightly, her eyes downcast. Then that half smile returned to her face.

"You think you know everything, don't you?" she said, and walked out of the room.

THIRTY-FOUR

My phone call to Whickam was short.

"I found her," I said, using the phone across the street from my apartment. "She's in your parents' place."

"Oh, thank God," Whickam said. "I will be down there as fast as I can."

"You might want to reconsider that." The phone, which had been sitting in the sun, was hot against my hand. People milled around me, going about their business. The day had grown unbearably muggy.

"She is my daughter," he said. "I need to bring her home, for my wife's sake. For my sake."

"That may be so," I said, "but right now, she needs a little time, and what I'm afraid of is that she'll move out and we'll have to start the search all over again."

Besides, I wasn't sure I wanted Whickam to walk into that mess. Not the messy row house; the possible bombs, the rhetoric, the strange uneasiness I'd felt ever since I stepped through that beautiful mahogany door.

"What about Daniel?" he asked.

"I'm going back later today. I hope to talk to Daniel then." And I hoped he would give me something. Some clue to what he was planning. Some idea of how dangerous he truly was.

"I worry about her, all alone there," Whickam said.

"She's not alone." I wiped the sweat off my forehead. I didn't like standing in the sun. "She's with a number of other people. I'm not sure how many."

"They are all in the house?" Whickam asked.

"I'm afraid so," I said.

"I could arrest them for trespassing."

"I'm sure you could try," I said. "But I don't know if you've noticed how run-down the neighborhood is getting. Even if you call the police, I doubt they'll come, and if they do, I doubt they'll arrest anyone."

At least not for that. The police might not go in for other reasons. If they suspected the group of militant activity, they might be spying on the row house, and they wouldn't go in if it compromised their investigation.

A trickle of sweat ran down my back. I hoped the house wasn't under surveillance. The last thing I needed was to be back in some police file.

Whickam sighed heavily. "Can you assure me that's she's in no danger?"

"Just give me a day," I said. "That's all I ask. Then you can come down here if you want."

"What if they leave? What if they decide it's not safe there and run, now that you have found them?"

"That's the risk we take," I said. "If you don't show up immediately, they might think everything's all right."

"I want my daughter back," Whickam said.

"I think you're going to have to realize that your daughter is an adult who makes her own choices. Whether you agree with them or not."

There was not much more to say after that. I promised to call him if anything else changed. Otherwise, I would get back in touch with him late the next day.

I let myself out of the booth, crossed the street, and headed into my new apartment. Jimmy and Malcolm were gone. They had planned to go to Central Park, and if they didn't enjoy themselves there, they would go to Morningside Park. They planned to end their day in the library, in air-conditioned comfort.

Air-conditioning sounded good to me, too.

There wasn't much I could do until later. I went into the back bedroom, clicked the air conditioner on high, and fell asleep.

I woke to the sound of thunder. The room was dark, even though the cheap alarm clock beside the bed told me it was late afternoon. The stress of the last few days had gotten to me, and so had the lack of sleep. I had slept for more than four hours, and my growling stomach told me that I needed something to eat.

I showered, got myself dinner, and headed back to the Whickam apartment. The sky had turned black, and a vicious wind made its way through the canyons between the buildings. I hoped that Malcolm and Jimmy had gone to the library already—I didn't want them caught in this.

The moment I had that thought, the heavens opened up, and water poured out of them. I climbed into a doorway, waiting for the rain to pass by.

After fifteen minutes, it became clear that the rain wasn't going to let up. I ran the last two blocks to the row houses. By the time I climbed the steps to the Whickam house, I was so wet that my shoes sloshed.

I pounded on the knocker. This time, the door swung back, and Daniel Kirkland faced me. He was taller than I remembered, and thinner. His Afro doubled the size of his head, making his face seem very tiny.

"I thought maybe it was you," he said without inviting me in. "Tell my mom I'm fine."

There wasn't a single breath of emotion in his words. He didn't care about Grace. I wondered if he cared about anyone.

"You tell her," I said. "She thought something horrible had happened to you. She doesn't hear from you, then she finds out you dropped out of school and you're going to lose your scholarship."

He shrugged. "It's my life."

"She's the one who worked hard so that you would get that scholarship. She's the one who sacrificed nearly twenty years of her life for you, and you're just walking away as if it doesn't matter."

His eyes were flat. "There's more important things than my mother right now."

"Like what?"

"This country," he said. "It's killing us."

I resisted the urge to roll my eyes. I had promised myself I would listen to him. I had hoped that he might let something slip.

"It's sending us to war," he was saying. "It's stifling us. It's destroying good people. You know that, man. You know how these things work. It's time to stop it."

He was giving me clues. I just had to get through the rhetoric. "How are you going to stop an entire nation?"

"Not just me," he said, not giving me the answer I had hoped for. "Lots of us feel this way. It's not enough to stop the war anymore. We got to stop the people who think that war is their right. This is a revolution. And in a revolution, everything changes."

Thunder boomed above me, and then the rain started to hurt. It made tapping noises as it hit the ground.

Hail, barely bigger than the raindrops themselves, but it stung.

I pushed the door open as wide as it went, and stepped inside, dripping on that fine wood floor.

"I didn't ask you in," Daniel said.

"It's a revolution," I said. "People do what they want."

He glared at me. I didn't care. We didn't like each other, which was fine. I didn't have to like him. I just had to find out what he was up to and stop it.

I walked past him toward the kitchen where I had last seen Rhondelle. A woman stood inside, heating refried beans on the hot plate. The smell was foul. Two young men sat at the table, eating a tabouli salad made with too much vinegar.

All three people in the kitchen were white. All three of them had long blondish brown hair, wore jeans and short tops, and had bare feet.

"Is this the man harassing you?" one of the young men asked Daniel, who had come in behind me.

I dripped on the tile floor. Without asking, I grabbed a towel and wiped off my face. "How many of you live here?"

"Who wants to know?" the girl asked, taking the pan of beans off the hot plate. She was classically beautiful, her features small and well drawn.

The power flickered. The lights dimmed for a moment, then came back up.

"He's a detective," Daniel said. "My mom hired him."

"Your mom?" the other young man asked. "I thought she didn't care about anything."

What a strange description of Grace. If anything, she cared too much.

"I see you've been lying to them," I said.

Daniel's right hand clenched into a fist, and then he forced himself to relax it. "You don't have any rights here. You barged into our place—"

"Actually, this place belongs to Professor Whickam's parents, not any of you. You're trespassing. I just might tell the police. If they come in here to evict you, what else will they find? Components for a Molotov cocktail, like I found in the Barn? More dynamite? Some blasting caps?"

The girl spun, looking at the boys as if they were at fault. They stared at me.

No one spoke for the longest time. I wasn't going to get them to admit anything, not without some work.

I balled the towel in my fist. "What did you plan to do with all that stuff at the Barn? Show the Administration how stupid it is by bombing New Haven?"

"It wasn't ours," Daniel said from behind me.

I turned. His face was impassive. If the stuff really wasn't his, he should have been shocked by my accusations. He wasn't.

"We weren't the only ones who used that place," one of the boys said.

I didn't turn toward him. I could tell by the tremble in his voice that he was lying.

This was between me and Daniel.

Daniel tilted his head ever so slightly. He looked almost bemused. "That's right. We've been in the city since May. Someone else could've stayed in the Barn since we left New Haven."

"So if I search this place," I said, "I won't find any bomb-making materials?"

"Of course not," Daniel said, this time remembering to sound shocked.

"What about guns?" I asked. "Will I find any of those?"

"Didn't say that," Daniel said. "A man's got to protect himself."

"Especially from people just barging into his home." The other boy stood. He was about half my size, but he knew how to hold himself so that he looked menacing.

I gave him a contemptuous look. "What are you going to do? Kick me so hard I have to go to the hospital?"

The boy flushed and glanced at Daniel. Daniel made a slight sound, almost like a growl, and I knew it wasn't aimed at me. He was angry at his friend for failing to lie well.

"He didn't kick anyone," Daniel said.

"Oh, that's right," I said, turning toward him. "You did. Unprovoked."

"I was provoked," Daniel said.

"By the Establishment and the Yale oppression," I said, letting all the contempt I felt into my voice. "Oppression most of us can't afford for our own child. Oppression that has to be earned."

"You don't understand," he said.

"I understand," I said. "You're angry because you don't get special privileges anymore. You're no longer Daniel the Smartest Person in the Room, and it upsets you. So you try to get special privileges for being the darkest person in the room, and when that fails, you decide to become a victim."

"Fuck you," Daniel said, and shoved me.

I pushed him against the wall, then held him there with one hand.

"I'm not liking anything I hear about you, Daniel. I thought maybe you were decent last summer when you helped me find your brother. Then you come back here and nearly kill a kid for no reason. You scare a bunch of people at various places, and the last place I go to, I find stuff that scares me. You kids have no idea what you're playing with. Revolution? Have you ever seen a revolution? Have you ever shot someone? Have you ever cleaned blood off a wall? Or carried a dead friend's body two miles holding him by his hips and his shoulders because his back has been blown away? Do you know what bombs do to people? Innocent people?"

"No one's innocent," Daniel said. "Not in this world."

It took all of my strength not to backhand him across the mouth.

"Your brother's innocent. And so's your mother. And so was that little boy we found murdered last summer. You set off a bomb, and people like that die. People who did nothing more than go to work or chose the wrong apartment. Do you really think that there's going to be a revolution in this country? That people like me are going to follow babies like you?"

I let him go. He staggered forward.

"We never said that bomb stuff was ours," one of the boys behind me said. "In fact, Danny said it wasn't. You heard him."

"Yeah, I heard him," I said. "I just didn't believe him."

Daniel had a hand on his chest. My handprint was purpling his bare skin. "You want a tour, man?"

"Yeah," I said. "I do. Then I want Rhondelle."

"Why?" Daniel asked.

"Because you haven't been treating her well, either."

"She makes her own choices," Daniel said.

"Where is she now?" I asked.

"Upstairs." His voice was scratchy. "Sleeping."

I looked from him to the other three. They all looked terrified. Maybe they'd never seen real violence before.

"You three sit down. I don't want to hear a peep from you while Daniel's giving me the tour. And if any of you threaten me, well, you've seen what I can do on a moment's notice. Think of what I can do with a little time to plan."

The boys backed toward their chair. The girl grabbed the counter, and leaned against it, her lower lip visibly shaking as if she were about to cry.

"I don't have to show you anything," Daniel said, finally rising to his full height.

It was his last stand.

"Yeah," I said as quietly as I could, knowing that Daniel heard the menace in my voice. "Yeah, you do."

THIRTY-FIVE

The row house was a mess. Clothing was strewn everywhere, and dishes cluttered every available surface. The bathroom hadn't been cleaned since Daniel's group had moved in.

I looked through each and every cabinet as we walked through the house, examined every closet, opened every box. I found evidence of more than five people living in the house—if I had to guess, I would have suspected ten or more—but I saw no bomb-making equipment, and only one shotgun, which Daniel assured me was for protection.

Rhondelle was in bed on the second floor. She was naked, and as I entered the room, she pulled covers up to her neck. I flicked on the overhead light, mostly to see if she had new bruises, and she cursed me.

The room smelled of sex.

"She's staying here," Daniel said.

"Is that true, Rhondelle?" I asked her.

There was an emptiness to her gaze as her eyes met mine. "Do I look like someone who wants to leave?"

"You like getting bruises on your face?" I asked her.

Daniel flinched beside me, but didn't move.

"We're in a war, man," Rhondelle said, and it sounded like the party line.

"The country's in a war," I said.

"*We're* in the war," Daniel said. "We're trying to stop something unjust—"

"I'm talking to Rhondelle," I snapped. Then I said, my voice softer, "I'll take you with me. You don't have to stay, no matter what he says."

"This is my home," she said.

"This is your grandparents' home, and your friends are ruining it. Just like Daniel ruined your pretty face. Come with me. No one'll hit you in New Haven."

"You so sure of that, man?" Daniel asked me.

But I ignored him. Rhondelle looked over my shoulder at Daniel, as if she were asking his permission.

"Come with me," I said again.

Slowly she shook her head, never taking her gaze off Daniel.

"I can keep you safe."

"Sure, man," Daniel said. "Like the government keeps us safe. Rhondi's better off here."

"Rhondelle's better off making her own decisions," I said.

"I'm staying," she whispered.

I stared at her for a moment. She stared back. After a moment, she closed her eyes and lay back down.

I sighed. I wasn't going to convince her to leave Daniel. So I searched the room.

I started with the closet. Then I looked under the bed, and even checked out the corner fireplace to make sure I hadn't missed anything.

Rhondelle said nothing. Daniel watched me as if I were some kind of lunatic who had invaded his house.

We finished the upstairs. I made Daniel take me into the attic where I found lots of boxes of old books and clothes, some of which had become mice nests. But I found no gasoline or bottles or anything that looked like it might be the stockpile for a revolution.

Even the cellar was empty, except for a wringer washer and clotheslines that someone had strung between the beams.

"Satisfied?" Daniel asked me when he finally brought me back to the kitchen.

"No," I said. "But I've done my job. I've found you. I've found Rhondelle. I told you both to contact your parents. I can't do much else."

"Damn straight," Daniel said. "We've got a life. We're actually fighting for something that means something. You can go back to your crummy apartment and dig through other people's garbage, but we're going to change this world. We're going to bring it down bit by bit."

"And then what?" I asked.

"What?" Daniel asked.

"When you tear down society, then what'll you do?"

"Build a better one," Daniel said.

"How?" I asked.

"You'll know," he said. "You'll know tomorrow."

I stiffened. "What are you doing tomorrow?"

"Partying." Only when he spoke, his voice was full of sarcasm. Then he ran his fingers over the bruise I gave him. "You're just like the rest of them, you know. You think just because you're stronger than me, you've defeated me. Shows you don't know a goddamn thing."

"That's right," I said. "I don't know anything. I don't know how a good woman like Grace Kirkland could have raised a loser like you."

"I'm not the loser," he said. "I'm not the guy who drags his kid from place to place because he can't hold a job."

"No, you're the guy who mooches off his girlfriend, and throws away his education."

"You ever read about revolution, man? You gotta go underground before you take action."

I studied him. "This isn't some backward colony in the eighteenth century. If you take action, you'll be arrested. Have you even seen a prison?"

"You think I'll get caught."

"If you don't die first," I said. "You're playing with things you don't understand."

"You assume that what you saw in New Haven is mine," he said. "You don't know a goddamn thing about me."

"Enlighten me."

He studied me for a moment, as if he were considering it. Then he said, "It's not my job, man. Now get the hell out of my house."

THIRTY-SIX

had no choice but to leave. I couldn't do anything else—yet.

As I stepped out of the row house, Daniel slammed the door behind me. I could feel the reverberation through the steps.

The rain had stopped, but water still dripped off every surface. I thought I saw movement to my right, but when I glanced that direction, nothing was there.

My heart pounded. I was usually good at spotting surveillance. I hoped I hadn't seen a cop. I hoped I was just being paranoid.

Still, I walked quickly away from the Whickam row house. About a block away, an expensive sedan with Connecticut plates was attempting a New Yorker's version of parallel parking—hitting the front bumper of the car in back, the back bumper of the car in front, until the new car had squeezed into such a small space that no one could move.

Finally the door opened, and René Whickam got out.

He seemed overdressed for the neighborhood. His suit was light, but stylish, and even though he wore no tie, his white shirt looked formal and out of place.

He was the last person I wanted to see.

"Professor," I said as I crossed the street to join him. "I thought I told you I'd call."

He shrugged. "I have to get Rhondelle."

"I was just there," I said. "She doesn't want to leave."

"I don't care what she wants," he said. "She is coming home."

He crossed the street, sliding slightly on the wet pavement. I hurried after him.

"There's a lot of kids in that place," I said.

"Then I will have them arrested," Whickam said.

"We already discussed that," I said. "I don't think the police'll listen."

"My family used to have a lot of clout in this neighborhood," he said. "The police will listen."

Whickam was living in some kind of fantasy world, one I didn't entirely understand. Still, I followed him as he strode down the block.

He took the stairs two at a time, then grabbed the doorknob and tried to shove the door open. The door was locked. He reached inside his suitcoat and removed his keys, quickly unlocking the door.

I stood beside him. I couldn't stop him, but I could protect him if he needed it.

The door swung open, only to reveal Daniel standing there. He pointed the shotgun at Whickam.

"Good evening, Professor Whickam," Daniel said.

Whickam took a deep breath, squaring his shoulders as if that gave him strength. "Where's my daughter?"

Daniel smiled. The smile was cold. His gaze never left Whickam, but I knew that Daniel saw me as well.

Perhaps he thought he could control me by ignoring me.

"You're not welcome here, Professor," Daniel said.

"It's my home," Whickam said. "I was born here. You have no claim to the place."

"Your daughter invited me. Then you sent this thug in." Daniel nodded toward me. "See what he did to me?"

He used one hand to show Whickam the bruise.

"There are scary stories about Mr. Grimshaw," Daniel said. "He took on an entire gang once in a schoolyard, and won. You didn't know that, did you?"

Whickam looked at me in surprise.

"So isn't it understandable that I feel threatened?" Daniel asked. "Any good law student knows that when a man feels threatened in his own home, he has the right to defend himself."

Whickam straightened. Daniel had obviously played the wrong card.

"This is not your home. It is mine. So I can defend myself here as you say. Do you really want to battle this in a court? Because to figure out which of us is right would take a shot, and maybe a death."

Daniel's smile grew colder. He wanted Whickam to provoke him. I was beginning to believe that Daniel wanted to pull that trigger; he was just waiting for the right time.

"Daniel doesn't want to take this to court," I said, "because he doesn't believe in the authority of the U.S. government, do you, Daniel?"

He glared at me. "Does my mother know how violent you are?"

"She certainly doesn't know how violent you are," I said.

Whickam ducked under the gun barrel and went into the house. "Rhondelle!" he shouted. "Rhondi, honey, it's Daddy."

Daniel started to swing the shotgun toward Whickam.

I grabbed the gun, and with one swift wrench, removed it from Daniel's hand. Then I unchambered the shells and dropped them in my pocket.

Daniel gave me a look filled with pure hatred. He rubbed his right arm as if I had hurt it.

"Don't play with guns if you don't know how to hold onto one," I said softly. I knew how. I made sure my grip on that gun was unbreakable.

The three white kids hovered around the kitchen door. They were staring at this whole thing as if they couldn't believe what was happening.

Whickam hadn't noticed the violence behind him. He was peering into the front parlor. "Rhondi, it's Dad. Please come out."

Daniel moved away from me. He crossed his arms and leaned against the wall, pretending that I hadn't rattled him. He was watching me, as if he were trying to gauge how to get the shotgun out of my hands.

"Rhondi!" Whickam shouted.

From the upstairs landing, someone cleared her throat. We looked up. Rhondelle was staring down at us. She had wrapped herself in a blanket. Her face was in shadow, the bruise not visible.

"Rhondelle, honey," Whickam said, and started toward the stairs.

"Stay there, Daddy," she said.

He stopped. I wondered if her tone chilled him as much as it did me.

"I'm not going anywhere, Daddy," she said. "If you want us to move out of here, we will. But I have to warn you, if we have to leave, you won't hear from me again."

Whickam held out his hands. "Rhondi, come home. We can talk there."

"No," she said.

"Your mother and I have been so worried. That's why we hired Mr.

Grimshaw here. That's why we have been searching for you. We were so afraid that something bad had happened to you."

"Well," Rhondelle said, her tone flat. "Now you can see I'm fine."

Whickam shook his head. "This isn't fine, Rhondi. You have so many opportunities. Come back to school. You can go anywhere you want, and I promise, I will not say anything about your politics or . . . your boyfriends."

Daniel snorted, but I was the only one who looked at him. His gaze met mine, and that cold smile had started to hover around his lips again.

"I don't want to live that life, Daddy," Rhondelle said. "I'm not some trained puppet who does what everybody tells her."

That was true, I thought. Now she only did what Daniel told her.

"Rhondi, please," Whickam said, but he didn't finish the thought. He didn't have to.

"Look at it this way, Daddy," she said. "You don't have to shell out for my college anymore. You're not responsible for me. I'm responsible for me. All I'm asking is some time to stay here while we find a place of our own. Then we'll leave. We'll even pay rent if you want it."

Daniel rolled his eyes, but he was behind Whickam's back. Whickam couldn't see the contempt.

"No." Whickam spoke with deep sadness. His shoulders slumped. "You can stay."

Rhondelle gave him a bright smile. I had a hunch that if Daniel weren't standing right there, she would have run down the steps and hugged her father. But she didn't move.

"Thanks, Daddy," she said.

He sighed, then looked at all of them. "You want to tell me what this is all about?"

"We've tried," Daniel said. "You don't listen."

"Try me now," Whickam said.

"I don't believe in repeating information," Daniel said. "If you don't get it the first time, you won't get it."

From the smiles around the room and the look of utter humiliation on Whickam's face, I realized that Daniel was quoting Whickam himself, probably something he had said in class.

"I have been so worried," Whickam said to Daniel.

Daniel shrugged. "Sometimes you have to let go, man."

"I'm all right, Daddy, really," Rhondelle said.

"So just give us back the gun and you can leave," Daniel said.

Whickam looked at me. "Maybe you should give it back."

"You don't need the gun," I said to Daniel.

"It's mine," he said.

"Not anymore." I gave him the same cold smile he had given me.

Daniel looked at my hands, then back at me, as if debating whether or not he could take the gun by force. Finally, he shrugged one shoulder. "I can always get another gun."

"Danny, stop," Rhondelle said. "Daddy's letting us stay. Don't antagonize him."

"Sorry, Professor," Daniel said with complete sarcasm. "Didn't mean to insult you."

"If you hurt my daughter," Whickam said, "you'll answer to me."

Daniel didn't move. He clearly wasn't intimidated.

"I promise, Professor," he said, "that I won't hurt her any more than you did."

Whickam's light brown skin reddened. He glanced at his daughter, the look filled with humiliation.

She didn't jump to his defense. No one did.

Finally I used my free hand to touch him lightly on the back. "Come on. Let's leave the children to their games."

And somehow, I managed to get Whickam out of that house.

THIRTY-SEVEN

I cracked open the shotgun, but I still felt awkward walking into the street. The shells clicked together in my pocket. I wanted to get rid of them and the gun as soon as possible.

Whickam didn't seem to notice the gun or the lightning still flaring in the distance. He walked, head down, toward his car. This time, I didn't have to struggle to keep up with him.

When we reached the car, Whickam leaned against the door as he unlocked it, looking more defeated than any man I had ever seen.

"I had visions of carrying her out," he said. "All the way down here, I imagined myself carrying her out like she was a little girl."

"She doesn't want to go," I said.

He shook his head. "That was the thing. If she screamed for help, or didn't say anything, I would've been up those stairs. But she wants to stay in the filth with that boy. I don't understand it."

"She knows where to go if she needs help," I said.

"She wouldn't even come down the stairs," he said. "She wasn't even dressed. It's nearly night, and she wasn't even dressed."

"I know," I said.

"How did she become this person? What happened to her?" His voice broke. He leaned his head on the car door.

212

I didn't move. I didn't know what to say, and any kind of physical sympathy—a touch on the shoulder, a hand on the back—seemed out of place.

After a moment, he straightened. "I owe you. I owe you for finding her. At least we know she's all right. That is more than we had yesterday."

"I wish it could have been different," I said.

He reached into his back pocket. "I brought money. It was going to be for her, but I couldn't give it to her, not with him there. They might use it for . . . the wrong things. So let me pay you what I owe."

I didn't want to take his money at the moment. He wasn't in any condition, and it didn't feel right.

"Let me bill you," I said.

He shook his head. "We had an agreement. Expenses, right, and your rate? I figure with coming to New York, you and your son, the hotel and meals, expenses are already at least two hundred. Then there's the rate."

"Professor—"

"Let's settle this," he said. "I don't want to have to think about it when I get home."

So this was where Rhondelle learned her ability to ignore the things she didn't want to see. I had suspected as much, but I had never really seen Whickam's talent in action.

"Two hundred is generous," I said. "Our expenses haven't come close to that."

He handed me four. I tried to give the other two back, but he wouldn't let me.

He had planned to give out that money today, and he was going to do so no matter what.

"I can't give you a receipt," I said. "I don't have anything on me."

"Mail it." Then he seemed to notice the gun. "That's my father's, you know."

"I think it's yours now," I said, handing it to him.

He took it as if he had never held a gun before. Maybe he hadn't.

"He always said he kept it to keep us safe. I never thought I'd see it turned on me." He shook his head. "My father would be appalled at Rhondelle."

"I know," I said quietly.

Whickam went to the back of the car, opened the trunk, and put the shotgun inside. At least he was thinking clearly about that.

Then he slammed the trunk and came back to the driver's door. "I'd like to ask you to check up on her, but you're leaving soon, aren't you?"

I didn't answer him. That last encounter with Daniel worried me. When he swung that gun toward Whickam, I actually thought Daniel might shoot.

I no longer had any doubt that he would use those explosives.

"Rhondi never changes her mind," Whickam was saying. "That's the problem. She'd go straight into hell if she thought that was the course she needed to take, no matter how many people told her she was wrong."

Like him this afternoon. When I had pleaded with him not to come, he had anyway.

I wasn't sure I would be so different.

"You still need to give her the chance," I said.

Half of Whickam's mouth rose in a sad smile. The expression was so like his daughter's that I felt surprise at the resemblance.

"When I first met you, I thought you were cynical," he said. "But you're not, are you? You like to believe the best of everyone."

"Your daughter's smart," I said. "Smart people figure things out."

"Not always," he said, and got into the car. He rolled down the driver's side window and leaned out of it. "I should not have let her stay there, should I? They may think I'm condoning what they're doing."

"I'm not sure what they're doing," I said. "I sure didn't like that shotgun, though."

"I did not like any of it," Whickam said, and started the car. It rumbled softly, almost inaudible against the noises of the city. "Thanks for your help, Mr. Grimshaw."

"Any time," I said.

But as I watched him drive away, I wondered if he really was grateful. Was it better to know that his daughter was living with an obsessed group of young people who seemed out of control? Or better to think she was missing?

I had no idea. But I couldn't condemn Whickam for giving in to her. Nor was I really upset that he had come for her, even though his attempt to bring her home had failed.

We had no idea what the future would bring, what would happen to our children, and how we could protect them. We could only do our best.

And sometimes our best simply wasn't good enough.

THIRTY-EIGHT

On the walk home, I thought about a lot of things. I worried that someone had seen me with that gun. I hoped no one was watching the apartment. I certainly didn't want to show up in some file, looking angry, a
shotgun clutched in my hands.

That slight movement I had seen near the apartment still worried me. A lot
of these militant groups had undercover agents inside the organization or surveillance outside. I could only hope that no one had discovered Daniel's group
yet, or if they had, they hadn't taken any photographs of me.

But there was nothing I could do about it now. Even the hope felt futile,
and it took a moment to understand why.

That conflict I'd felt earlier, between my duty to Grace and my responsibility as a person who knew about a potential crime had just increased. I no
longer doubted Daniel's capacity for violence.

I didn't even know how to talk to her, which was probably why I hadn't
called her yet. I wasn't sure she'd believe me if I told her who Daniel had become and what he was doing. I was afraid she'd spend money she didn't
have to come to New York, only to get turned away the way that René
Whickam had.

The next day was the Fourth of July, followed by a long weekend. People would be out of town. Offices would be closed. I could do some investigating, but not a lot.

And then I stopped.

What had Daniel said? He had said something would happen tomorrow. I had to concentrate to recall the context.

When you tear down society, I had asked him, *then what'll you do?*

Build a better one, he'd said. I asked how, and he had said, *You'll know tomorrow.*

Tomorrow. The Fourth of July.

That map I had found in the Barn had had a seven and a four written next to the circled site marked with the exclamation point. I had thought those numbers meant 74. But what if they meant 7/4—the Fourth of July?

I went cold. I hadn't kept the map, but I had memorized it. Only I didn't know what was at that location. It was on the southern tip of the island, near Battery Park. A lot of government buildings were there. But what was on the corner of Whitehall and Pearl?

I needed to find out.

Our maps were in the van, which was in Newark. I went down to the nearest subway platform, but the subway map didn't tell me what was at that corner either, although there was a stop nearby.

I would have to go there myself.

The holiday was already starting. Someone posted the subway's holiday hours all over the booth. People were pushing each other, smiling despite their hurry.

I had to get back to the apartment. I had two boys to take care of, a federal holiday to deal with, and a possible bombing target.

What I needed was a plan.

I had one by the time I reached 114th Street. If Daniel's group decided to bomb a building at Whitehall and Pearl, they were probably planning to plant the bomb tomorrow, when most people were out of town.

If I watched the area, I would see them arrive. I could call the police anonymously and stop the bombing. I'd be able to report who planted the bombs as well, and then let the authorities make a case against Daniel and his friends.

The plan had a lot of flaws. For example, Daniel could have already planted the bomb, and he—or someone else—would detonate it tomorrow. I would have to keep a reasonable distance from the building itself, just in case.

And there was also a good chance that the seven and the four on that map did mean 74. Whether that was a measurement, an address or a code, I wouldn't know.

But if I was right about the date, I might be able to stop something ugly.

Malcolm and Jimmy were already home when I arrived. They were sharing some lemonade at the kitchen table, the door to the hallway open so that the cool breeze from the air conditioner could filter into the room.

They looked surprised to see me. I told them that I had seen Daniel, and the case was as hopeless as Malcolm had feared. Then I told them about the possibility of a bomb, and my plans to stop it.

Jimmy pushed his lemonade away. "I don't want you to go."

"I know," I said.

"How come it's always gotta be you? How come nobody else can do this stuff?"

"Just call the cops," Malcolm said. "Let them deal with it."

I had poured myself a glass of lemonade and joined them at the table. "And be on record making a bomb threat? I don't think so."

"They'd know it's not a threat," Malcolm said.

"No, they wouldn't," I said. "A lot of groups call in the threats as warnings, just like I would be doing."

"They wouldn't know it was you," Malcolm said. "Right?"

"In a city this big, if I don't identify myself, they might not check the site."

"Why don't I go?" Malcolm said. "You can stay with Jim, and be safe."

I smiled at him. It was a generous offer, but just as fruitless as calling the police. I didn't say that, however.

"I have surveillance training," I said. "I know how to spot unusual activity, and how to stop it. You're good, Malcolm, but not quite ready for an all-night stake-out alone in a strange city."

"So what if they bomb some place we never seen?" Jimmy asked. "It's not our problem. You know where Daniel is now. Call Mrs. Kirkland and let's go home."

I sighed. A lot of people would not only accept Jimmy's reasoning, but act on it. I couldn't.

"We can walk away." I put my arms on the table and leaned toward him. "There's a good chance that nothing will happen. But what if something does? What if we find out on Saturday that a bomb went off and destroyed an entire building? What then?"

Jimmy shrugged. "Too bad, I guess."

"What if people were in that building? What if they died?"

"We don't know nobody here, Smoke." He frowned. "It'd be sad, but we don't know them."

"We should only help people we know?" I asked.

He stared at me. His lips were pressed tightly together. He knew the answer I wanted him to give, and he wasn't going to say it.

"Okay," I said into his silence. "What happens if among the people in that building was someone we know, like Laura or the Grimshaws or—"

"They're not here."

"Or maybe Laura's lawyer, Mr. McMillan. You know him, but you don't know where he is today. What happens if you find out he was in the building, and you could have saved his life by letting me go down there tonight?"

Jimmy's eyes filled with tears. "I don't like him."

"Does that matter?" I asked. "Liking or disliking, when he died in a way that could've been prevented."

"Stop," Malcolm said. "We get the point. You're not going to browbeat Jimmy into agreeing with it, because he's not willing to sacrifice you."

Jimmy wiped his eyes with the back of his hand.

"It's a civil responsibility thing," Malcolm said. "You gotta do what's right."

"Yeah," I said.

"Stupid argument," Malcolm said, "because most people don't do what's right."

"I know that, too," I said, "and I don't want to be like those people."

Malcolm's gaze met mine. Jimmy buried his head in his arms.

"If something goes wrong," I said, "and I don't come back, you know where the van is. Take Jimmy back to Chicago. The Grimshaws will know what to do."

"After we know what happened to you," Malcolm said.

I shook my head. "Wait a few days. No one knows you're here. If I can't get back to you right away, I'll meet you in Chicago. I don't want you confronting Daniel. Stay away from him."

"I can handle myself," Malcolm said.

"I know, but I brought you along to take care of Jim. And that's what I expect you to do."

Malcolm gave me a half smile. "That's *my* civic responsibility."

"That's right," I said, "and I can't think of anything more important."

THIRTY-NINE

An hour later, armed with prepackaged snack food and two sodas, I left. I took the subway downtown. The train was mostly empty. The handful of people who rode it stared out the windows at nothing, looking miserable, as if they regretted still being in town this late on the night before a holiday.

Jimmy had hugged me as I walked out the door, but he hadn't entirely forgiven me for going. He considered the case closed now that Daniel was found, and nothing would change his mind. I understood Jimmy's opposition, but for the night, he was safe. I simply wouldn't have been able to live with myself if I hadn't tried to do something.

I got off the subway at the South Ferry Station, took the stairs up, and stopped when I reached the street. It took a moment to get my bearings.

Battery Park looked the same as it always had, but the skyline to the north had changed somehow. I wasn't sure what was different, because I wasn't completely sure what had been there. But the air smelled the same: a combination of gas fumes, and the Upper Bay, exacerbated by the muggy night.

It was just past twilight, and the streetlights had come up. I walked to Water Street and saw what had changed. An entire group of buildings was gone. The streets had changed, too. What I remembered as a warren of tiny blocks had become one big construction site.

The steel frame of a huge building towered above me. I couldn't tell exactly how tall this was, but I could tell the steel work wasn't yet finished. A sign marked this the work of William Lescaze & Associates, and behind the name was an architectural drawing of a skyscraper. One New York Plaza, they called it, unoriginally, with offices for rent in the fall.

I doubted they'd make their rental date, considering how much work was left on the building. This would have been a good target—Lord knew how many historical buildings had disappeared—but it was a block away from the corner of Whitehall and Pearl.

I continued along Whitehall, crossing Water, and stopped, my breath catching. The building targeted on the map was so obvious that it hadn't even crossed my mind.

The Armed Forces Induction Center. Of course, it would be closed on the Fourth of July; all government buildings were. A bomb planted on that day, exploding that day, would have incredible significance.

With the right kind of explosives, the building itself might just crumble. It had an old-fashioned air—a brick Victorian with a two-story granite foundation. Time hadn't served it well: The foundation was dirty and cracked, the windows fogged from the day's humidity, and some of the bricks above the second story had come loose.

The neighborhood looked abandoned. I was sure there were apartments above the shops across the street, but none of the building's lights were on. I made myself keep walking so that I wouldn't look like I was casing the place.

I needed to settle in a spot that would give me a good view of the army building. It was large, but it looked impenetrable. Someone would have to work hard to get inside, especially with the place locked up the way it was.

I finally settled on a building halfway up Pearl. The building had an old wrought iron fire escape that reached all the way to the ground. From my vantage, it seemed like the fire escape went to the roof. I hoped no one was up there, trying to cool down. If so, I would have a heck of a time explaining what I was doing.

The iron was covered with a layer of rust that flaked onto my fingers as I grabbed the railing. I pulled myself up, hoping the supports that attached the escape to the building would hold. The entire fire escape shook as I moved. It also rattled, the sound so loud that it seemed like people could hear it all the way up in Central Park.

But I made it to the top without incident, climbed over the roof's lip, and stepped into the white granules that some places used for roofing material.

From this roof, I could jump to the next, and then the next, but I wouldn't have to. I had a good view of the Induction Center, particularly the front door.

Since the bombing site had been picked for its symbolism, I suspected the bombers would want to use that symbolism to its fullest. Either they'd destroy the entire building, or damage it near the recruitment signs.

There was no one else on the roof, and no evidence that the residents ever came up here. I glanced at the other rooftops and saw no one.

Then I found the perfect spot and settled in for the night.

FORTY

About three in the morning, I saw movement to the south. Someone had climbed on the steel frame of the new skyscraper and was wandering along the beams. The person wasn't on the upper level of the new structure. He was on a lower floor, peering over the edge.

He was probably a night watchman. It was necessary for larger construction areas to hire someone to keep an eye on the property, particularly over a long weekend like this one.

I didn't move as he surveyed the area to the west of the building. I didn't want anyone to see me.

But I watched him. I couldn't see how big he was from this distance. I couldn't really tell that I was looking at a man, but given the job, I doubted a woman would be up there. The light from the street did give him an outline, however, and I noted that he didn't have long hair or an Afro.

He wasn't one of the young men I had seen at the Whickam apartment.

Still, I remained motionless. He seemed to be moving a few things—because they were dangerous? In his way? I couldn't quite tell. Then he disappeared, probably to continue his rounds.

I doubted I'd see him again. Judging from the size of that unfinished building, he had a lot of ground to cover during one night.

But that was the only disturbance during the darkness. Dawn came—a beautiful sunrise over the water, illuminating the buildings beyond, reminding me again how much I had once loved this city and its environs. I stretched and shook my limbs, careful not to get stiff.

I had eaten a few of the snacks I brought, and finished an entire bottle of soda. Later, I'd used the empty bottle as a urinal, an old military trick that I'd used before on stakeouts.

During the night, I had found other exits off the roof, and I double-checked them in the light. The door leading into the building was locked, but the lock was flimsy. Two buildings over, another fire escape led to a different street, one impossible to see from Pearl. And all the way at the other end of the block, on Whitehall, I found an open door that seemed to lead into another group of apartments.

I felt better now that I had backup plans.

The neighborhood remained surprisingly quiet as the morning progressed. I expected to see Daniel or someone from his group shortly after dawn, but they didn't show.

Instead, a trickle of men, all in uniform, made their way from South Ferry Station to the army building. At least fifteen people were inside by seven-thirty, which surprised me. I would have thought the building would be empty on the Fourth of July.

I saw no one else until about nine, when a few people crossed out of the park. They seemed like tourists, laughing and joking as they walked partway up Pearl. When they realized that the businesses down here were closed, they went back the way they came.

Then, at ten, my breath caught. A ratty green car, covered in peace signs and antiwar bumper stickers, crawled down Pearl. It parked just below my perch, and five people got out.

I recognized three immediately—the white girl and the two young men from the Whickam apartment. They wore ripped blue jeans and had their hair tied back.

Then Rhondelle got out of the front seat, and Daniel got out of the driver's side.

"Told you it'd be empty down here," one of the white boys said.

"Better to be cautious," Daniel said.

The other boy said, "Still think we should've—"

"Shhh," said the white girl. "Windows are open. It's hot."

"I want to look around." Daniel put a hand on the white girl's arm, pulling her toward him. Rhondelle stood on the curb, then sighed. After a moment, she followed.

The group crossed the street, then walked along the army building to Whitehall. They moved as a unit. If they were scouting the place, they were doing a terrible job of it.

They obviously weren't military. Anyone military would have shown up before dawn, scouted locations, and left before daylight. This group had slept in. The way they were laughing as they walked they seemed to see what they were doing as a lark.

It clearly wasn't. If I hadn't seen that map, I might have doubted their intentions, but I didn't now. Not with the map, the dynamite in the Barn, and the date.

I hadn't wanted to be right, and it seemed that I was.

The group hadn't quite reached the main door when a shot echoed. The group seemed to collapse in on itself. Someone was screaming, and at least two people were on the ground—one was prone, the other kneeling.

I couldn't quite see what had happened.

Then Rhondelle ran, and so did one of the white boys. The front door to the army building opened, and a soldier beckoned. "Bring her in here," he yelled.

The shot obviously hadn't come from there, then. I looked around, but saw no one.

Then I looked at the steel frame. Did something glint over there? I couldn't tell. I kept my own head low, not wanting anyone to see me.

Another soldier joined the first. "We have a doctor inside. Hurry!"

The person kneeling was Daniel. The brown-haired girl was on the ground. Daniel held up bloody hands.

"You did this, man. I'm not bringing her in there so you can finish her off."

He slipped his hands underneath her back, and lifted her. I knew exactly how that felt, the hot viscous liquid, the slowly chilling skin. Her eyes were closed, and her arms dangled.

"Careful," the soldier yelled. "You could hurt her worse. We're sending out the doctor. Just stay there until he—"

"Stay away!" Daniel screamed. He staggered under the girl's weight, then stumbled toward me.

Except for the shouting, the area was quiet. No more shots, no one else moving. Rhondelle and the two boys had reached the car and were tugging the doors open.

Daniel ran toward them, the girl's body bouncing in his arms. "Make room for her, make room!" he screamed. "Somebody start the car."

Rhondelle got into the driver's seat, and the car rumbled to life. Soldiers poured out of the building—about ten in all—shouting, telling Daniel to bring the girl inside, they'd already called an ambulance, they had someone there who might save her life.

I clutched the edge of the roof, feeling helpless. I couldn't see who had fired the shot. And I couldn't go down to the street to help the injured girl. I was trapped up there, unable to move.

Daniel shoved the girl into the car and then crawled in beside her. The car peeled away as someone pulled the back door closed. Two soldiers stopped in the middle of Pearl Street. Another chased after the car, yelling at them to stop.

I couldn't stay where I was. It would only be a matter of time before the police arrived and searched the entire area. I grabbed the urine-filled bottle, put it in the sack with the rest of my garbage and the one still-full soda bottle, and crawled to the next roof over.

I hurried down the second fire escape, pausing at the bottom only to toss the urine-filled bottle down a sewer grate. Then I walked up Broad Street to the old Standard Oil Building. I knew there was another subway stop somewhere nearby, and I had to take it.

I had to leave before I got blamed for the shooting. Still, it felt strange to walk away from a crisis instead of help with it.

The subway was on Broadway, right near the Standard Oil Building, just like I remembered. I hurried down the steps and took the first northbound train.

I studied the other passengers, memorizing their faces. I wanted to know if someone had followed me.

I got off at Times Square, tossed the bag into a nearby garbage, and walked north. The streets were empty. Only a few people straggled by, looking at closed shops.

It felt very surreal. I was shaking, trying to figure out what exactly had happened. The soldiers hadn't shot anyone. Contrary to Daniel's accusations, a soldier wouldn't have offered to help if the offer weren't sincere. Someone else had fired that shot, and it had echoed like a rifle report.

Then I remembered the night watchman. Had he been doing what I had been doing? Staking out the area, waiting for Daniel and his group to arrive?

Why shoot one of the girls? Why not shoot Daniel?

Or had that shot been meant for Daniel, and had it somehow missed?

I picked up the train again at Columbus Circle. I saw no familiar faces, either in the station itself or in the train. No one had followed me. I leaned my head back against the scratched window.

Daniel had obviously planned something for the Army Induction Center. The map, and their conversation, confirmed that. Someone—a sniper?—had thwarted the plan, but the shots had come from some place other than the army building.

Daniel, however, believed the army was behind it, and that would probably provoke him to attack again.

I had to find out what was going on. I just wasn't sure how.

FORTY-ONE

I realized my next step the moment I walked into the apartment. Jimmy was sprawled on the living room floor reading the newspaper. Tomorrow's paper would report the incident. It would list the name of the girl who had been shot, and what hospital she went to—if Daniel had been smart enough to take her to a hospital.

As panicked as he had been, he probably had. After all, he hadn't shot her. No one in their group had. He just hadn't trusted the soldiers nearby to take care of her.

Jimmy was very glad to see me. Malcolm had just made them lunch, and I joined them, hungrier than I expected to be. I told them what had happened.

"Is that girl gonna die?" Jimmy asked.

"I don't know," I said. "I certainly hope not."

But she had lost a lot of blood. And I wasn't sure that she would survive Daniel's rough treatment either. The reason I dreamed about carrying my fallen comrade wasn't because of the ordeal, but because I had never been sure that my actions—my desperate attempt to save him—hadn't caused his death.

I had lost my chance to get Daniel and his group arrested. But I might be able to get information out of the wounded girl, provided she survived the night.

Jimmy was happy I had returned. He wanted to do something special for the Fourth, and Malcolm had been resisting. I saw no reason to resist. Jim was getting very little enjoyment out of this trip; the least I could do was help him celebrate, even though any sort of celebration felt odd after the last twenty-four hours.

After I took a short nap, I discovered there would be no parade, and no local fireworks. New Yorkers went out of town for that kind of celebration, although one neighbor said she believed we could see some from New Jersey if we went up on the roof.

I couldn't handle another roof. Instead, we walked through Harlem, which seemed unusually deserted. No flags flew, except for one or two from apartment windows.

So in lieu of a parade, I used the day for an impromptu civics lesson, one I felt both boys needed. I showed them houses where famous black Americans had lived. I explained how a black man, Scott Joplin, started an entire musical subgenre—ragtime—which led to blues and jazz and ultimately rock and roll. I showed them where the jazz musicians lived, and the writers of the Harlem Renaissance. I taught them about important black political leaders who helped change America, and who also lived in Harlem—Marcus Garvey and Thurgood Marshall and Malcolm X.

I showed them Madame C. J. Walker's house, and told them that, even in America, a black woman could become the rich head of her own company. I spent the day helping these boys respect their heritage and hoping that some of it, at least, would sink in.

We ended our tour at Mount Morris Park, expecting that we would be able to climb the only remaining fire watch tower in the city. From there we might be able to see some fireworks. But people already sat on its three levels and the stairs leading up to the top, and I didn't want to fight for our place.

So as twilight fell, we slowly walked back to our apartment. At Jimmy's insistence, we bought some firecrackers and sparklers. By the time we reached our street, we had hot dogs, root beers, and two armfuls of sparklers for a midstreet celebration.

Kids were already out there, running with sparking light trailing behind them, making images in the darkening air. Jimmy crammed the rest of his hot dog into his mouth, and grabbed a box of sparklers from me, then ran into the middle of the street toward kids he didn't know to get a light.

Soon he was laughing with pure joy and writing his name in the sky. Malcolm grinned at me, took a box of his own, and walked out there, too, deciding that for once he didn't have to be cool.

I sat on the steps and watched, staring at the phone booth across the street. Would Grace be home, or would she be at Jackson Park with Elijah, watching the fireworks there? I knew I should call her, but I couldn't summon the courage.

Instead, I leaned my elbows on the cool concrete step behind me and thought about my strange day. It had certainly turned my investigation upside down.

Now I had to figure out three things: not just what Daniel planned next or how to stop him, but also who had shot at his group, and why.

FORTY-TWO

The next morning's newspaper said that a student named June D'Amato had been shot while taking a walk near Battery Park with four of her friends. According to the paper, the friends panicked, and drove her to St. Vincent's Hospital. No one seemed to know why she had been shot.

I had no more arguments from Malcolm and Jimmy. They knew I had to investigate on my own. They went back to the Harlem branch of the library while I headed down to the Village to see if June D'Amato was angry at Daniel for allowing her to get hurt, and whether she would tell me exactly what she and Daniel had been up to when she got shot.

I arrived at St. Vincent's sprawling complex at the start of visiting hours, but my promptness did me no good. June D'Amato was in a drug-induced sleep after her second emergency surgery. The nurse on her floor told me that June wouldn't be up to visitors for at least twenty-four hours.

I thanked the nurse and headed back toward the main floor. I had thought June D'Amato my best chance of getting information quickly. Now I realized I would have a lot more work to do.

At least it was still early in the day.

As I headed toward the hospital's main exit, a white man in a suit approached me. He reached into his pocket, pulled out a wallet and opened it, revealing a badge.

My mouth went dry, but I managed to smile, nod, and look slightly confused, like any innocent black man would when approached by a plain-
clothes police officer.

"You the man who just asked to see June D'Amato?" he asked.

I took the badge from him, looked at it, and saw that it was legitimate.
I would have thought the police had finished with June D'Amato yesterday.
The case had to be important for someone to hang around the hospital.

I thought about lying about why I was here. But I decided it would be easier to cooperate. It might also get me some more information on Daniel.
"Yes, I asked about her."

"Why?" the man said. "You're clearly not family."

He was balding, with care lines around his mouth, but the suit fit him
well even though it was cheap. He looked five to ten years younger than I
was, obviously on a career track, and maybe more open-minded than some
of his longer term colleagues.

That was a gamble I was going to have to take.

"I heard she's a friend of Daniel Kirkland," I said.

The cop raised his eyebrows, asking a question without bothering with
the words.

"I'm from Chicago," I said. "I know Daniel's mother. He went missing
several months ago, and I've been looking for him. I just came down from
New Haven. He'd been attending Yale, but he dropped out."

"And you think June D'Amato knows about him."

"I had heard they were close," I said.

The cop stuffed his badge back in his breast pocket. "Where'd you hear
that?"

"In New Haven. I think I went to every hippie house and drug den in the
city, trying to find Daniel."

"You a private detective?" the cop asked.

"Kinda," I said. "I'm a freelance investigator for a number of Chicago
businesses."

If he wanted to check on me, he could. I'd give him the numbers if he
doubted me. "This is a far cry from Chicago."

"Yes, it is," I said. "Grace didn't have anyone else to turn to, and I had
some time coming to me, so I took it as a vacation, to see if I could find her
son."

"This Grace," he said, "she single?"

"Why the third degree, officer?" I asked.

"Detective," he said, correcting me like I knew he would. Then he sighed, relaxed his shoulders, and extended a hand. I was relieved to see it. Many white Chicago cops would never have shaken the hand of a black man. "Detective Mackey O'Conner."

"Bill Grimshaw," I said, shaking his hand.

"You know that June D'Amato was shot."

I wasn't quite sure how to play this. "I knew she was injured."

"Shot," he said. "Right outside the Army Induction Center yesterday. Some friends of hers brought her to the emergency room, then took off. This Kirkland, I take it he's colored?"

"He's black, yes," I said, adding a correction of my own.

"He might've been the one who brought her in. One of our guys talked to a black kid for a minute before he ran."

"But why are you here today?" I asked again, hoping I wasn't pushing too hard. I was trying to play the insurance investigator who did claim fraud and was out of his depth in the big city. I hoped the act convinced. "Is she in trouble?"

"I suspect so. She's the fourth person in her circle of friends to get shot."

I started. I knew nothing about this. "Was Daniel shot?" I asked, even though I knew he hadn't been.

O'Connor shook his head. "The victims are Ned Jones, Victor McCleary, and Joel Grossman. Names ring any bells?"

"No," I said, making a note of the names. "Were they all shot this week?"

"Over the summer," O'Connor said.

"They die?"

"No."

"You have any idea why they were shot?"

He shrugged. "They've been associating with some unsavories. Protesting—which ain't against the law—but this group—D'Amato's group—it's starting to get violent. There've been some assaults, and some threats, and one unexploded bomb."

"June has a group?" I asked, sounding as naïve as I could. "And it's violent?"

"We think so," O'Connor said. "We're watching a number of these militant antiestablishment groups. Your girl here, she just might've gotten some of her own medicine."

"You think someone she knew shot her?"

"I don't know what to think," he said. "First, there's the location. There's a lot of military folk down there, even on the Fourth, and not all take kindly to these kids, you know? But that's a long way between shouting at some kids and shooting at them. You got any military background, Mr. Grimshaw?"

"I served in Korea," I said.

"So no sniper training," he said.

That was an interesting statement. He sounded almost disappointed. In that statement was an assumption I had heard before. The younger vets seemed to believe that snipers were only used in Vietnam. I wasn't going to dissuade him.

I thought again of the echoing rifle shot, and that figure, standing on the steel girders outlined by streetlights. A sniper had crossed my mind yesterday. O'Connor simply confirmed one of my own suspicions.

"You think I'm a sniper and I came here to finish the job?" I asked, pretending an affront I didn't feel. "I came here to talk to her, just like I told you."

"I figured as much, but it doesn't hurt to check," he said. "Where were you yesterday?"

"With my son and a friend, walking through Harlem," I said. "My son's eleven, so if you want to verify my alibi, I suggest you talk to him before I do."

"No need," O'Connor said. "Have to ask everyone, you know."

"What makes you think a sniper shot her?" I asked. "Did you find a nest?"

His eyes met mine for half a second, measuring, evaluating. After a moment, he said, "What we found is police business."

I shook my head, as if I were out of my depth. "If June is involved with a group," I asked as if I were trying to get things straight, "does it have a name?"

"We think so, but we're not sure," he said. "These kids change their allegiances as fast as they change their clothes. Initially, we thought we had an offshoot of the Students for a Democratic Society. Then we hear about Black Panthers, but most of these kids are white. Then we hear about the War at Home Brigade, dedicated to bringing Vietnam to America."

I thought of that graffiti we had found in the Barn in Fair Haven.

"You know something about that?" he asked.

"I'd heard it," I said. "Up in New Haven, something about bringing the war home. It never made sense until now."

"I thought these college kids were local," he said. "D'Amato's going to City College. But we get lots of wackos down here in the Village. This's become some kind of gathering place. It's hard to keep track of all of them."

"That's why you can't tell me if she's been with Daniel," I said.

"All I know is that in the last month or two, I've seen more coloreds in her group. It'd been pretty white before that. But we've been having mixing, if you pardon the expression, ever since the Panthers got arrested."

"The Panthers in New Haven?"

He squinted at me. "Here. They call themselves the Panther 21. You don't know about this?"

"Actually, I don't."

"They threatened to bomb some department stores, the Botanical Garden, and a few police stations."

More bombs. I didn't like this.

"The Botanical Garden?" I asked, struck by the incongruity.

"Don't ask me to explain these nutballs," O'Connor said. "I just read about them. But I did notice after they got arrested, lots more Afros down here, folks trying to get involved, I think, you know, fight for something I guess, even if it is a bunch of criminals."

"So you think June is somehow involved with militants."

"We know she is," O'Connor said. "That's why I'm here, seeing who comes to visit her."

"Do you have anything on them?"

"Not enough to arrest most of them," he said. "Just some suspicions. But a few questions might get to the bottom of that dud bomb. You let us know if you find this Daniel. We'll want to talk to him."

"All right," I said. "If you answer me one question."

"Go ahead," he said.

"If you found a sniper's nest, why did you think she was shot by one of her own?"

His smile was slow, almost as if he found my question amusing. But his gaze had some respect in it. "Didn't say we found a nest. But suppose we did, a what-if, if you will, we can't trust it to be accurate. These kids are good at street theater, and we sure know that they're not above using one of their own to make a point. After all, they want to bring the war home."

That chill ran right through me. This sounded very familiar. It was the same technique Daniel had used at Yale. He had falsely accused someone and attacked him, trying to make his story more believable. That had backfired. Yale hadn't kicked out the people Daniel wanted, but it had also worked in an odd way. Daniel had learned that he could upset an entire group of people with a big lie.

"This ring some kinda bell to you?" O'Connor asked.

"It certainly makes me wonder," I said, "what these kids were doing at the induction center on the Fourth of July. You think they were trying to bomb the place?"

"Possible," O'Connor said, "but more likely I think they were scouting, looking where they could make the most ruckus during the week, where they could cause the most trouble and get the most attention."

"Then your street theater theory doesn't make sense," I said. "Why call attention to themselves yesterday? Why not wait until these offices were open?"

"They might've been practicing that, too. These kids aren't trained. A real sniper would've hit that girl and killed her right off, but she's gonna live through this. All four of these kids have survived. Either that's one bad sniper, or someone who's playing at it."

I wondered if O'Connor had ever tried to shoot like a sniper. Firing a rifle over a long distance, adjusting for wind velocity and trajectory, was an advanced skill not many good shots could manage. The fact that the shooter had actually hit someone, not the street or the building, led me to believe that the shooter was not playing.

"If I were you, I'd watch your back," O'Connor said. "In fact, I'd go home to Chicago, tell that woman you're interested in that you couldn't find her kid, although you'll probably get tons of points for trying, and then let it go. If he's involved at all—and it sounds like he very well might be—then you're in way too deep. Let us professionals handle this."

He pulled a small notebook out of his pocket, flipped the notebook open, and grabbed the matching pen from the protector in the breastpocket of his white shirt. He scrawled Daniel's first name, then asked me how to spell Kirkland.

I told him.

"How's about the names of those companies you freelance for?" O'Connor asked.

"I'll give you two," I said, and gave him the contact names, the address, and the phone number for Bronzeville Home, Health, Life and Burial Insurance, and the address, phone number, and Laura's name at Sturdy. Just saying her name made me long for her. I missed her more than I wanted to admit.

"You never told me what division you work for," I said to him.

"Homicide," he said, and flipped the notebook closed.

"Someone's died, then," I said.

He shook his head. "We handle attempted murder, too, and that's this case. Then there's the War at Home Brigade. We think we got a badly beaten security guard at a construction site we can tie to them. The feds want to take this, but we're holding them off."

"The FBI?" I asked, hoping that my sudden feeling of panic didn't come out in my voice. I had just given my address to this man, and he might have ties with the FBI. I didn't want them to notice me ever again.

"Not the febbies, but the Bureau of Alcohol, Tobacco, and Firearms. The night the security guard got attacked, someone stole a lot of dynamite. That gets regulated by the feds, and they want a piece of this. We've been giving them evidence, but they're busy enough. Kids are setting off bombs all over the country right now, and the ATF oversees a lot of those investigations. They're shorthanded—they weren't designed for this kind of long-term warfare." O'Connor shook his head. "I'm not sure what this country's coming to, but I have to tell you, it's not the place I was born in."

It wasn't the place I was born in either. In that world, I never would have had this conversation with a white cop. I would have been arrested on suspicion of something immediately, maybe even the shooting of June D'Amato.

But O'Connor wasn't making a move against me. He seemed to take me for the man I had presented myself as, although I knew he would go back to the precinct and check my credentials.

"You find this Kirkland," O'Connor said, "you let us know."

"I will," I said.

"And don't get involved in the D'Amato investigation," he said. "It's a police matter now."

"Can I at least go down to the site?" I asked.

"What are you, ghoulish?" he asked.

I shook my head. "I'd just like to see if anyone saw Daniel there."

"You got a picture of the kid?"

I fished in my pocket. I hadn't had to use Daniel's pictures through most of this investigation, but I had put it in my wallet after needing it a few times. I took out the shot. It didn't look much like Daniel now: The eyes were calmer, happier, his face thicker, his hair tamer. He looked like a wild-eyed revolutionary these days.

"Never saw this kid, but I'll keep my eye out," O'Connor said. "Can I keep this?"

"It's the only one I have," I lied.

He handed it back to me. "One more thing. I need a local contact address for you."

I had hoped he would forget that. I gave him a fake address, and told him I didn't have a phone.

"We need you, there are other ways to get you," he said with a grin. "Don't get in trouble now."

He tapped his notebook against his hand, then walked back into the main area of the hospital.

My heart was pounding. I hadn't noticed that during our discussion. But I had been concentrating on the words and my half-truths instead of on how I felt.

A sniper's nest. Probably with some shell casings, so the police knew that the nest had been used when June was shot. Which meant that the police had the trajectory of the shot, as well as some secondary evidence to lead them to the place where the shot had originated.

Someone trained, shooting at a militant group of college kids, wounding four of them.

I had three other names, three more places to go.

O'Connor had given me more of a gift than he realized.

FORTY-THREE

I left the hospital, and went to the New York Public Library on Fifth Avenue. I loved the huge building with the stone lions guarding the entrance. It was, to me, everything a library should be: grand, and gorgeous. I went inside, enjoying the coolness, and then went to the periodicals room.

O'Connor had given me the names of three victims, implied they were all students, and told me they'd been shot over the summer. It was a limited time range.

I skimmed the *New York Daily News,* which seemed to adore shootings, going backwards from July third to the beginning of summer.

Gradually, I got the information I needed. Victor McCleary had been shot near a bar on Christopher Street on June 27, during something the *Daily News* called the Queer Riot. Joel Grossman had been shot in Washington Square Park earlier in the month, during a meeting about the Lower Manhattan Expressway. Ned Jones had been shot in Central Park, at a protest rally just after Memorial Day. No one at the paper seemed to think the shootings were related.

Obviously O'Connor had information that the police hadn't given to the media.

The *Daily News* listed all three men's addresses. I wrote the addresses down on some scrap paper, pocketed it, and left, feeling better than I had in hours. Those three might tell me more about Daniel, give me a hint as to his plans, and, perhaps, have information about the shooter.

Before I talked with them, though, I went back to Battery Park. I wanted to see the shooting site up close, to see if there was anything I had missed.

The neighborhood looked like a completely different place. People filled the streets. The barbershop across the street from the army building had men in both of its chairs and more waiting against one wall. Even the haberdashers next door had a few customers. Cars drove tentatively along Whitehall, most of the drivers looking toward the park and the Upper Bay, probably trying to figure out how to get there, through the double-parked cars and past the DO NOT ENTER signs.

The main doors to the induction center were open. Two military police stood guard, their uniforms crisp, their heads straight ahead, as if they were statues. A number of military personnel went in and out: soldiers, their uniforms wrinkled with the heat, showed their degree of experience in the way they moved. Most had crew cuts and carried their caps under their arms.

Several young men, their hair so freshly mowed that their skulls shone, went inside carrying paperwork. But there were no recruits standing in line. Either they had already gone in to begin their day-long wrangle with the U.S. government, or the main part of the induction center was closed on this holiday weekend.

I remembered how it felt to go to an induction center that first day: the strange commands, the harsh sergeants, the unexpected humiliation. My strongest memory was standing in a bland room with fluorescent lights, stripped to my underwear, a bunch of skinny white boys—also nearly naked—standing beside me, a few of them swearing at me under their breath because they felt embarrassed and had to take it out on someone.

I moved a little farther down the street, looked up, and scanned the rooftops. If O'Connor had been right, and there had been a sniper, any one of the roofs on these nearby buildings would have made a perfect nest. The nearby stores would have worked as well. If the sniper gained the proper access, it would have taken little to shoot from one of the doorways or an upstairs open window.

But I hadn't seen anyone in those places, just on that partially finished skyscraper to the east. I faced it, saw that the level where I had seen the man was visible, even from this spot.

One of the military police saw me and, with a slight movement of his right hand, beckoned someone from inside. An officer came out, his uniform crisp despite the heat. He was black and had that official don't-fuck-with-me attitude that I had taken for confidence before I joined the service.

"Help you?" he asked.

"Yeah," I said, deciding I had nothing to lose. I had already given my information to the police, and O'Connor knew I'd be down here. "My name's Bill Grimshaw. I'm a private detective from Chicago. I'm looking for a young man who might have been here yesterday when that girl was shot."

The corners of his eyes narrowed, and I hoped he wouldn't ask for my PI license.

"That young man wouldn't be here today," he said, not denying there had been a shooting, as I had expected.

"I thought maybe he might be. I was playing a hunch. I figured he got his notice to report. I figured he might have been here yesterday to plan something to shut the place down so that he wouldn't have to."

"If that's what they were planning, those kids weren't here long enough yesterday to get anything done."

So the officer had been here. Good. He might be able to give me more information than O'Connor, provided I didn't ask too many leading questions.

"Really? I thought they were here for a couple of hours. I couldn't tell from what I'd heard. I thought that it was some kind of Fourth of July protest."

"Nope," he said. "We were prepared for that after last year."

"What happened last year?"

"Some distraught mother put the blame on the army instead of the Communists for the loss of her son. She chained herself to the building, along with a few other protestors. I always thought it a shame. Her son died a hero. He wouldn't've wanted her to tarnish his legacy."

"So you were prepared for the same thing this year," I said.

"We had some people stationed inside, and no," he said, seeing my next question, "they couldn't have had anything to do with the shooting. The girl was shot right there."

He swept a hand toward the closest corner of the granite. It was whiter than the rest, and had obviously been cleaned.

"No one from inside the building could've made that shot," he said.

"I wouldn't have expected it," I said. "I'm a veteran, too. I know we don't go around shooting people for expressing opinions, as much as we disagree with them."

For the first time, he smiled at me. "Where'd you serve?"

"Korea," I said.

"You volunteer?" he asked.

"Yeah," I said. "Truman inspired me."

His smile was wistful. "Me, too."

"But you stayed."

"I fit. At least we can get promoted on merit here," he said. "The rest of the world isn't like that."

"I know." I glanced at the cleaned-up wall. "Kids today are different, aren't they?"

His gaze followed mine and he sighed. "Some aren't. I'd say the majority of kids we get are ready to serve. Some are scared, but that's healthy to me. Then we get these . . ."

He paused, obviously censoring himself.

"It's all right," I said. "I've heard it before."

He shook his head. "You said it already. They got a right to their opinion, even if I don't agree. And I don't agree. We all owe this country. If we're called to serve, we serve. We don't lie about our intelligence or try to get out of it. Some of these kids come in and haven't bathed for days. Some of them purposely stain their underwear and don't wash them, trying to make us believe they're too crazy to know hygiene. Most of them got out in the early years. We're on to them now. Them and those doctors who write phony passes, and the goofy drugs they take to make them seem weirder than they are."

I shook my head. Maybe someone had thought to do that to get out of Korea, but I had never seen it. Once upon a time, I wouldn't even have been able to imagine it.

"However," I said, "I do understand these kids' desire not to get shot."

The MP laughed. "Hell, we all felt that at one time or another." Then his smile faded. "But you know that sometimes freedom is worth dying for."

I knew that, too. I knew a lot of people who had died for freedom in our own country, including my friend Martin.

"I talked to a cop a little while ago about the shooting," I said. "A detective O'Connor."

The MP spat, then wiped his mouth with the back of his hand, making his opinion of O'Connor known without saying a word.

"He told me that—"

"A soldier did it, right?" The MP couldn't wait for me to finish. "Bastard has no clue what it's like down here. None of the people in our building would've shot anyone, and no one would've climbed on any roof to hit those kids. I *told* him that."

His anger surprised me. I decided to run with it instead of asking my original question.

"He blamed you?" I asked.

"Me and all the others in the building. But like I said, anyone who understands how sniping works would've known that we didn't shoot that kid." He glanced at the wall. People walking past us looked curiously at me, then looked away. They seemed to think I was in trouble. "It was bad enough that those kids wouldn't even let us help her. We had a medic in the building, but the kids wouldn't let us near her. One kid picks her up and hauls her off like she's a sack of flour. I mean, don't they teach kids anything in schools? He could've made her worse. I'll bet he did."

"It's possible," I said. "She had a second emergency surgery this morning."

"I wasn't even sure she'd make it to the hospital the way she was bleeding. Those kids were lucky they had a car." He shook his head. "How'd we end up the enemy here? You know? The kids think we'd hurt the girl, the cops think we shot her. We're just doing our job—and that does not include shooting young people, no matter how irritating they are."

I had found some well within him, or maybe he'd reached his last straw yesterday. I decided to push.

"I'd heard," I said slowly, "that the young man, Daniel, was involved in a group called the War at Home Brigade."

"Yeah, they've been leafleting us. A coupla other places, too. Telling us to pull out of Nam or they'd show us what it was like to experience war."

"Just recently?" I asked.

"The last month or so. But we get so much nutty stuff, we just put it in a file and hope it never becomes useful."

"It makes me wonder," I said. "Perhaps these kids are living up to their name."

It wasn't hard for him to make the leap. "And shooting one of their own? That's a hell of a thing to accuse them of."

"They don't trust the police or the military and these are kids of privilege, not raised the way you and I were."

"Except maybe a couple of them," he said. "There were one or two blacks in the group, including the kid who ran off with the girl. They might have reasons for distrusting uniforms. That's one of the reasons I got one, so our people have something to trust."

I nodded. I remembered that impulse too. Only it had failed for me. "I was just thinking that maybe they're trying something, maybe they're trying to use a creative method to shut you down."

He frowned, then glanced over his shoulder to see if he was needed at the main doors. People were still going in and out—a secretary carrying files like they were schoolbooks, a young man with his head down, his hair flopping over his eyes, as he carried a briefcase inside, a middle-aged man with perfect posture walking with military precision—but the other two MPs weren't moving at all.

This MP had made that move to give himself time to think about what he'd say to me. I wondered if he was beginning to regret the conversation.

"You know," he said as he turned back toward me. "If it'd happened any other day, I might've thought you were right. But no one's here on the Fourth. The building would've been locked up tight, no one around, if it weren't for last year's protests, and no one knew that there'd be soldiers anywhere near the place. We didn't announce it. And even if they knew, they'd need witnesses, and there were none. Maybe if they'd done something in Battery Park or near the Statue of Liberty, maybe then. But the timing's off. And it doesn't fit with the threats."

"The leaflets?" I asked.

He nodded. "Those things threaten to wipe us off the map. You can't do that with a rifle. I've been thinking bombs."

I felt my breath catch. "Can I see the leaflets?"

"Sure," he said. "Let me get them for you."

It only took him a minute to get me the leaflets. He let me look at them, watching me the entire time.

The leaflets were crude. Mimeographed on yellow paper, they all seemed to be the work of the same machine if not the same hand. Some of the drawings looked familiar—giant soldiers hovering over tiny Vietnamese people, an evil-looking Uncle Sam squashing an tiny Asian child, and drawing after drawing of explosions.

Some of the leaflets were just rhetoric, obviously written by an educated person:

> *The genocidal war in Vietnam continues, even if the futility of America's military effort there and the aroused conscience of the American people have forced the government to make gestures toward a negotiated peace....*

I skimmed most of it, having seen similar arguments before. When the MP had handed me the leaflets—extra copies that he didn't need—I had been stunned at the number of them. He said they'd been receiving dozens of them every week, often on different color paper and with different wordings.

Finally, in the middle of the stack, I found it. Buried in a page of argument against Vietnam was this:

> We also cry out against the other war, the war against black America. The funeral of Dr. Martin Luther King, Jr., was followed by close to forty black funerals...

> ...We demand that black intellectuals in our country be given the opportunity to speak to the young generation, through schools and other platforms, in terms of black cultural tradition, dignity, and militancy...

The document ended with a demand to stop both wars—the war on blacks and the war in Vietnam.

That smacked of Daniel to me, and jibed with what I'd been hearing about his concerns at Yale and in New Haven. I folded that leaflet up and tucked it in my back pocket. The rest I handed back to the MP. I didn't need them, and if anyone else wanted them, I knew where to direct them.

I thanked the MP for his time, then left the induction center, feeling more disturbed than I had when I entered it.

The War at Home Brigade had certainly left its mark on this neighborhood. And Daniel's reaction to that shooting hadn't given me any additional confidence in the rationality of his actions.

I found a coffee shop nearby on Pearl Street and had a light lunch, mostly because I wanted the chance to sit and think rather than because I was hungry. The day had turned oppressively humid, and I was glad to get off my feet.

I pulled out the list I had made of names and addresses, seeing which were near my location. None of them were real close. I'd either have to walk some distance in this heat or take an even hotter subway ride.

But I couldn't stop now. I had to finish this.

I had to find out what Daniel was planning, and I had to stop him.

FORTY-FOUR

The nearest victim, Joel Grossman, lived on Macdougal and West Eighth, not far from Washington Square Park. I had walked from the coffee shop, deciding to avoid the subway in the heat. Even though the train cars were air-conditioned, the stations were not, and the hot air grew foul by midday.

When I reached the park, I found more construction signs, all of them announcing that the western end of the park would be closed starting on July 15. Graffiti covered the official words, mostly spray-painted swear words, although on one sign someone had written: *Its about freakin' time*.

Grossman's address was in a group of brick houses that seemed quaintly Village to me. They had been carved up into tiny apartments and had discreet buzzers near the door. I pushed the button next to Grossman's name but got no answer. I waited for some time, tried the main door once, and discovered it was locked.

A white woman with long brown hair poked her head out of a nearby window. "You buzzing for Joel?"

"Yeah," I said.

"Thought so," she said. "I can hear the buzzer in my place."

"Is he all right?" I asked.

"He was hurt a few weeks back," she said. "He couldn't stay alone so he went up to stay with his folks in the West Nineties."

"Do you know exactly where?" I asked.

"No," she said, "but his dad's Jerome, so I suppose you could look it up."

I thanked her and headed down the block. The West Nineties were a far cry from here. The Village always prided itself on being bohemian. If Grossman's neighbor thought anything of my skin color, she didn't show it. In the West Nineties, I'd be as suspect as I was on Chicago's Lake Shore Drive.

No one was home at the next address on my list either—Victor McCleary, the young man who'd been shot a week before. He lived in an old tenement apartment on Perry Street. The address wasn't far from the Christopher Street shooting site.

None of McCleary's neighbors had seen him, and none of them seemed interested in him either. I gave up and took the train north. The last address wasn't far from mine. The very first victim lived in Morningside Heights in a student apartment. Which made sense, since the paper said he had enrolled at Columbia University.

The apartment was in a drab white stone building not too far from the park. I trudged there, feeling grimy from the subway and a day in the heat. I had forgotten how hot this city could get: It didn't have the benefit of cooling breezes off the lake, the way Chicago did.

The doorbells for the apartments were inside the stone arch. Someone had rigged the bells haphazardly. A simple snip of the wires and I could have knocked out the entire system.

I pressed the button for Ned Jones. To my surprise, someone yelled from above, "Whozzit?"

I backed out of the archway and looked up, shielding my eyes. A shirtless redheaded white man, wearing a sling over his left arm, peered down at me from a landing on the fire escape.

"My name's Bill Grimshaw," I said. "I'm investigating some shootings. I'm looking for Ned Jones."

"That's me."

"I was wondering if I could talk to you."

"Sure," he said. "C'mon up."

He slid the fire escape bars down toward me. I stepped into the nearby alley, grabbed the ladder, and tugged it down. Then I climbed up, hand over hand, until I reached the landing with Jones on it. A large window opened into his apartment. He sat on the sill. He was wearing a pair of cutoff jeans and nothing else. A lawn chair sat on the far end of the landing, its metal legs braced precariously on the landing's iron bars.

"You want a beer?" he asked.

"No, thanks," I said, "but water'd be nice."

"You're in luck," he said. "We got that."

He swung his legs inside the apartment and padded off. I looked around. The landing had a good view of the alley and the apartments on the other side. If I craned my neck to the right, I caught the edge of the Columbia campus. If I craned farther to the left, I saw only more apartments and the street beyond.

When he came back, Jones had a glass in his good hand. I took the glass from him and extended an arm to help him onto the landing, but he shrugged me off.

"I'm getting used to this. It's healing slow. The bullet did a lot of damage." Jones tilted his head as if he were investigating me. His eyes were a dark auburn, matching his hair. His skin was pale, almost translucent, in the sunlight. "It's about time someone started looking into my shooting."

He didn't ask to see any identification, and I didn't offer any.

"You know there've been others," I said.

"In the park?" He sounded surprised.

"I don't know about that," I said. "I do know a number of young people have been shot in the city. The most recent was June D'Amato."

"Junie." He swung onto the windowsill, and frowned. "She okay?"

"She's had two emergency surgeries since yesterday," I said. "She's not conscious yet."

"Jeez," Jones said. "When'd this happen?"

"Yesterday morning, at the Armed Forces Induction Center on Whitehall."

"Idiots," he mumbled.

"Who?" I asked.

"The gang, whatever the hell they're calling themselves. I suppose they went down there to show their might."

"I was told they were planning something."

Jones shook his head. "These guys don't know when to quit."

"I thought you were part of the group."

" 'Were' being the operative word," Jones said. "I was planning to drop out when this happened. In fact, the last thing I remember before the shooting was arguing about the direction of the movement. I'm yelling something about nonviolence being the only way to fight, and whappo! I get zapped with a bullet, knocked to the ground, and I am out of it. Next thing I know, I'm in Columbia Presbyterian with IVs in me and a doctor hovering over me, telling me not to panic."

"Sounds serious," I said.

"Shock," he said. "That bullet went through my upper arm and destroyed some nerves. For a week there, they thought I might not have use of the arm. Now I will, but it'll never be up to normal. I don't have feeling in three of my fingers, probably never will."

I found myself looking at the arm in the sling. His fingers looked thinner and paler than the others, almost bluish.

"What else do you know about the shooting?" I asked.

"The cops say it was random. Someone was probably illegally firing off a gun in the Ramble. Now you're here telling me others have been shot, so I don't know. All I know is that I got hit."

"Three others," I said. "Besides June D'Amato, Joel Grossman and Victor McCleary got shot. All on separate occasions. All lived through the initial shooting, although I haven't been able to talk to any of them to see how they're doing."

"All at 'actions'?" he asked, putting a sarcastic emphasis on the word.

"June and Grossman's were," I said. "McCleary got shot after a riot down on Christopher Street last week."

Jones rolled his eyes. "That damn bar. I told him to stay out of it."

"So you were good friends with him?"

Jones shrugged. "I don't know about that."

"But you were planning to leave the group."

"Oh, yeah," Jones said. "There was new blood, and I really hated the direction. We were an offshoot of the SDS here on campus. We moved away from the militant stuff when some of the students held some buildings on campus hostage last year. Maybe you heard about that?"

Of course I had heard. The Columbia takeover was often cited as the beginning of violent student unrest on campuses all over the United States.

"You didn't participate in that?"

"I was at the early meetings," he said, "and I thought it was stupid. We want to stop the war in Vietnam, so we shut down a building on campus? What does that mean? So I gathered up some like-minded people, and we went our own way, publishing a newsletter, leafleting, giving speeches."

"But that changed," I said.

"Gradually." He propped himself up on the sill. "Some of the guys got caught in the glamour. They rejoined Mark Rudd and those guys—the true SDS they were calling themselves. We were just the other guys for a while. We didn't really have a name. I dropped out—we all did—and worked on stopping the war full-time. I was writing for the *Voice* and for *Rat* and some of the other underground papers, going to marches, you know the drill."

"What changed?" I asked.

"Everything," he said. "Bobby got killed, then the Democratic National Convention, then Nixon got elected. Some of our people began thinking nonviolence wasn't the way—it sure wasn't the way to get noticed any more—and we kept losing people. The new folks coming in had a different agenda."

"Which was?"

"Fight the war at all costs. That's what we were arguing about that afternoon. They wanted to escalate—bring the war home, stop the exploitation of the third world, all that crap. They wanted to work outside the system, and I said I believed in the system, even though it could get really fucked sometimes. You gotta change things from within, you know?"

"Sometimes it takes a while," I said.

"Everything of value is hard," Jones said. "But these new kids, they didn't understand that. And to be fair, no one's talking like that anymore. You been hearing about the fires in Providence? I'm convinced that's some student group, trying to make a point. I met a few of their people. They're just as radical as everyone else."

I hadn't heard about any fires in Rhode Island, but I didn't want to admit it and get him off track. "So you dropped out of the organization."

"It's not for me, man, and the gunshot proved it. It was karma." He grinned at me as he said that last, and tipped his beer my way. He took a long swallow.

"Do you know Daniel Kirkland?" I asked.

"Know him? Hell, I was arguing with him when I got shot. Bastard."

The strong negative reactions to Daniel no longer surprised me.

"He was one of the ones who wanted to move toward violence?" I asked, as if I didn't know.

Jones nodded. "Said he had everything they needed. They just needed a plan."

"Everything?"

Jones shrugged. "I didn't ask him to explain. I got out before I could be implicated. But I'd check out his place. You've gotta find something there."

"What kind of violence was he talking about?"

"What does anyone talk about? Blowing stuff up, mostly."

"Did he have any plans?"

"I don't know. I was stuck on the violence-nonviolence thing. The minute they started talking about bombs, I was outta there."

"But you said that you left because you were shot."

"No, I said I was thinking about leaving before I got shot. In fact, I was telling Daniel I was going to leave. I didn't much like him. And then he's screaming about discrimination, when he came down from Yale, of all places. He wanted to add black issues to the Vietnam stuff, and it just didn't fit—no offense, man."

"None taken," I said.

He tilted his beer at me again, then took another long drink. "I'm just glad to be out. I think I hung around too long as it was."

"Why?" I asked.

His smile became rueful. He balanced the beer on the sill. "I don't know exactly. You give yourself heart and soul to something, you're reluctant to give it up, I think. There was a camaraderie in the early days that I still miss, but it's long gone. It just took me a while to realize it, I think."

"Plus your political differences," I said.

He sighed. "On one level, these guys are right. The marches and the pickets and the newsletters aren't getting us anywhere. But holding people hostage on campus or bombing a building downtown? Seems to me that makes us just as bad as the people we're fighting against."

"Dr. King would've agreed with you," I said.

His gaze met mine. "I always admired him. I think that was the beginning of the end when he died."

It was certainly the end of one phase of my life, and it definitely put the country on a new path.

One bullet.

"What are you going to do now?" I asked him.

Jones held up a book that had been facedown on the landing. *The Federalist Papers*. "Majoring in government and international studies. The sooner we get those warmongering assholes out of power, the better off we'll all be."

I nodded my agreement and silently wished him the best, while not holding out a lot of hope. He hadn't even been able to control his small student organization. I had no idea how he thought he could make inroads in the government at large.

But I knew better than to discourage him. I'd been surprised by people before. I was willing to be positively surprised again.

"You sure you don't know any of Daniel's plans for the violence?" I asked.

Jones shook his head. "Like I said, I didn't want to know."

"Any ideas where he stored his supplies?"

"I figure they're in his girlfriend's apartment," Jones said with deep bitterness. "He brought stuff from New Haven around Memorial Day weekend, saying it was appropriate—a great way to remember the dead."

"Bombing supplies?" I asked.

"That's what I'm guessing. I made it a point not to know." He turned the book over and over in his hands before finally setting it back on the iron landing. "But he was pretty jacked on Memorial Day. Said he found a local supplier."

"Supplier of what?" I asked.

"I don't know that either," Jones said. "But if I had to guess, I'd say dynamite. Daniel was talking about going to some construction company's headquarters that night. And I can't think what a construction company would have that he'd need, except dynamite. Can you?"

O'Connor had said that dynamite was stolen from a construction site. And the Barn had been filled with dynamite from various construction companies. That fit Daniel's pattern.

"If that's what you thought he was doing, why didn't you call the police?" I asked.

Jones looked at me like I was crazy. "Pigs hated us, man. Going to the cops just wasn't our way. It's still kinda hard for me. Honestly, that's why I didn't invite you in. I'm trying to readjust my thinking. But after you've been teargassed a few times and hit on the head with a billy club, it's hard, you know?"

I did know. "I'm not offended. I just figured if you're concerned that Daniel and the others are going to do something harmful, why didn't you turn them in, even anonymously?"

"I just wasn't in that space, I guess." Jones finished his beer and set the bottle down. "Lucky for me, nothing in the city's been bombed in the last month. Then I might've thought of it. But until you came, it never crossed my mind."

"You gonna do it now?" I asked.

He shook his head. "I told you about it. Now it's your problem. I've done enough."

FORTY-FIVE

I left Ned Jones feeling shaken. He seemed like a good, responsible kid, yet he didn't think it his duty to report that people he knew were planning to bomb parts of the city.

I'd wandered into another world, one that made no sense to me. If I had been in Jones's shoes, I would have gone to the police. But at the moment, I had nothing new to offer. I knew that O'Connor was investigating the War at Home Brigade, and I knew that the military had reported the leaflets.

And so far, that was all. All but my suspicions.

I walked the handful of blocks to the place we were calling home. The street itself felt unfamiliar. The nearby precinct made me nervous. Even though some children were in the middle of the street, playing stickball, a number of older kids were huddled in a corner, talking to two young men wearing the signature black leather jackets and berets of the Black Panthers.

No one said hello to me as I hurried along the sidewalk. I took the steps two at a time, and let myself into the warm building. I made notes until dinner, trying to put myself in Daniel's crazy head, and then I went to the restaurant where I was supposed to meet Jimmy and Malcolm.

They were happy to see me, and we ate as if we were really tourists having a nice vacation.

A gunshot echoed through the neighborhood at three A.M. I scrambled awake, and was halfway out of my room before I even realized what I had heard. Malcolm and Jimmy hurried into the hall as well.

We stayed there, away from the windows, as more gunfire rang outside. We waiting until the shooting stopped, and then slowly, quietly, crept back to bed.

In the morning, no one discussed the shootings. I had to press a clerk in a nearby bodega before anyone acknowledged they'd heard anything.

"Saturdays," said the young man running the place, "it gets crazy sometimes. You get used to it."

I wasn't sure I'd get used to it, and I didn't want Jimmy to. I took the fresh bagels and the newspaper I bought back to the apartment.

I had another day of searching ahead of me. Malcolm and Jimmy had another day of finding things to do, away from the apartment.

"I could help," Malcolm said. "Maybe go talk to Rhondelle myself or head to this *Rat* place, see what I can learn."

"I don't want Jimmy anywhere near that row house," I said.

"It can't be worse than staying here," Jim mumbled from behind the comics.

I sighed. Shootings in Central Park, shootings on the block, shootings everywhere. Jimmy had a point.

But I wasn't going to give in.

"If you want to help," I said, "I have some tasks for you."

Malcolm glanced at Jimmy. "I have a hunch this isn't going to be fun."

"You asked," Jimmy said, folding the comics in front of him. "Whatcha need, Smoke?"

"Newspaper work, which you proved so good at in New Haven."

Jimmy rolled his eyes in disgust. "It's sunny. Can't we go to a lake or something?"

"There aren't any lakes close by." I didn't tell them about the beaches at Coney Island. I didn't want them to go that far today. "You're better off going to the library again. It's air-conditioned."

Jimmy brought up his paper. "I'm thinking I maybe'll go to church. I can't lie to Althea when I get home and she's not gonna like that you keep forgetting it's Sunday."

This time, Malcolm sighed. "Church."

I smiled. "It might do you some good."

There were a number of churches on Seventh Avenue, and the famous Riverside Baptist wasn't that far away either. I mentioned that, much to Malcolm's dismay. He knew that church at a strong congregation could last all day—with people coming and going as the spirit moved them.

"Library's better than church," Malcolm said.

"I promised." There was a whine in Jimmy's voice. "And I'm going even if you don't."

Malcolm looked at me, like he expected me to get him out of it.

I shrugged. "You guys have to stay together. I'm going to hunt for those bombing materials."

"And then we leave, right, Smoke?" Jimmy asked.

I nodded. "When I find them, and report them to the police, that's when we leave."

After I left the apartment, I walked until I found a pay phone outside of the neighborhood. Sometime during the night, I had decided that keeping my suspicions to myself wasn't a good idea. I had one more piece of information than the police did, and it was time they knew about it.

I dropped a dime into the phone, and called the police station. I had to go through two precincts before I found O'Connor's.

To my surprise, he was in.

"Look," I said after I identified myself. "I found out yesterday that Daniel Kirkland may be the one who stole dynamite from a construction site. I suspect he might have it in a location out of Harlem, but I don't know where that is."

"Why're you calling me?" O'Connor asked.

"Besides doing my civic duty?" I snapped. Maybe this was why Jones hadn't called the police. "I'm telling you because if you have Daniel under surveillance—and I trust you do—now's the time to watch him. Since I mentioned the dynamite to him, he might get scared and move it. Or try to use it."

"Figure he's that afraid of you?" O'Connor asked.

"I figure he's that paranoid," I said.

"You heading home now that you found him? Or are you gonna try to play the hero and get him out of trouble?"

This guy was good. He put together, just from one remark, that I knew where Daniel was. I had slipped up.

"I'm past playing the hero with this kid," I said. "I want to see him stopped. He's dangerous."

"Yeah," O'Connor said. "That's my take on him, too."

"You didn't tell me yesterday that you knew him."

"You didn't tell me yesterday that you'd already found him. We saw you going into that row house on the third, Mr. Grimshaw."

I froze. I hoped they only saw me, not that they had photographed me. And I hoped they hadn't seen me come out with that gun.

However, O'Connor had had a chance to arrest me the day before. He hadn't done it, and he already knew I had a connection to Daniel.

"We'll keep an eye out," O'Connor said. "I can't promise anything."

Then he hung up. I stared at the phone for a moment, then hung up too.

He had obviously checked the references I'd already given him, and the Grimshaw identity had held up, at least for the moment. But I had screwed up. If someone else saw me, if someone else recognized me, I would be in real trouble.

Jimmy would be in real trouble.

I rested my head against the phone. I was shaking. First thing in the morning, we would go to the rental agent, turn in the keys, then take the train to the Port Authority. I'd make sure we weren't followed, and then we'd take a bus to the van.

I didn't want to leave right after this phone call. I didn't want to call attention to us by skipping out on the rental agent. I wanted to act like the man I had pretended to be, the insurance investigator who was in over his head.

If we were lucky, O'Connor wouldn't investigate us further.

If we weren't lucky, we wouldn't be able to go back to Chicago either. And I would have to evaluate if Jimmy and I had to change identities—again.

FORTY-SIX

The neighborhood where Joel Grossman's parents lived was as different from my Harlem neighborhood as a street could get. Before I had taken the train here, I had called the Grossmans and asked if I could come up to the apartment to talk to Joel.

"We're happy to cooperate," Mrs. Grossman said. "My boy has had a rough time. Anything we can do to find the person who hurt him, we'll do."

They promised to leave my name with the doorman.

The apartment building was large and imposing—not a rehabbed mansion like some of the buildings facing the park, but actually built for apartments. The exterior, with its terra-cotta Egyptian accents and tapestry brick, made me guess the building had been built in the 1920s, not in the late nineteenth century like so much of the neighborhood.

The doorman, who was white, smiled at me as if I were, too, and told me that I was expected. He held the door for me, something no one did outside of Laura's place.

The building's interior was dark, done in red and golds. The golds were supposed to add richness, the red warmth, or so I guessed. Both colors overwhelmed the real mahogany desk, set up like a motel check-in, and the heavy men's club–style furniture.

The doorman had directed me to the tenth floor. As I got onto the small elevator, the doorman picked up the phone. I assumed he was calling upstairs so that the Grossmans knew I was coming.

The elevator opened onto a lush hallway, with red shag carpet, and ivory and gold wallpaper. The overhead lights were chandeliers, hanging every six feet like an interior decorator's nightmare.

At the end of the hall, a middle-aged woman stood in a doorway. She leaned against her open door, clasping ring-bejeweled hands together.

"Mr. Grimshaw?" she asked.

I nodded.

"I hadn't expected—I mean—" She interrupted herself and gave me an apologetic smile. She had obviously figured out halfway through her sentence that she had been about to insult me.

"I take it you're Mrs. Grossman," I said, making my voice as warm as possible. My appearance—not just my blackness, but my size and my scar—intimidated a lot of people. Kindness sometimes got them past it. "I can't thank you enough for taking time from your Sunday to see me."

She smiled. This time it was more relaxed. She had a round face, with dark eyes that had still held some of their youthful beauty. Her hair had gone gunmetal gray, and she wore it up, in an unflattering matronly style.

"My Joel, we nearly lost him," she said as she ushered me into a darkened cave of an apartment. "He just lies in his room, listening to that music and sometimes watching some news. Nobody visits, nobody calls. I think he feels abandoned."

She twisted her hands together as she spoke, the rings making a slight clicking sound as they touched.

"Is that the detective, Mother?" A man came toward me. He was smaller than I was, with delicate gray curls that fell around his face. His features weren't delicate, though. His eyes were heavy-lidded, his nose large. His face was lined, and I wondered if Mrs. Grossman didn't keep her hair up and her style old-fashioned so that her age difference with her husband wouldn't seem so obvious.

"Mr. Grimshaw," she said as we reached the man, "this is my husband, Dr. Grossman."

"Doctor," I said.

He took my hand, and shook it. "You are the lead detective on my son's case?"

"Actually, no," I said, deciding not to lie to these good people more than I had to. "Apparently your son's shooting is related to three others in the city. I'm working on all four, hoping to find a link."

"Three other shootings," Dr. Grossman said. "Did the victims live through them?"

"So far," I said. "Although the young lady shot on Friday has had a rough time of it."

"Her poor parents," Mrs. Grossman said. "Are they holding up?"

"I haven't met them yet, ma'am," I said. "She had just finished her second emergency surgery when I arrived yesterday, and no one was up to talking with me."

"Understandable," Dr. Grossman said. "Were they in the park when they were shot as well?"

"Actually, no," I said. "One of the shootings was in Central Park, another in a different section of the Village, and the last near Battery Park."

"So different," Mrs. Grossman said. "Why do you think they're related to my Joel?"

"Because they all took place during a protest, ma'am, and all of the victims are friends of your son."

"We taught him to be active in his community," Dr. Grossman said, "but the world is a different place than it was when I was a young man. Active now has another meaning. I am not in favor."

"I'm not sure I am either," I said.

"Papa," Mrs. Grossman said to her husband, "Mr. Grimshaw came for Joel. We should let him conduct his business."

"Yes," Dr. Grossman said. "This way."

He led me down a dark corridor. The narrowness of the hallways surprised me. I was used to Laura's apartment, filled with light and floor-to-ceiling windows. I glanced into the living room as I passed it here—there were large windows, but they were covered by heavy brocade curtains. All the doors in the hallway were shut, adding to the closed-in feeling.

Dr. Grossman opened a door at the end of the hall. A sharp odor of camphor and stale sweat wafted toward me.

I peered in. A small man lay in the center of a large bed. Nearly a dozen pillows rested around and behind him. An IV stood to one side, unused, and there were more medical supplies on a nearby table.

His neighbor had said he couldn't be alone, but I hadn't realized he was hurt this badly.

The young man looked at me from his bed, his face gray in the artificial light. "You're the detective?" he asked, and I could hear the same disbelief I had heard in his mother's tones.

"Yes," I said.

He shook his head slightly, then sighed. I went deeper into the room.

"Do you want me to stay, son?" Dr. Grossman asked.

"No, Dad," the young man responded. "It's okay. I can ring if I need you."

His hand moved tiredly toward a bell pull that hung down the wall beside the bed. I hadn't seen anything that old-fashioned outside of the movies.

"All right," Dr. Grossman said. Then he gave me a pointed look. "Go easy on him. He's still frail."

"I will." I went deeper into the room. Someone had moved an upholstered chair close to the bed. A book rested on the cushion. I picked it up and looked at it as I sat down. It was about the upcoming Apollo mission to the moon.

"Think they're gonna make it?" I asked, holding up the book.

"I think it's one of the riskier things we've done," the young man said.

"Me, too," I said. "And I'm not sure the expense is justified. I'm Bill, by the way."

"Joel." He glanced at the door, then back to me. "My folks told me you were coming. You're really investigating the shooting, huh?"

"There've been a few others," I said. "I'm investigating all of them."

He nodded. "I don't remember much. I already told somebody that."

"I know," I said. "But tell me what you can."

"The Lower Manhattan Expressway." He pushed himself up on the pillows, then winced. "People have been fighting it for years. I'd gotten my own place nearby, and it had become home. There were meetings about it, and I finally decided to go to one, in the park. I show up early, talk to a few friends, and then suddenly—nothing. I can't remember any more."

"You were there for the expressway meeting," I said.

He nodded.

"Not for the War at Home Brigade?"

His eyes narrowed. They were as dark and arresting as his mother's. "Who told you that?"

"That you were part of the group?"

"No, that I was there for WHB."

"One of the detectives said you were involved in it."

Joel pursed his lips. "I stopped being part of that group when they changed their name. When someone actually brought a copy of the military's bomb-making pamphlet to a meeting and started demanding that we take stuff out of it for future use. Feh. I told Daniel that I would have nothing to do with him."

"Daniel Kirkland?" I asked.

Joel nodded.

"What was his response?"

"He doesn't understand smaller goals. The expressway doesn't matter, he says to me, because the city doesn't matter. It's part of the capitalist system that oppresses all of us. And so on and so on. I am not a rhetorician. I am a man who gives to his community. I am against the war—who isn't?—but I am not going to kill for peace. There is no logic in that."

He wheezed, then closed his eyes again, taking shallow breaths.

"Are you all right?" I asked.

He nodded, but didn't open his eyes. "Just give me a minute."

I did. He breathed slowly, evenly, until the breaths got deeper. His face had gone even paler.

When he opened his eyes, I asked, "Is all of this from the gunshot?"

"Didn't even have to go to Vietnam to get my war wound." He said it lightly, but he didn't mean it that way.

"When did you drop out of the group?" I asked.

"I didn't drop out," he said. "I left. A number of us did. The ones who are left have come for the spectacle, for the fight, not for any real cause. Or maybe they're slightly crazy, I don't know. It's not for me to know."

"You left the group to Daniel," I said.

"No," Joel said. "Groups change. They follow the strongest personality. And I am not that. Daniel has a charisma, a gift. I call it a gift for lies, but that could be because I seem immune to him. I have a lot of friends—I had a lot of friends—in that group who saw nothing wrong with him, who believed what he had to say, even though it doesn't hold up to rational thought. They tell me that sometimes rational thought isn't enough. Sometimes emotion will turn the tide. Do you believe that?"

"The best leaders I've known have combined both," I said.

He gave me a sideways look. "But we shoot all of those people, don't we?"

Was that how he justified his own shooting? That he had spoken a truth, and the truth had somehow angered someone enough to shoot him?

"Did you think your shooting had political overtones?" I asked.

"One of the cops said that it might've been related to my political activities," he said. "Or it might have been random. They found some shell casings on a rooftop that came from the same kind of gun that fired my bullet, but that's all I know. You tell me. You've read the file."

"That's what I'm trying to figure out," I said. "First Ned Jones gets shot, then you, and then Victor McCleary—"

"Vic?" Joel shifted on the pillow. "When?"

"Last weekend," I said.

"Then it's definitely not connected. We left at the same time. Right after the refrigerator incident."

"The refrigerator incident?" I asked.

Joel rubbed his hand over his face. Then he shook his head slightly.

Feeling like I was about to lose the opening, I said, "I'm not here for any reason except the shooting. Everything else stays in this room."

Joel moved his hand away from his face. I didn't think I'd ever seen anyone whose skin was so white. The veins were outlined in blue, like a river of little bruises running through him.

"Promise?" he whispered.

"Promise," I said.

He glanced at the door. I did, too, but I didn't see either of his parents. Still, I got up and closed the door just enough to give us a little more privacy.

"We were at Daniel's girlfriend's apartment, and we were talking—arguing maybe—me and Vic. We're so damn naïve. We thought if we talked to Daniel, he might see reason. But he wasn't having any of it, although he gave a good argument. He's smart."

"Yes," I said, "he is."

"Sometimes I think that's part of the problem. He's so used to being the smart one. Then he went to Yale, and he wasn't the smart one anymore, so he had to be the radical one." Joel gave a small laugh. "Then I think I'm so full of it. What do I know?"

"Something radicalized him," I said, more to keep Joel talking than anything else.

"Anyway, we were having this argument, and I wanted a beer. So I walk over to the fridge and pull it open. It's full. I don't think I've ever seen a full fridge outside of this place—you know. My folks don't believe in ordering in. Which is beside the point. The point is the fridge was full, but it didn't have food. It had boxes. I crouch down and look at the side of them, and Daniel's yelling at me to close the door, and Vic's going 'What's going on?' and he comes over and Daniel yanks him away, then grabs me and throws me back, but not before I see the EXPLOSIVES written on the side, and the name of a construction company."

Had I looked inside the fridge at the row house? I wouldn't have thought of it. Keeping dynamite inside a fridge was a good idea, though, especially if the dynamite was older and the nitroglycerin unstable.

"Do you remember the name of the company?" I asked.

"Tucker," Joel said. "Tucker Construction."

Had I seen that name in New Haven? I couldn't remember.

"They're doing a bunch of projects around town," Joel was saying. "I think they're one of the crew working on World Trade, even. I know they got part of the Washington Square job, and they want to do the State Office Building in Harlem, but you know how that's going."

"Is that the protest on 125th?" I had seen it as I walked by.

"Yeah. No one wants that building finished any more than they want all this other stuff built. All we seem to be doing is tearing stuff down—important stuff—to build stupid stuff."

I had gotten him onto his soapbox, and I hadn't meant to. But I had been thinking of Tucker Construction. Maybe the name was familiar because I had seen its signs all over the city.

"The dynamite," I prompted.

"Daniel tells me that he's storing it for a friend. Vic says 'What friend?' and Daniel says his dad, which sounded really fishy to me because I distinctly remember Daniel telling me he barely remembered his dad and hadn't seen him since he was like three."

"He said his dad worked at Tucker?"

"And he said that his dad was on the crew working in the Village, and they needed extra storage space for the dynamite so they put it in the fridge. Which, I know, sounds really stupid, but Daniel was saying this, and I don't know if you've noticed, but when Daniel talks, things that are really stupid make a lot more sense."

I had noticed that Daniel had a gift for lying. I had fallen for some of his lies in New Haven, and I'd only heard them second-hand.

"What happened after you found the dynamite?" I asked.

"Vic and me, we hustle it out of there. I'm thinking we should call Tucker and ask for Daniel's dad, but Vic reminded me that Daniel's folks are divorced and his last name might be different. Then I got to thinking about it, and I wondered if maybe someone did ask Daniel to hold the stuff, but not his dad. So I was going to ask June, but I never got the chance. I had the Lower Manhattan Expressway meeting first, and that's it."

"You weren't going to call the police?" I asked.

"I should've. I've been thinking that ever since the drugs started clearing out of my system. I should've called. I should've reported it. I just hope Vic did. But you say he was shot, too."

"Do you think Daniel was involved in the shooting?"

"*Daniel?*" Joel slumped against his pillow. "Two weeks ago, I'd've said no. But with the military pamphlet and the dynamite, and me and Vic getting shot, I just don't know. What happened to Vic exactly?"

"I don't know exactly," I said. "He was shot last Friday night. I've been trying to track him down, too."

"Daniel didn't like Ned either." Joel sighed. "But Daniel was sitting right there when Ned got shot."

He looked at me as if I had answered. I shrugged. "Do you have other enemies?"

"Other enemies," he repeated. "I wouldn't've thought I had one. Weird. You know, my folks keep thinking that someone else fired the shot, you know, trying to hurt the meeting, not me."

"What do you think?"

He shook his head. His eyes were bright with tears. "I think my life is all fucked up. I think nothing's ever going to be the same again."

I couldn't say much to that. He was right.

I talked to him a little longer and got nothing more out of him. I felt guilty for tiring him, and for bringing his mood down even farther. I apologized, but he waved me off.

"What can I do?" he said. "What's past is past."

His words were resigned, but he wasn't. I told his parents on the way out that I had distressed him.

"We thought you might," his mother said, "but he needs to get this resolved."

"He's a smart boy," his father said as if his son were twelve. "He just has to pick his friends more carefully."

I wished it were as simple as that.

I thanked his parents for letting me disturb their day. I had probably disturbed more than the day. I wasn't sure what Joel would do, but I had a hunch his time of lying quietly in that room had ended.

FORTY-SEVEN

When I left the building, I blinked in the light. The heat of the day had grown, but the air was filled with moisture, making everything look shimmery and vague.

Now I had more pieces than the police. I had seen the map drawn in New Haven of New York targets. I knew that Daniel and maybe a few others had stolen dynamite, probably from a construction company named Tucker Construction, around Memorial Day. I knew that they had stored the dynamite in the refrigerator at the row house, and I guessed that the dynamite had been moved, or Daniel wouldn't have let me search the apartment.

Maybe June knew, if she was awake. Or maybe the other victim, McCleary, knew. If I could talk to one of them, I might get the last piece of the puzzle.

They were in the Village, so that was where I went.

St. Vincent's was filled with people, most of whom had suffered some sort of holiday injury. Most of those injuries had involved fireworks. I overheard one man at the information desk telling the woman behind the desk that it wasn't his fault his son had nearly lost his hand; he wasn't home when the boy had been lighting a cherry bomb to see how big a bang it made.

I shook my head, happy that Jimmy was content with sparklers.

This time no detectives haunted June's floor. Her room was dark and marked "private." I wasn't able to see anyone inside. I had to find a nurse, and have her check to see if June had been moved.

She hadn't. But she was still in a coma, and the doctors were beginning to get worried that this wasn't a healing coma, so they had taken her to X-ray to see if they could find something they might have missed.

From the hospital, I walked to Perry Street. My legs were getting tired and I had a blister on the side of one foot. I didn't walk this much in Chicago.

When I finally reached Perry Street, I found it filled with people. Most of them sat on lawn chairs on the sidewalk, several of them beneath oversized umbrellas. At the end of the block, several men wearing nothing more than tight swim trunks barbecued on five different grills. Smoke covered that end of the block. The smell of charred hamburger made my stomach growl.

An ice cream cooler filled with dry ice gave off more steam. Several women, all of them wearing bikinis, poured lemonade into tall glasses. A couple of women another table over would add a dash of vodka if the drinker wanted some alcohol in his refreshment.

A hi-fi sat on top of a wide banister, and a small man sat beside it, his lap filled with albums. He thumbed through them, looking for the next one. The current album, blaring out of two cheap speakers, was some kind of salsa music, adding to the festive air.

The entire scene, which looked almost impromptu, made me smile. I wandered in, then leaned next to one of the men, asking if he knew Victor McCleary.

The man pointed to a person sitting on one of the stoops. He had long curly hair pulled back in a ponytail. He wore cutoffs and a midriff top, and he was daintily eating corn on the cob, balancing a plate across his knees.

I thanked the man I'd been talking to and walked over to the stoop. Several women moved so that I could climb the stairs.

I sat down next to McCleary. He smiled at me, his mouth greasy with butter. He grabbed a napkin and wiped his lips.

"Victor?" I asked.

His green eyes were clear, and framed by long, black lashes. His nose was small and straight.

"Have we met?" His voice was soft. He had a slight Carolina accent that I suspected could become thick if he wanted it to.

"No," I said, and stuck out my hand. "Bill Grimshaw. I'm investigating some shootings."

"What are you, IAD?" He set the half-eaten cob on his plate and wiped his fingers, pointedly ignoring my outstretched hand.

"No," I said. "I'm a private detective."

He turned toward me and grinned. "Well, why didn't you say so straight off, sugar? Someone finally gonna put up some money so we can get those cops where they live?"

"You were shot by the police?" I asked.

"Didn't I just say that? Or was I merely thinking it? Lord, I forget sometimes. It's been a long week." The accent *had* gotten thicker. It felt like he was putting on some kind of performance for me.

He set the plate on the stone step beside him and stretched out his legs. The thigh nearest to me had a rectangular bandage, slightly stained with new blood, and a bruise that was flowering outward, one that promised to engulf the entire side of his leg.

"Is that where you got hit?" I asked, nodding toward his thigh.

"Hurt like a son of a bitch," McCleary said. Then his eyes twinkled as he looked up sideways at me. "Well, maybe not like a son of a bitch, but you catch my drift."

He was making me uncomfortable, and he was doing it on purpose. "Why don't you tell me what happened?"

"Why don't you tell me who you're working for," he said.

"I can't tell you who I'm working for, but I can tell you I'm not with the police. I'm actually from Chicago, and this is part of a larger case."

"Well, of course. You midwestern folks do know about police misconduct now, don't you?"

"I'm afraid so," I said.

He reached back, tugged on his hair, making sure the ponytail was in place. Then he rested his elbows on the step and looked out over the neighborhood as if it were his domain.

"Were you here for the riots?" he asked.

"Last Friday?"

He nodded, not looking at me. The light manner with which he had greeted me was gone.

"No," I said.

"You know anything about them?"

"A little," I said, "but honestly, last Friday I was in New Haven. What I know about the riots, I learned when I got to New York."

"Well, avoid the *Voice* coverage. I never expected them to be homophobic, but there they were, 'Full Moon Over the Stonewall' like we all were influenced by the tides." He shook his head. "Let me give it to you short and sweet: Judy's funeral was Friday afternoon—"

"Judy?"

"Judy Garland, sweetie. You are hopelessly out of it, aren't you?" He smiled at me sideways, but he didn't take his gaze off the street.

"Judy Garland," I repeated, not sure what I was listening to.

"Her funeral was an *event*," he said. "They say the city hadn't seen anything like it since Valentino died. It was a mob scene, right, Delores?"

One of the women who had been sitting a few steps down, looked up, nodded, and then said, "You bet, babe."

Her voice was much deeper than mine. I realized that I was looking at a man in excellent drag.

"A bunch of us went down to the Stonewall that night to drown our sorrows," McCleary was saying. "It's the Friday nightspot, very popular, and last Friday it was the busiest I'd ever seen it. The party had just gotten started when the police raided us."

"We didn't have a warning," the man named Delores said. I was having trouble putting that voice with the beautifully made-up face I saw before me. "Usually, the folks at the Stonewall knew a raid was coming. There's rumors the place is mob-owned or at least makes protection payments, so usually someone knows in advance."

"But this time, no one did," McCleary said, "and I don't know, I think it was just the last straw after one very shitty day. Instead of the police busting heads, we busted heads."

"Felt damn good," Delores said.

"Until they started giving back," McCleary said. "I was in the wrong place. I took off, and Rufio followed me—"

"Rufio?"

"He's a patrolman with the Sixth. He's had it out for me from the beginning."

"You did kiss him on the lips, doll," Delores said.

McCleary grinned. "He is deliciously cute."

My cheeks grew warm. "When was that?"

"Oh, hell, months ago? I don't know. He was hassling us, and I told him that he was too pretty to worry about a little nooky. That upset him, and—" McCleary gave me that sideways glance again, "sometimes it's so much fun to make you straight boys nervous."

The flush had worked its way deep into my skin. I was right. He had been playing with me. "So this Rufio followed you."

"Ye-up," McCleary said. "I was running off home, like a good little camper, and he told me to stop. I knew the way the tide was turning that if

I stopped he had me alone in an alley. He was going to beat the crap out of me."

The fun flirtatious tone was gone from McCleary's voice. So was any hint of femininity.

"I was frightened, I truly was, and I knew that I was going to pay for messing with him. I just didn't realize how much." McCleary turned slightly so that he faced me. "Rufio told me to stop again, and when I didn't, he shot me. I fell forward—it wasn't like it hurt. It didn't. But it felt like someone had hit me with a two-by-four right in the leg. I tried to move, and that's when I felt the blood. He was coming toward me, and I hadn't been that scared in my life. Truly."

"Wait until you hear this." Delores turned, wrapped his arms around his legs, and listened to the rest of the story as if it were being told for his benefit.

"I was near a subway entrance. I flung myself down the stairs, literally flung, because I couldn't really walk. I rolled down, then crawled across the platform, pulled myself up in time to see Rufio hurrying down the stairs. A train was just about to leave, but some of the kind passengers held the door for me. I got on, and the doors closed, leaving him behind. They—the passengers—were good Samaritans. They asked no questions, got me to a hospital, and there I had to deal with more police, who of course didn't believe me. I was briefly arrested for taking part in the 'Queer Riot' as the papers are calling it, but the charges were dropped because no one can prove I did anything. And, of course, everyone straight is saying I was shot by someone queer."

"Of course," Delores said, shaking his head.

"But I wasn't. It was Rufio. The bastard actually came to my hospital bed to see if I was all right. I screamed for the nurse and threw a bedpan at him." McCleary smiled. "A full bedpan."

"They had to keep Vic there for a couple of days," Delores said. "He picked up something from those stairs. The wound was pretty infected."

"Delores has been helping me since I got home," McCleary said.

"I told him he missed the best part. The riots went on for a couple of nights, and that's when we realized how strong we are. There's going to be a march." Delores reached up and touched my hand. It took all of my resolve not to pull away. "If you want to come out in support, you're more than welcome. We're hoping it'll be next weekend, but there'll be flyers."

"I may not be in town next weekend," I said, feeling slightly light-headed. The others I'd seen had mentioned McCleary's sexual preference, but I had actually thought it was tough talk—the way that people insulted each other when they didn't really like each other.

"I'm sure there'll be other marches," Delores said, and stretched out on the steps, looking up at me.

"So," I said to McCleary. "This had nothing to do with the War at Home Brigade?"

He raised his eyebrows at me. "You're actually using that name?"

I shrugged.

"I think it's pretentious and silly, and has nothing to do with antiwar protesting, only with violence and mayhem." McCleary shook his head. "You know, sometimes being an activist gets you in the worst situations."

"Are you referring to Friday or to the War at Home Brigade."

"Stop it," McCleary said. "Call them those violent motherfuckers or something else, but don't honor them with their own self-selected self-aggrandizing moniker."

"All right," I said, smiling. I was beginning to like him. "Do you know Daniel Kirkland?"

McCleary put the back of his hand to his forehead like a thirties serial heroine. "For my sins."

"And did you belong to a group that he ran, a group that proclaimed itself against the Vietnam war?"

"I belonged to an offshoot group of the SDS, run by Joel Grossman and Ned Jones," McCleary said. "We all met at Columbia, but I stuck with it even after I graduated. We were doing some good work. Mostly draft counseling and community education, but a few protests—we made all the big ones."

"Draft counseling?" I asked.

"Telling people how to legally avoid. Not everyone wants to flee to Canada, you know."

I nodded. "Is this a free service?"

"Why wouldn't it be?" McCleary said. "We couldn't very well hang out a shingle and tell people 'Hello! Draft Dodgers United Over Here!' now, could we?"

"But people found you," I said.

"People still find us. A number of us have continued the work, now that Ned's dropped out and Joel's too sick." He blinked at me. "Is that why you're here? Because Ned got hit with some random bullet in Central Park and Joel was attacked by one of those Robert-Moses-Destroy-the-City construction crazies?"

"Is that who shot him?"

McCleary shrugged. "I'd always assumed. And that's what the police said. Do you think it was someone else?"

"I honestly don't know," I said. "I thought so when I started. You know that June D'Amato got shot on Friday."

"Good Lord, Junie?" McCleary dropped all pretense. "Is she all right?"

"I really don't have a lot of information," I said. "She's at St. Vincent's, but I'm not family, so they don't tell me much. She's been in a coma since the shooting happened."

"God, Junie." McCleary shook his head. "How's Danny taking this?"

"Daniel?" I asked. "Why?"

McCleary looked at me like I had just asked the stupidest question he'd ever heard. "Because he's really got a thing for her. They hang off each other."

"June?" I asked. "What about Rhondelle?"

"Ah, you didn't know," McCleary said.

"Know what?"

McCleary nodded, almost as if he were having a conversation with himself. "They haven't given you the speech."

"What speech?"

"The one about property and ownership and how it affects relationships and how everything should *flow*, man, and how you know, you do what you *feel*, man, and if it's right, then it's right, and all that garbage."

I frowned at him. He was being sarcastic and judgmental, and I hadn't expected it of him. "You're saying that their relationship is somehow open?"

"I'm saying that Daniel has the right to sleep with whomever he wants. Theoretically, Junie and Rhondelle do, too, but the girls never seem to take advantage of it. Besides, Danny spent most of his time with June, at least what I saw, and only kept Rhondelle around because she was useful."

"Because of the row house," I said.

"Because she's his chemist," McCleary said.

I stared at him. The confusion had lifted, but I didn't trust my feeling of clarity. "Chemist? You mean she makes the drugs he's been giving away?"

I'd only heard he did that in New Haven. Was he doing it here, too? Was that where they got their money? Was he dealing?

"That, and the other thing," McCleary said.

"The other thing," I said, feeling slow again.

"She's in charge of the big bang, brother," McCleary said. "She knows more about how to make things go boom than anyone I've ever met. She's brilliant."

"I thought Daniel was the scientist."

"Maybe he is," McCleary said, "but Rhondelle's Madam Fucking Curie."

I sucked in a breath. I hadn't seen Rhondelle as anything but a victim.

Both Daniel and Rhondelle had played on my assumptions. Again, I had underestimated someone.

"Joel said you found some dynamite in Rhondelle's refrigerator," I said.

"He what?" Now it was McCleary's turn to look shocked.

"He said that—"

"I know what you said he said." McCleary made a small up-and-down movement with his right hand, signaling that we should be quiet. I had no idea how anyone except Delores could hear us. "We never found anything at Rhondi's."

Then I understood. Joel had said that they saw dynamite in "Daniel's girl-friend's apartment." Not the row house. It was at June's, not Rhondelle's.

"June doesn't live at the Harlem house, does she?" I asked.

"She's got her own place not far from here," McCleary said. "Or she did. I traded that little tidbit for freedom last Saturday."

"You told the police about the dynamite in the refrigerator."

"Yep," McCleary said. "They were happy to hear it, even though when they got there, the entire place'd been cleared out. It gave them enough evidence, though, to keep an eye on Daniel's little parade."

He stopped, then looked at me, his face going very pale.

"I didn't lead them to Junie, did I? I didn't make them shoot her? Jesus, what if it was the police? What if they shot her, like they shot me, and if she dies—"

"Stop," I said. "First of all, they would have arrested her if they had found anything, not shot her. And secondly, I'm not sure what's going on. Three of you were no longer friends with Daniel. Maybe June had a falling out with him."

"Or maybe Rhondi went all Whatever-Happened-to-Baby-Jane on him and decided to take out everyone who hurt him?" McCleary put the heel of his hands against his forehead. "Oh, this is giving me a sick headache."

I hadn't thought of Rhondelle, but I didn't believe it. Of course, I was having trouble believing that she was their chemist as well.

"Or maybe it was all random," I said. "Your shooting was clearly unrelated. Maybe the others are, too."

"It's a dangerous city," McCleary said. "But do you think it's that dangerous? Three people in such a small group getting shot like that?"

"No," I said. "I don't."

I sighed. The party had evolved along the street. Now some people were dancing—men dancing with each other, and the women in the bikinis had their arms around each other's waists and were swaying with the music.

"It bothers you, doesn't it?" McCleary said to me, very softly. I almost didn't hear him.

"The shootings?" I asked. "Yeah—"

"No," he said. "Us."

He nodded toward the street. Delores had gone down the steps. He had his hand on another man's neck, resting it there possessively, the way a man would do to a woman.

"I'm—not comfortable," I said. "That's true."

"And you probably think it was okay for the cops to bust up a bunch of queers." The humor had left McCleary's face.

"I didn't say that." I looked at him. "The police often go overboard, especially in situations they don't understand."

"So you been in a few police riots," he said.

"More than my share," I said.

"You understand, then, how it is when they go after you for being different."

"Yes," I said cautiously. I wasn't sure where this part of the conversation was going.

"I just wanted you to understand," McCleary said. "As you investigate all this stuff going on. I want you to know the reason I got shot is just because I'm different. That threatens people. You know that."

I still felt uncomfortable. I wasn't breathing very deeply, and I did want to move back up the steps so that I wasn't sitting so close to McCleary.

"You and me," he was saying, "we got a lot in common. We get attacked just for being who we are."

I couldn't keep quiet any longer. "Yes, but I can't dye my skin. You can change how you live."

The look he gave me was both triumphant and sad, as if he knew that an opinion he didn't like had lurked within me. "You think I can just change? You think I like being called names and being treated this way? You think I do it because I want to?"

I didn't answer him.

He leaned close to me. I remembered what he had said about kissing the cop and hoped he didn't try it with me.

"Being gay is as fundamental to who I am as being black is to you," he said. "And treating me as anything less than fully human is just as much discrimination as treating you the same way. I trust you'll remember that while you're looking into the various crimes around here."

272

I didn't move away, even though I wanted to. "I was brought up to believe something different."

His eyes glittered. "And I was brought up to believe that niggers were inferior. I got over my prejudice. When are you gonna get past yours?"

He tapped me once on the chest, lightly, not quite threateningly. Then he leaned back, and the moment faded.

"Thanks for telling me about Junie," he said. "She's a good girl in the wrong crowd. I'll go see her tomorrow."

And with that, I had been dismissed.

FORTY-EIGHT

I staggered out of the block party slightly ill. I wasn't sure whether my light-headedness came from the heat, the information that McCleary had given me, or the discomfort I'd been trying to suppress through the entire meeting. I walked as far from the neighborhood as I could before I found a café that advertised air-conditioning in the window.

I went inside, ordered a burger, a milkshake, and water. Then I asked the waitress for extra napkins, and I made notes.

Daniel was tied to all of the victims. But his attachment to June explained why he had panicked so badly when she got shot.

Had Rhondelle hired the shooter? I didn't know. It didn't seem likely, but I had underestimated her from the start.

The police? Possible. I wasn't going to rule it out. But Detective O'Connor didn't look like IAD and he seemed to be investigating the D'Amato shooting. However, he had given me Victor McCleary's name with the others, and he had to know that McCleary's shooting wasn't connected. I didn't dare underestimate the New York police.

After I had eaten and had a chance to think things through, I felt better. I was calmer. I still hadn't come up with the identity of the shooter, but I did have confirmation that Daniel, Rhondelle, and their little group had been collecting dynamite. The police knew it, and had acted on it once.

But that didn't mean they had found everything.

A refrigerator full of dynamite wasn't one-tenth the amount we had found in New Haven—at least based on the empty boxes. (And why were those boxes empty? What had happened to that dynamite?) If Daniel felt he needed a lot—and why would he?—then he needed some other place to store it.

Some place that wouldn't have been as easy to find.

I got up, left a five on the table to cover my tab and tip, and went to the back, carrying one of the napkins and a pen. Near the restrooms was a bank of pay phones. Someone had scratched names and phone numbers into the wall beside them, and the entire area smelled of urine. If I hadn't already eaten, I would have left without touching my food.

Still, I grabbed one of the phones, plugged a dime into it, and had the operator hook me up with St. Vincent's main line. Once I got the hospital's operator, I asked for the accounting department.

"You mean Billing?" she asked. "Or do you want Records?"

"Are they in tonight?" I asked.

"Billing is," she said.

"Then hook me up," I said.

She did. I heard the double click as she transferred me, and then I hung up.

I redialed the hospital, got the operator, disguised my voice slightly, and asked for the nurse's station on June's floor. When the nurse answered, I introduced myself as John from Billing.

"We need to confirm June D'Amato's address. We have 1 West Twelfth Street, but that address looks wrong to me. Do you think this kid could've faked her address when she came in? I don't want to send information to the wrong place."

"What are you billing for now anyway?" the nurse asked. "The girl's in a coma."

"It's policy," I said. "We get the file ready, send the preliminary information, just in case someone else is at the house and needs notification."

The nurse harrumphed at me. "Sounds like typical bureaucratic foolishness."

"I don't make the rules," I said with a verbal shrug.

"Just a minute." She put me on hold, and I crossed my fingers. A cook came out of the kitchen, pushed past me, and headed into the men's room, trailing the odor of cooking grease behind him.

"Got it," she said as she got back on the line. "And your address is wrong, or maybe mine is. I know she didn't fill out the paperwork because she's been unconscious from the moment she arrived."

"Give me the second address anyway," I said. "Between us, we might have the right one."

The nurse gave me a reluctant chuckle, and then she recited an address. I wrote it down, then repeated it back to her.

"You ask me," she said, "that sounds as suspect as your 1 West Twelfth Street."

"Yes, it does," I said. "You know how many of these kids give us fake addresses? What is she, an overdose?"

"No. Poor thing was shot on the Fourth of July. Have you ever heard of such a thing?"

"Wow," I said, sounding as surprised as I could. "What was she doing?"

"Just standing on the sidewalk, minding her own business." The nurse sighed. "Sure hope she lives through this. She's a pretty little thing."

I thanked her for her time and hung up, then stared at the address. It might have been the one the police raided, but it might not.

Daniel had been pretty shaken up when he carried June to that car. There was a chance he was even more upset at the hospital. There was also a chance that he wasn't the one who had filled out the paperwork—that someone else in his group, someone less devious than he was—had done so.

I needed to check out the apartment, but I didn't want to stay in the city, not now that O'Connor had told me about the surveillance.

I figured, however, that I could give it one more day.

FORTY-NINE

Early Monday morning, I took a train to the Village. Jimmy and Malcolm had one more day at the library. They weren't happy about the library, but they were pleased to learn that we'd be leaving the next morning.

The subway was filled with commuters holding coffee in Styrofoam cups, reading newspapers while standing, sitting with their briefcases shoved tightly between their legs. I pushed my way in and rattled along with everyone else as the train headed downtown.

Most of the commuters got off in midtown. I rode the train down to Washington Square. I wanted to see how far the park was from June D'Amato's apartment. The day was nice; the short walk from Washington Square Park to the address the nurse had given me on East Eleventh would be pleasant.

In this part of town, the commuters gave way to street people, hippies, and card sharks, all of whom sat at makeshift tables and tried to catch unsuspecting people. Graffiti covered many of the buildings. Transistor radios blared conflicting styles of rock music along the block, and near the intersection with Second Avenue, a teenage boy who looked like he hadn't had a bath in three months had another boy against the wall, a knife at his throat. Five other boys stood around them, egging them on, before a policeman walked through the group, slapping his truncheon against his hand, and shouting, "Break it up, break it up."

Two different hulks of burned-out cars sat near the curb, but no one seemed to notice them, which made me realize car burning had to be pretty common around here. The address the nurse had given me led me to an old tenement, its brick walls rough with time and neglect.

I walked up the steps to the stoop, past two kids who swore at me in Spanish. I answered them in the same language, telling them it wasn't polite to make fun of other people.

They ran away.

The door to the building was closed, but not locked. I pushed it open. The on-site manager's apartment was listed as apartment one. As I walked past the open wiring and the flaking paint, I found the apartment. Beneath the crooked number was a hand-scrawled sign that read MANAGER.

I knocked.

After a moment, the door opened, releasing a waft of tobacco and marijuana smoke. I could almost get high standing there. A middle-aged white man, his naked gut hanging over a pair of filthy blue jeans, peered at me.

"You don't live here," he said.

"No, I don't," I said.

"We don't got nothing," he said and started to close the door.

I put my hand on it. "I'm a detective. I'm here on a case."

"Oh." He gave me a greasy smile. "Why didn't you say so? Just a minute. Lemme get a shirt."

He closed the door, and I knew he was doing more than putting on a shirt. He was getting rid of the joint that had been smoldering on the table behind him, and probably hiding a few other things as well.

Then he opened the door again. He was wearing a T-shirt that was too big. It floated around him like a nightdress.

"Sorry," he said, as he slid in front of the door, not letting me inside. "The wife's not decent."

I bet, I thought, but I didn't say anything.

"Whatcha need?"

"I suppose you heard that one of your tenants is in the hospital?"

"If you mean little Junie D'Amato, she ain't my tenant no more."

"She isn't?" I asked.

"What, don't you guys at the force talk to each other? I just told some official types this a coupla days ago."

"Apparently they left it off the report," I said.

"Apparently. Jeez, for all the work you guys are supposed to do, it don't make sense for you to repeat each other's work."

"When did June move out?" I asked, not willing to hear the complaints. The hallway was close and hot, and he stank of sweat and marijuana.

"I don't got the slightest. First I know about it is when I'm taking your buddies up there to see the place, it's been cleaned out. Not cleaned, mind you—her and those friendsa hers wouldn't know cleaned—but it was emptied, you know? Even took a couch belonging to us. So I'm not paying back the deposit no matter what her old man says."

"You talked with her father?"

"No, but I will. Whenever there was a problem with the rent, the old man sent a check. You know he's the kind who'll probably spit blood if he don't get his due."

"You've met him?" I asked.

"Just by phone. That's plenty." The manager hitched his pants up. "If that's all—"

"Actually, no, it's not," I said. "Do you have a forwarding address?"

"Jeez, you guys are all the same. If I knew she was moving, I woulda got it, but I didn't, so I don't. Now are we done?"

"No," I said. "I'd like to see the apartment."

"It's empty," he said. "There ain't nothing to see."

"Humor me," I said.

He rolled his eyes, then pushed the door to his own apartment open. "I gotta get my keys."

He disappeared inside. I heard his voice, faint, chastising someone—"For chrissake, there's a cop out there!"—and then the door opened again. He clutched a gigantic ring of keys in one hand. They clanged against each other. He slid his fist through the ring and led me up the steps.

Cockroaches scuttled across the molding, and a spiderweb caught my hair. I stopped and swiped at it, making an inadvertent sound of disgust.

The manager didn't seem to notice. He walked ahead of me, passing the landing and making a lot of noise as he went up the second flight of steps.

I wondered who he was warning.

I followed him. The steps were steep. I could only see his legs as I started up them. I heard a key turn in the lock and his shout, "Manager!" as he stepped inside.

Did he allow squatters? I had no idea, and I wasn't about to get into the middle of anything. I slowed, peering up as I walked, hoping that I wouldn't see anything too far out of the ordinary.

The hallway was as narrow as the one downstairs. Someone had put a fist through the wall, revealing wires and plaster. The overhead light had been pulled off the ceiling and dangled there like a forgotten kite.

The manager stood just inside the apartment. He had his arms crossed. "There ain't nothing else to see here," he said, which was enough to tell me that if I had been working Vice I might have found a lot to see.

I gave him a nod, then walked deeper into the apartment. Once it had been two railroad flats, but someone had converted it into one by tearing out a wall. Whoever had done the conversion hadn't tried to make transition between the two apartments look like part of the design. If I peered carefully enough, I could see bits of wallboard still trapped in the floor.

There wasn't any furniture, but there were a lot of dust bunnies. The walls were covered with scraps and leftover bits of yellowed tape. Footprints showed in the dust—some of the prints bare, and others long and official, like cop shoes.

I wandered through, saw the converted kitchen, and, holding my breath, opened the refrigerator door. Nothing except the stale smell of old food. I looked inside the cupboards, the stove, and under the kitchen sink, but found nothing.

"You looking for something in particular?" the manager asked.

I shook my head, then glanced at the fridge again. It was small, even by apartment standards. An old 1930s Frigidaire, with a rounded top, it barely came up to my chest. If it had held boxes of dynamite, it couldn't have held more than three.

I walked through the remaining rooms, saw nothing of interest, checked out all four fireplaces, which seemed like an odd feature of an odd apartment, and then returned to the manager.

"Told you they was gone," he said.

That was the second time he'd referred to others in the apartment. "These friends of hers," I said, "did they live in the building or in the apartment with her?"

"She swore to me she lived alone, but she had a guy up there a lot, and they seemed to know everybody. It was like one big party. But it sometimes is like a party around here. We ain't far from St. Marks Place, and it's been crazy for the past two, maybe three years. That crazy spills this way."

"Crazy?" I asked.

"Hippies, freaks, druggies. You name it, they come around here. Now we got the Spics—pardon my French—and it's all going to hell."

"Since you don't seem to like your neighbors," I said, "why don't you just move?"

"Where else would I find a job that gives me free rent and pays me? Hmmm? I get janitorial pay."

"And you do a fine job for it," I said sarcastically.

He crossed his thick arms. "Hey, if you had to deal with what I got to deal with—all them junkies coming in here wanting a place to bed down, trashing the place—you wouldn't be so quick to judge."

"So it's their fault this place is falling apart."

"Damn right," he said, then blinked at me. He couldn't tell if I was making fun of him.

"Did any of her friends live in the building?" I asked.

"How should I know? I didn't keep a list."

"I was just wondering if you saw anything that made you a little suspicious."

He shook his head. "That's impossible to answer. All the stuff around here, it's suspicious from a cop's perspective."

"Do you ever report any of it?"

"Sometimes," he said. "When it gets bad."

I wasn't sure I wanted to know his definition of bad. "In the last two months," I said, trying one last time, "did you have any tenants who moved in with a pile of same-size boxes and very little else? Maybe they brought some coolers or a table or some equipment—"

"Why do you ask?" He frowned at me in such a way that my heart skipped a beat. He knew something. He just wanted to know what was in it for him.

"Because if I'm right, everyone in this building could be in danger."

"Yeah, sure, from what?"

"Explosives," I said.

He went pale. "You're shitting me."

I shook my head.

"You think little Junie was doing stuff like that?"

"Yes, I do," I said. "I understand she kept boxes of dynamite in that refrigerator."

I nodded toward it. The manager looked at it like it might explode at any minute.

"You gotta be kidding," he said.

"I wish I were."

"Christ on a crutch," he said. "The only people who fit your description are the Castro brothers. But they've never been no trouble. They pay their rent on time and they never complain about nothing."

"The *Castro* brothers?" I asked, unable to keep the disbelief from my voice. "Ché and Fidel?"

"I'm not dumb," the manager said. "Michael and John. They had ID. You know, I do check driver's licenses."

"Do you see these guys a lot?" I asked.

He shook his head. "Sometimes they came by with this beautiful nigra chick. She was just . . ."

His voice ran down as he realized what he said.

"Tell me about this beautiful girl," I said.

"She had real delicate features, you know. She seemed kinda breakable. Last week, she tripped on the way out, fell against the step. I heard her fall, and helped her up. I have a hunch she had a mother of a shiner. She really walloped herself."

Rhondelle.

"I told her we could put some ice on it," he said, "but she laughed and told me she'd just blame it on her shit-ass boyfriend. Her word 'shit-ass.' Don't sound like she liked him much."

"If she's the same girl I'm thinking of," I said, "she doesn't have much reason to like him."

"You know her?"

"I know a beautiful black girl with an incredible shiner. She's also a friend of June's and is known as the group's chemist."

"Well, she was on something that day she tripped down the steps, but you know, if I had to guess, I woulda thought it was glue. She had that whiffer smell, you know? Like she was sniffing airplane glue like we did when we were kids."

I must have been a dull child. It never crossed my mind to sniff glue. "Can you let me into their apartment?"

"Not without twenty-four hours' warning," he said.

"And if they do have dynamite in there like I think they do, it'll be gone in twenty-four hours. You know it, and so do I."

He shrugged. "I can't violate code without the owner's permission."

I smiled at him, crossed my arms, and took a step toward him. I was nearly half a foot taller than he was, and although he outweighed me, his extra weight was fat.

"If you let me in there, I'll overlook the marijuana in your apartment.

I'll also fail to report all the building code violations when I get back to the office."

He swallowed once, and looked up at me nervously. "The other cops didn't threaten me," he said, his voice shaking.

"But you didn't tell them about the Castro brothers, did you?"

"I don't got no real proof that you are a cop," he said.

"You gonna risk making me mad now?" I asked.

Small beads of sweat formed on his forehead. His body odor, which hadn't been light before, was getting stronger.

"Shit, man," he said, "if I lose this job, I'm sunk. I can't get nothing else."

"You're gonna lose it," I said, "if you don't cooperate with me. In fact, you're gonna lose a lot more. You're gonna lose your freedom. Vice isn't really happy about any kind of drug these days, and I have a hunch the joint I saw in your place was just the tip of the proverbial iceberg."

His eyes moved from my face to the refrigerator to my face again.

"All right," he whispered. "But you tell people you gave me twenty-four-hour notice, okay?"

"Just take me to the apartment," I said.

He nodded, then scuttled down the damaged hall of this apartment. He waited for me at the door. When I stepped out, he locked up, his hands shaking.

"That way," he said, nodding down the corridor.

"You lead," I said.

He put his head down and trudged, as if I were making him go to prison. His keys jangled in his right hand.

When he reached the apartment at the very end of the hall, he knocked. "Manager!" he shouted.

We waited a minute. There was no movement inside.

"Manager!" he shouted again.

Then he glanced at me.

"Open it," I said.

He took a deep breath, unlocked the door, and stepped back. A blast of cold air hit us. He gave me a surprised look.

I stepped in first.

"Manager!" he shouted again from behind me.

I nearly hit him.

"Don't do that," I whispered. I wanted to listen, to see if I heard anything besides the rattle of an overworked air conditioner.

The rattle seemed too loud, and as I turned to the right, into the main room of the apartment, I saw why.

Both windows had air conditioners, and both conditioners were set so high that they vibrated. Beneath them, someone had placed newspaper and big soup pots to catch the condensation as it dripped off the units.

Both pots were nearly full.

But that wasn't what caught me. What got my attention were the boxes, stacked floor to ceiling in the half kitchen off the main room. All of them had Tucker Construction stamped on the side. I knew if I turned them around, they would read "Explosives."

"Izzat it?" the manager asked from behind me.

"You stay there," I said, wishing for the first time on this trip that I had my gun. I had left it in Chicago, not wanting the trouble, not expecting it.

I made my way through the kitchen, and into the back bedroom. There was only one, and it was dark. Light came in around the third air conditioner, also set on high. This place was as cold as a refrigerator.

I flicked on the light with the back of my hand. A table was pushed against the back wall. Lined up on it were nails, thumbtacks, screws, and duct tape. Several squares of muslin were cut and resting next to those items. On the very edge of the table, someone had wrapped muslin around a package, and secured it with duct tape.

I walked close, looked, but didn't touch. Inside the muslin were the nails and screws and thumbtacks, held in place with what smelled ever so faintly like airplane glue.

My stomach turned. I swallowed hard and scanned the rest of the room. More newspaper, another pot beneath the air conditioner, and on the far wall, two rows of alarm clocks, still in their packages. Electrician's wire hung from a large nail someone had pounded into the wall.

"Oh, shit," the manager said from behind me.

I just about jumped out of my skin.

"Didn't I tell you to stay in the living room?" I asked, barely controlling the urge to hit him.

"I just had to see," he said. "Goddamn, those little fuckers lied to me. They were such clean-cut white boys, too."

"White boys?" I asked.

"You expected colored?" he said, then put a hand to his mouth. "Colored's okay, right?"

I didn't answer him. "What did these boys look like?"

He shrugged. "Dark hair on the one. The other one had brown hair, long, and he was really thin. I only seen them a coupla times. I was starting to wonder if maybe they rented it out to that pretty ni—colored lady and her boyfriend, not that I woulda approved the sublet. But that happens a lot here. You know, kids think they got the money and they don't, so they find a way to make a quick buck."

"These guys were young?" I asked.

"Twenty, maybe. Maybe more. It's hard to tell."

"And they had a black girl as a friend."

"And her kinda scary boyfriend. He had one of those . . ." The manager put his hands around his head, signifying a lot of hair.

"An Afro," I said.

"Yeah, but he tied it back with a headband sometimes. He was real polite. Spoke like a normal person, too."

"Probably in better English than you use," I said, the sarcasm hard to control.

"Much better," he agreed, without catching the sarcasm. "He had education, that kid, though he liked his speeches. Wanted me to come to some march."

I went back into the kitchen and used the back of my hand to turn on the light in there, too.

And it was right there, on the table, a mimeograph machine, with the discarded masters in the garbage can beside it. I grabbed a paper towel off the counter, picked up one of the masters with the towel and looked.

Written backward, in purple, on the back were the words "The genocidal war in Vietnam . . ."

And they were in the same strange script I'd seen at the induction center.

I knew it. I knew that all it would take was one more day.

Finally, I had enough to put Daniel Kirkland away.

FIFTY

N ow what're we gonna do?" the manager asked from behind me. This time, he didn't startle me.

I let the mimeograph master drop back into the garbage can, wiped off my hands, and stuck the paper towel in my pocket. Then I turned around to face him.

His skin was blotchy with sweat. His eyes had sunk into his face. His T-shirt, which had looked somewhat clean, was now covered with big wet splotches that centered on his armpits.

"I mean," he said, "do we evacuate the building or what?"

"We call for backup," I said. "We'll lock this place up and then we go downstairs and you won't say a single word to anyone else, not even your wife, you got that?"

"Sure," he said. "Sure."

He looked at all the equipment, then back at me.

"You sure it's safe?"

"It's safe enough just sitting there," I said, wondering if we'd missed any gasoline or motor oil. I didn't see the makings for a Molotov cocktail, but that didn't mean they weren't here. "Let's go."

The manager scurried out of the apartment as if he were being chased. I moved slower, taking in all the details.

Daniel and his group had been smarter this time. They hadn't left a lot of trace evidence of themselves here, probably because they weren't living here.

There hadn't been any bombings to my knowledge in New York in the past two months, and none in New Haven that I had heard of. But people were mentioning a lot of activity in the East Coast Corridor. It wouldn't take a lot to build some small bombs, like the one on that table, put it in a suitcase, and have someone take it to, say, Philadelphia on the train.

Maybe Daniel and Rhondelle hadn't been selling drugs. Maybe they'd been selling bombs.

I felt colder than I ever had in my life, and it wasn't just because of the three overworked air conditioners. I had stumbled onto something that I wanted no part of and that I had to stop right away.

I got out of the apartment and rubbed my arms, feeling gooseflesh. The manager looked at me, apparently waiting for my approval to shut the door.

"Lock it up," I said.

He sighed, his hands shaking so badly that he almost dropped the keys. He tried to find the right key twice, then finally had to go through the ring one by one, staring at the tiny numbers taped to the keys' sides before finding the right one.

I waited until I heard the deadbolt thunk into place. We hurried down the stairs, and he led me to his apartment.

"Shirl," he shouted as we got near it. "I'm baaack."

I had a hunch that wasn't his normal greeting. "It doesn't matter what she's doing. I need to use your phone."

He nodded, and pushed his door open. The apartment was filthy. Marijuana buds covered the coffee table, and a woman sat near it, her dirty feet crossed on the tabletop. She wore a loose housedress, her hair was tousled around her face, and she held a very fat joint in one hand. In the other, she had a lighter.

She stared at me in surprise.

"He a cop?" she asked the manger.

"Don't worry about it, Shirl. He's gonna use the phone."

"Shit, man, you screwup. He's—"

"Ma'am," I said with the firmest tone I had. "We have a much more serious problem than your little habit there. Be quiet, stay calm, don't light that thing, and nothing will happen, all right?"

She blinked at me. "Sure, I guess," she said, then she set the joint on the table, knocking some buds off of it.

The manager took the lighter out of her hand. His hands were still shaking. I wondered if he was afraid that tiny lighter would somehow ignite all the dynamite upstairs.

"Where's the phone?" I asked.

The woman pointed toward her left. "We got one in the bed—"

"In the kitchen," the manager said, and gave her a pointed look. He nodded in the opposite direction. "Just down the hall."

I walked that way. He followed.

The kitchen was U-shaped and small, with barely enough room for one person, let alone two. The phone sat on the edge of the counter, half buried in cellophane wrappers, aluminum containers for frozen dinners, and dirty cups.

Apparently the manager didn't get a lot of phone calls.

I picked up the receiver, winced at its slimy texture, and dialed O'Connor's precinct. When someone answered, I asked for O'Connor by name.

The manager swallowed hard, then turned around and left. I had a hunch he had had run-ins with Detective O'Connor as well.

The person I spoke to set the phone down for a minute, then came back. "Sorry," he said. "O'Connor's not here. Need to leave a message?"

"No," I said. "I need to talk to his captain."

"Ah," the man at the other end said. "We don't bother the captain unless it's important."

"This is important," I said. "I found where the War at Home Brigade keeps its dynamite."

"Shit," the man said, and set the phone down again. This time, I could hear him as he made his way through the halls. "Captain! Hey, Captain . . ."

It took a few minutes, but someone picked up another receiver. "Captain Donato," an official sounding voice said.

"Captain Donato," I said turning toward the wall so that my voice wouldn't carry into the main room. "My name is Bill Grimshaw. I'm a private detective who met Detective O'Connor last week. We're working on similar cases. I've been tracking Daniel Kirkland from Chicago through New Haven to here."

"I'm familiar with you," Donato said. My heart started to pound. I hoped the familiarity was only through my contact with O'Connor.

"I was tracking down a lead in June D'Amato's old building, and I played a hunch. I asked the manager if there were any people who had been carrying small boxes in and out. He mentioned two boys who fit the description. He rented to them, and then told me a few stories about their friends that led me to believe Daniel Kirkland and his group had been in their apartment as well. The manager let me into their place—"

"He had no right to do that," the captain said.

"Well, that's just one reason you'll have to operate as if you got an anonymous tip on this, all right?" I said.

The captain sighed on the other end. "Go on."

"The apartment has at least twenty boxes of dynamite in the main room, equipment in the back, including electrician's wire and some alarm clock works, one almost-completed bomb, and a mimeograph machine with discarded masters that ties it to the War at Home Brigade."

"And I can trust you didn't plant any of this."

"Why would I?" I asked. "I work for Daniel's mother. This is terrible news for me."

The captain grunted. "You're sure this is dynamite?"

"I've seen it before," I said. "Even if I hadn't, it'd be hard to miss. They left it in the original boxes."

"Where are you?" he asked.

I gave him the address. "I'd suggest sending someone right away, maybe even a beat cop to secure the site. I'm not sure how trustworthy this building manager is."

"I'll see what we've got. You stay put. We'll have to talk."

Then he hung up, promising to have someone here immediately. I set the receiver down, then frowned at it. Twenty small boxes was a lot less than Daniel had taken in New Haven. Twenty small boxes might not even have been noticed missing from a construction site.

I rummaged around in the mess, looking for a phone book. Moving some of the cellophane wrappers discharged odors so foul I couldn't even identify some of them. One made my eyes water.

I finally found the book and looked up the number for Tucker Construction. There was a general contracting office in Manhattan and several smaller offices in the other boroughs. I dialed the Manhattan number, got a secretary, and asked for the owner of the company.

I identified myself as a detective—that seemed to be working in this city, better than it had in Chicago—and said that I wanted to discuss the big dynamite theft of a few weeks ago.

She put me right through.

The owner of Tucker Construction was Albert Tucker. As he picked up the phone, his greeting was gruff. He asked right off if I was a regular detective or private. I told him that I was private, and he nearly hung up, but

I managed to catch him by saying that I knew where some of his dynamite was.

"We just located it," I said, giving him the address. "The police'll be here at any minute, and I had a hunch they probably wouldn't tell you they recovered it."

"Probably not," he said, but he didn't sound as gruff as he had a few minutes earlier. "How come you're telling me?"

"Because I need some information they won't tell me," I said. "When was the theft?"

"Memorial Day weekend," he said.

"And how many boxes did they steal?"

"Boxes?" he asked. "They didn't steal boxes. They stole cases. At least a pallet's worth. I'm not sure how they got it out of here."

Just as I suspected. We'd only found a small amount of what had already been stolen.

"Didn't you have a security guard on your construction sites?"

"This wasn't one of my sites. It's here, at the warehouse. And yeah, I had a guard. He was a great guy, too. Those kids, they had scouted the place. They knew when he made his rounds. They got him and I'm not sure how because he was military, you know? But they managed it. I think it was dumb luck. They knocked him out, tied him up, and fucked him over."

"What do you mean 'fucked him over'?" I asked.

"I don't know, he was spouting crazy talk when we found him," Tucker said. "Like he was seeing things. I think they drugged him."

"With what?"

"Coffee, something. It's just this guy's big. You don't tussle with him. So they had to've done something. They couldn't've taken him on one-on-one."

"Can I speak to him?" I asked.

"I wish," Tucker said. "I gave him a few days off right after, and he never came back to work. Won't answer his phone, won't come to his door. Not that I blame him. He was in pretty rough shape when we found him that Tuesday. I never knew for sure, but I think he might've been lying near the guard shed since Sunday night, tied up and half out of his mind."

I frowned. I could hear sirens in the distance. "You said he was military? He was army then?"

"I don't know. Wounded three different times, so they finally sent him home."

"Vietnam?" I asked.

"Yep. Good guy, too. Smart. Never had a minute's trouble in the year plus that he'd been working for me. I don't even blame the theft on him. The cops said, and I agree, that those kids were not only determined, they were experienced. This break-in was clearly orchestrated by some pros."

Pros. Daniel had clearly taken that brilliant mind of his and turned it in the wrong direction. Which was a serious problem. The best thing about criminals was that most of them were stupid.

Daniel's brain made him one of the most dangerous people I'd ever encountered.

"Do you have the name and address of the security guard handy?" I asked.

"Actually, I do," Tucker said. "The cops wanted it just this morning. Weird coincidence, huh?"

"Yeah," I said. "Did they say why?"

"Nope, just that they were following up." I heard paper rustling, then he said, "Here it is. Calvin Jervis. Just off Astor Place."

He gave me the address, and I wrote it down. The sirens stopped outside the building. The police were here.

I thanked Tucker, told him he might want to come down here, and then hung up. I washed my hands in the sink—that slimy stuff from the receiver had gotten on my palms—and shook them dry as I walked back into the living room.

It wasn't the same place. Except for the buds still littering the floor, there was no sign of marijuana at all. The manger had opened his windows and stuck fans in them. The coffee table was cleaned and polished, and the mess throughout the room had been straightened. His wife had put on blue jeans and a tight shirt, and combed her hair. Her feet were still bare, though, but she looked a lot more presentable.

Someone knocked on the door.

It was time for my little tap dance to begin.

FIFTY-ONE

The first two cops on the scene were beat cops. The captain had taken my advice and brought in people to secure the building. The manager and I showed them to the dynamite, and while they were figuring out how to best handle the situation, I slipped out, relieved that the dynamite and the War at Home Brigade was now someone else's problem. I had done my duty, maybe saved some lives. I couldn't do anything more.

My goal had simply been to get enough information to the right people to get Daniel arrested, and, I hoped, put away for life. My conversation with the security guard might provide the very last piece of the puzzle, the thing that conclusively linked Daniel Kirkland and his gang to a very real act of violence as well as the dynamite itself.

I hurried to the address that Tucker had given me. It was just a few blocks down on Third Avenue, a brownstone in terrible repair. I had to step over some people sleeping on the sidewalk. A few kids hanging out near the door of one of the buildings disappeared inside as they saw me.

The street was remarkably empty, especially compared to Eleventh. Eleventh had looked pretty quiet, though, when I left: the sirens must have scared people off.

I hurried up the steps and into the building. The door was half off its hinges, and the names scrawled beside the mailboxes were fading. I did see Jervis's name, but someone had tried to write over it.

The apartment number placed it on the fourth floor. I let myself in, overwhelmed by the stench of stale beer and vomit. I stepped around the pile of goop that looked like it caused the smell.

Some of the lights were out in the hallway. The main area was wide, with four apartments on either side. Through an open door, the stairway loomed.

A white man in a police uniform stood at the base of the stairs with his arms crossed. He looked at me suspiciously.

I played a hunch.

"Detective O'Connor's on the fourth floor, right? He told me to meet him at Jervis's place, and I've been in three other buildings. This is the right one, right?"

The officer nodded. "They just went up."

"They?"

"Him and the manager. Nobody's answering the door."

"Thanks," I said, and walked past him. I could hear footsteps on the wooden stairs above me, and the low grumble of voices. I would let the two men open the door, and then I'd join them in Jervis's apartment.

The stairs wound crazily, finally stopping on a landing just shy of the second floor. There they widened, taking up most of the hallway. I walked up, getting closer to the voice. From this point, the steps were more traditional—about fifteen, then a landing with a window overlooking the street, a turn, and another fifteen steps, cross the main floor, and go up again.

This part of the building looked like it had been grafted on to an earlier building. Or perhaps the first-floor stairway wasn't supposed to come up this far when the building had been built. This part of the building was cleaner, too, but it was clear that no one who lived here had a lot of money.

I reached the third floor as the footsteps above me stopped. I moved as quietly as I could, so that they wouldn't think anyone was behind them.

"He added an extra deadbolt," someone said. I didn't recognize the voice, so I assumed it was the manager. "I know he gave me the key. Give me a second."

"Be quick about it." O'Connor's voice was low.

"Got it," the manager said.

I could hear the key click against the lock, startlingly loud in the small space. I started up the next flight of steps. I figured I'd be on the landing by the time they got inside the apartment.

"He hasn't been any trouble. Just a nice guy, a little quiet—"

The explosion sent me backwards. I hit the wall on the third floor so hard that the breath left my body. Debris came flying at me, and I tried to cover myself, but I couldn't move.

Something hit me in the head, and I closed my eyes—to protect them, I thought—but maybe I was closing them because I had gone unconscious.

Because I don't remember part of that afternoon, still. All I know is from the moment the explosion boomed outward to the moment I actually started to move again seemed like a very, very long time.

Hours, maybe days.

When, in fact, it was probably only minutes.

FIFTY-TWO

I was choking on the dust. It came at me in clouds, billowing from what remained of the wall.

The wall that had protected me. If I had been on the landing, I probably would have died.

I couldn't see very far ahead of me. My eyes burned from the grit that filled them, and chalky-tasting plaster fragments filled my mouth.

My entire body ached from a thousand bruises. The air had been knocked out of my body. It took a long time to catch my breath. My left arm burned, and something—probably blood—dripped into my right eye. My ears rang, and I couldn't hear myself breathe.

I pushed debris off me—wood, nails, that odd metal that some doors were made out of, and more blood. My pants were covered with dust. A jagged piece of wood stuck out of my thigh—a small piece, thank heavens, and I pulled it out without feeling a thing. I made myself look at the wound, to see if the wood had punctured anything important, but it was scarcely bleeding.

The dust billowed past me, one cloud, then another, almost as if a breeze was pushing it toward me. But I couldn't feel anything.

The world was strangely silent.

I patted myself down, and was startled to discover that I was okay.

Still, standing was difficult. My balance was gone. I swayed, nearly fell, and caught myself. There was a Smokey-size hole in the wall, showing how very hard I hit. I would feel that in the morning.

I would feel all of it.

I was moving slowly and thinking even more slowly. Shock. I cursed it—I needed all my faculties here—but I couldn't force the thoughts any quicker.

The stairs above me seemed intact, but I couldn't see much beyond them. The landing had vanished in a cloud of white. I didn't know if there were stairs above it or not. That ninety-degree angle from the landing had saved my life, but it made seeing what was ahead impossible.

I shook, remembering how I picked up colleagues in Korea, carried them, how cold it had been, the way the light had played on the frozen ground, the snow—

I closed my eyes, forced myself to breathe like I had trained myself over a decade before, reminded myself: New York, I was in New York, someone had just set off a bomb in New York, and that made me open my eyes.

They were scratchy with dust. One eye watered. The other stuck together—that blood again. I was afraid to touch my face.

I bent slightly at the waist, pulled myself up the stairs using the shaky banister. My feet kept slipping on things that I didn't initially see, sometimes couldn't see when I looked down, and I knew, without checking that I was slipping on blood or remains or something organic. Wood, metal, scrap wouldn't feel like that.

Finally, I reached the landing. It seemed shaky. The white clouds were even thicker here, and what I saw of the stairs was chunks of wood and debris. I got on my hands and knees, crawling to distribute my weight. With luck, I wouldn't fall through the destroyed staircase.

With luck, I'd make it to the fourth floor.

It seemed to take ten years to make it to the top step. My sense of time had vanished along with the sense of sound. I hadn't realized how much I relied on both: My hearing was my safeguard, the way I knew if something was behind me, in front of me, hiding.

I didn't know if someone lurked around the next corner with a gun, ready to shoot whoever came up here.

But I couldn't stop. What if O'Connor was lying on the ground, bleeding to death, and all it would take was a little pressure in the right spot to save him? What if the manager hadn't been hurt after all, what if the blood belonged not to him but to the bomber?

I wasn't thinking very clearly. I knew I wasn't thinking very clearly when I reached the top step, came through the debris cloud as if I had emerged from a snow storm, and saw the open hole where the apartment across the hall had been, saw the hole that went farther in, the furniture moved, the bits of clothing and charred wood, and the cat on its side, the lower half of its body severed and slammed against the remaining wall, and that vision meant little to me. I saw it; I didn't process it. I hadn't yet realized how much impact the blast had.

If I had thought it through, I would have known there was no one alive in that rubble. I wouldn't have gotten down on my hands and knees and started searching through the wood, the hot nails, the even hotter metal shards of the door, digging like a mad thing, looking for O'Connor, the manager, anyone—even the owner of that poor, unfortunate cat. I searched and searched, and then I found it.

The hand. It looked so small and unassuming, not like an adult hand at all. I picked it up as if it were an artifact, and until it dripped blood on my leg, until I felt the warmth of the blood hit my skin through my pants, I didn't realize what I had.

I let out a yelp, dropped the hand, and backed away. At that moment, I knew the search was futile.

Someone touched my back, and I yelled again. It was the cop from downstairs. He was even whiter than he had been before. His uniform was white, his face was white, even his hair was white. The dust coated him as it probably coated me.

He spoke to me. His lips moved, his face registered concern, but I couldn't hear him. My ears kept ringing.

I couldn't read lips. He patted me, pointed to the stairs, indicated that I should go down them, get away. But I couldn't. There were men under the rubble. And a dead cat, meaning someone had lived in that hole across the hall. Fire was burning one of the curtains in the back, a trail of embers led toward it.

The cop touched me again, pointed to the stairs.

I shook my head, put a hand against the hot wall, and stood. I had to see what caused this. I had to look.

I took a few more steps forward and looked at the apartment that O'Connor and the manager had tried to get into.

Jervis's apartment.

The door was gone, blown outward with the force of the explosion, but the rest of the apartment was intact. The windows were covered with blackout cloth, but a bit of light came in from the side—a spyhole—and a rifle leaned against the wall. Wind blew in from somewhere else—somewhere inside.

I looked at the side of the door, saw something both unexpected and completely expected: a homemade bomb. It resembled a claymore, only it wasn't. Instead of using shotgun shells, wire, and a hammer, he had set it up with something more powerful, something that got triggered when the door opened, something that would blow outward to destroy the enemy but leave the good guys intact.

We'd learned that. I'd learned it long ago.

This wasn't an apartment. It was a bunker. And that meant there was an escape route.

I started to step inside, but the officer held me back. I tried to shake him off, and he still held me, and it showed how very weak I was that I couldn't fight him off.

"There's an escape route," I said, or I think I said, my lips moving awkwardly, my mouth tasting of blood.

He nodded, but it was that nod people use when faced with someone crazy.

"He set up a bunker," I said. "His hidey-hole. He has an escape route. He was here. You have to catch him."

The officer moved his lips again, gave me a fake smile, led me to the stairs. I kept looking over my shoulder at that blown-away door, the impact of the explosion, going outward, the hole that had been an apartment just across the hall.

What had caused all the debris on the floor? I looked up as I reached the stairs, saw that the ceiling was mostly gone, too, and so was the ceiling over the other apartment.

What had Jervis used? Whatever it was, it had been ingenious, and effective, and oh so wrong.

The next thing I knew I was lying on an ambulance stretcher in the street below, being strapped in. Two ambulance attendants in bloodstained white were leaning over me.

My ears were popping and my head hurt, and my eyes felt like they were on fire. A man not much older than Malcolm was winding a bandage around my left arm, telling me the bleeding would stop soon. At least, I think that was what he was saying. His lips were easier to read than the officer's.

Words were fading in and out, sirens hitting, missing, like the needle of a record player hitting a scratch in the album. Sound, then nothing, then different sound, then nothing, then sound again.

I was incredibly thirsty and panicked. I couldn't go to any hospital. What would happen to Jimmy? Malcolm and Jimmy needed me. I had to find them. I had to meet them.

I must have been saying some of this, because the attendant pushed me back. He gave me a calm look, nodded at me, and assured me I would be fine. The easiest sentence to mouth-read in the English language: *You'll be just fine.*

But I wouldn't be.

Jervis had built a bunker.

O'Connor was dead.

And Jimmy didn't know what had happened to me.

Jervis had blackout cloths in the window. A spyhole. A bunker.

He was military. He'd been beaten, drugged, left for dead.

He'd been in Vietnam.

He had built a bunker.

And now he was loose in the city, thinking the enemy had finally arrived.

The enemy was here, and he was at war.

FIFTY-THREE

St. Vincent's emergency room: a whirl of lights, and plastic curtains, and screams. A baby whooping like it couldn't get its breath. Someone crying. The stench of rubbing alcohol and pee. Fake wood paneling on one wall, a nurse's station that seemed tiny: behind it, the word EMERGENCY in a small lighted sign.

They left me in the hall next to a pile of dirty laundry. Across from me, a desk. A phone with a lot of cords coming out of its back sat in the center, surrounded by medical equipment, seemingly abandoned in the middle of some task.

The bulletin board above the desk was covered with papers: instructions—How to Bandage a Suppurating Wound; employee sheets—names followed by phone numbers and sometimes an order *Do Not Call Unless Serious!!*; a half-completed prescription form with the words *Forget Something?* scrawled in red; and patient ID bracelets tacked together.

My hearing still wobbled in and out, hurting with each sound. A nurse flew past me, her white dress marked with sweat, her starched cap sliding back on her head. Behind her, a stretcher, and a little girl, white, her back arched, eyes floating into the back of her head. Two orderlies held her down, but they could barely control her. She was convulsing.

". . . Valium! . . ." the nurse shouted as she went into the exam room.

The girl followed, the orderlies doing their best to keep her still. ". . . tongue depressor . . ."

I was still strapped to my stretcher, forgotten, like the laundry, as other emergencies floated by me. I faded in and out of consciousness, too exhausted to be frightened by my lack of energy.

Finally the nurse who had worked with the little girl was bending over me. Her mouth moved, but once again, I heard no words.

"I'm sorry," I said. "My hearing only works sometimes."

She looked in my right ear, then in my left. Shook her head, nodded toward an exam room. Someone shoved the cart forward.

The exam room was smaller than I expected. A vinyl sliding door covered a supply closet, and a sink hung against the wall. Above it, a medical cabinet had a lock on it.

She unstrapped me, helped me sit up. My balance was still gone.

". . . the doctor will be here shortly. I don't think your eardrum is ruptured. You wouldn't be able to sit up. Do you remember . . ."

"I heard part of that," I said.

She smiled at me, wiped a damp cloth over my face. Moved her lips again.

I shrugged. The sound had gone out again, like a bad signal on the radio. And the ringing. It wasn't a better substitute for real sound. It wasn't a substitute at all.

A doctor came in, a big white man with stubble on his chin, his white coat flowing behind him. He looked as stressed as I felt. He spoke to the nurse, and I wished I could hear. I couldn't even see their lips.

She gestured toward me, then turned.

"I pulled some wood from my leg," I said. "It didn't seem to bleed much."

They continued to talk. He looked in my ears, at my eyes, in my mouth. She wiped off my left arm, then stuck a needle in my elbow. I started. He held me back.

I looked at the arm. A gash ran from my shoulder to the elbow, over an inch wide. They were going to give me stitches.

". . . and a tetanus shot. I don't know if he ever had one, so we may as well do the whole spectrum," the doctor was saying. He sounded like he was inside a bottle, his words garbled.

"Just a booster," I said.

"You heard that?" he asked.

"Barely. My ears ring. The sound fades in and out."

"That's common after a blast like that," he said. "You have some bleeding, but the drum is fine. Your other wounds are worse. We gave you a local so that I can stitch up your arm. I'm going to look at the rest of you. I'm afraid of shrapnel. That blast sounded awful. We even heard it here. I think half the city did . . ."

The ringing grew even more intense, and I had trouble concentrating on his words. He threaded a needle, moved a tray close, set some small metal tools on it. The nurse was working behind him, getting the booster ready.

He started to stitch. I looked away. My shirt was ripped. I hadn't realized that. I wasn't wearing a hospital gown, though, and I was still wearing pants and shoes.

That didn't last long, however. They helped me strip, examined the rest of me, gave me the booster, which hurt worse than the stitches, and found another long cut in my thigh. Another local, more stitches.

I closed my eyes, opened them in a hospital room. A clock in the hall, barely visible above the nurse's station, read 7:18, the second hand ticking away.

Jimmy. Malcolm. I had to meet them. If I didn't get there, they'd think something had happened to me.

I couldn't do that to Jimmy, not again. I'd nearly died on a case in December, and at first I thought he wouldn't forgive me. If Malcolm had to drag him to Newark, Jimmy would be terrified.

I had to keep them safe.

I wasn't keeping them safe here. If the doctors gave me something for the pain, I might be out for days.

I couldn't be. I couldn't leave Malcolm and Jimmy alone.

Not here. Not now.

I staggered out of bed, opened the metal cabinet, saw my clothes—including my ripped shirt—neatly folded on a shelf, my shoes beneath them. An old man slept in the bed near the window. He snored as if he were congested. A tube ran from his nose to a machine beside the bed.

I was dizzy, but I managed to get the clothes out of the closet. My wallet still had money; there was change in my pocket.

I had to sit on the bed to pull up my pants, and I had to wait until another dizzy spell passed before putting on my shoes.

"Mr. Grimshaw," a nurse said as she hurried into the room. "You need to lie down. You've been through a terrible experience."

"I have to go home," I said. "My son doesn't know where I am."

"We'll call your family," she said. "We were waiting for you to wake up."

"There's no phone." The ringing wasn't as bad, but the dizziness was awful. "Do I have a concussion?"

She checked my chart. "No. But you're not recommended to leave. The doctor wanted you to stay the night for observation. After something like that—"

"I need to leave," I said. "My son's only eleven."

"I'm sure your wife can handle it."

"I'm not married."

She frowned. "Can't you call a neighbor?"

I shook my head, had to grab the tray table to catch my balance, and had to choke back the nausea.

"Will it kill me to leave?" I asked.

"Probably not," she said. "But if you have internal injuries—"

"They'd've shown up by now. Even I know that. And if there's more trouble, then I'll check back in."

"Mr. Grimshaw, you can't leave."

"Can't a man check himself out in the State of New York?" I asked. "Even if it's against doctor's orders?"

"Yes," she said, and looked helpless. "But it's not recommended. You can hardly stand."

"I have to go," I said. "You don't understand about my son."

"Maybe we can find someone to go there."

"No," I said, envisioning the police arriving at the apartment, Jimmy in terror, screaming, afraid they were going to take him away for life. "I'm leaving."

I slipped my shirt on, felt for my wallet again, found it, and sighed with relief. Then I stood, cautiously. The ringing grew louder.

"Mr. Grimshaw, this isn't recommended—"

"I know," I said. "And believe me, if I had a choice, I'd do something else entirely."

The door to the room seemed very far away. I would have asked her to call me a cab, but even I knew that cabs wouldn't go into Harlem. Not with white drivers, not at night, and not from here.

She left the room ahead of me and went to the nurse's station, picking up the phone. Probably calling the doctor. But if I wanted to check out, I could.

"Give me a form to sign," I said.

She looked at me, then sighed, and reached into a drawer, removing a form. She filled out the top quickly, and I signed it, barely looking at it.

Then I staggered toward the elevators, my walk as uneven as a drunk's. My balance was badly off, the ringing was growing worse, and the hearing was subsiding. Black spots crossed my vision.

I made myself breathe as I pushed the button for the main floor. That helped the black spots fade. The wall inside the elevator held me up all the way to the ground floor. I tried to walk with determination, but people stared at me. My shirt was ripped and I wondered how much blood and plaster dust still covered my face.

The subway was only a block up, but that block stretched for miles. Then the stairs went all the way down to hell. I managed to get to the platform, managed to pull myself onto a train, and remembered to check once I was sitting down to see if I was on the right line. Miraculously, I was.

People didn't sit next to me. The train wasn't that full, but people got on, looked at me, and moved to the other end of the car. A few women gave me sideways glances, as if they expected me to hurt them. Some men cringed when they saw me, their gazes sliding away from my face as if they'd seen something hideous.

I didn't close my eyes. I had to struggle to keep them open. The ringing had gotten worse, and I knew I wouldn't be able to hear the announcement.

I stared at the door, at the designations, counting the stops to 116th Street, praying I had enough energy to walk the two blocks south to the apartment.

I barely remember those blocks. Someone asking if I was all right. A small boy running in front of me, then looking at my face in horror. A woman putting her hand to her mouth as she passed me.

I turned onto 114th, saw the apartment building, the people who had become familiar in the last few days. I staggered toward it, so dizzy that the entire world was spinning. I counted the steps, forced myself to breath with each movement, deep breath, step, deep breath, step, knowing I had to make it, praying I would make it.

As I tripped my way into the building, I realized my keys were gone. Wallet intact, keys missing. No local address, so they couldn't do anyone any good. But no way to get into the apartment, not if Jimmy and Malcolm weren't here.

I didn't care.

I fell going up the steps, caught myself, crawled like a child the last few stairs, leaned against the door and closed my eyes.

I'd made it.

And that was all that mattered.

FIFTY-FOUR

When I opened my eyes again, a woman leaned over me. She seemed vaguely familiar. Her hair, in a modified bouffant, was shiny and smooth and black, her skin the color of dark chocolate. She smiled at me.

"Welcome back, Smokey," she said quietly. "You scared us."

I had the worst headache I'd ever had in my life. My ears still rang, but the sound was fading. I looked to my left, saw a window with an air conditioner, and Jimmy, sitting in a chair, a book in his lap.

"How come you always get hurt?" he asked me.

"What day is it?" I asked.

"Tuesday," the woman said. She put a cool hand on my throbbing head. "You weren't out for long."

"Where's Malcolm?"

"In the kitchen." Jimmy stood. His hands were small fists at his side. "You got hurt again. You promised you wouldn't."

Had I? I didn't remember. "This is the apartment, right?"

"Yes," the woman said. "And you don't know who I am."

I swallowed, looked at Jimmy, saw panic on his face.

"You said he'd know you," Jimmy said. "You said—"

"It's Gwen, Smokey," the woman said, ignoring Jimmy's growing tantrum. "A little older, a little fatter, but it's Gwen."

It was Gwen. Her cheeks had filled out. She had crow's-feet beside her eyes. She used to wear her hair long. She would iron it. And she'd been tiny.

She wasn't tiny anymore.

"How'd you find us?"

"Not hard," she said. "Although the fake name threw me. I recommended the apartment broker, remember? When he didn't have a Smokey Dalton, I asked about a man and two boys that he rented to recently."

"She come here yesterday afternoon, asking for Smokey Dalton," Jimmy said. "Good thing she talked to me before Malcolm heard. I told her not to use that name."

I shouldn't have called her. I shouldn't have used that name. Now someone could put me together with the apartment broker and this place, and then tie Smokey Dalton to Bill Grimshaw.

So many mistakes.

"But he didn't tell me why," she said. "Are you going to tell me why, Smokey?"

"You've been here since last night?" I asked.

"Yes," she said. "I got here just in time to see these boys dragging you into the apartment. They were terrified. I wanted them to take you to a hospital, but they wouldn't. They wanted to leave town. I convinced them to stay."

I looked at Jimmy. He shrugged and looked away.

"Don't blame them, Smokey. They needed help. They're little more than children, and they thought you were going to die."

"I said you couldn't die," Jimmy said. "I *lied*. I said you were too stubborn to die."

"If it had been life-threatening, they wouldn't have let me out of the hospital," I said, and then realized that sentence wasn't as comforting as I meant it.

"You were in the hospital?" Jimmy's voice went up. "And you left?"

"Because I couldn't call you," I said. "I'm just bruised."

"And stitched," Gwen said. "Something got you but good."

I closed my eyes again. The conversation was tiring. "Is there a paper?"

"Food first," Gwen said. "Malcolm's cooking up some eggs. He says he's good at it. You're going to eat if I have to stuff the food down you."

Old flashback: too many nights drinking, Gwen beside me, giving me hair of the dog, making me eat, holding my head while I puked. Poor thing. She always got the worst of this relationship.

"I'm sorry, Gwen," I said.

"I always figured you'd get your life together, Smokey," she said. "I never figured on this."

That took enormous faith on her part, figuring I would get my life together. By the time I'd moved in with her after I finished my master's, the nightmares controlled me. Sometimes I lost touch with reality; I thought I was in Korea. I was convinced of it.

I often slept on the couch so my shouting wouldn't keep her awake. If I drank, I slept, but I could still be startled.

I woke one night with her son's arm in my hand, the thought in my mind that a simple snap of the wrist would give me the information I needed.

He had been six.

I moved out the next day.

"It's not as bad as it looks," I said.

I opened my eyes. She was sitting beside me, her figure fine and full. The extra weight looked good on her, made her seem more like a woman than the girl I remembered.

Jimmy was standing beside us. "So you do know her."

I nodded, then wished I hadn't. The dizziness was lurking there, waiting beneath the headache.

"Old friend," I said. "I'd called her from New Haven, asking for help finding a place to stay."

"When you didn't call," Gwen said, her tone light but forced. "I figured you were too shy, so I would contact you. Had to wait until yesterday when the office reopened. Then I learn that you don't have a phone. What's with that?"

"I didn't think we'd need it. I wasn't expecting this." I moved my left arm to indicate my injuries and wished I hadn't. The stitches pulled. That awakened all the aches and pains and the throbbing in my thigh from the other stitches. "How bad do I look?"

"Like it was one hell of a fight," Gwen said.

"It wasn't a fight." I scooted up. There were a pile of pillows behind me, and one on the floor, along with a blanket. Someone had slept in here, keeping an eye on me.

"Is he awake?" Malcolm stood at the door. His eyes were sunken in his face. He hadn't gotten much sleep.

"Yes," I said.

"Jesus, man. You said you were going to talk to someone. What happened?"

I wouldn't be able to hide it from them, so I supposed there was no point in trying.

"It was why I didn't want you along. What I was worried about from the beginning."

"Daniel," Malcolm said. "He hurt you."

I shook my head once, and stopped, the dizziness growing fiercer. "He wasn't anywhere near me. It was an accident."

"You got hit by a car?" Jimmy asked.

Such a simple lie, but it didn't go with my injuries. And I had promised him, more than once, that I'd never lie to him.

"A bomb," I said. And oddly enough, it wasn't Daniel's. It had been Jervis's.

"The bomb in the Village?" Gwen said. "The one that's all over the news? The one that killed the cop?"

It was on the news? Did they report the names of all the victims? Or did they wait, pending notification of relatives?

"Yeah," I said.

Gwen frowned at me. The panic must have shown on my face.

"What?" she asked.

But I couldn't tell her. I glanced at Malcolm. He was watching me. Somehow I had to let the boys know that we were leaving. We had to get out of town now.

"You're one of the survivors?" Gwen's voice went up. "What were you doing there?"

"Trying to join the cop. I wanted to talk to the guy who lived in the apartment."

"For heaven's sake, why?" she asked.

"Because I thought maybe he would know who was shooting young people on the streets of New York." That sentence sounded too harsh, too. I obviously wasn't myself. I wasn't usually that blunt.

"You thought he was the guy who was going after Daniel?" Malcolm asked.

I almost nodded, but caught myself. "I'm convinced of it now."

"But the police are handling it, right?" Gwen said. "There's nothing more for you to do."

But there was something. I just couldn't remember it. Something that they probably wouldn't figure out. Something that I had seen.

I knew better than to force it. The blast had blown away bits of my memory, and I had to trust that those bits would return.

"How about lunch?" Malcolm asked.

Lunch. I had been out a long time.

"Do we have a paper?" I threw the covers back, trying not to wince as the stitches pulled in my left arm.

"Yesterday's," Malcolm said as he hurried to my side.

I waved him away. I was wearing only boxers. The wound on my leg looked red and angry.

"We're going to need some hydrogen peroxide," I said. "And some cotton balls. Would you mind getting that along with a paper?"

"What for?" Jimmy asked.

"I don't want to go back to the hospital with an infection," I said. "I've still got things to do."

"You don't gotta do nothing," Jimmy said. "They arrested Daniel."

I looked at him. "How do you know that?"

"Radio news," he said.

I glanced at Gwen. She seemed somewhat oblivious to the conversation. She had moved to the side of the room and was looking through my pile of clothes for something for me to wear.

I had seen her do that a hundred times. Having her here was a flashback, an unpleasant one. I hadn't treated her well.

Malcolm vanished into the hallway. "I left the eggs on the stove," he said. "There's toast, too. I'll be right back."

"Do you have money?" I asked, but the door closing was my answer.

Gwen had found a shirt that was still folded. The pants I had worn yesterday were ruined. They were in the garbage, along with the remains of my shirt.

"I can get it, Gwen. Thanks." My tone was gentle.

She smiled at me. "I'll set the table," she said, and left the room.

"I'll help," Jimmy said, and followed.

I put on the shirt she found, moving my left arm cautiously so that I wouldn't reinjure it. My leg was sore, but I managed to get pants on over the wound. The cotton rubbed against the stitches, making them hurt.

My ears still rang, but my balance was back. I got up slowly, feeling the blood rush to my head. The headache was fierce. I had to use the wall to support myself.

Before I went into the kitchen, I used the bathroom. I washed up, careful to avoid the stitches—it helped having had them before; I knew how to take care of them—and then I looked in the mirror.

My face was covered with scrapes and scratches. A thin cut ran across my right eyebrow—too small for the doctors to do more than tape shut. Another cut ran under my browline, and still another along my right ear. No wonder I had felt so much blood. A lot of it had been mine.

I left the bathroom and walked slowly into the kitchen, feeling like an old man. The headache combined with seeing Gwen in a Harlem kitchen felt like a flashback—a moment from my past that I didn't want to relive again.

Flashback. Something floated across my brain and vanished again. Close. Almost there. If I didn't push, the memory would return.

"I'm sorry, Gwen," I said as I sat at the table. "This couldn't have been what you expected when you came here last night."

She set a plate of steaming scrambled eggs in front of me. My stomach growled. They smelled fantastic. Two pieces of heavily buttered toast rested on either side. Malcolm's days as a short-order cook had served him well.

"I had hoped for more," she said as she went back to the stove. "You always had so much potential, Smokey."

She sounded like my adopted mother.

"I been telling her, Smoke, that you're not always like this. That we got a home and a job, and that you take real good care of me," Jimmy said.

"He's been quite the defender," Gwen said, setting a place in front of him. "You have a wonderful child here, Smokey. I hope you realize that."

"I know it," I said.

"He's homesick, and trying valiantly to live with whatever crazy idea you got into your head this time." Gwen took a small plate of eggs for herself and sat across from me. "Going after murderers and bombers? What were you thinking, Smokey?"

"I work as a private detective, Gwen," I said.

"And bringing your son along—"

"Gwen, you haven't seen me in a long time. Don't pretend to understand my life."

Jimmy raised his eyebrows at me. I had just done something I always yelled at him about: I had snapped at someone, seemingly without provocation.

But the provocation—and the embarrassment—with Gwen was more than a decade old. We fought a lot, mostly about me, and she had mostly been justified. I had been a mess in those days. The war still haunted me, and so did some of the work I had done afterwards.

I wasn't sure if I had been entirely sane in those days. Anything could make me slip back into the past. Korea was more real to me than New York had been, than Gwen had been.

Add to that the fact that I hadn't known how to use the varied skills I'd gained from my education, my military service, and my unhappy childhood. It took years, and some extra training in Memphis, before I found that I worked best alone, on my own schedule, and in my own way.

"I just look at the evidence I see," Gwen said. "You're badly injured, that new scar on your cheek, some other scars I don't recognize. You're doing dangerous work, and you brought a child into the middle of it."

"I'm fine," Jimmy said.

"Gwen," I said. "I owe you a great debt for what you've done here, but my life has changed a lot in the past fourteen years."

"I see that," she said, giving Jimmy a sideways glance. She wanted me to explain him. I wouldn't. I was glad he hadn't.

"You scared him, you know," Gwen said, as if Jimmy weren't there.

Jimmy bowed his head and dug into the eggs.

"I know," I said. "It would have scared him worse if a police officer had come here to tell him I was in the hospital."

All the color left Jimmy's face. "You wouldn't've done that."

"I considered it. The hospital wanted me to do something like that, since I was so stupid and didn't get us a phone. Speaking of which," I said to Gwen, changing the subject, "didn't you tell me Alex was home? Does he know where you are?"

Jimmy's hand was shaking. Even the idea of having the police show up had terrified him.

"I called Alex from the pay phone," Gwen said. "He told me not to get involved. He never really forgave you, you know."

"For that night?" I asked, still remembering how his small hand felt in mine.

"For leaving, I think," Gwen said. "He liked you, Smokey."

"I scared him," I said. "I scared him a lot."

"He would have understood."

I shook my head. "It took me a long time to understand. Drinking didn't help. Nothing helped, except time and a little less pressure. The nightmares will never entirely go away, and I'm not good at intimate relationships."

"Yet you have a son," Gwen said.

"Jimmy and I are about as similar as two people can get," I said.

Jimmy glanced at me in surprise.

"And a fiancée," Gwen added, with a touch of bitterness.

"A fiancée?" I asked.

"A woman named Laura," Gwen said.

My eyes met Jimmy's. He was looking at me defiantly. He had told a lie, and he wanted me to support it.

"Laura's a special woman," I said, "but we're not engaged."

Jimmy rolled his eyes and gave me a disgusted look.

"You're not?" Gwen asked, with hope in her voice.

"Our lives are very different," I said. "If I can figure out how to mesh them, I would. But there's that intimacy thing, at least for me."

"And Jimmy," Gwen said.

"Laura loves me," Jimmy said.

"She does," I said. "If this were just about Jimmy, I'd marry Laura in a heartbeat. But there are a lot of other issues involved."

I waited for Gwen to make a derogatory comment about a white woman in my life. But apparently Jimmy and Malcolm hadn't seen fit to tell her, which was good. They also hadn't told her that Laura was rich, which was also good.

"Issues," Gwen said.

"What about you?" I asked. "You're single again?"

She said yes, and told me what happened to her last two relationships. I ate slowly, only half listening, trying to see if that feeling would return—the memory that had eluded me so far.

The headache was fading as I ate something and had some juice. Part of the headache remained: the part that came from the blow to the head. But the rest slowly eased, making me feel somewhat human.

Malcolm returned partway through Gwen's recital. He glanced at her, then at me, and didn't say anything. I think he understood what I had done.

He set the newspaper on the counter, then dished up the last of the eggs, and sat down.

"You did all the work to cook them," I said, "and you only get cold."

"A cook's life," Malcolm said. "I put the other stuff in the bathroom."

I thanked him, then bid Gwen to continue. She told us about her boyfriends and her job as a secretary, but no one really paid a lot of attention until she got to Alex.

"He's heading out on his second tour," she said. "I worry about him."

"He's in Vietnam?" Malcolm asked.

She nodded.

"He was just a boy when I saw him last," I said. "I can't believe he's full grown."

"Full grown and promoted. A sergeant. He's good at what he does," Gwen said with pride.

"What does he think of being over there?" Malcolm asked.

"He doesn't talk about it much," Gwen said. "You could ask him."

I glanced at Malcolm. "If you want to," I said. "It might be good to get an outside perspective."

"Are you thinking of volunteering?" Gwen asked.

"Something like that," Malcolm said.

They continued the conversation while I ate the last of the toast. I got up from the table, poured myself a cup of coffee, and looked at the newspaper.

The bombing had made the front page because a policeman had died. My name was not mentioned. I was apparently included in the handful of people injured, none of whom were identified.

So far so good. But that didn't mean the television or radio news hadn't identified me. Or that the cops hadn't started to investigate me.

My hands shook so much the paper rattled. I braced them on the counter-top and kept reading.

O'Connor got his own article, a full-dress uniform picture, and a lot of coverage. He'd been an impressive man. He'd been doing a lot of work tracking down "dangerous militant groups," and had had a lot of success at it.

"Even on the day of his death," the article's anonymous writer said, "he still completed his work. The arrests of the War at Home Brigade in their Harlem apartment [see article page 25] occurred because of his tireless efforts."

I turned to page 25. Under the headline "Militant Group Captured" was a photograph of Daniel and Rhondelle being led from the row house in handcuffs. The article said that ten members of the group had been arrested, with more arrests to follow. The arraignment would be held on Wednesday morning at the Federal Court House.

The article mentioned nothing about the bomb-making equipment, although it did mention the group's threats to various organizations, including the Armed Forces Induction Center. The only note to any of the things I had discovered yesterday was this: "Evidence seized yesterday strongly suggests that the group would have carried out its threats against these organizations within the week."

Somehow I had managed to stop Daniel just in time.

"Smokey?"

I turned. Jimmy, Gwen, and Malcolm were looking at me.

"Are you all right?" Gwen asked in that tone people used when they'd asked a question more than once.

"Yeah," I said. "Just looking at the write-ups about yesterday."

"Are you in them?" Jimmy asked. I heard fear in his voice.

He was as worried as I was.

"Not so far," I said, "but I think it's time to leave the city."

"Are you in trouble?" Gwen asked.

"I haven't made friends," I said.

She studied me for a moment. Then, to my surprise, she said, "What can I do to help?"

"Nothing," Malcolm said. "You've already done too much."

And in his voice I heard impatience.

"Actually," I said, "we can use your help."

She frowned.

"Can you return the keys to this place for us? Let your friend know that it didn't work out after all? I don't want him to see me like this."

The disappointment she always felt in me showed in her face. "The name you're using, it's Grimshaw, right?"

"Just tell him the apartment number," I said. "That's enough."

"And your deposit?"

"It'll cover the extra time," I lied. I didn't want her to know that he had my address in Chicago.

"All right," she said. "When should I go?"

"This afternoon," I said.

"You can't leave now. You're hurt."

"We have another place to stay in New Jersey," I said, not willing to tell her more. "We'll be all right."

Her lips thinned.

"We will," Malcolm said. I could hear the relief in his voice.

"I don't like this," Gwen said.

"I know," I said, and turned back to the spread-out paper.

Only two people had died in the bombing—O'Connor and the building manager, whose name was Roy Wallace. Seven other people were wounded, including the woman who lived across the hall. She had lost her right eye.

The rest of the article focused on Jervis. He had served in Vietnam, received an honorable discharge after getting a Purple Heart. He also received a Bronze Star for bravery, for heroics in an action that remained classified. There was no photograph of him beside the article, and the paper noted that the military had yet to release one.

Upon his return to the States, he started work at Tucker Construction. He worked there for nearly a year before failing to show up for work at the beginning of June.

The article made no mention of the attack on Jervis at the warehouse or his tenuous connection to the War at Home Brigade. According to the article,

314

no one knew what Jervis had been doing for the past month or why he hadn't showed up for work.

Some anonymous source speculated that he had been storing military equipment in the apartment illegally, and it had accidentally gone off when Wallace opened the door.

"That's it," I said.

The memory came back: the homemade bomb—designed to explode outward, protecting the person inside. The blacked-out window, the spyhole.

It was a modified sniper's nest inside a makeshift bunker. The breeze coming in the hall from the apartment meant that a window on the far side of the building was open.

Jervis had escaped from his bunker when the bomb went off, just like he planned.

He wasn't operating like a man returned from service. He was operating like a man still at war.

Something—the attack, maybe, or something else—triggered him, the way that the nightmares sometimes triggered me. In his mind, he probably wasn't even in New York, but in some city in Vietnam, some place he'd been sent to get a particular enemy.

He'd probably made Daniel that enemy, Daniel and the War at Home Brigade. After they had attacked him, after they had put a drug in his coffee.

The difference between me and him was that I snapped out of those memory delusions after a minute or two. He had been in his for more than a month.

It wasn't unusual. I knew some guys who never came home, not in the mental sense. In the World War I, they were called shell-shock victims. In World War II they called them victims of battle fatigue. Korean veterans didn't get a label, and who knew what was going on with Vietnam, except that some of these guys were experiencing it, too.

"What's it?" Malcolm asked.

"I just remembered something," I said. "It's not important."

But it was important. I stared at the paper so that the others thought I was reading.

I was actually thinking. McCleary's shooting had nothing to do with Jervis. But Jervis had clearly shot Jones, June, and Grossman. When Jervis shot Jones, Jones had been arguing with Daniel. When Jervis shot June, she and Daniel had been standing close together.

Judging by that bomb, Jervis probably hadn't received sniper training. He probably worked with munitions. Only someone with experience could have modified a claymore design like that.

His sniper skills were minimal. He had probably been aiming for Daniel when he shot Jones. Daniel had been the one who hurt Jervis at the construction site, and Jervis had probably seen him.

Jervis must have tracked Daniel all over the city, shooting at him twice—the first time hitting Jones, the second time hitting June.

Which left only Grossman unexplained, and I figured I had a handle on that as well. Grossman fit the description of one of the Castro brothers. He and someone else had rented that apartment for Daniel. Once Grossman found out what it was being used for, he left the group—which didn't matter, because his real name wasn't on that lease.

Maybe Grossman had been involved with the robbery. He had certainly been reluctant to speak to me about the dynamite. Maybe he was in deeper than he said.

That would explain his shooting, which happened at a time when Daniel wasn't present.

If I had the energy, I would have investigated. But I didn't. The case no longer belonged to me. I had to get the boys out of New York. We had to disappear as suddenly as we had arrived.

I couldn't tell them how this mattered. But it did. And it wouldn't make sense to most people, only to someone who'd been through something similar.

"I've got to make a phone call," I said.

"Let me do it," Malcolm said.

I shook my head and immediately wished I hadn't. I had to clutch the counter while the room spun. "I have to. While I'm in the phone booth, you guys pack. We'll leave when I get back."

"Smokey, can't I talk you out of this?" Gwen asked.

"Gwen," I said gently, "have you ever been able to talk me out of anything?"

And for the first time that day, she smiled her real and beautiful smile, the one that had made me fall in love with her.

"You are the most stubborn man I know," she said.

"And you're the kindest woman."

I hadn't deserved her back then, and I didn't deserve her now. I knew no way of telling her that, or thanking her for all she had done.

But I had more pressing concerns. I had a phone call to make and boys to get out of the city.

And after that, I had one last thing to do.

FIFTY-FIVE

Sometimes I was too stubborn even for my own good. I should have listened to Gwen and taken a day of rest, but I was worried, worried that everything was going to crash around me.

Jervis was just another crazy criminal to the police—one of those loner types who seemed to lose it one day for no apparent reason. But he wasn't without reason, at least in his own mind. He was fighting a war in a way that I understood all too well.

If I hadn't had Gwen, I might have ended up just like him, lost in my delusions. I hadn't; I had been lucky. But I understood those delusions. They weren't random. They made sense, at least to Jervis, and the indications to me were that, after the assault at the construction site, he believed he was under enemy attack.

The bomb in his apartment hadn't been set to destroy the building. What he had done was set up a device that would protect his hidey-hole.

We had all been trained to do that if we were alone in a bunker. Rig a device that would hurt the enemy should he enter without warning.

Have an escape route.

Use it.

All part of the training.

Even the way he stalked his victim. He had had the patience of a soldier who somehow knew where the enemy would be. He had studied Daniel as if Daniel were prey—which, to Jervis, Daniel had become.

Only his lack of long-range rifle training—sniper shooting—had caused Jervis to hit two nearby targets. But he had nearly killed Joel Grossman. On that, Jervis had almost succeeded.

It took more effort than I liked to reach the pay phone across the street. The day was warm, but not hot, the humidity relatively low. Even so, I broke out into a sweat. I moved like an old man, and I made an easy target for anyone who wanted to hurt me.

Fortunately for me, I didn't look like someone with money to the junkies who hung out at the corner. I wasn't even sure, on this day, whether I could defend myself against them.

No one was using the phone, although someone had recently. That person had left their gum melting on the built-in metal shelf.

I plugged in my dime and dialed O'Connor's precinct. When the desk sergeant answered, I asked to speak to Captain Donato. When the sergeant asked for my name, I said simply, "I'm his anonymous tipster from yesterday."

"You weren't at the D'Amato building when we got there," Donato said as he picked up the phone. "How the hell did you know to go to Jervis's apartment?"

"I was following up another lead," I said.

"I'm asking what the lead was," Donato said.

"I'd talked with the head of Tucker construction and asked about the security guard. When he said the guard hadn't been in to work for a month, I decided I wanted to talk to the guy. Simple as that."

"And wrong place wrong time. You vanished from the hospital, too," Donato said.

"Yeah," I said. "I have a kid to take care of."

"They said you're in no condition to take care of anyone."

"Well, they were wrong." I hoped my voice sounded stronger than I felt. "Listen, I wanted to tell you a few things I discovered, just in case you didn't know them."

"You thinking we can't do our jobs?" he asked.

"I'm thinking I've been on this case longer than anyone now," I said.

Donato didn't respond. After a moment, he said, "What've you got?"

I told him about the extra dynamite. I told him my suspicions about Daniel selling the stuff all over the East Coast.

"What proof you got of that?" Donato asked.

"None," I said. "Except one of Daniel's old friends calling Rhondelle a chemist. I know that they use that term for people who make drugs, but you know, her specialty seemed to be bombs. And chemists tend to sell their specialties."

"I'll get a guy on it," Donato said.

"You also might want to talk to the New Haven Police Department. Before I left, I called in an anonymous tip about a place called the Barn—"

"You like this anonymous stuff," Donato said.

"It keeps me out of court," I said. "Anyway, this place called the Barn was also filled with explosives. It looked like someone had cleared out of there fairly quickly. But I've been thinking about it. New Haven isn't far from here. The Barn would be a great secondary storage area."

"You saying when they ran out of something, they'd drive up to New Haven and get it?" Donato asked.

"That's exactly what I'm saying."

"You got proof?"

"I'm not sure," I said. "I seem to remember boxes from Tucker Construction in there, but I'm not trusting that memory. Contact New Haven. They probably have all of this stuff inventoried. If there's dynamite from Tucker in the Barn, then that might be confirmation enough."

"How come you don't want to testify? You got something to hide?"

I noticed that never once did he use my name. He was respecting my choice to be anonymous, even though I hadn't told him why I was.

"I have a lot of history," I said. "I'd make a terrible witness. It's better if you retrace my steps so that your people can testify about this stuff. Besides, this way I get to go home when the case is finished and not worry about coming back here."

He grunted. "You got anything else?"

"I'm curious. Have you found Jervis?"

"No," he said. "You know where to look?"

"No," I said. "But he seems to have a heck of a grudge against the War at Home Brigade. What did they do to him when they robbed Tucker Construction?"

"Drugged him, tied him up, kicked him a few times. Nothing that doesn't happen to security guards all over the city."

"Drugged him with what?" I asked.

"LSD. You know it?"

"Yeah," I said. "It's a hallucinogen. I know a few guys who weren't right ever again after they took it."

"Making excuses for him?"

"No," I said. "I doubt anyone could defend the man now. He killed a cop."

"You got it. Half the cops in the city are looking for him."

"They won't find him," I said.

"You know that how?"

"His training," I said. "He's special ops. He knows more about hiding than all the rest of us combined."

"How do you know he's special ops?" Donato asked.

"The bomb he made. The way he kept his apartment. You don't learn that in basic training."

"You sure?" he asked.

"Positive," I said. "He's at war with these guys. He built a bunker to protect himself. They're the enemy, as far as he's concerned."

"That's why he was trying to pick them off?" Donato asked.

"Yeah," I said. "He obviously wasn't trained as a sniper—he missed too often—but he's good enough not to get caught. He's probably dangerous one-on-one."

"You find him, you bring him in," Donato said. "No cowboy stuff."

"I don't care about him," I said. "He's your problem."

And then I hung up.

Maybe if I had been in Chicago, I might have helped the police find Jervis. I had a friend on the force who would have listened to me.

But I wasn't in Chicago. I had no options here. Daniel had been arrested, which was all I wanted. And people were dead, which was what I had feared.

And I had placed Jimmy in danger. Again.

I leaned against the phone for a moment, making myself breathe, waiting for the dizziness to pass. When it finally did, I stood up.

I had to get the boys out of the city. One more trip.

And then I could rest.

FIFTY-SIX

The trip out of the city took longer than I expected. First, I had to clean myself up as much as possible. That meant a shower, even though I shouldn't have because of the stitches. I wrapped plastic wrap around my arm and my leg, and cleaned up as best I could.

By the time I got out, Gwen had straightened the apartment. The boys had packed everything, including my belongings. The suitcases were waiting by the door.

Gwen was going to help us get to our new "hotel" in New Jersey. I talked her out of it, reminding her that she had to go to the apartment agent.

"Are you in legal trouble?" she asked. "Because if you are, I have a friend—"

"It's a long story, Gwen," I said.

"Tell me the Reader's Digest Condensed Version."

I owed her something, but I couldn't tell her the truth. Jimmy stared at me. Malcolm was frowning.

"I volunteered to find the son of a friend," I said. "It turns out that he's been playing with explosives. I'm afraid he knows where we're staying."

That last was a lie, but I didn't want to tell her that I was afraid the cops might figure out who I was.

"He's the one who bombed you?" Gwen asked. "I thought it was some vet."

"That's what the police think, too." Which was the truth. But I was using it to mislead her.

Gwen sighed. "We never seem to find the right time, do we, Smokey?"

"It's my fault," I said.

She shook her head. "It sounds like you have a woman at home who can handle you. She must be special."

"She is." I put a hand on Gwen's face, then I pulled her close. We hugged for a minute, and then she stepped away.

"Good-bye, Smokey," she said.

"Thanks, Gwen." I gave her one last look, and then I opened the apartment door. No one was in the hall. The boys left first. Gwen went next, and I followed.

The suitcase seemed heavier than it had before. Malcolm offered to carry it, but I wouldn't let him.

When we reached the outer door, the boys waved to Gwen. She waved back, then turned away and left my life for the second time.

We retraced our steps, taking the subway to the Port Authority and the bus to Newark. The bus ride was a welcome rest for me. I had to doze.

At least no one stared at me on this trip. I had cleaned up enough to look presentable, at least to the average commuter.

Our walk to the van was longer than I remembered, but the van was intact when we found it.

The interior was hot, but I didn't care. All of our possessions were there.

"Lemme drive," Malcolm said as he loaded the suitcases in the back.

"Not yet," I said.

Both boys looked at me.

"I want to stay one more night," I said.

"Smoke," Jimmy said. "You promised."

"We have to get out of here, Bill," Malcolm said.

I swallowed. I had thought about this all day. "I want to go to Daniel's arraignment. I want to make sure they don't let him out on bail. There's still dynamite missing, and he's angry."

"You can't go to the cops," Jimmy said.

"I'm going to the courthouse," I said. "It's okay. The cops know that I found the dynamite, and they know I was at the bomb site. They have been looking for the bomber. They're not interested in me. After the arraignment, I'll come back here and we can go home."

"I'm going with you," Malcolm said.

I shook my head. "You and Jimmy are spending the morning in the airport, eating some breakfast and reading a newspaper. That way I can have you paged if I need to. Otherwise, we'll meet back at the van about noon."

"You don't need to be there," Malcolm said.

"I do. It's also something I need to do for Grace."

"Mrs. Kirkland," Malcolm said and leaned his head against the van's back door. "What're you going to tell her?"

"If Daniel hasn't called her, I'm not going to say a word," I said. "If he has, I'll tell her the truth."

"She won't believe you," Jimmy said.

I looked at him. I certainly wouldn't have believed any story like that about him.

"I know," I said. "And she'll probably be angry at me for not doing more. But I have to remember—we all have to remember—that Daniel made these choices. We had nothing to do with who he is."

"It's going to break her heart," Malcolm said.

"That's why I'm taking this one last trip," I said. "I want to make sure I do what I can for her."

"You hate him, don't you?" Jimmy asked.

"Who? Daniel?" I said.

Jimmy nodded.

I thought about that for a moment. "Hate's not the right word," I said. "He's scary. He's scary because he's so smart."

"You're afraid he'll find a way out of this," Malcolm said.

"Yeah," I said, "and I want to be there to prevent it."

FIFTY-SEVEN

That night it was too hot to sleep in the van. We had to drive several miles away from the airport before we found a deserted patch of grass where we could sleep outside. We used the sleeping bags as ground cover and slept until dawn.

I didn't wake refreshed, but at least I wasn't as exhausted as I had been. I still didn't have a lot of energy to spend. It would take a great deal of effort to go into the city, but I didn't see any other choice.

We had breakfast at a nearby restaurant, used its bathroom to brush our teeth and wash our faces, and then I dropped the van and the boys back at the airport. I promised them I'd return by noon. If I was delayed, I would page Malcolm and let him know.

Then I took the bus back to Manhattan.

The United States Courthouse was in the center of a series of government office buildings anchored by City Hall. Just off the wide-open Foley Square, the courthouse was one of the stranger buildings in the city.

The courthouse had a thirty-two-story tower roofed in gold leaf that looked like someone had just glued it to the top of a typical turn-of-the-century granite government building. The result made it look like the tower was part of a building behind the courthouse, even though it wasn't.

As brave as I had sounded to Jimmy the night before, I felt nervous entering this large building. There might be FBI at the arraignment, and they would be looking at people who had showed up to watch the War at Home Brigade plead. I could only hope that they would assume I was Daniel's father or a simple bystander who had wandered in off the street.

I couldn't imagine they would think I was Smokey Dalton from Memphis.

The worst thing I could do, however, was look nervous. I arrived early enough to find the courtroom, and just late enough so that I wouldn't seem anxious.

I slipped in ten minutes before the proceedings started and found a packed courtroom. The room itself was large, with murals on the walls and the thick brown wood that marked it as a 1930s construction. Obviously, lots of WPA help went into this building. But the room itself was faded and musty with overuse, and the air smelled faintly of an added air-conditioning unit not properly installed.

A group of elderly people lined the back wall. I had learned early in my detecting days that if you wanted to find out anything about the inner workings of a courtroom, talk to the retired folk who spent their days watching trials.

Up front, reporters sat in a designated area. Many of them already had notebooks out and were scrawling details to be used later in articles that would cover this case.

The jury box was empty, except for some purses and a briefcase tossed casually on some chairs. A lot of reporters used the jury box for extra space when there weren't any jury trials. Most judges discouraged the practice, however, and frowned on any reporter who dirtied up the courtrooms.

Professor Whickam and his wife sat in the first row behind the tables. They were the only black couple. The rest of the War at Home Brigade's family members—equally well dressed, just as obviously from money—were white.

I planned to slip in behind Professor Whickam so that I looked like family as well. But I waited a minute, preferring to view the others from the back so they couldn't see me watching them.

The remaining people in the courtroom were either hobbyists, like the elderly, or people who had other relatives in other cases on the docket after the War at Home Brigade. I saw no young people, nor did I see anyone who looked familiar.

A middle-aged white man turned slightly and looked at me, obviously having felt my gaze on his back. He had a beak nose, short hair, and wide, intelligent eyes. He nodded to me. I nodded back.

Then he turned around again.

I didn't recognize him, but his action made me nervous. Did I know him? Was he someone from my past?

I couldn't very well leave now, not so soon. I would simply play this by ear.

A few other people looked, probably because he had. I felt conspicuous, so I went and sat down.

I touched Whickam on the back. He jumped slightly as he turned.

"I'm sorry, Professor," I said softly.

He sighed. "I did not expect this."

"I know," I said.

"We hired an excellent attorney. Rhondelle would not take him unless he represented Daniel, too. So he is taken care of." Whickam sounded annoyed.

"Thank you for that," I lied. I hoped the attorney wasn't as wonderful as Whickam thought he was.

"I don't think it will do a lot of good. They have got a lot of evidence, and they are getting more." He ran his hand through his hair, revealing drops of sweat against his scalp. "That girl died, you know."

"June?" I asked.

He nodded. He didn't sound sad that June D'Amato had died. I wondered how Daniel was taking it. Was that why Rhondelle wanted him to have a good attorney as well? Because her competition was out of the way?

Or was she afraid that Daniel would lie, blame everyone else, and get himself off the hook, leaving the rest of them to hold the bag? Was she doing her best to control him?

The prosecuting attorney arrived next, along with an assistant, which surprised me. Several police officers entered, most of them sitting near the elderly in the back.

Then the defendants came in. There were twelve, and most had their own attorneys. Rhondelle and Daniel entered last, a well-dressed white man following them, his suit so expensive that it shone.

Daniel's hair had been cut and he wore a suit that didn't fit well. Rhondelle was in the dress she had been photographed in for the *New Haven Register* long ago, back when she'd been a pretty and innocent high school student who had just received a scholarship. She looked a lot like that student now—or would have, if it weren't for the bruise still coloring her face.

"All rise!" the clerk shouted.

And we did.

The judge, an overweight middle-aged white man, balding and impatient, hustled into his chair. He had a stack of files with him, and he scattered them across his desk as he sat down.

He motioned for all of us to sit, then with a minimum of fanfare, began the proceedings.

The clerk called the cases, starting with the War at Home Brigade. The nice thing about places like New York, places that were used to public trials, was that everyone knew to get the high-profile cases out of the way quickly so that they could get back to the business of the court.

The War at Home Brigade defendants appeared in the order they had arrived. The prosecutor read the charges, the individual kids pleaded—not guilty, all of them—and the prosecutor asked for remand in each case.

The defense lawyers protested. None of the kids had a record, and most were excellent students.

"The prosecutor only has a supposition, your honor," said Daniel's lawyer, "that these young people were even involved."

"Enough supposition to get some warrants and make arrests," the judge said.

"Certainly not enough to put these exemplary young people in jail while awaiting trial," Daniel's lawyer said.

"Your honor," the prosecutor said, "we haven't found all of the bombing materials. These aren't kids. Daniel Kirkland nearly kicked a man to death in New Haven, and then beat up a security guard here while stealing dynamite. If we let them go now, they might try to bomb the jail or the courthouse or the police station. No one is safe while they're on the street."

"One hundred thousand dollars bail each," the judge said, and brought his gavel down. "Next case."

Rhondelle looked at her father. He nodded wearily. My stomach twisted. Judging by the row house and his attitudes, Whickam had enough money to cover both Rhondelle and Daniel.

I didn't want Daniel on the street. I didn't want Rhondelle free either.

I had to stop this somehow.

Half the courtroom stood, and started to leave. Whickam made his way to the defense table. I followed, wanting to overhear his promises.

Daniel saw me, and his eyes widened slightly.

The bailiffs were gathering the defendants, trying to move them back into the system until their bonds could be assured. The attorney leaned toward Daniel, and asked him a question.

He seemed to be ignoring me.

Someone bumped me. I turned to see the man who had nodded at me.

His expression was grim and determined. He shoved his way through the families gathered around the defendents. The bailiffs didn't notice him; they were trying to break up the bail conversation, trying to get their young charges out of the courtroom.

The man had reached the railing that separated the gallery from the defense table. Then he raised his arm.

He was holding a gun.

He was staring at Daniel.

Daniel, who might go free that very afternoon on one hundred thousand dollars bond.

I hurried forward, trying to reach the man, but people kept shoving at me, trying to hold me back.

No one seemed to notice that man except me.

Then the gun went off, and Daniel jerked forward. People screamed. I shouted at everyone to get down.

I hit the ground, pulling Whickam and his wife down with me.

Around us, more gunshots.

I lifted my head to see three different cops shooting the man. He crumpled, hit a bench seat on the way down, and then slid into the railing.

The shooter's eyes were open.

On the other side of that railing, Daniel was sprawled on the marble floor.

I slid out of the aisle and made my way to Daniel. He was bleeding heavily. He looked at me. His lips moved, but I couldn't hear him. For a moment, I thought the deafness had returned, but it hadn't.

Daniel couldn't get enough air to speak.

I didn't give him comfort. I couldn't. Jimmy had been right after all. I hated this man.

People were running out of the courtroom. Behind me, someone was screaming.

A policeman crouched beside me, then another, and another. Some moved aside the shooter. A man in black, with a medical kit, knelt in Daniel's blood, touched his neck, and shook his head.

A man I didn't know moved me away from Daniel.

"He's dead," the man said. "I'm so sorry."

I looked down. Of course he was dead. His skin was gray, his blood pooling with the shooter's on the marble floor.

A camera crew arrived. I made my way to the back of the courtroom, careful to stay out of the sight. The other defendants had disappeared into the back. The bailiffs must have hustled them out when the shooting started.

The judge peered up from underneath his desk, astonishment on his face. His clerk stood beside him, equally stunned. The bailiff finally convinced them to go inside the judge's chambers.

Daniel was dead, and there had been a single shooter.

A man who had waited until he had his chance, waited with patience and a plan.

A man who was at war and knew it.

A man who had known where his enemy would be, just like he had known all along.

Jervis had come here—and he had ended it, once and for all.

FIFTY-EIGHT

I stayed in the courtroom, waiting for an opportune moment to disappear. Everything was chaos. Whickam was shouting for his daughter, who was probably back at the jail. The crime-scene people were trying to shut down the room.

The camera crews had gotten footage of the dead before the police shoved them outside. I remained in my chair until someone sat down beside me.

Captain Donato, a slender middle-aged man, said he recognized me from my injuries. "I thought you might be here."

"I didn't want those kids back on the streets," I said.

"Looks like you got your wish."

He seemed quiet, even though he must have known there was a shitstorm brewing in the corridors. The reporters were already asking how a man with a gun had gotten into the courthouse. The answer was simple: He had gotten in the same way the rest of us had. He had walked through the front door, found the courtroom, and sat down. No one patted us down; no one checked for weapons. Somehow people assumed civility in a courtroom.

Our assumptions were false.

"I checked your information yesterday," he said. "You were right."

I nodded.

"We've reconstructed everything, but I'd still like you to testify."

"I'm not well," I said, running my hands along my torso to indicate the injuries. "I just want to go home."

"Figured you'd say that," he said. "Figured you might say that even if you hadn't been injured."

He was silent for a moment, maybe waiting for me to tell him my real reasons for wanting to leave.

I didn't say anything.

He put a hand on my shoulder. "We owe you."

I shook my head. "I just gave you a starting point. You'd have found your own."

"Maybe," he said. "Maybe not."

Then he stood, squared his shoulders, and left, ready to face the crowd.

Apparently he'd given word to the crime-scene people, because I was allowed to stay until the corridors were empty. It wasn't quite eleven. If I was careful, I'd make it back to Newark in plenty of time.

But before I left, I took care of one last thing. I was afraid Grace would turn on the news, see the footage of the dramatic New York courtroom shooting, and find herself looking at the face of her dead son.

For all I knew, Daniel had called her the night before, letting her know he had been arrested. If so, she'd be frightened.

I didn't want her to hear the news from an impersonal source. I used a courthouse pay phone to call her.

She sounded hopeful when she answered the phone.

"I was getting worried," she said. "I hadn't heard from you in so long."

I didn't know how to do this. I didn't want to do it. "I found some things, Grace."

"Things?"

"Daniel. He . . ." I paused, uncertain which tense to use. "He had gotten in with some violent people."

"Gangs?" Her voice was filled with fear.

"No," I said. "You've been hearing how the protestors, the antiwar protestors, have been having violent demonstrations?"

"What's going on, Bill?" she asked. "Just tell me what's happened."

I took a deep breath. "Daniel's dead. He was shot this morning. He was in a courtroom. He'd been arraigned, and a guy got in with a gun, and just started shooting . . ."

I made it sound random. God help me, I was still protecting Grace.

"He's dead?" Grace's voice shook.

"I'm sorry."

"Dead?"

"I'm so sorry, Grace, really. He—"

She screamed. I'd never heard a sound like that in my life. I held the phone away from my ear and listened to her wail.

It seemed to go on forever. I clutched the receiver, my forehead resting against the wall, my breath shallow.

Finally, the sound faded.

"Bill?"

"Grace, I can stay if you want me to," I said, even though I didn't want to. "I can get him transferred home, I can—"

"No," she said.

"It's probably the easiest—"

"You've done enough," she said, and hung up.

FIFTY-NINE

By two that afternoon, Jimmy, Malcolm, and I were on the road home. I drove. I was operating on adrenaline, but I didn't care.

I wanted to get as far away from New York as possible.

We talked a little about Daniel, but mostly we rode in silence.

All I'd wanted to do when I left Chicago was find Daniel, to give peace to his mother. Instead, I had given her heartache.

I was smart enough to know that Daniel was the one responsible for his mother's heartbreak.

But I also knew that if I hadn't acted, if I hadn't reported the dynamite, someone else might dead. Or a lot of someones. That had been a risk I had been unwilling to take.

Daniel did teach me one thing: He had shown me something I had left unfinished.

Just inside the Pennsylvania border, I stopped the van at a gas station. While Jimmy and Malcolm used the restroom, I went to the pay phone.

I dialed a number that was so ingrained in my memory I didn't even have to look as I spun the rotary wheel. Even the clicks were familiar.

And the hello, from a rich, warm female voice, one that made me shake when I heard it.

"Mom?" I said.

"Smokey? Smokey!" She shouted into the kitchen, yelling at my dad to pick up the extension.

I could picture her in the hallway, holding the phone tight to her chest.

"We've been so worried about you, baby," she said. "Are you all right?"

"Didn't Henry Davis contact you from Memphis last year?" I asked.

"Yes," she said. "He told us exactly what you did, how you saved that little boy. But he didn't know how long you'd be gone. Are you back now, Smokey? We missed you so much."

"No, Mom," I said. "I'm not back. I can't talk very long—"

I heard a click as my adopted father picked up the phone.

"Smokey?"

"Yeah, Dad," I said.

"It's so good to hear you."

"It's good to hear you, too. But as I was saying to Mom, I can't talk long. I'm sure your phone is bugged."

"Me, too," my father said. "We've been having all sorts of troubles with it—weird clicks, voices, hang-ups. You're still in trouble, son?"

"I'm not in trouble," I said. "That's what I wanted to tell you. I'm fine. Everyone—everyone involved is fine. But we're being safe. We're staying low."

"Oh, Smokey, this isn't what we wanted for you," my mother said.

"I know," I said. "But it's okay. I'm learning some things, and I wanted to tell you something quickly."

Jimmy had returned to the car. Malcolm was inside, buying some gum. Jimmy frowned at me. He didn't understand why I was on the phone.

"I wanted to tell you," I said, "that I'm beginning to understand the sacrifices you made, taking in a damaged little boy who had just lost his parents—"

"Smokey," my mother said.

"—and," I said, "I wanted you to know that all the lessons—the good lessons you taught me, about responsibility and taking things day to day and about family, I'm putting them to use."

"Are you all right, son?" my father asked. "Physically, I mean."

"Yes," I said. "Are you?"

"We've been worried," he said, "but our health is fine."

"If you need me," I said, "leave a message with Shelby Bowler. He's an attorney in Memphis."

"He knows how to reach you?" My father asked.

"Yes." Shelby had instructions to contact Andrew McMillan, Laura's attorney. Drew would contact me. I had set this up last December, after I'd been injured. That put two layers of attorney-client privilege between me and the authorities. "Only use it in emergencies."

"We will, son," my father said.

"I have to go," I said. "I stayed on too long. But I wanted to tell you that I love you. I'm sorry if this call causes you to get a visit from the FBI."

"It's all right," my mother said. "They've been here before. We don't know a damn thing. Except that you're all right."

And I could hear the smile in her voice.

It carried me long after I hung up, long after we left that little gas station in Pennsylvania.

The drive to Chicago seemed to take forever. On one long stretch of highway in Ohio, Malcolm told us his news.

He was going to the draft board. He was going to enlist.

I wasn't sure I would have made that choice. Not with this war. Not after what I'd been through with Gwen, with Jervis.

"If this is about getting into college," I said, "there are other ways. We can find something."

"That's not it," Malcolm said.

"Then what is it?" I asked.

Malcolm looked straight ahead, at the road filled with cars. "It's the right thing. If Daniel had done the right thing, he'd be alive now."

"It's not the same," I said. "You're going to a very dangerous place."

Malcolm shrugged. "It's my civic responsibility."

"Malcolm, this is a little different—"

"You know I'm right," he said. "If not me, then someone else'll go."

"Yeah," I said. "But I don't know that someone else."

He looked at me then. His dark eyes were more open than I had ever seen them. "You're the one who always talks about living up to your responsibilities, no matter how tough they are. That's all I'm going to do. I can't live with myself otherwise."

He had turned my own words on me. I didn't like how it felt. But I didn't try to argue with him anymore. He knew the risks, and he was taking them. It was his life to live, his choice to make.

I simply wished I could keep him from it—and I was smart enough to know that I couldn't.

We were silent much of the rest of the trip. But Jimmy grew happier and happier the closer we got to Chicago. He didn't realize how much had changed.

I was feeling nothing. I felt empty, just like I had when I returned from Korea. Dislocated, distant, at a loss without really knowing why.

I was returning from a different war and, like the first, I didn't entirely comprehend it.

The only thing I knew was that in some very fundamental ways, we had all lost.